I0642002

Robinson Ellis, Avianus

The Fables of Avianus

Robinson Ellis, Avianus

The Fables of Avianus

ISBN/EAN: 9783744776769

Printed in Europe, USA, Canada, Australia, Japan

Cover: Foto ©Andreas Hilbeck / pixelio.de

More available books at **www.hansebooks.com**

THE FABLES OF AVIANUS

ELLIS

London

HENRY FROWDE

OXFORD UNIVERSITY PRESS WAREHOUSE

AMEN CORNER, E.C.

THE

FABLES OF AVIANUS

EDITED, WITH

PROLEGOMENA, CRITICAL APPARATUS, COMMENTARY

EXCURSUS, AND INDEX

BY

ROBINSON ELLIS, M.A., LL.D.

FELLOW OF TRINITY COLLEGE, OXFORD
UNIVERSITY READER IN LATIN

𝕺𝖝𝖋𝖔𝖗𝖉

AT THE CLARENDON PRESS

1887

PREFACE.

THE publication in 1883 of Mr. Rutherford's *Babrius* determined the present edition of *Avianus*. The Elegiac version, if not equal to its Greek original, is sufficiently good as a specimen of Latin in the fourth and fifth centuries A. D. to deserve a revived study[1]. For me the work had a special attraction. Not only is it contained in good and early MSS, but in many of these MSS it follows or precedes the Elegies of Maximianus, which had engaged my attention as far back as 1878 (when I collated the Eton MS of Maximianus), and on which I have since written two articles printed in the American Journal of Philology (vol. v. 1–15, 145–163). As is there observed, the two works, the Fables of Avianus and the Elegies of Maximianus, seem to have been studied together in the Middle Age. To both of them I feel grateful for leading me for a time away from the beaten paths of philology to the comparatively neglected literature of the Decline, to the History of Ammianus Marcellinus, the Epistles of Apollinaris Sidonius, the poems of Ausonius, Claudian, Rutilius Namatianus, as well as of Prudentius and Orientius: in a word to that cycle of writers to whom Prof. E. A. Freeman has recently called (and not, I trust, vainly) our attention. It is indeed impossible to believe that an Age of Research like ours will content itself with the amount of illustration which these authors have received from the editors of the past. No adequate edition of Ammianus exists; Savaron's edition of Sidonius, published in 1599, is still the only one which can be recommended. New commentaries on Symmachus, Ausonius, Claudian, Rutilius, are loudly called for, all the more that the Germans, while exhausting their energies in publishing new texts, are almost indifferent to the equally important task of comment and elucidation.

On Avianus the only existing Commentary is that of Cannegieter, published in 1731. Judged by modern standards, Cannegieter performed his task only tolerably well. His notes are cumbrous and loaded with useless citations, as well as unnecessary or improbable con-

---

[1] Lachmann's critical editions of Babrius and Avianus appeared in 1845.

jectures. He was also guilty of the serious mistake of habitually illustrating Avianus (whom he pre-dated by at least two centuries) from
writers of the Ciceronian or Augustan age. I have taken warning
from his example, and have made my commentary as illustrative as I
could of the later literature to which the Fables undoubtedly belong.
It is something merely to recall to the reader's mind the existence of
an historian as great as Ammianus or a poet as finished as Merobaudes.

I must record my obligations to the librarians of the Bibliothèque
Nationale at Paris, of the public library of Trèves, and of S. Peter's
College, Cambridge, for the loan of valuable and early MSS of the
Fables. Also to the distinguished archaeologist, M. Wilhelm Fröhner,
for the free use which he allowed me to make of his collation of the
two Paris MSS *A* and *P*, as well as of the Carlsruhe fragment (*K*).
I have not availed myself of his generous permission to reprint the
Latin Paraphrast, thinking it better to refer the reader to Fröhner's
own edition (Teubner, 1862). For the Index of words I am indebted
to my friend Mr. Charles Bradburne of Trinity College.

OXFORD, *March* 1887.

INDEX.

PROLEGOMENA.

I.

THE AGE OF AVIANUS.

At what period were the forty-two fables of Avianus written? Do they belong to the age of the Antonines, as Cannegieter and Lachmann both thought, or are they the product of a much later time, the fourth, fifth, or even sixth century of the Christian era?

It is only within the last forty years that any adequate answer could be given to this question. It was not till 1844 that the Greek scazons of Babrius, the original which Avianus paraphrased, became known to the philological world; and no really critical edition of the text of Avianus had been published till 1862, when the eminent archaeologist and savant, Wilhelm Fröhner, exhibited for the first time the readings of the three earliest MSS in the National Library of Paris. Lately our data for forming an opinion have been largely augmented by the MSS which Bährens collated for his edition (Poet. Latin. Minor. v. pp. 31–70), to which I may now add my own four, *BORX*.

It is unlucky that the earlier of the two Leyden MSS (Bährens' *V* of the ninth century) does not give the poet's name either at the beginning or end. But in *C*, perhaps the best of Fröhner's Paris MSS, and hardly later than the tenth century, in *O*, a Bodleian codex of the eleventh century, in the Galeanus of the same date in the library of Trinity College, Cambridge (O. 3. 5), in two others of the same period, Bährens' *L* and *R*, belonging respectively to the Laurentian Library at Florence and to the Vatican, lastly in two MSS exhibited by me for the first time (*B* and *X*), the name is given uniformly (in the genitive) *Aviani*. I know of only one early MS in which it appears as *Avieni*—my Bodleian *R* (XI–XII century), which ends with the words, *Expliciunt fabule auieni poete aegregii.*

To come to external authorities. It is remarkable that the fables of Avianus are never quoted by any of the grammatical or metrical writers included in the first six volumes of Keil's edition [1]. It is only

---

[1] This is much more remarkable when we remember that Symmachus, a pagan of the most pronounced type is, like Claudian, not unfrequently quoted by the Grammarians, e. g. iv. p. 488 Keil, v. 588 twice, vii. 458, 489. The author of the short treatise De Dubiis Nominibus (Keil v. 588) quotes Symmachus with Prudentius, Sidonius, Ausonius, Iuvencus, Paulinus, Lactantius, Dynamius, Sedulius, Ambrosius, Avitus, Cyprianus, Fortunatus, Claudianus. Probably Symmachus was treated as a classic from the connexion of his memory with Prudentius, who while combating his anti-Christian views eulogises his learning and eloquence.

in the later treatise edited by Hagen in his Anecdota Heluetica (vol.
vii of Keil's Gramm. Lat.) that they appear, pp. 174, 182, 185. In the
first of these passages ix. 19 is cited from Avienius; in the latter two,
vii. 8, ix. 19, are quoted each with the introductory *illud Auieni.* I
have myself found one citation from them in the twelfth century Phillipps
Glossary (4626) s.v. *Citisus* (see on XXVI. 5) where the author is called
in the nominative Avianus.

This exceptional Avienius or Avienus of the grammatical treatise
edited by Hagen from cod. Bern. 83 ought not to be lightly dismissed.
Hagen believed that treatise to be written ' intra saeculorum noni deci-
mique fines,' and its author was obviously a man of learning. It may
be assumed, therefore, that he found in a MS probably earlier than
any now extant, *Fabulae Auieni* or *Auienii.* This agrees, not only with
the heading *Auienus Theodosio* affixed to the Praefatio, as copied in
cod. Vindob. 3261 (Endlicher cccvi) from an early source (Schenkl
Zeitsch. f. Österreich. Gymn. xvi. p. 400, Ausonius p. xxxiv), with the
Prologus Auieni incipit of Paris 8093 f. 94^b where the Preface as far as
coartauit is written by itself, and with my own Bodleian MS *R*, but
with the additional name *Festi* in the Bodl. codex *O*. Festus is
well known as one of the names of the poet Rufius Festus Avienus,
the translator of Aratus, and author of two geographical poems, the
Descriptio Orbis Terrae, a version in Latin hexameters of the Περιήγησις
of Dionysius, and the *Orae Maritimae liber I* in Latin iambics. The
ascription of the Fables to him, common in modern times, was no
doubt started in antiquity. *O* retains part of this ascription, but
otherwise follows the prevailing spelling of the name, Avianus.

A comparison of the Index to Mommsen's Corpus Inscriptionum
Regni Neapolitani (*CIRN*) with that of the C. I. Africae shows
that Avianius, Aviania are far commoner than Avianus, Aviana, or Avienus. In the *CIRN* there are nine Avianii for one Avianus, three
Avianiae for one Aviana; Avienus is only recorded once. In the
C. I. A. there are ten Avianii, four Avianiae, for one Aviana, one Avi-
en(us). Hence there is some plausibility in Fröhner's conjecture
(Kritische Analekten, p. 60) that the writer of the Fables was really
not Avianus, but Avianius. The latter name occurs as early as Inscript. 577 in the volume of Republican Inscriptions, C. I. L. 1 *M. Aui-
anius M. F. Coniunctus :* four Avianii Flacci are mentioned in Orelli's
Onomasticon as among the friends of Cicero, one of whom, the C. Avianius of Acad. ii. 25. 80, was long written Avianus, and has only recently been restored to his rights by the sagacity of Bergk and the
evidence of the best MSS. In the fourth century of the Christian era
the name became famous as borne by L. Avianius Symmachus, *inter
praecipua nominandus exempla doctrinarum atque modestiae* Amm. xxvii.
3. 3, father of the illustrious orator and epistolographer Q. Aurelius
Symmachus: see Seeck's ed. of Symmachus, pp. xli sqq. Four epi-
grams, each of six lines, are extant by Avianius Symmachus in the
collection of his son's Epistles (i. 2): they are dry, with no charm of
style or diction, and exhibit defects of metre, of which there is no trace
in our *Auiani Fabulae.*

If, however, the name was Avianius or Avienius, it seems unlikely that all trace of the genitive in -*ii* would have disappeared from the MSS of the Fables, most of which have *Aviani*, an exceptional few *Avieni*. The more real question seems to be whether the names Avianus, Avienus were not confused with each other, whether the preponderance of the former name in our MSS is not accidental, or at least not decisive against a plausible ascription of the authorship to an Avienus.

And here, at any rate, we seem to touch a certainty. The Oxford MS which I call *O*, adds the praenomen *Sextus*: an addition which points to a belief that the author of the *Fables* was identical with the well-known author of the *Aratea* and *Descriptio Orbis Terrae*, Sextus Rufius Avienus.

One and one only of Cannegieter's arguments against this identification is of weight. The style of the *Fables* is unlike that of the *Aratea*. The fables, though saturated with Vergilianisms, bear unmistakable traces of a declining feeling of correct Latin : the diction of the *Aratea* is pure, exalted, and classical. But neither the age of Sextus Avienus (Proconsul of Africa 366. of Achaia 372, Teuffel Hist. Rom. Lit. 413), nor the MS data as to the name of the Fabulist, *preclude* such identification. The real argument against it is the complete distinctness of the simple *Aviani*, which is the prevailing MS title of the author of the *Fables*, from the *Rufi Festi Auieni, u. c.*, which is the MS description of the author of the *Aratea*.

There are, however, two other *Avieni* to whom the authorship of the *Fables* may justifiably be ascribed. The first of these is the young Avienus, who is introduced by Macrobius as one of the interlocutors in the *Saturnalia* ; the second is the pupil and correspondent of Ennodius, Bishop of Pavia.

The claims of the second of these may be discussed first.

Not only was he learned and the son of a learned father (Ennod. Epist. i. 5 Hartel *additur quod in principio uitae disciplinis optimis institutus uidetur meruisse quod adeptus est . . . naturae in decus scolas et litterarum studia consecutus, paternae perfectionis aemulator . . . quicquid Attica, quicquid Romana habet praecipuum lingua cognouit, aurum Demosthenis et ferrum Ciceronis expendit, utramque dicendi seriem Latinus relator impleuit.* ix. 32 *domnum Auienum superantem uota reddidimus: habet de origine eius Roma iactantiam, Liguria de profectu: ibi domno Fausto filius naturae lege concessus est, hic eruditione patefactus*), but his teacher Ennodius had trained him on the study of Vergil (Ennod. Ep. i. 18 *doctorum radix Maro, uestri formator eloquii*), and illustrates his devotion to his father's example by the fable of the young eagles trained by their parent to look upon the sun (ib.) : two points which might seem to suit the author of our Fables. But (*a*) whether the Theodosius to whom the fables are inscribed was one of the Roman emperors of that name, or Macrobius Theodosius, the author of the *Saturnalia*—in either case the time is earlier by nearly a century than the Avienus in question; (*b*) in the time of Ennodius sacrifices had long ceased, and the allusions in XXIII. 5, XLII. 8 would be out of date.

Far more is to be said in favour of the other Avienus. In the
Saturnalia he is described as a modest and virtuous youth (*uerecundia
probi adulescentis* vi. 7. 1, *mi Auiene, instituenda est enim adulescentia
tua quae ita docilis est ut discenda praecipiat* vii. 3. 23), and who rarely
speaks at much length himself, but keeps the conversation going by
questions, interruptions, or whispered objections (Ian, Macrob. i.
p. xxix). Yet so far as his personality is introduced it is well suited
to the character of a lover or writer of fables. Thus ii. 4 sqq. he tells a
number of witty stories with which his memory supplies him of J. Caesar, Augustus, and others, to the great delight of the company, who
hail with enthusiasm his 'bright memory and pleasant wit.' So again
in vii. 12. 3 he recalls the conversation, which had become too abstruse,
to lighter subjects more suited to the entertainment. It will be remembered that a large part of the *Saturnalia* is taken up with a discussion
on Vergil (see Nettleship's full examination, pp. xxxi-lvi in vol. I. of
Conington's Vergil); and no remnant of Roman literature is more
informed with the diction of Vergil than the Fables.

The probability of our hypothesis becomes considerably greater if
the Theodosius of the Preface to the Fables is Macrobius Theodosius
the author of the *Saturnalia*. This view was suggested by Pithou
(Poemat. Vet. p. 474), and subsequently maintained by Sirmond (Sidon.
p. 4), Gerard John Voss (De Histor. Latinis ii. 9), Colomies (Cimelia
Litteraria c. 38), Wernsdorf (De Carminibus Avieni, P. L. M. v.
pp. 669, 670), Lucian Müller (De Phaedri et Aviani Libellis, p. 32),
Bährens (P. L. M. v. p. 31), and Unrein (De Aviani Aetate, p. 60).

The elder critics, beginning with Lilius Gyraldus, thought that
Avianus addressed his Preface to Theodosius the Great. In doing
so they were not without support (1) from the MSS, (2) from parallels in literary history. (1) Two early MSS, Bährens' Reginensis
of the eleventh century and my Bodleian *R*, add to the words
ad theodosium of the Praefatio the title *imperatorem*. (2) It was
not uncommon to inscribe works to kings or royal personages.
Babrius, whose Greek fables were paraphrased by Avianus, dedicated
his work to an Alexander, probably Alexander Severus (Rutherford,
Introduction, p. 1); and Vegetius, in offering his *Epitoma Rei Militaris* to an *imperator inuictus* (Gibbon Seeck and Lang in his second
edition, thought Valentinian III; Bähr Jordan and Lang, first edition,
believed Theodosius I). uses words which may be quoted here : *Antiquis temporibus mos fuit bonarum artium studia mandare litteris atque
in libros redacta offerre principibus, quia neque recte aliquid inchoatur,
nisi post Deum fauerit imperator, neque quemquam magis decet uel
meliora scire uel plura quam principem, cuius doctrina omnibus potest
prodesse subiectis. Quod Octauianum Augustum ac bonos dehinc principes libenter habuisse frequentibus declaratur exemplis. Sic regnan-
tium testimoniis crebuit eloquentia, dum non culpatur audacia. Hac
ego imitatione conpulsus dum considero clementiam uestram ausibus litterarum magis ignoscere posse quam celeros, tanto inferiorem me antiquis scriptoribus esse uix sensi, licet in hoc opusculo nec uerborum
concinnitas sit necessaria nec acumen ingenii, sed labor diligens ac fidelis.*

These words belong to an age when Panegyrics were habitually addressed to the Roman emperors, an age when it would be hard to say where flattery paused, or what particular merit it forbore to dwell upon. We may form some idea of the extravagance which even good and estimable men allowed themselves in speaking of imperial virtues, from two orations, the first complete, the second fragmentary, which the rhetorician Ausonius and the orator Symmachus delivered in honour of Gratian. Ausonius had been appointed consul by his royal pupil, and had received the notification of his appointment in the following words : *cum de consulibus in annum creandis solus mecum uolutarem, ut me nosti atque ut facere debui, ut uelle te sciui, consilium meum ad deum rettuli. Eius auctoritati obsecutus te consulem designaui et declaraui et priorem nuncupaui* (Auson. Grat. Act. ad Gratian. § 44 ed. Schenkl).[1] The language of this imperial message would hardly stand the test of criticism—it is harsh and somewhat rude. But Ausonius, in a rapture of admiration, exclaims : ' When did speech ever show more lucid arrangement ? When was learning so careful to speak in the proper language of elections, and to avoid any admixture of foreign words with the terms sanctioned by antiquity ?' And he goes on to examine the whole clause by clause, and ends with asking, ' If I order this letter of yours to be hung like an imperial edict on every pillar and portico from which it may be read distinctly, surely I shall be rewarded with as many honorary statues as each copy of the letter has pages.' And again, § 68, 'I should go on to say something of your powers as a speaker were I not afraid of self-complacency. Not Sulpicius more violent in his harangues, not more admirable the self-restraint of the elder Gracchus, not your own father more authoritative or weighty. What grand tones in the vehement passages ! What fine modulation in the unimpassioned ! What happy blending of both when you deliver each alternately. Where is the orator who has either expressed, or, as he might do more freely, thought out gay ideas with such humour, eloquent ideas with such finish, contradictory statements with such compression, compressed statements with such volume ?' Symmachus is not less pronounced in his own way : ' Henceforth we believe antiquity. In the same tent of yours books and arms are handled equally. And as circumstances and times vary, you have abundant matter to pass in review. History is your amusement in fighting : when your men are to be addressed, you have hortatory harangues ; judicial pleadings when you are in conference ; poetry when you are triumphing' (Symm. Orat. ad Gratian. p. 331, Seeck). And again, in a letter to the same emperor (Seeck, p. 78) : ' Let your divine intellect, August prince, Glory of the Roman name, be borne on the chariot of its eloquence : as for myself, in the Return of Thanks I make, I do but creep on the ground, fitter to aspire to the comic sock than the tragic buskin, now that oratory has

---

[1] Ausonius is equally flattering to Gratian as a verse-writer Epigr. i. 11. 17. Gratian wrote on the battle of Achilles with the Amazons. Ausonius says *Exulta, Aeacide, celebraris uate superbo Rursum Romanusque tibi contingit Homerus.*

become an Imperial possession. For all I know, indeed, you have given the Muses lodging and entertainment in the Palace.' Similarly, Epist. i. 20, he calls Gratian *eruditissimus Imperator.*

Could this language be addressed to Theodosius the Great? Aurelius Victor, or whoever was the author of the *Epitome* of the Lives of the Caesars from Augustus to Theodosius, speaks of his learning in these words, c. 48 *Litteris, si nimium perfectos contemplemur, mediocriter doctus : sagax plane, multumque diligens ad noscenda maiorum gesta. E quibus non desinebat exsecrari quorum facta superba crudelia liber- tatique infesta legerat.* From this it would seem that Theodosius was a great reader; as may also be inferred from the words in which Claudian makes him address his son, *De Quarto Cons. Honorii* 396- 418, the beginning of which may be quoted :

Interea Musis, animus dum mollior, insta,
Et quae mox imitere, legas: nec desinat umquam
Tecum Graia loqui, tecum Romana uetustas.
Antiquos euolue duces, adsuesce futurae
Militiae, Latium retro te confer in aeuum.
Libertas quaesita placet: mirabere Brutum.
Perfidiam damnas: Metti satiabere poenis.
Triste rigor nimius: Torquati despue mores.
Mors inpensa bonum: Decios uenerare ruentes.

Zosimus tells us Theodosius encouraged μῖμοι γελοίων, dancers, and everything that contributes to this flagitious and irregular music (iv. 33). It is therefore probable that he was not averse to the lighter literature, whether the degraded comedies of his time, of which a curious specimen is still extant in the *Querolus*, or such *jeux d' esprit* as Ausonius' *Cento Nuptialis*, with the other pieces contained in his *Eidyllia* and *Epistulae.* Indeed there is a still extant *auto- graph* letter written by Theodosius to Ausonius, in which he begs him to send copies of his poems, not only such as were known to the Emperor already, but others of which report had informed him : and he compares himself to Augustus, declaring that his admira- tion for the poet was not less, and his love certainly more. (Cf. Ausonius' dextrous reply Epist. ii Schenkl.)

So far there is nothing in Avianus' preface which is incompatible with the ascription of the Fables to the Emperor Theodosius. If Theodosius had any[1] literary bent it would be in this direction: cf. Epitom. ib. *simplicia ingenia aeque diligere, erudita mirari, sed innoxia,* a good description of our fabulist. Again, the words of the Preface *habes ergo opus quo animum oblectes, ingenium exerceas, solli- citudines leues, totumque uiuendi ordinem cautus agnoscas* seem aptly enough to describe the brief hours of amusement which the cares of war and government would leave Theodosius. Nor is there any great difficulty in accepting the words *Theodosi optime* as meant for the Emperor. Cannegieter's remark that the style of *optimus* belonged in

---

[1] Pacatus in his elaborate panegyric of Theodosius says nothing of his literary tendencies.

a peculiar and special sense to Trajan (Plin. Paneg. ii) will hardly
bear the test of research, if it is meant to imply that no succeeding
Emperor was so addressed: but it is remarkable that the Epitomator
quoted above draws an elaborate parallel between Trajan and
Theodosius; and as the characters and even the features of the two
Emperors resembled each other, there would be an implied compliment in addressing Theodosius with the word which antiquity had
consecrated to Trajan[1].

The Preface however must be judged as a whole. So considered
it suggests, I think, rather the confidential, almost familiar tone of an
equal, than the deferential style of a subject. Avianus begins by
saying that being in doubt what form of literature to select for the
preservation of his name, he had chosen fables as making fiction
natural, and truth unnecessary. A prince would resent such language,
and justifiably. 'Why should this scribbler parade his wish to be
immortal? Why should he tell me that truth is unpalatable, and
fiction the only thing acceptable to kings?' Avianus proceeds with
an exaggerated compliment. He will not mention formal prose or
verse to so incomparable a master of Latin and Greek style as Theodosius: prose or verse, Greek or Latin, he is superior to the best critics
in either. Can we believe that the great and simple-minded Theodosius
would welcome so enormous a falsehood? It seems to me impossible.
It is far more likely that Avianus is addressing some acknowledged
leader in literature, whose name would be familiar to his readers and
serve as a guarantee for his own performance. He might speak to the
author of the *Saturnalia*, to Macrobius Ambrosius Theodosius, as Ausonius speaks to the greatest orator of his time, to Q. Aurelius Symmachus. Epist. xvii: *Quisquam ita nitet ut comparatus tibi non sordeat? quis
ita Aesopi uenustatem, quis sophisticas Isocratis conclusiones? quis ita
ad enthymemata Demosthenis aut opulentiam Tullianam aut proprietatem
nostri Maronis accedat? quis ita affectet singula, ut tu imples omnia?
quid enim aliud es quam ex omni bonarum artium ingenio collecta perfectio?*

It is not necessary to prove at length how fully the author of the
Commentarii in Somnium Scipionis and the *Saturnalia* comes up to
the words of Avianus, *cum in utroque litterarum genere et Atticos Graeca
eruditione superes et latinitate Romanos.* Ian shows from the *subscriptio*
still extant in some MSS that the Commentary on the *Somnium Scipionis*
was revised by Aurelius Memmius Symmachus[2], a *uir consularis*,
perhaps in the fifth century; that collections of excerpts were made
from it; and that it was translated in the fourteenth century into
Greek by Maximus Planudes, the translator of Ovid's *Metamorphoses*.

---

[1] Fröhner now (1886) inclines to think the Preface of the Fables was based on
the preface which Marcellus Empiricus has affixed to his work De Medicamentis.
Marcellus is there called 'uir ill. ex mag. off. Theodosii sen.,' and Teuffel concludes
that he wrote under Theodosius II. But I own that I fail to detect any sufficient
resemblance in the two prefaces to justify an hypothesis framed on the comparison.

[2] Paris 6371 gives the subscription thus at the end of the first book of the Commentary on the Somnium Scipionis. AVR. MEMM. SYMMACHVS. VC EMENDABAM
VEL DISIINS MEV RAVENKE CVMACROBIO. PLOVNO EVDOXIO. VC.

The larger and more important work of Macrobius, the *Saturnalia*, has not indeed come down to us in its entirety: but the considerable fragment which remains, particularly the discussion on Vergil and the sources which he imitated or from which he drew his materials (Books iv–vi), shows not only the extent of his reading both in Latin and Greek, but the exactness of his knowledge and the combined antiquarianism and freshness of his criticism. Prof. Nettleship, who has minutely compared the remarks of Macrobius on Vergil with those of Servius, declares that 'in the great majority of cases where Servius and Macrobius have identical notes, those of Macrobius are far the fuller, clearer and more logical;' and John of Salisbury (Polycr. viii. 10) says of the first book that, rightly viewed, it was such and so full as to be sufficient in itself for all purposes of reference. The physical discussions scattered through the *Saturnalia* prove a different kind of erudition; here Macrobius must have mainly drawn from prose sources, and those Greek: they have however no less than the rest of the work the double merit of proving the author's competence to deal with very difficult problems and of being written in an interesting style. If indeed the grammatical treatise *De differentiis et societatibus Graeci Latinique uerbi*, some extracts from which are headed *Theodosius Symmacho suo* in a MS at Vienna, cod. Vindob. 16 (Keil Gramm. Lat. v. p. 596), is rightly attributed to Theodosius Macrobius, we have a more special instance of his *erudition* as a grammarian dealing with the comparative inflexions of Greek and Latin verbs. It is observable that Avianus compliments his Theodosius on his *latinity*. Now this word is used several times in the above-mentioned treatise i. 3 *dualem nulla latinitas admisit*, ii. 3 *latinitas conpositi uerbi saepe primam syllabam mutat*, vi. 13 *ipsum autem Φ adeo latinitas non recipit, ut pro ea etiam in Graecis nominibus P et H utatur, ut Philippus Phaedon:* and not unfrequently in the *Saturnalia*.

I have shown that the preface of Avianus' Fables may well have been inscribed to Theodosius Macrobius. I have also made it probable that the names Avianus and Avienus being confused, not only in MSS of the Fables, but elsewhere (e.g. Sat. i. 4. 17 Ian's best MS *B* (the Bambergensis) gives *Auiene*), the Avianus or Avienus of the Fables may be the youthful Avienus of the *Saturnalia*. It remains to find approximately the probable period of the composition of the Fables.

Macrobius tells us, S. i. 1. 5, that some of the interlocutors in his dialogue did not reach maturity till after the period of Praetextatus (*uni aut alteri ex his quos coetus coegit matura aetas posterior saeculo Praetextati fuit*). Seeck's lucid biography of Praetextatus (Symm. Op. pp. lxxxiii–xc) makes it easy to fix this period within two dates, either from his proconsulate of Achaia in 362 to his death in 385, the year after he had been appointed Praefectus Praetorio; or, if the meaning of the term *saeculi* is slightly restricted, from 367 when Praetextatus was Prefect of the City to his death. Within this period of twenty-three or eighteen years we may suppose the banquet held which is the scene of the dialogue in the *Saturnalia*. Avienus at the time of the dialogue is described as *adulescens*: if he was seventeen in 370 or 375, he would have been born in 353 or 358, and would be twenty years of age in 373 or 378. Or reckoning from the earlier date 362 he would be twenty in 365, thirty in 375.

There is a passage in Ausonius' Gratiarum Actio to the Emperor Gratian, delivered in 379, in which I seem to trace an allusion to a fable not indeed contained in our Babrius but extant in several prose Greek versions (Halm Fab. Aesop. 270) and versified by Avianus, XXVI. A lion (the Greek has a wolf) seeing a she-goat standing on a precipice advises her to come down to the safe pastures of flowering shrubs below. The goat declines, pleading the greater danger of falling into the lion's jaws: ending with this distich

Nam quamuis rectis constet sententia uerbis,
Suspectam hanc rabidus consiliator habes.

Compare with this the words of Ausonius (x. 41) '*solus mecum uolutarem,*' *o profundi altitudo secreti! habes ergo consiliatorem et non metuis proditorem.* Not only the general aptness of the fable to the occasion, but the special introduction of the word *consiliatorem* make it probable that Avianus' work is here alluded to by Ausonius. It is true that the same word is used, though far less appositely for the purpose of Ausonius, by Phaedrus (ii. 6) in his fable of the Tortoise and the Eagle; and it is also true that Ausonius knew the Latinized prose fables of Julius Titianus (Epist. xvi. 2. 81, 92), and himself contributed an elegiac version of one fable of the Babrian collection (Epigr. 75, 71 Schenkl, Babr. 75). *If*, however, Ausonius is here referring to our Fabulist, Avianus, or, as we have seen reason for calling him, Avienus, had published his fables before 379. Not much can be inferred from Macrob. S. vii. 8. 6 where Disarius alludes to the well-known fable of the Oak and Reed in language which need have no reference to any particular version, yet has some resemblance to Av. XVI: *uento nimio abies aut quercus auellitur, cannam nulla facile frangit procella.* The date of the publication of the *Saturnalia* is uncertain, but it probably falls within 400–420.

More distinctly like a reference to our Fables is a passage from a letter of Symmachus i. 101 addressed to Syagrius in 380 or 381: *Video, Consul amplissime, quantum mihi amor tuus honoris imponat. Iubes te adeam et coram defruar magistratus tui gaudio. Quo pacto istud possum negare, nisi ea religione ignoueris qua uocasti? nam quid agam fortunae dubius, cum hinc inuiter ad obsequia honoris tui, hinc luctu amissi fratris impediar? Duae mihi simul personae dispares offeruntur. Qui fieri potest ut os unum contrariis adfectionibus induamus?* This is very like the language in which the Satyr in our Fabulist angrily dismisses the Traveller, who has put his mouth to the two different uses of warming and cooling. Av. XXIX. 21, 22:

Nolo, ait, ut nostris umquam successerit antris,
Tam diuersa duo qui simul ora ferat.

Again Unrein rightly points out (De Aetate Auiani, p. 60) that the words of the Preface *fabularum textus occurrit, quod in his urbane concepta falsitas deceat et non incumbat necessitas ueritatis* seem to be alluded

to by Macrobius Comm. Somn. Scip. i. 2. *7 fabulae, quarum nomen indicat
falsi professionem;* again §9, *ex iis autem, quae ad quandam uirtutis speciem
intellectum legentis hortantur, fit secunda discretio: in quibusdam enim et
argumentum ex ficto locatur et per mendacia ipse relationis ordo contexitur,
ut sunt illae Aesopi fabulae elegantia fictionis illustres;* and again § 10,
prior species quae concepta de falso per falsum narratur. Other points
in which the fabulist and the antiquarian illustrate each other will be
found in the notes on XII. 5, Introduction to IV.

It seems then more than probable that in 380-381 Symmachus had
the work of Avienus before him; nearly certain that early in the fifth
century Macrobius alludes to it; not unlikely that Ausonius (1) adopted
an allusion and a word from it in 379: (2) was possibly led by
imitation or rivalry to translate himself a Babrian fable into the same
Elegiac metre [1].

It follows that Avienus must have been quite a young man at the
time he published his forty-two Fables; and as the fame of Macrobius
belongs either to the beginning of the fifth or the later years of the
fourth century, it may have been between 370-379 that Avienus
dedicated them to him, already well known in the learned and literary
world. This was the period of revived opposition to Christianity,
the period of Praetextatus, Symmachus, and the other supporters
of the old Pagan creeds, whom Macrobius has introduced in his
elaborate dialogue the *Saturnalia.* The different characters of the
two men are exhibited in the scoffing reply of Praetextatus to Ambrose,
Bishop of Milan, ' I will turn Christian, if you will make me bishop of
Rome,' and the famous *Relation* which Symmachus, when urban
Prefect in 384, addressed to the Emperor Valentinian [Seeck p. xvi]
in behalf of the Senate for the restoration of the altar of Victory.
Seeck sums up the conflict in words which I will condense here
(pp. liii sqq.).

The Pagan rites in part suppressed by Constantius had been restored
by Julian (361) and were left undisturbed in the first years of Valentinian
I (364) and Gratian. Both religions still subsisted side by side: the Emperors were themselves Christians, but sacrifices (which as early as 341
had been made illegal and stigmatized as *sacrificiorum insania* by a law
of Constantius (Clinton, F. R. i. p. 402)) continued to be performed at
the expense of the state, and the altar of Victory still stood in the Curia.
Hence in the earlier Epistles of Symmachus the pagan ceremonies are
often alluded to; consultations and decrees of the College of Ponti-
fices are recorded, besides sacrifices for expiation of portents, solemni-
sation of the festival of the Magna Mater at Rome, and punishment of
a Vestal Virgin for unchastity. It is in these years that we may
suppose Macrobius to fix the scene of his Dialogue, at a time when
Paganism was still sufficiently in the ascendant to be interesting, and
when a discussion on the names and attributes of the ancient gods

---

[1] Prudentius Perist. v. 17-20 might seem to allude to Av. XLII *Ac uerba primum
mollia Suadendo blande effuderat, Captator ut uitulum lupus Rapturus adludit
prius.* Even more distinct is Perist. x. 1104, 5 *Aliter silere nescit oris garruli Vox
inquieta quam tubam si fregero,* cf. Av. XXXIX.

would find sympathetic readers. But with 382, the last year but one of Gratian's reign, a change set in. The Pagan worship ceased to be acknowledged; money spent on its ceremonies was claimed for the fiscus or the chest of the Praefectus Praetorio, the bread purveyed for the use of the Vestals and other attendants or priests was withdrawn, the altar of Victory removed. Then the Senate sent Symmachus to protest, but he failed to obtain even a hearing. The gods avenged themselves by a dearth which cut short the bread-supply of Rome, and by the violent death of Gratian in 383. The Pagan party took heart. Praetextatus and Symmachus were conjointly appointed *praefectus praetorio* and *praefectus urbi* for 384; and a decree was obtained commanding the restitution of all ornaments taken from temples or other public buildings. In the summer of 384 they tried to obtain a repeal of the law of Gratian, and to have the Pagan worship placed on its former footing. The *Relatio* of Symmachus on the altar of Victory followed: but though the whole of the imperial *consistory* was deeply moved by its eloquence, the representations of Ambrose prevailed, and the altar was not restored. Soon after followed the series of Theodosian edicts, by which sacrifices were prohibited, the temples closed, instruments of idolatry seized or destroyed, and the privileges of priests abolished (Gibbon, c. xxviii. vol. iii. p. 9 of Milman's Edition).

If then Avienus wrote his fables at any time between 365 and 379 he might naturally speak of temples, altars, sacrifices, sacrificing-priests, victims, incense, and images of the gods as still existing and in habitual use. Isis still had her worshippers, and baldness, which forms the *motif* of the tenth fable and of a learned discussion in the last book of Macrobius, was still a common sight in Roman streets. Such a hypothesis is not indeed necessary: for the fables descend not only from the epoch of Babrius, which Otto Crusius shows to be the reign of Alexander Severus, (222–235), but in some cases from the Aesopic age, the sixth or seventh century B.C. And fables are repeated from one narrator to another with little if any change of scene or surroundings. Yet in reading the forty-two apologues which our author selected from the far longer collection of Babrius, it is difficult to escape the impression of a homogeneous whole, worked up with a purpose, and using as a back-ground the circumstances of every-day life as it existed at the time. If my view is right as to the authorship of this little work, which though widely read in the dark and middle ages, has in modern times almost fallen out of view, and only been brought into renewed notice by the still recent discovery of the Greek text of Babrius on which it was founded, the author was a member of a literary coterie which treasured as sacred every surviving remnant of ancient Roman usage, its religion no less than its language. He was therefore not a Christian, of which belief the fables certainly offer no hint, though it is possible that XXIII represents a point of view peculiarly, if not exclusively, Christian.

II.

THE PROSODY OF AVIANUS.

Cannegieter in his Dissertation on the age and style of Avianus argued that he wrote in the second century of our era and during the reign of the Antonines. The same view has in our own time been held by one of the greatest of philologists, Lachmann; and it is necessary to examine what are the grounds for this opinion.

Cannegieter's first argument was a historical inference. In the preface to his work Avianus gives a short account of his predecessors. *Verum has pro exemplo fabulas et Socrates diuinis operibus indidit et poemati suo Flaccus aptauit, quod in se sub iocorum communium specie uitae argumenta contineant. Quas Graecis iambis Babrius repetens in duo uolumina coartauit. Phaedrus etiam partem aliquam quinque in libellos resoluit. De his ego ad quadraginta et duas in unum redactas fabulas dedi.* Besides Horace, who has occasionally introduced fables into his Satires and Epistles, Phaedrus is the only Roman fabulist alluded to. Yet we know from Ausonius (Epist. xvi. 2. 81, 92) that a collection of Greek Aesopic fables in iambic trimeters (whether the scazons of Babrius, as Cannegieter, Wernsdorf, O. Crusius (De Babrii Aetate p. 238 note) believe, or as I think a version in ordinary iambic trimeters like those which diversify the ordinary Greek prose of Halm's collection (e. g. 20, from Aristoph. Vesp. 1402 sqq., 33[h], 77, 252, 280, 334[c], 391; cf. 248[h], which, though in prose, shews traces of an iambic original, cf. Rutherford, p. xxii) had been translated into Latin prose by Julius Titianus. Auson. Epist. xvi to Probus *Apologos Titiani et Nepotis Chronica, quasi alios apologos (nam et ipsa instar sunt fabularum) ad nobilitatem tuam misi:* and again in the *Epodi* which his friend is to read as the fore-words to the fables (*antelogium fabularum*) he says v. 74 :—

> *Apologos en misit tibi*
> *Ab usque Rheni limite*
> *Ausonius, nomen Italum,*
> *Praeceptor Augusti tui,*
> *Aesopian trimetriam*
> *Quam uertit exili stilo*
> *Pedestre concinnans opus*
> *Fandi Titianus artifex.*

And again 102

> *Sed iam ut loquatur Iulius*
> *Fandi modum inuita accipe*
> *Volucripes dimetria.*

This Julius Titianus was identified by Casaubon (on Capitol. Vit. Maximin. Iunioris c. i) with the *Titianus senior*, whom Capitolinus calls father of a Titianus who taught oratory to the younger Maximinus. This elder Titianus was nicknamed the ape of his Epoch (*simia temporum suorum* Capitol. *l.c.*), and may therefore be plausibly identified with the Julius Titianus who, as we learn from Sidonius (Epp. i. 1) was

called *oratorum simia* by the other Frontonians. He would thus
have been a follower of the famous orator Fronto, the preceptor of
M. Aurelius; and as Maximinus, the father of the younger Titianus'
pupil, became Emperor in 235, the elder Titianus may be assigned to
the immediately preceding reigns of Elagabalus (218), Macrinus (217),
Caracallus (211), and perhaps may be pushed back as far as Com-
modus (180). Now as Avianus in the list of his predecessors in Latin
Fable does not allude to Julius Titianus, he cannot have known him,
and must therefore have lived before him. Hence his own period
may be the age of the Antonines, with which the diction of the
Fables would agree.

To all this Wernsdorf's reply seems sufficient (De Carm. Aviani in his
Poet. Lat. Min. v. pp. 664 sqq.). Avianus in his Preface does not give
an exhaustive list of his predecessors. He mentions only representative types, Socrates, Horace, Babrius, Phaedrus—the two former as
introducing apologues to illustrate their subject, the two latter as
writers of apologues in verse. If Cannegieter's reasoning were valid,
we might as well conclude that Babrius lived intermediate between
Horace and Phaedrus. But as we now know, Phaedrus, a contemporary of the Emperor Tiberius, preceded Babrius by nearly two
centuries. I assume, what since Otto Crusius' Essay I suppose no
one will deny, that the Alexander to whom Babrius addressed his
Fables is Alexander Severus. (See Rutherford, pp. xi–xxiv.) Or
again we might with equal plausibility maintain that Phaedrus lived
after Seneca, because he is ignored in a well-known passage of the
Consolatio ad Polybium, viii. 27 *Non audeo te usque eo producere ut
fabellas quoque et Aesopeos logos intemptatum Romanis ingeniis
opus, solita tibi uenustate conectas.*

But, in truth, though there is much probability in Casaubon's
identification of Ausonius' prose writer of Latin Apologues, Julius
Titianus, with the elder Titianus of Capitolinus, we have nothing
to *prove* that they were the same. Gerard John Voss (De Historicis
Latinis ii. p. 173 ed. 1651) thought the *younger* of Capitolinus' Titiani
was the Apologue-writer; and O. Crusius remarks that such an
occupation would better suit a schoolmaster, such as the younger
Titianus, than a man of literary distinction like his father (p. 244).

Cannegieter's other argument, from the diction and prosody of
Avianus, requires a fuller and more detailed examination. It will be
convenient to take these in reversed order.

The first scholar who subjected the Fables to a close metrical
review was the eighteenth century philologist and critic, John
Hildebrand Withof. In his *Encaenia Critica* published in 1741,
most of which is occupied with a critical examination of the text of
Lucan, a section is given to the Elegies of Maximianus, and another
to the Fables of Avianus. Of Maximianus, and Withof's valuable
services to his often vitiated text, I have spoken in the American
Journal of Philology (vol. v. pp. 1–15, 145–163). His remarks on
Avianus are not less acute; but his corrections are less happy. Yet
it should not be forgotten that his criticisms anticipated Lachmann by

a complete century, and that several of his emendations have now a permanent place in the best editions of the Fables.

If we look at the Elegiacs of Avianus as a whole, the general impression is one of correctness marred by occasional licences. Deviations from classical prosody of a serious kind are rare: omitting a certain number of cases in which the first half of the pentameter is allowed to terminate either with hiatus or on a positionally short syllable (which cases will be considered later), the only violations of strict metre are *uelis* III. 6, XXIII. 10, *dispăr* XI. 5, XXIII. 8, *impăr* XVIII. 10, *Paeŏnio* VI. 7, *fābella* VIII. 2, *nŏlam* VII. 8, *prŏfundens* XXXV. 1, *alteriŭs* XXXV. 4, *herĕs* XXXV. 14, *exstinctŭs ut* XXII. 15.

Lachmann (Kleine Schriften pp. 51 sqq.) argued from *prŏfundens* and *herĕs* in XXXV, the former of which is rare, the latter impossible, that the fable in the shape our MSS give to it is corrupt; that part of it may be restored by conjecture; part is mere interpolation of a later age, probably the seventh and eighth centuries. Hence he changed *geminum profundens* to *geminum una profundens*, and bracketed vv. 3–6, 13–16 as spurious.

Again analysing XXIII he concluded from *dispăr* in 8, *uelis* in 10, as well as from numerous faults of language scattered throughout the fable, that 8 and 9, as well as the epimythion 13, 14, are an interpolation, that 10 must be changed to *Sine decus busti seu decus esse uelis*, and that 1, 5, 7, 11 are to be restored by reading *insignem arte ferens, Alter ut ornatis, ambiguo, Subdita nempe tibi est.*

In these violent changes he had some support from Bentley, who observing that the Epimythia were not in the Gale codex (since collated for Bährens by H. A. J. Munro), concluded that they were all spurious (on Horace A. P. 337).

Here however, since Fröhner's collation of the three oldest Paris MSS, we are able to meet Lachmann on firmer ground. The *promythia* and *epimythia* which these exhibit are at any rate of an early date, for the MSS themselves can scarcely be later than century x, and may be earlier, as Fröhner, a good judge, believed. On the other hand MSS of a decidedly later date contain epimythia which do not occur in any of the best: and these are undoubtedly spurious. It is these *later* epimythia which are omitted in the *Galeanus*: but no argument can be drawn from the *Galeanus* against the genuineness of the others, for like all the other early MSS it contains them.

Lachmann however argued on general principles. Visible to his eye as the substratum of the Fables was 'nobilior aliqui antiquitatis color;' and where language or metre palpably contradicted this view, a later hand had been at work, and conjecture must restore the original but defaced fabric.

The problem is not a very easy one to decide. Lachmann may have failed to restore the original Avianus, but defects of execution do not disprove a hypothesis as a possibility. And at least some part of his hypothesis appears to me indubitably true. The general correctness of Avianus' prosody throws the occasional exceptions into strong, almost glaring, relief. To take the most prominent instance; out of

321 pentameters there are two in which hiatus is admitted in the
middle of the verse, XXVIII. 12 *Quam ferus in domini ora sequentis agit,*
XLI. 8 *Immemor illa sui' Amphora dicor' ait*: XXVII. 10 (Unrein p. 20)
is very doubtful. There are ten in which the first half of the pentameter
ends with a syllable which as standing before a vowel or *h* is positionally short. They are :—

III. 12	Alterius censor ut uitiosa notes.
XI. 6	Incertumque uagus amnis habebat iter.
XIX. 12	Et nostris frueris inperiosa malis.
XXII. 4	Namque alter cupidus, inuidus alter erat.
XXII. 6	Obtulit et precibus ut peteretur, ait.
XXVII. 10	Qua coeptum uolucris explicuisset opus.
XXXIV. 10	In propriis laribus umida grana legit.
XXXV. 16	Spes humiles rursus in meliora refert.
XXXVIII. 6	Verbaque cum salibus asperiora dedit.
XLI. 18	Subdita nobilibus ut sua fata gemant.

To which may be added as at least exceptional—

XXIX. 22	Tam diuersa duō qui simul ora ferat.

It is remarkable that only three of these XXVII. 10, XXXV. 16, and
XLI. 18 occur in epimythia: the remaining seven are in the body of
the fable. But of these three, the last is now, on the authority of my
excellent and uninterpolated British Museum codex *B*, to be written
with *ne* for *ut*: XXVII. 10, XXXV. 16 admit of easy correction,
the former by substituting *cornix* for *uolucris*, the latter by reading
Rursus spes humiles. Yet it must remain a question, whether they are
not accretions of a later age, as Lachmann thought: what is nearly
certain, is, *that they are not the casual or intended slips of a generally
correct writer.*

Of the remaining seven the greater part admit of easy and almost
certain emendation; XIX. 12, XXXIV. 10 by simply transposing two
consecutive words; XI. 6, XXII. 6 by readings found in MSS not
before known: for in XI. 6 *uagans* for *uagus* rests on the authority of

ut peteretur
B; in XXII. 6 my Bodleian codex *X* gives *precibus confiteretur,*
whence I restore the manifestly true reading *precibus quom peteretur.*
XXII. 4 Withof emended by substituting *liuidus* for *inuidus,* a conjecture admitted by Lachmann and all subsequent editors. Two remain
which must be considered doubtful, III. 12 and XXXVIII. 6; that
they are so does not prove that they come from Avianus, but that the
lines of conjecture are insufficiently defined. III. 12 may be a later
accretion, as Lachmann thought: XXXVIII. 6 belongs to a fable
which on other grounds is open to suspicion, notably from the use of
debile in 12. As for *duō* in XXIX. 22, which L. Müller and Krenkel
show to occur more than once in Prudentius, it can hardly be thought
a certain test of lateness, and may fairly be compared with the rare
modō which, as Munro after Lachm. shows, is found in Plautus, Terence,
Lucilius, Lucretius and Cicero's Aratea (on Lucr. ii. 1135).

We may now return to the ten violations of classical prosody
mentioned on p. xxiv. They are *uelis dispăr inpăr Pacŏnio făbella*

nōlam prōfundens alterīūs herēs exstinctūs. Of these ten, two,
Pacōnio prōfundens, cannot be taken into account: for *Paconius,* as
Dr. Ingram shows (Hermathena ix. 407) is regularly used with short *o*
in the Latin poets, Verg. Aen. vii. 769, xii. 401, Ovid M. xv. 535, Sil.
xiv. 27, Stat. S. i. 4, 108, Claud. B. Get. 121, in II. Cons. Stil. 173,
in Eutrop. ii. 12, Apon. 67, for in spite of Ramsay (Prosody p. 118),
Conington (see however the doubtful note on xii. 401), and others, I
cannot but agree with Lachmann's view (Lucret. v. 85) that synizesis
in a Greek word of this kind is unlikely, if not impossible: and
prōfundere is found certainly in Cat. lxiv. 202, Claud. Nilus 12,
perhaps Luc. vii. 159 (Luc. Müller de R. M. p. 363). Again *fābella
alterīūs exstinctūs* though supported by most of the earliest MSS
cannot be thought to come certainly from Av.; for the tenth century
Paris codex *C* has *fabula nostra* written as a v. l. over *nostra fabella;*
for *alterius* several MSS as early as century thirteen give *Alteriusque;*
and *exstinctūs ut,* if indeed it is not accus. plural of a noun, may so
easily be corrected (see App. Crit. on XXII. 15) as a participle, as to
give no difficulty. The remaining five stand on a different footing.
It is perhaps noteworthy that *uelīs* and *dispār* both occur in XXIII, a
fable which on grounds of syntax and unusual obscurity is open to
suspicion. Still both *uelīs* and *dispār* (as well as *infār*) occur again,
III. 6, XI. 5, XVIII. 10; and none of them can be said to belong to
classical prosody, though *uelīs* as a word of frequent occurrence is
more excusable than *possis* of most MSS of Juv. v. 10 (*possit* the
Pithoeanus); and the shortening of the *a* in the inflected cases of
făr[1] had a natural tendency to react on the nominative, cf. *pēs
tripēs,* but *bitēs tripēs quadrupēs* in one v. of Ausonius. *nōlam* in
VII. 8, though not quite certain, for the Lunensis has *notam,* and
one of the Peterhouse MSS *uolam,* was the reading of the early
MS from which the author of the Grammatical treatise in Hagen's
Anecdota Heluetica quotes it, i. e. of a MS at least as early as the
eighth or ninth century. It is, I think, the most outrageous of the
violations of correct prosody which the Fables present, and like *herēs*
(for which Lachm. wrote *heris,* I do not know on what authority),
could not possibly be assigned to any but a late writer.

Lachmann disposed of all these cases either by emendation or
the supposition that they were interpolated. They did not, in fact,
come up to the required standard of purity which he traced in
the real Avianus. But suppose them all genuine; may not a Lach-
mannian hypothesis not indeed of a second century Avianus, coeval
with the Antonines, but of an Avianus closely following Babrius, be true?

Prof. E. A. Freeman (Methods of Historical Study pp. 197 sqq.) has
called attention to the fact which we are too ready to ignore, that there

---

[1] The reading of the Ilias Latina 901, 2 *Occurritque uiro, sed non cum uiribus
aequis, Aeacidae nec compar erat* is doubtful: the MSS give *corpus,* though one of
Wernsdorf's Wolfenbüttel MSS has *compar* written over, and C. Barth, no light
authority, thought the poet wrote *compăr.* The date of the Ilias Latina is assigned
by Lachmann and L. Müller to the age of Nero, by Bücheler, who thought Silius
Italicus wrote it, to the beginning of the second century.

was a stage in the history of the Roman Empire when Latin nearly gave way to Greek. 'For a season, even in the western lands, Latin seemed to have passed away as the tongue of anything that claimed to be literature. . . . If the feeble thread of the Augustan History did not bind together the age of Trajan and the age of Diocletian, we might almost say that it was by the Christian writers of Roman Africa that the Latin tongue was kept alive.' The Letters of Fronto and his pupil M. Aurelius, the *Noctes Atticae* of A. Gellius, the *Golden Ass* of Apuleius, in prose : in verse the *De Medicina Praecepta* of Q. Serenus Sammonicus, the fine fragment of Nemesianus' *Cynegetica*, the *Peruigilium Veneris* which Bücheler assigns to the second or third century, and the *Concubitus Martis et Veneris* of Reposianus are the best surviving representations of the literature of this epoch. No doubt many poems of the *Anthologia Latina* belonged to it besides ; but the dates of most of these are unknown or uncertain. Hence we are left with a very inadequate knowledge of the gradual modifications by which the metre and prosody of Silius, Statius, Val. Flaccus, Juvenal, and Martial passed into the wholly different metre and prosody of Ausonius and Prudentius. There is therefore no *a priori* improbability in the view that the original Avianus belonged to the age of Alexander Severus or his immediate successors. And it would be very rash to assert that the violations of classical prosody just examined were impossible in 250 A.D. because they were impossible in 120.

Let us look at the two indubitable specimens of the poetry of this interval, the 1107 hexameters of Serenus Sammonicus (circ. 200–235 A.D.) and the fragm. of Nemesianus' *Cynegetica* edited by Haupt. The only departures from strict prosody which Serenus Sammonicus exhibits are the short -*to* of the imperative *confunditō curatō iungitō permulcetō*, etc., the lengthening (if MSS may be trusted) of *poterīs* 12, and of *uōmica* 738. In diction he is more distinctly unclassical, *fimus* as neuter 599,714, *penitis* as dat. plur. of an adj. *penitus* (448), perhaps *absorbitur* (so Bährens) for *absorbetur* 460. Elision, though not over frequent, is pretty regular : in 221 verses I have counted 65 elisions, which gives an average of 2 for 7 lines. The metre and diction of Nemesianus (255–284 A.D.) are, as might be expected in a didactic poem imitating Vergil and Gratius, more severe ; *denotō exercetō*, hiatus once *catuli huc* 150, *feruida zonae* as the end of a hexameter 154, with the rare words *inocciduus, cibatus*. Elision is very sparingly employed : the 325 vv. contain, it is true, 52 elisions, an average of about 1 to 6 lines : but long passages occur (e.g. 96–124) without any ; and a large majority are cases of elided *que* or *atque*. On the other hand the hexameter poem of Reposianus (253 in Riese's Anthol. Latina), which Teuffel seems rightly to assign to the third century, exhibits two violent transgressions of correct prosody, *tū* monosyllabic in 93, *gratiosa* seemingly a palimbacchius ($- - \cup$) in 126. But as the text of this poem rests on one MS only, and the metre is otherwise carefully correct, no great weight can be given to these two errors. Elision occurs 21 times, i.e. an average of 2 in 17 lines, or rather more than 1 in 8.

Such an estimate, based on very scanty materials, and those of quite a different kind from the work of Avianus, must needs be rough and cannot *prove* anything. Yet so far as it goes, it seems to shew that the tradition of classical prosody remained substantially unaltered in good writers up to the age of Diocletian. It is of course true that writers such as the Christian poet Commodianus (238–250 A.D.), in whom all laws of metre are set at defiance, were beginning to tell upon literature ; and it is very probable that much of the Latin Anthology which we might be willing to assign to a period of barbarism, really dates from the second or third century. Still, taking the more formal productions of the interval from the Antonines to Diocletian as a standard of the correctness of literary works, we may perhaps say that the five cases of abnormal prosody which a review of the Fables left unaccounted for would not have been tolerated in a set work of the period under consideration.

If then the original kernel of Avianus is to be placed in the latter half of the second or again in the third century, we must first eliminate at least seven verses which are inconsistent with an age of metrical purity. Now allowing that two of these verses XXIII. 8, 10 fall under reasonable suspicion, from the rough and obscure style of the fable as a whole, and that the distich containing XVIII. 10 seems unnecessary and may be an interpolation, it is impossible to remove III. 6, XI. 5, VII. 8, XXXV. 14. from their place without virtually destroying in each case the whole fabric of the fable. It seems safer to believe that they are real evidences of a declining feeling of metrical correctness, and are the production of a later time.

The sum of the above argument is that Lachmann's hypothesis of an early and purer text of which our extant Avianus is a barbarized depravation, is quite borne out as regards metre by the general correctness of the verse and by the variations of the MSS : but that the violations of classical prosody, which after a critical examination still remain unaccounted for, do not justify us in pushing the first composition of the Fables back to a period either as early as the Antonines (which the probable date of Babrius makes impossible) or to the time between Alexander Severus and Diocletian.

III.

THE DICTION AND SYNTAX OF AVIANUS.

The style of Avianus has been variously estimated by different critics. Eberhard of Bethune in his *Labyrinthus* (iii. 9) written in the thirteenth century speaks of his *pauperior stylus*. Lilius Gyraldus (De Poetis Dial. iv) dismisses him with a few words, as unworthy of serious attention. Nevelet found the fables full of faults which must be condoned as written in a debased period and on which it was useless to waste thought or time. Caspar Barth in one mood lauds him as an elegant poet comparable with the best (Aduers. xxvii. 4, xxxix. 7, especially xxxix. 13), and with Atticisms of style (xxxix. 13), in another censures him as an unskilful and rustic writer of the meaner kind, full of barbarisms, with no judgment, and crassly ignorant of metre (Aduers. xix. 24, xxvii. 4, xxix. 13). Nicolas Heinsius (Adu. 611) says 'quoties incido in Avieni fabellas, elegantes sane lepidasque, toties indignor aut oscitantibus ac inscitis librariis, aut aliis hominibus male feriatis tam multum in eas licuisse. Adeo soloecismis syllabisque nunc contra legem metricam productis, nunc correptis sunt inquinatae.' Cannegieter distinguished the true Avianus from the false; the true was polished pure Vergilian, and might well belong to the age of M. Aurelius: the false was mainly the work of school-masters, who in their eagerness to point a moral for the edification of their young pupils, added promythia and epimythia which have disguised the simple proportions of the original. Withof (Encaenia Critica, p. 231 sqq.) while declaring that the corrupt state of Avianus' text was such as might well draw tears, ascribed these faults to the copyists and set himself to the task of removing them by conjecture. Wopkens[1], by far the ablest scholar who has examined the language and grammar of the fables, accepted them as a genuine product of a very late period, and did great service by recalling critics from the rash attempts at emendation which Cannegieter's edition had encouraged, to a sober examination of the Latin of the fourth and fifth centuries. Wernsdorf (P. L. M. v. p. 669) confesses that the 'childish and inarticulate talk' which Withof had denounced is after all attempts too palpable and unworthy of any but a declining epoch.

In the present century, Édélestand du Méril in the short notice which he has given of Avianus in his *Poésies inédites du Moyen Âge* (pp. 95—97) describes him in these severe words, 'Le style traînant, embarrassé, sans unité ni aucune propriété d' expression, quelquefois même véritablement barbare, trahit un esprit encore grossier et trop inexpérimenté des choses littéraires pour ne pas ignorer les usages de la prosodie.' L. Müller de Re Metr. p. 55, censures Lachmann for *introducing* into Avianus' text metrical faults from which they are quite free, but considers their real deviations from strict prosody and pure Latin to point to the latest period of the Empire, the period of Maximianus and Arator. This opinion he seems in his treatise De Phaedri et Auiani Fabulis, p. 32, to modify so far as to place the date not later than the fifth century. The style he considers to have some merits, but to be far inferior to Babrius, and even to Phaedrus. Fröhner

---

[1] Wopkens' Notes on Avianus were first printed in Miscell. Observatt. Critt. in Auct. Vet. et Recent. vol. vii. Tom. 2, pagg. 197-253 Amstelod. 1736. Withof's Encaenia Critica appeared in 1741. Both Withof and Wopkens were men of great acuteness. Wopkens in particular, as will be evident to anyone who examines his Aduersaria (published collectively in 1834), was as an exponent of Latin construction and syntax far in advance of his time. Bährens' criticisms of Avianus in his Miscellanea Critica (1878) do not seem to me up to his ordinary mark.

(Praef. p. xii) calls Avianus a very rustic story-teller of the fifth century undeniably.　Schenkl (Zeitsch. f. Österr. Gymn. xvi. p. 398) finds none of the grace of Babrius in our collection: but considers it interesting as a monument of fifth century language, and perhaps as containing lost fables of Babrius.　Bährens, accepting the views of L. Müller as to the late date of composition, finds much to be tolerated, yet much that is too rough and coarse, as well as too incoherent and absurd, to belong to any time but the Middle Age (Misc. Crit. p. 137).　Unrein De Auiani Aetate (Iena 1885) believes the work to have been dedicated to Macrobius the author of the *Saturnalia*, and identifying him with the *praefectus praetorio Hispaniarum* of 399 A. D. (cod. Theod. xvi. 10. 15, viii. 5. 61), *Proconsul Africae* 410 (cod. Theod. xi. 28. 6), *praepositus sacri cubiculi* 422 (cod. Theod. vi. 8. 1) fixes the date of Avianus from 400-420 A. D.　Sittl considers the diction of Av. essentially barbarous and pronounces him in his want of finish and the awkwardness with which he connects his verses on a par with Dracontius and Corippus.

Before attempting to mediate between views so opposed as those of Heinsius and Du Méril, it will be worth while to clear the ground, in other words to consider how much of the 42 fables can safely be thought to come from Avianus.

Fabricius (Bibl. Latina iii. p. 155 ed. Ernesti) with whom Du Méril seems to agree (p. 97) thought that some of the Fables were of a later date than most of the Collection; these had been introduced in place of others which were in the original 42 published by Avianus, which latter were ousted for the new-comers, in order to keep up the specified number of 42.　This seems to be supported by a gloss on Dig. xvii. 2. 29, where Aristo is quoted as stating that Cassius used to call a partnership in which one only gained, the other lost, a *leonine partnership*.　A gloss on this passage speaks of '*fabulam Aniani de societate leonina*,' obviously the fable of the lion hunting with a cow, she-goat and sheep (Phaed. i. 5), or as in the prose Greek versions (Halm Fab. Aesop. 260) with an ass and a fox.　It is not in our Avianus: yet it may have been in the Avianus which the Glossator had before him. This is true; but the date of the gloss is uncertain, and a slip of memory in quoting a fable as Avianus' (if he is alluded to in *Aniani*) which was not in his, but in some other collection, would be very easy.

There are however some few distichs and one or two whole fables which are unlike the usual style of the rest.　The most notable example is XXIII, which the Commentary will show to be from first to last involved in construction, awkward in language (*referens* in 1, *omen* in 7, *spes* in 8, *praestare* in 14) and licentious in metre (*dispär. uelis*). Rather less objectionable, but open to grave suspicion, is XXXV.　It accumulates four metrical faults, *profundens* 1, *Alterïus* 4, *herës* 14, *rursüs* 16; while as regards language, *Fama est quod* 1, *caro amore* 3, *quoque* 13, perhaps *exsaturata* 4, seem to point to a different author.　A similar doubt attaches to XXXVIII; for though *salibus* has been plausibly emended, the use of *laboratis* for 'got-up,' 'artificial' in 7, and still more of *debile* in 12 for 'ignoble,' 'mean,' betrays a very late authorship.

Bentley (on Hor. A. P. 337) maintained that the Epimythia or additional verses in which the fable is applied to a didactic purpose were all spurious, and he asserted that they are not in the Gale MS. The collation of this MS made by H. A. J. Munro for Bährens proves however that all the Epimythia which are found in Fröhner's three earliest MSS, as well as in the Vossianus L. Q. 86 (Lachmann's *antiquissimus*), are also in the *Galeanus*; and this is also true of the Promythia, or moral introductions. There are however in many of the more recent MSS Epimythia of later genesis and obviously forged: it is one of Fröhner's greatest services to have shown that these must be distinguished from the earlier as quite on a different level.

The genuine Epimythia are—

I. 15, 16	Haec sibi dicta putet, seque hac sciat arte notari, Femineam quisquis credidit esse fidem.
II. 15, 16	Sic quicumque noua sublatus laude tumescit, Dat merito poenas, dum meliora cupit.
XVI. 19, 20	Haec nos dicta monent magnis obsistere frustra, Paulatimque truces exsuperare minas.
XXVII. 9, 10	Viribus haec docuit quam sit prudentia maior, Qua coeptum uolucris explicuisset opus.
XXX. 17, 18	Haec illos descripta monent, qui saepius ausi Numquam peccatis abstinuere manus.
XXXIII. 13, 14	Sic qui cuncta deos uno male tempore poscunt, Iustius his etiam uota diurna negant.
XXXVI. 17, 18	preceded by two vv. which end the dialogue. I give all four:
	'Proderit ergo grauis quamuis perferre labores, Otia quam tenerum mox peritura pati.'
	Est hominum sors ista, magis felicibus ut mors Sit cita, cum miseros uita diurna regat.
XLI. 17, 18	Haec poterunt post haec miseros exempla monere Subdita nobilibus ut (ne *B*) sua fata gemant.

XXIII, XXXV are suspicious as wholes: I therefore omit the epimythia belonging to them. The last two vv. of III are not an epimythion proper, but an epimythiastic addition.

The Promythia are the following—

V. 1–4	Metiri se quemque decet propriisque iuuari Laudibus, alterius nec bona ferre sibi, Ne detracta grauem faciant miracula risum, Coeperit in solis cum remanere malis.
VII. 1–2	Haud facile est prauis innatum mentibus ut se Muneribus dignas supplicioue putent.
VIII. 1–4	Contentum propriis sapientem uiuere rebus, Nec cupere alterius, nostra fabella monet. Indignata cito ne stet fortuna recursu, Atque eadem minuat, quae dedit ante, rota.

XXXIV. 1-4   Quisquis torpentem passus transisse iuuentam
                Nec timuit uitae prouidus ante mala,
              Confectus senio, postquam grauis adfuit aetas,
                Heu frustra alterius saepe rogabit opem.

This conspectus will suffice to shew that the Epimythia and Promythia in Avianus do not stand on the same footing with those in Babrius. Rutherford seems to have decided rightly in rejecting the latter *en masse;* they are usually very transparent forgeries, and could not possibly come from Babrius. Yet even amongst these there are some which are less pronouncedly spurious than the rest : I may mention xxiv, xxxv, xcviii, civ. Still, speaking of them as a whole, it seems true that 'every kind of error in metre, accidence, and syntax is represented in them' (Rutherford, p. lxxxviii). And whatever causes were at work to prompt didactic or gnomic *additamenta* to Babrius, would be equally true of Avianus. The school-boy would ask the meaning of a fable ; the schoolmaster would supply this answer and suggest, if he did not himself fabricate, the verses which expressed it. The πτερνίσματα and ἐπικαττύματα, as Phrynichus tells us they were called (Rutherford p. lxxxvi), would be forthcoming all the more readily in proportion to the moral purity of the work. It is indeed certain that the fables of Avianus, doubtless for this reason, almost supplanted those of Phaedrus in spite of the literary charm of Phaedrus, and the comparatively early period of the Latin language when he wrote. We know too what care was necessary to keep the text of favorite authors uncontaminated, and to what accidents in spite of all care they were liable. Vettius Praetextatus, the friend of Symmachus, and like him a determined opponent of Christianity, is stated in the iambics with which his wife Paulina addresses him in the Sepulchral Inscription to his memory (C. I. L. vi. 1779 cited in Seeck's ed. of Symmachus p. lxxxiv) to have revised and emended the texts of many authors both in prose and verse :—

              Tu namque quidquid lingua utraque est proditum
              Cura soforum, porta quis caeli patet,
              Vel quae periti condidere carmina,
              Vel quae solutis uocibus sunt edita,
              Meliora reddis quam legendo sumpseras :

and a *subscriptio* appended to several MSS of Macrobius' Commentary on the *Somnium Scipionis* states that this work had been revised and punctuated by Aurelius Memmius Symmachus. Sidonius (Epp. vi. 15) in sending to his friend Ruricius a volume of the Prophets, tells him it had been cleared from much rubbish, yet that the counter-reader (*contra legente*) who had undertaken, it would seem, to compare it with another copy, had from ill-health or some other cause not performed his promise. In some cases, indeed, a work was revised and in part re-written long after the author had passed away. The hexameter poem of Dracontius *De Creatione Mundi*, written circ. 425 A.D., was re-edited by Eugenius, about 220 years after his death (Clinton, F. R. ii. p. 472). Ildefonsus (middle of seventh century), on whose authority this statement rests, gives some particulars so highly illustrative of the casualties of literature at that time as to deserve quotation: *Libellos quoque Dracontii de Creatione Mundi conscriptos, quos antiquitas protulerat uitiatos, subtrahendo immutando uel meliorando in pulchritudinis formam coegit ut pulchriores de artificio corrigentis quam de manu processisse uideantur auctoris. Et quia de die septimo idem Dracontius omnimodo reticendo semiplenum opus uisus est reliquisse, iste et sex dierum recapitulationem singulis uersibus renotauit, et de die septimo quae illi uisa sunt eleganter dicta subiunxit* (Ildefons. de Scriptor. Ecclesiasticis c. 14). If Eugenius thought he might 'subtract,' 'change,' or 'improve' on a poet who lived 220 years before him, it is perfectly possible that the same thing might happen to the fables of Avianus.

It is necessary, in judging on this question, to consider the Epimythia and Promythia, (1) *en masse*, (2) singly.

(1) Looked at collectively, they can hardly, I think, be said to stand out from the rest of the work in any marked way. Omitting XXIII and XXXV, which are open to doubt as wholes, the rest of the Epimythia are very much in the prevailing style. In sixteen verses there is only one metrical fault (*uolucris explicuisset* XXVII. 10). The only peculiarities of diction are *descripta* XXX. 17, *diurna* XXXIII. 14, XXXVI. 18.

The Promythia are very similar. In twelve verses there is one false quantity *fábella*, for which however *C* gives a v. l. (see above, p. xxvi). In language *miracula* V. 3, *passus Nec timuit* XXXIV. 1, 2, are hardly classical: but have parallels in the literature of the fourth century.

On the other hand it is noticeable that all the Epimythia are in two vv., all the Promythia except one in four. Rutherford shows that there was a tendency to *tetrastichism* in the interpolators of Babrius; and it may have become part of a received tradition.

(2) Judged singly, they cannot all be placed on the same level. I. 15, 16 are inseparable from the rest of the fable. To end on v. 14 would be abrupt: 15, 16 round off the narrative. II. 15, 16 are not so necessary: the fable might well end with 14. But in themselves 15, 16 are unobjectionable: if anything calls for suspicion it is the rare passive use of *exosae* in 13: which however has a parallel in XXXIII. 6. XXXIII. 13, 14 are similar to II. 15, 16: unobjectionable in themselves, and required to prevent the fable ending suddenly. The epimythion XVI. 19, 20 seems to correspond closely with the similar epimythion of Babr. 36:

κάλαμος μὲν οὗτως· ὁ δέ γε μῦθος ἐμφαίνει
μὴ δεῖν μάχεσθαι τοῖς κρατοῦσιν, ἀλλ' εἴκειν.

Yet the variations of the MSS lead me to doubt whether the original reading was not
Haec nos dicta monent magnis obsistere fluxa;
and if this conjecture is right, the moral of the Latin fable is not that it is useless to resist the great, but that the weak at times stand against the strong. Here too again there is some abruptness in the ending of the fable *Motibus aura meis ludificata perit* if vv. 19, 20 are withdrawn: an argument which applies even more forcibly to XXVII. 9,

10, which cannot possibly be wrenched away from their context.˙ The fable, we may be sure, did not end with the abrupt statement

<blockquote>
Nam breuis inmersis accrescens sponte lapillis
Potandi facilem praebuit unda uiam.
</blockquote>

The metrical fault *uolucris* may easily be corrected by substituting *cornix ;* for I cannot believe that Avianus would have ended the first half of a pentameter with a short syllable.

On the other hand, XXX. 17, 18 are quite comparable with the Babrian interpolations: they spoil the effect of the fable, which otherwise ends with an epigrammatic question completely worthy both of Avianus and Babrius at their best. The same may be said of XLI. 17, 18 : they are unnecessary, the fable having already ended effectively with the declamatory

<blockquote>
Infelix, quae magna sibi cognomina sumens
Ausa pharetratis nubibus ista loqui.
</blockquote>

More puzzling are XXXVI. 17, 18. For not only is the curious assonance

<blockquote>
Est hominum s o r s i s t a, magis felicibus ut m o r s
Sit c i t a
</blockquote>

alien to the sober style of Avianus, but the two vv. which precede them can hardly, in their existing form, have come from him: both the inversion *grauis quamuis* and the combination *otia pati* are abnormal.

In the Promythia I seem to detect a forger. Three of them are tetrastichs, and all contain the word *alterius*. He would seem to have wished to leave his mark on the bastard children of his creation. The fourth is a distich, the Latin of which is faulty ; either *muneribus* or *dignas* is strained.

The conclusion of the above examination is that the Epimythia in our Fables, though at times and to some extent questionable, are not, like those in Babrius, so decidedly inferior to the bulk of the work as to justify us in rejecting them altogether. In most cases they cannot well be removed without leaving a gap more or less perceptible. Yet, as they are sometimes combined with verses which from their peculiarity suggest a different authorship,—as, besides, three of the promythia point visibly to a self-conscious, self-betraying fabricator, and all of them are easily removable, it is more than probable that at some time after the life of Avianus a new editor revised the fables in accordance with the debased standard of his time, and with additions adapted to the increasing illiteracy of an age falling more and more into darkness.

The ground having thus been cleared of doubtful or spurious additions, we may proceed to judge the language of the genuine remainder. There is, I believe, enough of undeniable uniformity in this to justify a pronounced verdict.

Avianus himself says in his Preface that he had written in rude Latin (*rudi latinitate*). This is not the first impression to a modern reader. The general effect is a complex one : there is a blending of two quite distinct styles. The prevailing tone of the language is not only elaborately poetical, but specially Vergilian. Every fable has

echoes or actual imitations of the Aeneid. Even where not distinctly
modelled on Vergil, it is artificial and worked up; in no sense rude or
commonplace. And doubtless, had Avianus wished, he might have
woven his fabric throughout on this model. But writing in an age
when the Latin language was not only senescent, but visibly on its
way to destruction, writing too on a subject which appealed to simple
or childish understandings, one in which trees talk, beasts and men
converse, birds dispute, fishes cry, he could not but adapt his language
to suit in some degree both his subject and his hearers. Hence side
by side with the prevailing poetical style of the fables is a style which
breaks through it somewhat incongruously, in which the words belong
to the decadent diction of the epoch, and the grammatical construction is allowed to follow the increasingly lax usage of popular speech.
In proportion as this latter element asserts itself, the fables seem
unfinished or even rude ; and there are hardly any in which the
mixture of the two kinds does not produce a constrained effect. In
this respect Avianus is far below Babrius ; he has none of the playful
grace of his Greek model. But it is more than probable that his very
weakness is in part the cause of his popularity: the strange unclassical
words and constructions are the signs of his sympathy with his
time.

It is not necessary to speak at length of the former of these two
elements of Avianus' style. It has much that is common with other
poets of the same period, such as Claudian and Prudentius, or the
somewhat later writers, Rutilius Namatianus and Maximianus. As
compared with Ausonius, we are able to speak more definitely. The
seventy-fifth epigram of Ausonius is a translation of the seventy-fifth
Babrian fable :

> Languentem Gaium moriturum dixerat olim
>   Eunomus: euasit fati ope, non medici.
> Paulo post ipsum uidet aut uidisse putauit
>   Pallentem et multa mortis in effigie.
> 'Quis tu?' 'Gaius' ait, 'uiuisne?' hic abnuit, 'et quid
>   Nunc agis hic?' 'missu Ditis' ait 'uenio,
> Vt, qui notitiam rerumque hominumque tenerem,
>   Accirem medicos.' Eunomus obriguit.
> Tum Gaius 'metuas nihil, Eunome : dixi ego et omnes
>   Nullum qui saperet dicere te medicum.'

Had Avianus translated Babrius in this style, we may feel sure he
would long since have perished. With the exception of brevity (ten
lines for Babrius' twenty) Ausonius' version has no merit at all. It
fails to preserve any part of the charm of the original. The Latin, to
be sure, is classical, but the rhythm is that of the Greek Anthology,
sometimes as in v. 9 even beyond the Greek Anthology in licence.
All the pentameters end in trisyllabic or quadrisyllabic words: *i* is
elided in *fati ope, dixi ego et*, twice in the compass of ten lines, and in
the latter instance with a second elision in the same dactylic foot.
Whereas Avianus has only allowed himself to elide *i* five times in
642 lines *fragili et, breui est, tibi est, fieri exstinctam, sibi abrupti*,

and of these five *tibi*, *sibi* are doubtfully long. The comparison is instructive: art has had a good deal to do in preserving our Fables from oblivion.

Other points of care there are in which Avianus contrasts favorably not only with Ausonius, but with Maximianus, approaching even Rutilius. For instance, the second foot of the hexameter is allowed to terminate on an elided syllable *Dispar erat fragili et* only once by Avianus in 642 vv.; whereas Ausonius in 634 elegiacs (Parentalia, Eclogae, Elegiacs to Theodosius, to the Reader, to Syagrius) has six such cases, Maximianus in 686 has 2; while Rutilius goes beyond the strictness of Avianus, and in 712 elegiacs has none.

In another point, again, which in an especial sense marks the poetry of the fourth century A.D., I mean the shortening of nominatives in *-es*, whether by writing them *-is* or simply allowing *-es* to count as a short syllable, a phenomenon which occurs five times in Ausonius (*Thalĕs, bipĕs, tripĕs, quadrupĕs, ederipĕs*), once in Maximianus (*Vlissĕs*), more frequently in Prudentius, *pubis, luis, famis* (each twice), *Ioannis* (three times), *prolis* once. the fables of Avianus present only one, *herĕs*; *uulpis* is found as early as Phaedrus, and can hardly be counted as an example.

On the other hand the fourth century tendency to end the pentameter with a nomin. sing. participle, a departure from classical usage of the most marked kind, seems to be more affected by Avianus than by any writer of the fourth or fifth centuries. Claudian admits it very sparingly, Prudentius in his single Elegiac poem (Perist. xi) only three times in 123, Merobaudes only once (*ouans*) in 21 pentameters. Maximianus is freer: he has five instances in 343 pentameters, while Avianus in 321 has twelve.

This, however, is a metrical digression. I return to the more marked features of Avianus' *language*, viewed on its distinctively *poetical* side.

A. The following points are noticeable:

(1) Transformation of a sentence naturally expressed by a passive verb followed by an abl. to a nomin. with an active verb. The best instance is I. 6 *Spem quoque raptori sustulit inde fames=spes raptori sublata est famis explendae.* A less violent case is XV. 11 *Quamuis innumerus plumas uariauerit ordo=quamuis innumero ordine uariatae sint plumae.* Cf. XIX. 4. This transformation of a passive to an active construction, with its attendant change of subject, is not uncommon in Latin poetry. Propertius' *adspergat tempora sudor* for *adspergantur tempora sudore*, Claudian's *necdum festiuos regia cantus Sopierat* for *necdum in regia festiui cantus sopiti erant*, are typical instances; but it is not so often that the new nominative is a mere *state* or *quality*.

(2) Tentative uses, in which the poet seems to be playing with language, so that the words suggest more than one meaning, according as they are taken in a classical or in a post-classical sense. This was possible when Latin words were passing into wholly new significations. It was, perhaps, connected with the tendency observable in some Christian writings, such as the letters of Ennodius and Sidonius, to

use words with an esoteric or at least a non-natural meaning. To this class belong

positi capilli X. 11, in the classical sense = placed on purpose; later Latin 'artificial.'

tantorum XVIII. 10, cl. 'so great': l.l. 'so many.'

praesumptus uigor V. 10, cl. 'assumed in advance': l.l. 'presumed upon.'

fatigans XXXI. 7, cl. 'worrying': l.l. 'joking.' Cf. our 'bantering.'

diurnus XXXIII. 14, cl. 'of the day': l.l. nearly = *quotidianus.*

(3) Affected uses of single words, but which are not unclassical—e. g. *nullus*, where we should say 'never,' 'nowhere,' 'not at all,' VII. 3, XXVII. 5, XXXVI. 7, XL. 3, *pecus* of a single animal V. 16, XXVIII. 4, *semina* of plants XII. 4, *munera* followed by a gen. of the thing offered XIV. 2, *munera natorum, caespes* = a tuft of roots XVI. 7, cf. XXI. 2, *conuenire*, 'to encounter,' 'cross the path' XVII. 15, IX. 6, *onus* used with slight if any meaning XX. 2, and in the odd combination *auris onus* XXX. 6, VIII. 12, *difficilis* 'intractable' XX. 14, *datur* is said III. 4, XXV. 10, *breuis* 'small' or 'scanty,' *b. simia* XIV. 9, *unda* XXVII. 7, cf. XXXIV. 6, XXXVIII. 12 (see Cannegieter's Discussion, pp. 314-315), *moles* of a heavy mist, *m. nimborum* XXIX. 3, *pharetratus* of the clouds charged with hail and rain XLI. 16, *iubar* of the peacock's sheeny tail XV. 8.

(4) Grecisms.

XXIV. 15, 16   Tunc hominem aspiceres oppressum murmure magno,
           Conderet ut rabidis ultima fata genis.
           Εἶδες ἂν τὸν ἄνθρωπον ὡς τέλος ἔχοι τοῦ πότμου.

XI. 9, 10   Illa timens, ne quid leuibus grauiora nocerent,
           Et quia nulla breui est cum meliore fides.

Here *breui* = τῷ βραχεῖ.

B. I come to the second part of the subject, i. e. to those words, expressions, or combinations of words, which Avianus has admitted in his Fables not as poetical, but as part of the development of Latin in his own time. This point has been discussed but very partially by Unrein, and cursorily by Sittl.

1. Use of *quoque.* Av. delights in this adverb, and has introduced it in many of his fables, often in a lax or even weak way, e. g. XVIII. 5 *Hos quoque collatis inter se cornibus ingens Dicitur in siluis pertimuisse leo*, where it simply introduces a new statement about the oxen which are the subject of the fable, 'Besides.' See notes on XXXV. 13, I. 6, IX. 21.

2. *nimius* = strong, deep, *nimiam sitim* XXVII. 4, *nimias aquas* IV. 8, *nimiae quieti* I. 5, *nimio igne* IV. 12.

3. *exosus* 'hated' II. 13, XXXIII. 6. Found also in Macrobius.

4. *discutere* 'to examine' XIV. 8 : also in Symmachus. Av. also uses this verb in its literal sense, *d. crines* XXVIII. 14.

5. *differre* 'to disperse,' 'rout,' X. 10, XXXI. 8.

6. *ferre iurgia* 'to quarrel' XIII. 8, *f. uulnus* 'to wound' XVII. 11, but *ferre uulnus* 'to be wounded' XX. 4.

7. *relidere* 'to dash' III. 2, X. 10. Unrein shows that Sallust ap.

Serv. on Aen. iii. 414 used the word in his *Historiae* = 'dash back':
but as used by Av. it is unclassical.

8. *referre* twice in a doubtful meaning XXIII. 1 *referens de marmore
Bacchum*, XXIX. 14 *Siluarum referens optima quaeque dabal*. No
word is so common in Av. or other writers of the time. In the
prose Panegyric of Merobaudes to Aetius, p. 10 N. two consecutive
sentences end with this word in two wholly different significations.
*Iam considera, ductor inuicte, quanta tibi haec agenti praemia debeantur,
pro quibus mihi tanta sunt collata referenti. Tibi quidem nullum
commune praemium, nec par ceteris honor, aut laus aliqua usitata
referenda est.*

9. *recurrere* nearly = *redire* VI. 3.

10. *dare uerba* ' to speak ' IX. 20, XXIV. 10, XXXVII. 2, XXXVIII.
6. Once only in its classical sense to deceive I. 14.

11. *cupere* ' to claim ' or ' assert,' ἀξιοῦν, VII. 16, XXIV. 12.

12. *defremere* ' to cease raving ' XXVIII. 4. The word is found in
Plin. Epist. ix. 13, and is so printed by Keil, following the Medicean
MS, but others give *deferuissel*. It is not till Sidonius that it comes
into frequent use. (Unrein.)

13. *tanta* for *tot* X. 9 *tantis milibus*.

14. *substantia* ' property ' XXXIV. 17.

15. *prosus* adj. ' direct,' ' straightforward,' *proso tramite* III. 8.

16. *inmensus* 'large,' 'full grown,' *i. leonem* XIII. 1, *i. iuuencis* XVIII. 1,
i. aratro XXVIII. 5. where see note: and cf. C. Barth Aduers. xxxix. 13.

To these Unrein adds the following :—

1. *debilis* XXXVIII. 11, *debile uulgus*, ' the ignoble rabble,' for which
he says no instance can be found earlier than a law of King Childebert
in the sixth century. I am inclined on other grounds to doubt the
genuineness of this fable as a whole : not only *debile*, but *laboratis* in
v. 7, is suspicious.

2. *resultans* XXXIX. 13, which Unr. interprets ' recusans': a
sense which he states to be found first in the Letters of Sixtus
(Xistus), Bishop of Rome, 8 (Tom. L. p. 611 Migne), *nullus obuiet salu-
bribus constitutis, nullus praeceptionibus his resultet*, ib. *si huic uoluerit
Ecclesiae resultare ;* afterwards in Cassiodorius, and Gregory of Tours.
But in XXXIX. 13 this is not the meaning: see my note.

3. *sperare* = *rogare* in two passages VIII. 11 *Iuppiter arridens, postquam sperata negauit*, XXII. 9 *nam quae sperauerit unus*. But in the
former place *sperata* is simply ' his wish'; in the latter most of the
MSS give *nam quaeque rogauerit*, and either this, or, as I prefer, *quae
namque rogauerit* is probably what Av. wrote.

4. *Expositus* in XXXVI. 4 *Ferre nec expositis otia nosse iugis.*
Here Unr. explains *expositis* as = *depositis ;* and it seems to be so used
in Tertullian, Arnobius, Lactantius, Cyprian, Paulinus of Nola, and
Dracontius. But in Av. XXXVI. 4 nothing proves this meaning :
it may quite as naturally signify ' open' (so Withof), and refer to
the hill-ridges over which the steer left to itself ranges at liberty. But it
is more than possible that *expositis* is a corruption of *haec positis ;* see
my note.

C. It remains to notice the peculiarities of syntax and construction in the Fables.

1. Use of *quod* with finite verb for infinitive.

I. 1, 2   Rustica deflentem paruum iaurauerat olim,
              Ni taceat, rabido *quod foret* esca lupo.

XXXV. 1 Fama est *quod* geminum profundens simia natum
              Diuidat.

Dräger, Historische Syntax, ii. p. 225, shows that this construction is observable in writers from the middle of the 2nd cent. onwards. Roby shows it is common in the Digest (Introd. to Dig. p. ccxvii). If the view of those who maintain that Av. wrote in the 5th or 6th century were true, it is wonderful that a phenomenon of such common occurrence at that time as this construction should occur so very rarely in the Fables. On the other hand *nolo ut* XXIX. 21 seems to be unexampled.

2. Late use of participle in -*dus*, as a future passive participle. *Non timor ex animo deculiendus erit* XI. 12.

3. Anomalous or anacoluthic constructions modelled on the language of the people. Of these there are two main types.

(*a*) II. 1   Testudo locuta est,
              Si quis eam uolucrum constituisset humi,
              Protinus e rubris conchas *proferret* harenis.

IX. 2–4   Cum socio quidam suscipiebat iter,
              Securus, quodcumque malum fortuna tulisset,
              Robore collato *posset* uterque pati.

Wopkens seems right in explaining these as a conversational change from oblique to direct narrative. The two subjunctives would be in orat. obliqua infinitives: but the normal grammar is violated, and the apodosis proceeds independently.

(*b*) Anacoluthic introduction of *que* or *atque* into two clauses, the first of which is connected with the second as nom. participle with finite verb.

XVII. 13 Illa gemens fracto*que* loqui uix murmure *coepit.*

XVI. 11   Stridula mox blando respondens canna susurro
              Se*que* magis tutam debilitate *docet.*

XXV. 5   Ille sibi abrupti fingens discrimina funis
              A*tque* auri *queritur* desiluisse cadum.

To this perhaps belongs the peculiar use of *nec* in XXXIV. 2
              Quisquis torpentem passus transisse iuuentam
              Nec timuit uitae prouidus ante mala,
for it seems improbable that Av. has here used *passus=passus est.*

IV.

THE MSS OF AVIANUS.

The MSS of Avianus are numerous and to be found in every part of Europe. The *Fables* were much read in the Middle Age, and scholia of varying extent and goodness are extant in most of them.

Both Fröhner's C as well as the Trèves codex have short glosses superscribed or in the margin. Those in C 1 had originally intended to publish : but on examination rejected as too trivial. The glosses in T are valuable and have been, with one or two exceptions, inserted in the Commentary.

Fröhner has published (pp. 67-84 of his edition) from two Paris MSS (347^h 347°) a prose paraphrase of the Fables, of uncertain date. It can hardly however be early, as it contains some of the spurious epimythia, besides additions not known to the uninterpolated MSS. For this reason I have not printed it, though its interpretations are usually sound, and occasionally merit quoting.

The MSS which I have used may conveniently be grouped by their locale.

     1. The Paris codices, $A = 8093$, $C = 5570$, $P = 13206$, first examined by Fröhner (1862). Fröhner considers A and P to have been written in the first half, C towards the close of century IX. Bährens assigns C to century XI. From a careful examination which I made of it for some months in the Bodleian, I believe that it cannot be later than century X. It is in my opinion the best of the three Paris codices, although both A and P seem to be earlier. I have used Fröhners' collation of A and P, checking it in some points where I was in doubt by personal inspection. A full description of all three will be found in Fröhner's ed. pp. i-vii.

     2. The Oxford codices $O =$ Auct. F. 2. 14. $R =$ B. N. Rawl. 111, $X =$ Auct. F. 5. 6, first examined by myself for the present edition. Of these the oldest is O, a MS of century XI. Where the *manus prima* can be ascertained, O is of value ; but some centuries after it was written a later hand made many erasures and corrections, all of which are wrong. It is in consequence of less importance than either R (of century XI-XII) or X (circ. 1300). R is a very good, completely trustworthy, MS : X is chiefly valuable for occasional variants which point to the true reading.

     3. The Cambridge codices, G (Gale O. 3. 5, in the Library of Trinity College, of century XII) and the two Peterhouse, Pet^1 Pet^2.

G was collated for Bährens by H. A. J. Munro. It was examined by Bentley. It has special variants which are interesting, but not certainly right. I quote these from Bährens' edition (P. L. M. v. 30 sqq.).

Pet^1 (4 in James' Catalogue) is imperfect, the leaves containing Av. I-XXII having been torn out. The fables are followed by the Elegies of Maximianus.

Pet^2 (James 25) contains all Avianus, with Maximianus. These two MSS perhaps are of century XIII-XIV.

     4. The British Museum codices. I have examined five, and collated four of these (B, b, b^2, b^3). The fifth Reg. 15 A. VII. is cited on XXXIX. 11.

$B =$ Harl. 4967. A MS of unique importance, though not written (so Mr. E. M. Thompson believes) much before 1300. The *m. prima* may generally be made out, in spite of the many corrections and additions added subsequently. I consider it the most interesting of the new MSS which I have collated. It has no *Praefatio*. In one case the normal arrangement of the Fables is disturbed; IV precedes III.

$b = 21,213$ (century XIII) of secondary importance, and often interpolated.

$b^2 = 15$ A. XXXI (circ. 1300) uninterpolated, and worth consideration, but imperfect, omitting XVII, XVIII, XIX, XX, XXI.

$b^3 = 10090$, interpolated. I only quote it occasionally.

5. *T.* Trèves 1464, of century x. This codex, an enormous folio, containing also Prudentius, is one of the best sources of the text. The short scholia are excellent and may come down from an early period. I collated it in the Bodleian.

6. *S.* St. Gallen, 1396, a fragment of century XI. It contains XXI. 1–13, XXII, XLI. 13–XLII. 16. I collated it at St. Gallen.

7. *K*, a Carlsruhe fragment (85 in the Hof Bibliothek) which Fröhner assigns to century IX. It contains XXXIV. 8–XL. 9.

On these I have based my text. I have not seen either of the Vossian MSS at Leyden, and wherever they are quoted, cite from Bährens who describes them thus: 'Voss. L. Q. 86 saec. ix. est Lachmanni antiquissimus' 'Voss. L. O. 15, saec. xi:' nor the Ashburnham (Libri 1813) of cent. XI–XII. Nor can I profess to give much weight to the reported readings of a 'codex uetustissimus' reprinted from the papers of a Danish clergyman named Cabeljau by Cannegieter in D'Orville's Miscellanea Noua for 1734 : still less to reconstitute the orthography of Avianus on so precarious a foundation. (See Fröhner's Praef. p. ix, Bährens P. L. M. v. p. 32.)

ERRATA AND ADDENDA.

P. 33. In XXIX. 22, for *semel* read *simul*.

P. 42. The speech of the lion does not end with XXXVII. 18, as printed, but with XXXVII. 20.

P. 75. Add to the passages quoted on XIV. 4, Aristot. de Mundo p. 400^b τῶν τε ζῴων τά τε ἄγρια καὶ ἥμερα, τά τ' ἐν ἀέρι καὶ ἐπὶ γῆς καὶ ἐν ὕδατι βοσκόμενα, cited by Stobaeus Ecl. Phys. i. p. 45 Wachsmuth.

P. 76. Read Ian for Jahn, and so on p. 79.

P. 94. Add on XXIII. 7, Possibly *omen* itself = 'a bid,' cf. English *bode* = (1) presentiment, (2 an offer of a price, a bid J. A. H. Murray in New English Dictionary, p. 961).

P. 120. Add on XXXVII. 2. Tibull. i. 1. 73, 4 *dum frangere postes Non pudet, et rixas inseruisse iuuat.*

AVIANI FABVLAE.

AVIANI FABVLAE.

INCIPIVNT FABVLAE XLII AVIANI POETAE.   EPISTOLA EIVSDEM AD
THEODOSIVM.

Dubitanti mihi, Theodosi optime, quo*i*nam litterarum titulo
nostri nominis memoriam mandaremus, fabularum textus occurrit, quod in his urbane concepta falsitas deceat, et non
incumbat necessitas ueritatis. Nam quis tecum de oratione,
quis tecum de poemate loqueretur? cum in utroque litterarum 5
genere et Atticos Graeca eruditione superes et latinitate
Romanos? Huius ergo materiae ducem nobis Aesopum
noueris, qui responso Delphici Apollinis monitus ridicula
orsus est ut †legenda firmaret. Verum has pro exemplo
fabulas et Socrates diuinis operibus indidit et poemati suo 10
Flaccus aptauit, quod in se sub iocorum communium specie
uitae argumenta contineant. Quas Graecis iambis Babrius
repetens in duo uolumina coartauit, Phaedrus etiam partem
aliquam quinque in libellos resoluit. De his ego ad quadraginta et duas in unum redactas fabulas dedi, quas rudi lati- 15

B

nitate compositas elegis sum explicare conatus. Habes ergo
opus quo animum oblectes, ingenium exerceas, sollicitudinem
leues, totumque uiuendi ordinem cautus agnoscas. Loqui
uero arbores, feras cum hominibus gemere, uerbis certare
20 uolucres, animalia ridere fecimus, ut pro singulorum necessi-
tatibus uel ab ipsis *in*animis sententia proferatur.

elegi sum *P* ablactes *P* sollicitudines *P* totum qui *P* agnuscas *P*
loqui uero—proferatur] *Lachmannus uncis inclusit* singularum *P* inanimis *Pithoeus in adnotatione* mimis *Pithoei textus* animis *codd.*
exanimis *Neueletus* proferratur *P* EXPLICIT PRAEFATIO *C* *deinde*
fab. I. *In OR post praefationem secuntur uersus hi* (PROLOGVS AVIANI *O*
Prefatio sequentis opusculi *R*) Lector non fabulas spectes (quaeras *O*)
sed tende magis quid. Rure morans quid agam respondi pauca rogatus.
Mane deum exoro, famulos post arua (paruosque *R*) reuiso, Partitusque
meis iustos indico labores. Inde lego Phoebumque cio musamque lacesso.
Tunc oleo corpus fingo mollique palestra Stringo libens animo gaudens-
que ac fe(oe *O*)nore liber. Prandeo poto cano ludo lauo ceno quiesco *qui*
septem uersus Martiali ab aliis adsignantur. Eosdem uersus habet Galeanus.
Tum fab. I.

AVIANI FABVLAE.

I.

DE NVTRICE ET INFANTE.

Rustica deflentem paruum iurauerat olim,
  Ni taceat, rabido quod foret esca lupo.
Credulus hanc uocem lupus audiit et manet ipsas
  Peruigil ante fores irrita uota gerens.
Nam lassata puer nimiae dat membra quieti.   5
  Spem quoque raptori sustulit inde fames.
Hunc ubi siluarum repetentem lustra suarum
  Ieiunum coniunx sensit adesse lupa,
'Cur,' inquit, 'nullam referens de more rapinam,
  Languida consumptis *sic* trahis ora genis?'   10
'Ne mireris,' ait, 'deceptum fraude maligna
  Vix miserum uacua delituisse fuga.

I.

DE NVTRICE ET INFANTE *C*   DE LVPO ET MVLIERE *O*   FABVLA
AVIENI Poętę· De rustico & lupo fraudato *R.*
  1. deflentem *ACTR m. pr.*   defluentem *P*   deflenti *OR m. sec.*
paruum *A*   paruo *OR m. sec.*   deleri puerum *Lachm.*   iurauerat
codd. praeter Pet²   iuuauerat *Pet²*   iurgauerat *Froehnerus secutus
Cabeliauium cuius haec uerba sunt* 'Iurgauerat pro iurauerat est in N.
(? nostro) et placebit illud forte ob us. 14.'
  2. rapido *A m. pr. O.*
  3. audit *OT Pet².*
  5. nimium *edit. Bodleiana intra* 1470–1480 *impressa*   menbra *C.*
  6. famis *P cum Vossianis duobus nisi quod in antiquiore m. sec. correxit* fames
fami *T ex* fames   Spem quoque raptoris sustulit inde fami *Wopkensius.*
  8. sentit *B Pet².*
  9. referis *C*   referis *T*   referes *A*   referes *R*   referens *Galeanus
cum Voss. L. O.* 15   defers *Pet²*   praefers *Froehnerus*   An retines?
  10. sed *codd.*   sic *Baehrensius.*

Nam quae praeda, rogas, quae spes contingere posset,
     Iurgia nutricis cum mihi uerba darent ?'
Haec sibi dicta putet, seque hac sciat arte notari,   15
     Femineam quisquis credidit esse fidem.

II.

DE TESTVDINE ET AQVILA.

Pennatis auibus quondam testudo loquuta est,
     Si quis eam uolucrum constituisset humi,
Protinus e rubris conchas proferret harenis,
     Quis pretium nitido cortice baca daret.
Indignum sibimet tardo quod sedula gressu   5
     Nil ageret toto perficeretque die.
Ast ubi promissis aquilam fallacibus implet,
     Experta est similem perfida lingua fidem.
Et male mercatis dum quaerit sidera pennis

Ioannes Sarisburiensis Prolog. Policratici Neque enim adeo excors sum ut
pro uero astruam quia pennatis auibus quondam testudo locuta est.

13. rogo *b²*   Namque rogas praedam *Pet² B*   possit *P.t² BR*.
14. cõ *C.*
14, 15 *uncis inclusit Lachmannus.*
15. uocari *Pet².*
16. adesse *b num* asse ?

II.

DE TESTVDINE ET AQVILA *ACO*   De aquila et testudine *R.*
1. Pennatis *BCORT cum cod. Bodl. Policratici* (F. 1. 8)   Pinnatis *P*
locuta *om. est ed. Bodl.*
2. uolucrum *A m. pr. CORT*   uolucrem *P et corr. A*   destituisset *Pet² B Galeanus*   restituisset *Withofius*   humo *O*   ait
Lachmannus   ibi *Baehrensius*   *Post* uolucrum *duos uersus excidisse
censet Georgius Murray, ut* constituisset *pro* pactus esset *infinitiuum ex se
pendentem habeat.*
3. concas *C*   deferre *B*   auferret *Lachm.*   harenas *Voss. L. Q.* 86
m. pr.   bac a *C*   bacca *ABORT.*
5. Indignum *A m. pr. CT*   Indignans *BO A m. sec. et Galeanus*
Indlingnans *Pet².*
6. *deest in P*   perficeretque *ACOT*   proficeretque *Pet² Galeanus,*
R sed post rasuram, Bbb² cum codicibus Cabeliauii   totum diem *Galeanus.*
8. *Cf. Prop. III.* 13. 66 Experta est ueros irrita lingua deos. Experta
est *marg.* exple *C.*
9. sidere *A m. pr.*   sydera *C.*

†Occidit infelix alitis ungue fero. 10
Tum quoque sublimis, cum iam moreretur, in auras
    Ingemuit uotis haec licuisse suis.
Nam dedit exosae post haec documenta quieti
    Non sine supremo magna labore peti.
Sic quicumque noua sublatus laude tumescit 15
    Dat merito poenas, dum meliora cupit.

III.

DE CANCRO ET MATRE EIVS.

Curua retro cedens *d*um fert uestigia cancer,
    Hispida saxosis terga relisit aquis.
Hunc genitrix facili cupiens procedere gressu
    Talibus alloquiis *e*monuisse datur.
'Ne tibi transuerso placeant haec deuia, nate, 5
    Rursus in obliquos neu uelis ire pedes.
Sed nisu contenta ferens uestigia recto
    Innocuos proso tramite siste gradus.'

---

10. Decidit *b et ed. Bodl. Lachm.* Excidit *Baehrensius* ungui *ACP.*

11. Tunc *OT* sublimis *CR* sullimis *Galeanus* sublimes
BP Pet[2] *T* in auris *R* in auris *Gal.*

13. ex sese *Baehrensius ex Vossiano L. O.* 15 *qui habet* ex semet An aegrotae? quieti *O Pet*[2] *R m. sec.* quietis *PAT sed in AT* s erasa *C legi non poterat Versum cum tribus sequentibus uncis inclusit Lachmannus.*

III.

DE MATRE & FILIO *C sed post* DE *usque ad* & *litterae euanuerant, ita tamen ut* MAII *legere uiderer. Aliter ratus est Froehnerus* DE CANCRO *AR* DE CANCRO ET MATRE EIVS *O.*

1. Cum *ACOPRT* dum *Pet*[2] *b*[2].
2. terra *T* resilit *C* tergora laesit *Cannegieterus.*
3. procedere *CT* praecedere *ABOR Pet*[2] *cum Galeano.*
4. alloquiis *ABCOR Pet*[2] *T* emonuisse *ego* e *in* I *abierat* praemonuisse *codd.*
6. neuelis *BC Pet*[2] *bb*[2] neu uelis *APRO m. pr. T* ne *uel* neu iuuet *Withofius* neue tuere *Froehnerus Versum cum* 7 *delebat Lachmannus.*
7. conptempta *Pet*[2].
8. pro se *C* proso *AP Vossianus L. O.* 15 presso *Galeanus* prono *ORT Pet*[2] *Bbb*[2].

†

Cui natus 'faciam, si me praecesseris,' inquit,
'Rectaque monstrantem certior ipse sequar.   10
Nam stultum nimis est, cum tu prauissima temptes,
Alterius censor *si* uitiosa notes.'

IV.

DE VENTO ET SOLE.

Inmitis Boreas placidusque †ad sidera Phoebus
Iurgia cum magno conseruere Ioue,
Quis prior inceptum peragat : mediumque per aequor
Carpebat solitum forte uiator iter.
Conuenit hanc potius liti praefigere causam,   5
Pallia nudato decutienda uiro.
Protinus inpulsus uentis circum tonat aether,
Et gelidus nimias depluit imber aquas.
Ille magis lateri duplicem circum dat amictum,
Turbida summotos quod trahit aura sinus.   10
Sed tenues radios paulatim increscere Phoebus

---

9. Qui *C*   inquit *CRT*   inquid *O Pet*² *Froehnerus*.
     ᵐᵒˢ
10. monstrantem *C*.
11, 12 *uncis inclusit Lachmannus*.
12. cens *pro* censor *P*   sensor *Bb*   si *ego*   ut *codd*.

DE VENTO ET SOLE *A*   DE VENTO ET SOLE ET VIATORE *O*   De Sole et
uento *R*.
                          ᵃᵈ
     1. pladusque *P*   sidera *B*   ad cetera *Lachmannus*   ad
ludicra *Baehrensius*̄   *num* adsidere ? *an* ad sibila ?
     2. *om. P*   ioco *pro* Ioue *Lachm*.
     3. *super* aequor *quod ex parte erasum est in C eadem, ut uidetur, manus
scripsit* orbem   orbem *cett*.   aruum *Wopkensius*.
     5. litis *Pet*²   lita *A m. pr.*   litei *Froehnerus*.
     6. discusienda *b*²   discuscienda *B*.
     7. inpulsus *A m. sec. BCOR*   inpulsis *A m. sec. PPet*²   inpulsu uenti
Baehrensius   uentus *B*.
     8. gelidas nimius *B*   depulit *B b b*² *Pet*².
     9. lateri duplicem *BCR*   dupplicem lateri *O et plerique*.
     10. quod *ACP Vossianus L. O.* 15   quo *O m. pr. RT*   qua *Galeannus
Pet*² *quod recepit Lachm*.   quia *B*   *In Vossiano L. Q.* 86 (*saec. IX*)
manus prima dispici nequit, teste Baehrensio.
     11. crescere *B Pet*² *bb*².

Iusserat ut nimio surgeret igne iubar.

Donec lassa uolens requiescere membra uiator

Deposita fessus ueste sederet humi.

Tunc uictor docuit praesentia numina Titan 15

Nullum praemissis uincere posse minis.

V.

DE ASINO PELLE LEONIS INDVTO.

[Metiri se quemque decet propriisque iuuari

Laudibus, alterius nec bona ferre sibi.

Ne detracta grauem faciant miracula risum

Coeperit in solis cum remanere malis.]

Exuuias asinus Gaetuli forte leonis 5

Repperit et spoliis induit ora nouis.

Aptauitque suis incongrua tegmina membris,

Et miserum tanto pressit honore caput.

Ast ubi terribilis *m*imo circum stetit horror,

Pigraque praesumptus uenit in ossa uigor, 10

Mitibus ille feris communia pabula calcans,

Turbabat pauidas per sua rura boues.

---

12. suggeret *ed.* 1494   *an* et n. suggerit?   spargeret *Wopkensius.*
13. lassata *T.*
14. Deposita *T*   resedit *Galeanus R*   recedit *Pet²b².*
15. tytan *O.*
16. praemissas *b² m. pr.*   minas *b² m. pr.*   minus *B.*

V.

DE ASINO PELLE LEONIS INDVTA *C*   DE ASINO *AR*   DE ASINO
ET DOMINO EIVS ET PELLE LEONIS *O.*
1–4 *delebat Cannegieterus, uncis incluserunt Lachmannus et Froehnerus.*
3. Nec *C*   miracula *codd. nisi quod b habet* pericula   *Num* umbra-
cula? *h. e.* σκεπάσματα.
4. solis *ACOPRT*   solitis *Pet²b*   remeare *R post rasuram, Pet²bb²*
ụemiare *B.*
5. getuli *CO*   getuli iam *T*   defuncti *P et Vossianus L.Q.* 86.
6. Reperit *B.*
8. tanto   P̄ssit *C relicto sic spatio*   onere *P*   capud *Pet².*
9–12 *uncis inclusit Lachmannus.*
9. animo *codd.*   mimo *Cannegieterus probabiliter*   uano *Schenkelius*
an limbo?
12. pauidos *ORTb²*   per sua lustra feras *Pet² Bb.*

Rusticus hunc magna postquam deprendit ab aure,
  Correptum uinclis uerberibusque domat,
Et simul abstracto denudans corpora tergo,   15
  Increpat his miserum uocibus ille pecus.
' Forsitan ignotos imitato murmure fallas,
  At mihi, qui quondam, semper asellus eris.'

VI.

DE RANA.

.

Edita gurgitibus limoque immersa profundo
  Et luteis tantum semper amica uadis,
Ad superos colles herbosaque prata recurrens,
  Mulcebat miseras turgida rana feras.
Callida quod posset grauibus succurrere morbis,   5
  Et uitam ingenio continuare suo.
Nec se Paeonio iactat cessisse magistro,
  Quamuis perpetuos curet in orbe deos.
Tunc uulpes pecudum ridens astuta quietem
  Verborum uacuam prodidit esse fidem.   10
' Haec dabit aegrotis,' inquit, ' medicamina membris,
  Pallida caeruleus cui notat ora color?'

13. ' Rusticus ex Rusticolus.' *Cabeliauii schedae.*
14. *An* Correctum uirgis? *cf. Prud. Perist. XI.* 792.
15. abstrato *C*   corpore *B Pet² m. pr.*
16. petus *PR m. pr.*
17. mutato *O Galeanus Pet² b².*
18. Et *Pet²*   eras *C*   om. *Pet².*

VI.

DE RANA *C*   DE RANA ET VVLPE *OR.*
  1. olimque *codd. nisi quod Vossianus L. O.* 15 *habet* = limoque *h. e. erasa una littera* olimoque   limoque *Neueletus.*
  2. lutis *Cabeliauius enotarat ex codd.*
  4. turgida *ORT*   turbida *C et sic Cabeliauius.*
  5. quo *CRT Pet²*   quod *O cum Galeano*   succurere *B.*
  7. Nam sepe onio *C*   Nec se peonio *OR*   pionio *Pet²*   Paeoni *Lachmannus.*
  8. curạt *B*   in orbe *codd.*   is arte *Withofius.*
  9. uul *P*   arguta *Lachm.*
  11. inquid *B Pet² Froehnerus*   menbris *C.*
  12. calor *Pet².*

VII.

DE CANE.

[Haud facile est prauis innatum mentibus ut se
Muneribus dignas suppliciouc putent.]
Forte canis quondam nullis latratibus horrens,
  Nec patulis †primum rictibus ora trahens,
Mollia sed pauidae summittens uerbera caudae,   5
  Concitus audaci uulnera dente dabat.
Hunc dominus, ne. quem probitas simulata lateret,
  Iusserat in rabido gutture ferre †nolam.
Faucibus innexis crepitantia subligat aera,
  Quae facili motu signa cauenda darent.   10
Haec tamen ille sibi credebat praemia ferri,
  Et similem turbam despiciebat ouans.
Tunc insultantem senior de plebe superbum
  Adgreditur, 'Tali cingula uoce mones?

8. *Hageni Anecdota Heluetica (supplementum est Keilii Grammat. Latin.)*
p. 182 Nola et Campanella unum est, id est schilla, ut est illud Auieni de
cane Iusserat in rabido gutture ferre nolam.

VII.

DE CANE *ACR*   DE CANE QUI NOLVIT LATRARE *O.*

1-2 *uncis inclusit Lachmannus.*
2. Muneribus *codd.*   Verberibus *Withofius*   Vulneribus *Froehnerus.*
3. quidam *ed. Bodl.*   quoidam *Lachmannus.*
4. *fortasse* simum   ratibus *C*   rectibus *A.*
5. submittens *OR Pet*[2]   sumite *A*   sumittens *C*   summittens *T.*
6. conscius *cod. Campensis Nodelli et ed.* 1494: *cf. Verg. Aen. XI.* 811, 12.
8. rapido *B Pet*[2] *P*   nolam *ABCORT*   mollam *P*   uolam
Pet[2]   notam *Lunensis*   nolam *etiam Hageni Anecdota Heluetica,*
p. 182. *Sed Auianum* nolam *correptam scripsisse uix credibile ratus Petren-*
sem sequerer, (*cf. prouerbium* nec uola nec uestigium) *nisi Cataldus Iannel-*
lius in commentario huius loci monuisset Prudentium Nolanus *corripuisse*
Peristeph. XI. 208 Campanus Capuae iamque Nolanus adest, *sic enim*
scriptum est in codice peruetusto Bodleiano Prudentii T. 2. 22, *nec probabiliter*
emendarunt Ianicolanus.
11. ferre *PT cum Galeano.*
12. dispiciebat ou *P.*
13. Hunc *Pet*[2].
14. Adgreditur *CT*   Aggreditur *AOR cum Galeano*   Agreditur *B*
cingula *ego*   singula *codd.*   sibila *Lachmannus*   paucula *Froeh-*
nerus   seria *Schenkelius*   uoce seuera *uel* sinistra *Baehrensius*
monens *ACOPRT Galeanus Pet*[2]   inouens *Laurentianus LXVIII.* 24,
Puteaneus Froehneri, et ed. 1494   maonens *B*   mones *b*[2].

Infelix, quae tanta rapit dementia sensum,   15
   Munera pro meritis si cupis ista dari?
Non hoc uirtutis decus ostentatur in aere,
   Nequitiae testem sed geris inde sonum.'

VIII.

DE CAMELO.

[Contentum propriis sapientem uiuere rebus,
   Nec cupere alterius, fabula nostra monet,
Indignata cito ne stet fortuna recursu,
   Atque eadem minuat, quae dedit ante, rota.]
Corporis inmensi fertur pecus isse per auras   5
   Et magnum precibus sollicitasse Iouem.
Turpe nimis cunctis irridendumque uideri,
   Insignes geminis cornibus ire boues,
Et solum nulla munitum parte camelum
   Obiectum cunctis expositumque feris.   10
Iuppiter arridens postquam sperata negauit,
   Insuper et magnae sustulit auris onus.

15-18 *uncis inclusit Lachmannus.*
16. qui putes ista dare *Cabelianii schedae. Fueratne* qui potis ista dari?
17. ostendatur *OP Pet²*.
18. Nequities *et* Nequitii *enotarat Cabelianius ex suis codd. Vide Neue*
Formenl. I. pp. 387–390.

VIII.

DE CAMELO *ACR*   DE CAMELO ET IOVE *O.*
1-4 *uncis inclusit Lachmannus.*
1. sapienter *ed. Bodl.*
2. fabula nostra *C supra lineam sed ut uidetur a m. pr.*   nostra fabella
C in uersu ABOPRT bb² Gal.   nostra flabella *Pet² m. pr.*
3. Indignatio est et fortuna *P.*
4. qua *A*   Fortasse Indignata citos ne det fortuna recursus Atque
eadem minuat quae (? qua) stetit ante rota.
5. auras *COT cum Galeano*   auras *R*   aras *b fortasse recte* 'Non
uolauit in caelum camelus, ut Iouem alloqueretur, nec opus erat.' *Withofius*
arua *Pet² uitiose.*
6. sollicitasse *CORT*   soliscitasse *B*   solicitasse *Pet².*
7. irridendumque *ACORT Pet²*   iridendumque *B*   uidere *B.*
8. geminis *Pet².*
9. Et *R*   Se *Cabeliauii schedae*   At *Cannegieterus.*
11. arridens *COT*   adridens *AP*   irridens *BR Pet²*   at ridens
Froehnerus   spostquam *Pet².*
12. aurisonus *C*   auresonus *P*   honus *B Pet².*

Viue minor merito cui sors non sufficit, inquit,
Et tua perpetuum, liuide, damna geme.

IX.

DE DVOBVS SOCIIS ET VRSA.

Montibus ignotis curuisque in uallibus artum
  Cum socio quidam suscipiebat iter,
Securus, quodcumque malum fortuna tulisset,
  Robore collato posset uterque pati.
Dumque per inseptum uario sermone feruntur,   5
  In mediam praeceps conuenit ursa uiam.
Horum alter facili conprendens robora cursu
  In uiridi trepidum fronde pependit onus.
Ille trahens nullo iacuit uestigia gressu,
  Exanimem fingens, sponte relisus humi.   10
Continuo praedam cupiens fera saeua cucurrit,
  Et miserum curuis unguibus ante leuat.
Verum ubi concreto riguerunt membra timore,
  Nam solitus mentis liquerat ossa calor,

---

14. geme *C*   geme *ORT*   tene *B m. pr. quod manus alia mutauit in* geme.

IX.

DE DVOBVS SOCIIS ET VRSA *C*   DE VRSA ET DVOBVS SODIBVS (*sic*) *O*   DE DVOBVS VIATORIBVS ET VRSA *R*.

1. ingnotis *Pet²*   altum l *erasa R*.
3. quocumque *B*   quod cuique *Cannegieterus*   quod cum qua *Lachmannus*   quod quoique *Froehnerus*   cum, quodque *Baehrensius an* quoicumque ?
4. collecto *B male*   possit *P*   pater *C*.
5. inceptum *ACR*   inceptum *O*   incepto *B*   incertum *T Cannegieterus Lachm. Froehn. Bähr.*   inseptum *ego cf. Paul. p.* 111 *M*. Inseptum non septum, ponitur tamen et pro non aedificatum.
6. In medio *b³*   In media . . . uia *Lachmannus*   conuenit *codd.* en uenit *Cannegieterus*   conuolat *uel* conmeat *Baehrensius*.
7. Alter horum facili comprehendens *Pet²*.
8. fronte *B*.
10. exanimen *A est, eraso quod fuerat*   relisit *Bb²*. *Etiam in Pet²* relisus *ex correctore* humi *Pet²* i *correcta ex eo quod fuerat*.
11. seua *R*.
13. contracto *b²*   menbra *C*.
14. Non *C*.

Tunc olidum credens quamuis ieiuna cadauer, 15
  Deserit et lustris conditur ursa suis.
Sed cum securi paulatim in uerba redissent,
  Liberior iusto, qui fuit ante fugax,
'Dic, sodes, quidnam trepido tibi rettulit ursa?
  Nam secreta diu multaque uerba dedit.' 20
'Magna quidem monuit, tamen haec quoque maxima iussit,
  Quae misero semper sunt facienda mihi.
Ne facile alterius repetas consortia, dixit,
  Rursus ab insana ne capiare fera.'

X.

DE CALVO EQVITE.

Caluus eques capiti solitus religare capillos
  Atque alias nudo uertice ferre comas,
Ad campum nitidis uenit conspectus in armis
  Et facilem frenis flectere coepit equum.
Huius ab aduerso Boreae spiramina praeflant 5
  Ridiculum populo conspiciente caput.

19. *Hageni Anecd. Heluet. p.* 174 Sodes aduerbium est deprecantis, non sodaliter, ut quidam uolunt. Vnde dicit Auienius Dic sodes quidnam trepido tibi dixerit ursa? Nam sodalis breuis est so. *Ib. p.* 185 Sodes aduerbium non significat sodaliter, sed aduerbium est precatiuum, ut illud Auieni Dic sodes quidnam trepido tibi retulit ursa? So uidelicet producta, cum sit in sodali correpta.

---

17. paulatim securi *O.*
19. retulit *ABC Pet²*   rettulit *OR a m. pr. sed in utroque prior* t *erasa est.*
21, 22 *delebat Lachmannus.*
21. hoc *R m. pr.,* T   maxime *CR Pet²T*   maximę *O*   maxima *A m. pr., P Galeanus*   maximę̂ *B*   quasi maxima *Baehrensius*   Num cum maxima?
22. merito *T*   sunt *codd. nisi quod in Vossiano L. O.* 15 si/nt *scriptum est teste Baehrensio, in* T sunt *erasa altera parte litterae* u.

X.

DE CALVO FQVITE *AOR*   DE CALVO *C.*
1. capitis *Pet² m. pr.*   religasse *PR*   reliquare *coni. Cannegieterus.*
3. Ad Campum *Cannegieterus*   conspectus uenit *A.*
4. equum *O m. pr.,*   equm *Pet².*
5. praestant *codd. nisi quod* persl/ant *exhibet Ashburnhamensis*   praeflant *scripsi, nam ab aduerso uentus flabat.*
6. Ridiculo *C*   capud *Pet².*

Nam mox deiecto nituit frons nuda galero,
    Discolor adposita quae fuit ante coma.
Ille sagax, tantis quod risus milibus esset,
    Distulit ammota calliditate iocum,   10
'Quid mirum,' referens, 'positos fugisse capillos,
    Quem prius aequaeuae deseruere comae?'

XI.

DE DUABVS OLLIS.

Eripiens geminas ripis cedentibus ollas
    Insanis pariter flumen agebat aquis,
Sed diuersa duas ars et natura creauit,
    Acre prior fusa est, altera facta luto.
Dispar erat fragili et solidae concordia motus,   5
    Incertumque uagans amnis habebat iter,
Ne tamen elisam confringeret aerea testa,
    Iurabat solidam longius ire uiam.

7. ẹiecto *R*   derepto *B*.
8. adposita *C*   apposita *BORT*.
9. *Ab hoc uersu incipit X*   mentis *pro* tantis *b*.
10. Disstulit *R*   Dispulit *Lachmannus*   amota *C*   admota
ORTX Pet[2]   calliditate *BX Pet*[2] *m. pr.*

XI.

DE DVABVS OLLIS *OR, quamquam in R omissum est* OLLIS. *Eundem titulum
fuisse etiam in A reor, quamquam euanida scriptura uix legi potuit*   DE
OLLIS *C*   *In O haec fabula post* Inpulsus uentis (*XLI*) *scripta est, estque
in serie tricesima nona.*

1. Exripiens *A m. pr. teste Froehnero*   Eripiens *BCORX*   Aripiens *b*[2]
Arripiens *b*   geminans *B*.

3. diuersẹ *B*.
4. tacta *CX Pet*[2] *b*[2]   ficta *TOBb*   ficta *R*   fincta *Cabeliauius
enotarat*.
5, 6 *uncis inclusit Lachmannus*.
5. et *om. X bb*[2] *fortasse recte*   solido *CPT*   fragilis solide *b*   fragili
et solideque *B*   motu *C, erasa s ut uisum est Froehnero, quamquam id mihi
non liquere confiteor*.
6. uagus *codd. praeter B*   Incertum uagans ampnis *B Sed et in X
post* uag *rasura est, ut suspicer a prima manu scriptum fuisse* uagas. *An
scribendum erat* uagis?   agebat *X*   agebat *codex Campensis Nodelli*.
7. elesam *B*   allisam *Barthius*   illisam *Schenkelius*   testa *Pb*
testam *ABCORTX*.
8. solitam *codd.*   solidam *ego. Cf. Ovid. Trist. I. 2. 54*   sociam
Neueletus   solito *Schenkelius*   *Fortasse* solita.

Illa timens ne quid leuibus grauiora nocerent,
  Et quia nulla breui est cum meliore fides,   10
'Quamuis securam uerbis me feceris,' inquit,
  'Non timor ex animo decutiendus erit.
Nam me siue tibi seu te mihi conferat unda,
  Semper ero ambobus subdita sola malis.'

XII.

DE THENSAVRO.

Rusticus impresso molitus uomere terram,
  Thensaurum sulcis prosiluisse uidet.
Mox indigna animo properante reliquit aratra,
  †Semina conpellens ad meliora boues.
Continuo supplex telluri construit aras,   5
  Quae sibi depositas sponte dedisset opes.
Hunc fortuna nouis gaudentem prouida rebus
  Admonet, indignam se quoque ture dolens.
'Nunc inuenta meis non prodis munera templis,
  Atque alios mauis participare deos;   10

10. est *om. X b*   nulla fides cum meliore breui *B uitiose.*
11. inquid *Pet²*.
12. discutiendus *BOX Pet² b b²*   decutiendus *AC Vossianus L. Q.* 86
detutiendus *Vossianus L.O.* 15.
13. conterat *Cabeliauius.*
14. subruta *Lachmannus.*

XII.

DE THESAVRO *C*   DE INVENTO THESAVRO *A*   DE RVSTICO ET
THESAVRO *O*   *In O haec fabula quadragesima est.*
1. inpresso *O Pet²*   mollitus *T Pet².*
2. Thensaurum *A m. pr. ut nisum est Froehnero*   in sulcis *R m. pr.*
3. relinquit *A*   reliquid *Pet²*   arata *b².*
4. Semina *codd. Fortasse* Stramina *uel* Vimina. *Cannegieterus coni.* Gra-
mina   cōpellens *C*   conpellens *O*   compellens *RT Pet².*
5. telluris instruit *PC, sed in C superscripto* construit   telluri construit
BORTX Pet².
7. Tunc *OR.*
8. Admonet *ABCTX Pet²*   Ammonet *OPR m. pr. Fortasse* indiguam ...
docens   Admonuit dignam ... docens *Lachmannus.*
9. Nunc *codd. nisi quod b* Qum *exhibet*   prodi *P*   pro *Vossianus
L. Q.* 86   non prodest urnula *Lachmannus*   non prosunt munera
Baehrensius   An promis *h. e. in publicum profers* ?

Sed cum subrepto fueris tristissimus auro,
Me primam lacrimis sollicitabis inops.'

XIII.

DE HIRCO ET TAVRO.

Inmensum taurus fugeret cum forte leonem,
  Tutaque desertis quaereret antra uiis ;
Speluncam reperit, quam tunc hirsutus habebat
  Cinyphii ductor qui gregis esse solet.
Post ubi summissa meditantem irrumpere fronte   5
  Obuius obliquo terruit ore caper,
Tristis abit, long*um*que fugax de ualle locutus,
  (Nam timor expulsum iurgia ferre uetat)
Non te demissis saetosum, putide, barbis,
  Illum, qui super est consequiturque, tremo.   10
Nam si discedat, nosces, stultissime, quantum
  Discrepet a tauri uiribus hircus olens.

11. Ast *B Pet*² *m. pr.*
12. sollicitabis *X Pet*³.

XIII.

DE HIRCO ET TAVRO *C*   DE TAVRO ET HIRCO (HYRCO *O*) *AO*
DE TAVRO ET LEONE ET HIRCO *R*.
  1. fu*n*geret *Pet*².
  2. iugis *b*.
  3. Speloncam *A*   repperit *O Pet*²   reperit *X*   repetit *C R m. pr.*   abebit *B*.
  4. Cyniphei *C*   Cinifei *BO*   Cyniphii *RT*   Ciniphei *X Pet*² solet esse gregis *B*.
  5. Ppost *C*   Post *AO m. pr., PR*   Ast *BX Pet*² *b*²   Hunc *Galeanus* Huc *Lachmannus*   submissa *BOX Pet*²   rumpere *X*.
  6. caput *P*.
  7. obit *P Froehnerus* longinqua *scribens*   ßabit *Pet*²   longum-que *ego*   longaque *codd. praeter b et Pet*²   longamque *b*   longa *Pet*²   longeque *Cannegieterus*   longinqua *Lachmannus*   locutus est *X*.
  8. expulsas *B*   *Fortasse* expuls*n*ans.
  9. de(di *T*)missis setosum *BOTX*   s(f *Pet*²)etosum demissis *R Pet*² *Cabeliauius*   demissums/etosis *C m. sec. eraso quod fuerat* demissis saetosum   putride *b b*² *Pet*² cum *Treuirensis m. prima*.
  10. consequiturque *codd.*   insequiturque *paraphrastes Lachm. Froehn.*
  11. discedast noscis *X*.
  12. Discrepat *BOPT b*² *Pet*².

XIV.

DE SIMIA.

Iuppiter in toto quondam quaesiuerat orbe,
  Munera natorum quis meliora daret.
Certatim ad regem currit genus omne ferarum,
  Permixtumque homini cogitur ire pecus.
Sed nec squamigeri desunt ad iurgia pisces,   5
  Vel quicquid uolucrum purior aura uehit.
Inter quos trepidae ducebant pignera matres,
  Iudicio tanti discutienda dei.
Tunc breuis informem traheret cum simia natum,
  Ipsum etiam in risum conpulit ire Iouem.   10
Hanc tamen ante alios rupit turpissima uocem,
  Dum generis crimen sic abolere cupit.
'Iuppiter hoc norit, maneat uictoria si quem'
  Iudicio super est omnibus iste meo.'

XIV.

DE SIMIA *C*   De ioue et cunctis animalibus *AR*   DE IOVE ET
DE EXQUISITIONE NATORVM *O*.
   1. quaesierat *BX Pet²*.
   2. Pignora *coni. Guietus*   natorum *ex* naturum *C*   an naturae?
quis *BORX cum Galeano et Pet²*   qui *ACPT*   quoi *Lachmannus*.
   3. currit *BX Pet²*   genus *om. P*.
   4. homini *codd*. eodem *Withofius*   cicur *Baehrensius*   Mihi permixtum
homini genus *tamquam cicur feris opponi uidetur, quae ab hominibus discretae
uiuunt*.
   6. Et *X*   Vt *Galeanus*   quic quid *O*   prior *P cum Vossiano*
L. Q. 86 m. pr.   ueit *B*.
   7. In tergo *Baehrensius*   pignera *R*   pignora *BOX*.
   8. uiri *X*.
   9. traeret *B*   simea *B*.
   10. etiam *om. X*   et *Pet²*.
   11. Hanc *ACPOT Pet²*   Haec *BRX*   alias *BO Pet² m. pr.*
rūpit *CP*   rupit *RX*   rumpit *O et T m. pr.*   rūppit *B*.
   12. Cum *O*   genetrix *P cum Vossiano L. Q. 86 m. pr.*   genitrix
TX b²   abholere *Pet²*.

* Frochnerus ex *A* uitiose pro CVNCTIS dedit . . . NOTIS, sequente Baehrensio.

XV.

DE GRVE ET PAVONE.

Threiciam uolucrem fertur Iunonius ales
  Communi sociam *de*tinuisse cibo,
Namque inter uarias fuerat discordia formas,
  Magnaque de facili iurgia lite trahunt,
Quod sibi multimodo fulgerent membra decore,   5
  Caeruleam facerent liuida terga gruem.
Et simul erectae circumdans *a*gmina caudae,
  Sparserat arca*t*um *s*ursus in astra iubar.
Illa, licet nullo pennarum certet honore,
  His tamen insultans uocibus usa datur.   10
' Quamuis innumerus plumas uariauerit ordo,
  Mersus humi semper florida terga geris.
Ast ego deformi sublimis in aera penna,
  Proxima sideribus numinibusque feror.'

XV.

DE GRVE (GVRE *A*) ET PAVONE *ACOR.*
2. contenuisse *P*   continuisse *AOT sed in T a supra scripta* continuasse *CXB b¹ b² Pet²*   non tolerasse *Withofius Lachm.*   non tenuisse *Baehrensius*   conripuisse *Froehnerus*   detinuisse *uel* commonuisse *ego.*
3, 4 *uncis inclusit Lachmannus.*
3. Nam *O.*
4. litte *A.*
5. fuls(c *B*)erunt *B Pet²*   menbra *C.*
6. Ceruleam *COXT*   Caeruleam *R*   liuida *ex* umida *uel* inuida *B.*
7. agmina *ego*   tegmina *codd. nisi quod* circumdan temina *habent P et Vossianus L. Q.* 86 *a m. pr.*
8. arcatum *Barthius*   arcanum (archanum *TOR Pet²* canum *P*) *codd.* sursus *Lachmannus*   russus *B*   rursus *cett.*
9. nulla *B m. pr.*   pinnarum *P*   certe *P*   certat *RX.*
10. insulstans *A.*
11. innumeras *X Pet²*   *fortasse* in numerum   uariauerat *C* uarieuerit *P*   uariauerat *X.*
12. florda *Pet² m. pr.*
13. deformis *O m. pr.*   deformo *Vossianus L. Q.* 86 *m. pr.*   aera *BORX*   aere *ACT.*   pinna *P*   pennis *AOXB m. pr.*
14. syderibus *C*   omnibus ipse *pro* nominibusque *b².*

XVI.

DE QVERCV ET HARVNDINE.

Montibus e summis radicitus eruta quercus
  Decidit insani turbine uicta noti.
Quam tumidis subter decurrens alueus undis
  Suscipit et fluuio praecipitante rapit.
Verum ubi diuersis inpellitur ardua ripis,   5
  In fragiles calamos grande residit onus.
Tunc sic exiguo conectens caespite ramos
  Miratur liquidis quod stet harundo uadis.
Se quoque tam uasto rectam *n*on sistere trunco,
  Ast illam tenui cortice ferre minas.   10
Stridula mox blando respondens canna susurro
  Seque magis tutam debilitate docet.
'Tu rapidos,' inquit, 'uentos saeuasque procellas
  Despicis et totis uiribus acta ruis.
Ast ego surgentes paulatim demoror austros,   15
  Et quamuis leuibus prouida cedo notis.
In tua praeruptus *se fu*ndit robora nimbus,

XVI.

DE QVERCV ET HAR(AR *R*)VNDINE *AR*   DE HARVNDINE ET QVERCV *O*
DE ROBORE ET CALAMO *C.*
  1. radicitus *PORTX Pet*[2]   tradicitus *B*   radicibus *C.*
  2. Descidit *B*   nothi *codd.*
  3. timidis *C*   timidis *BX.*
  6. resedit *ACORTX Pet*[2]   residit *BP Vossianus L. Q.* 86   honus *X.*
  7. Tum *A*   Tunc *BCOPRTX*   nectens *C*   conectens *RT*
connectens *OX Galeanus*   conuertens *B an* conuerrens?   cepite
PB   cespite *CORTX.*
  8. quos *B*   stat *OX*   arundo *OPRX*   harundo *C.*
  9. uesto *C*   rectam *ego*   rectum *C*   nec dum *ABOPRTX*   nec
enim *Lachmannus*   consistere *codd.*   asistere *Pet*[2]   non sistere *ego.*
  10. Atque *Bb.*
  11. respondit *RX Pet*[2]   respond t *b*[2].
  12. Sequi *P*   docens *Lachmannus.*
  13. rapidos *C*   rabidos *T*   seuasque *ORX.*
  14. Dispicis *PA m. pr. Vossianus L. Q.* 86 *m. pr.*   tutis *C*   alta *O.*
  15. paulatum *P*   pālatim *B num* palatim?   astros *B.*
  16. cedo *C.*
  17. praeruptus *codd. praeter X Pet*[2]   praerumpens *X*   praeruptis

Motibus aura meis ludificata perit.'
Haec nos dicta monent magnis obsistere fluxa,
Paulatimque truces exsuperare minas.　　　　20

XVII.

DE VENATORE ET TIGRIDE.

Venator iaculis haud irrita uulnera torquens,
　　Turbabat trepidas per sua lustra feras.
Tum pauidis audax cupiens succurrere tigris
　　Verbere commoto iussit adesse minax.
Ille tamen solito contorquens tela lacerto　　　　5
　　'Nunc tibi, qualis eam, nuntius iste refert,'
Et simul emissum transegit uulnere ferrum,
　　Praestrinxitque citos hasta cruenta pedes.
Molliter at fixum traheret cum saucia telum,
　　A trepida fertur uulpe retenta diu.　　　　10

Pet² 　　 offendit *codd. praeter X* 　　 ostendit *X* 　　 se effundit
Lachmannus 　　 se fundit *ego* 　　 robura *P* 　　 *Fortasse* prorumpens
offendit *uel* praeruptis offendit robora nimbis.
　19, 20 *uncis inclusit Lachmannus.*
　19. subsistere *O* 　　 fluxa *ego* 　　 frusta *b* 　　 lustra *B* 　　 rebus *b*³
frustra *cett.*
　20. Paulatim *BC* 　　 exuperare *CO.*

XVII.

DE VENATORE ET TIGRIDE *CR* 　　 DE VENATORE AC TIGRI *A* 　　 DE
VENATORE *O.*
　1. haut *BT.*
　2. pauidas *BORX cum Galeano et Pet²* 　　 rapidas *Laur. LXVIII.* 24
rabidas *ACPT* 　　 tacitas *codex Moldauianus Cabeliauii* 　　 trepidas *Lachmannus.*
　3. Tunc *B* 　　 succurc *BX* 　　 tygris *OR.*
　4. commotas *ABCPRT* 　　 commoto *O* 　　 submotas *X* 　　 Verbera
conmotans *Froehnerus* 　　 abesse *A b* 　　 abire *X* 　　 minas *codd.*
minax *Froehnerus.*
　5. solido *Cabeliauii schedae et sic Wopkensius* 　　 contorques *B.*
　6. eram *codd.* 　　 eam *Froehnerus et sic corrector Treuirensis* 　　 qua
lateam *Lachmannus* 　　 nuncius *C.*
　7. uulnere *A* 　　 uulnera *potius quam* uulnere *C* 　　 uulnera *BOPRT*
Pet² 　　 uiscera (uicera *X*) *X b b*³.
　8. Perstrinxitque *PR m. sec. X m. pr. Pet²* 　　 Pertinxitque *B* 　　 /uos *X*
fueratne duos? 　　 asta *C.*
　9. ad fixum *B* 　　 adfixum *APT* 　　 affixum *COR* 　　 at fixum
Cannegieterus.

Nempe quis ille foret, qui talia uulnera ferret,
  Aut ubinam iaculum delituisset agens?
Illa gemens fractoque loqui uix murmure coepit.
  Nam solitas uoces ira dolorque rapit.
'Nulla quidem medio conuenit in aggere forma,   15
  Quaeque oculis olim sit repetenda meis.
Sed cruor et ualidis in nos directa lacertis,
  Ostendunt aliquem tela fuisse uirum.'

XVIII.
OR
DE IIII IVVENCIS ET LEONE.

Quattuor immensis quondam per prata iuuencis
  Fertur amicitiae tanta fuisse fides
Vt simul emissos nullus diuelleret error
  Rursus et e pastu turba rediret amans.
Hos quoque collatis inter se cornibus ingens   5
  Dicitur in siluis pertimuisse leo,
Dum metus oblatam prohibet temptare rapinam,
  Et coniuratos horret adire boues.
† Sed quamuis audax factisque inmanior esset,

---

11. Dum quis ille *ACPT*   Dumque quis ille *B*   Namque quis
iste *b*   Dic quis et ille *X*   Ecquis et unde *Withofius*   Cuias
Lachmannus   Vnde, quis *Froehnerus*   Nempe quis *ego*   foret *C*
ferret *B*.
12. dilutuisset *B*.
13. fracto *BX*   Num reloqui?   loquens *ed. Bodl.*   coeptans
Lachmannus uix probabiliter.
15. quidem et *B*   agere *P*.
16. Quodque *B*.
17. in me *X*.

XVIII.
OR
DE IIII IVVENCIS ET LEONE *C*   DE LEONE ET QVATTVOR IVVENCIS *O*
De quattuor bobus & leone *R*   *Deest titulus in A.*
1. immensis *C*   inmensis *ORT*   perpetrata *P*.
3. emissor *B*   deuelleret horror *BX*   orror *Pet²*.
4. ab epastu *B*   ouans *B.X b Pet²*.
5. collatis *CORTX Pet²*   tollatis *B*.
7-10 *uncis inclusit Lachmannus.*
7. Nam *Froehnerus*   proibet *B*.
8. in ire *Pet²*.
9. Sed *codd.* Et *editio Bodleiana, uulgo*   quam *B*   factis *B*.

Tantorum solus uiribus impar erat.   10
Protinus aggreditur prauis insistere uerbis,
  Collisum cupiens dissociare pecus.
Sic postquam dictis animos disiunxit acerbis,
  Inuasit miserum diripuitque gregem.
Tunc quidam ex illis 'uitam seruare quietam   15
  Qui cupit, ex nostra discere morte potest.
Neue cito admotas uerbis fallacibus aures
  Impleat, aut ueterem deserat ante fidem.'

XIX.

DE ABIETE AC DVMIS.

Horrentes dumos abies pulcherrima risit,
  Cum facerent formae iurgia magna suae.
Indignum referens *dumis* certamen haberi,
  Quos meritis nullus consociaret honor.
'Nam mihi deductum surgens in nubila corpus   5

---

10. Taurorum *cod. Campensis, et ed.* 1494 *cum Bodleiana*   ueribus *B*
impar *ACORX*   inpar *B*   imperaret *P*   *Versus* 9, 10 *ante* 7, 8
fortasse collocandi erant.
    11. aggreditur *COR cum Galeano*   agreditur *BX Pet*[2]   adgredi-
tur *T.*
    12. Collisum *COR Pet*[2]   Collectum *BX.*
    13. Sic *ACOP Pet*[2] *Cabeliauius*   Sed *BRX*   disiungit *A*
disiunexit *PR*   diuisit *Cabeliauius*   amaris *Pet*[2].
    14. Inuasit *BX Pet*[2]   Inuadit *ACOPRT*   dirripuitque *X*   disri-
puitque *Pet*[2].
    15. Tunc *ABCORX Galeanus Pet*[2]   Tuṇ *P*   Tum *AT*   quidem
A Pet[2]   quidem *X*   quietiam *P.*
    16. cupit ex *BTX Pet*[2]   cupiet *CR*   cupit e *O Baehrensius.*
    17 *deest in A*   admotos *P Vossianus L. O.* 15 *et Voss. L. Q.* 86 *m. pr.*
    18. Impleat *CORTX*   Inpleat *B Pet*[2]   ut *AT Froehnerus et ed.*
1494   inde *Froehnerus.*

XIX.
DE ABIETE (ABIETTE *A*) AC DUMIS *AC*   DE ABIETE ET DVMO *OR.*
    1. Horentes *B*   dumas *P.*
    2. sererent *Cabeliauii schedae*   iuria *P.*
    3. dumis *ego*   cunctis *codd.*   cuctis *B*   haberi *ABOPRTX*
habere *C*   obiri *Froehnerus.*
    4. Quos *ORTX Galeanus*   Quod *C et sic AP teste Froehnero*   meriti
Colbertinus[3] *Cannegieteri quod malebat Schenkelius, et nuper Baehrensius*   nullis
OB m. pr.   nullis *ante* meritis *O*   honos *P.*
    5. Nam indeductum *B.*

Verticis erectas tollit in astra comas.

Puppibus et patulis media cum sede locamur,

   In me suspensos explicat aura sinus.

At tibi deformem quod dant spineta figuram,

   Despectum cuncti praeteriere uiri.'   10

Ille refert 'Nunc laeta quidem bona sola fateris,

   Et frueris nostris imperiosa malis.

Sed cum pulchra minax succidet membra securis,

   Quam uelles spinas tunc habuisse meas.'

XX.

DE PISCATORE ET PISCE.

Piscator solitus praedam suspendere sacta,

   Exigui piscis uile trahebat onus.

Sed postquam superas captum perduxit ad auras

---

6. Verticis *cum erasum esset in B, infra simili scriptura restitutum est.*

7. *Ab hoc inde uersu C breuioribus inter lineas spatiis scriptus est, manu tamen aut eadem aut certe persimili. Sed et turbatus est ordo foliorum.* Nam fol. 58ᵇ *finitur* XIX. 6, 59ª *incipit a* XXII. 12 Seque ratus solum munera ferre duo *unde continuantur fabulae ad* XXXIV. 20 Cantibus est quoniam uita peracta prior. *Quo uersu clausum est fol.* 60ᵇ. *Dein f.* 61ª *habet* XIX. 9–XXII. 11, 61ᵇ *Auiani nihil sed soluta quaedam oratione; quorum ultimum hoc est.* Prosa *dicitur quae producta et recta est oratio* Prosum *enim antiqui productum dicebant et rectum. Siue prosa dicitur quod sit profusa.* Tum a fol. 62ª *usque ad extremam columnam priorem folii 63 ceterae Auiani fabulae secuntur* XXXV. 1. Fama est quod geminum—XLII. 16 Expedit insignem promeruisse necem.

7. in *pro et* O   medea B.

9. At CRT   Ast ABX Pet²   A P et Vossianus L. Q. 86 m. pr. deformen A   dent C.

10. Dispectum P   cunti B.

11. Illa *ex* ille C   Illa B m. pr. R   Ille OPTX Pet²   est *pro* refert P   letu P   fateri P Vossianus L. O. 15 *et* Voss. L. Q. 86 m. pr.

12. Sed P *cum Vossianis*   nostris frueris codd.   fueris b³   frueris nostris Lachmannus.

13. Set Bb   pulc̃ra C   succidat C   succidit PRT   succidet ABOX *cum Galeano*   sequuris C.

14. uellis P.

XX.

DE PISCATORE ET PISCE ACR   DE PISCATORE O.

1. solitis B   suspentare P.

2. pissis B   tracbat honus B   onus C.

3. deduxit R.

Atque auido fixum uulnus ab ore tulit,
'Parce, precor,' supplex lacrimis ita dixit obortis,   5
'Nam quanta ex nostro corpore *dona* feres?'
Nunc me saxosis genitrix fecunda sub antris
Fudit et in propriis ludere iussit aquis.
Tolle minas, tenerumque tuis sine crescere mensis.
Haec tibi me rursum litoris ora dabit.   10
Protinus immensi depastus caerula ponti
Pinguior ad calamum sponte recurro tuum.
Ille nefas captum referens absoluere piscem,
Difficiles queritur cassibus esse uices.
'Nam miserum est' inquit 'praesentem amittere praedam,   15
Stultius et rursum uota futura sequi.'

XXI.

DE ALITE ET MESSIONE.

Paruula progeniem terrae mandauerat ales
Qua stabat uiridi caespite flaua seges.

4. audo *P*   *An* auidum fixo?   trahit *Pet²*.
5. obortis *CPT*   abortis *ARX Pet²*.
6. Heu *B*   Heu *b³* ᵖ·ᴺᵃᵐ   ex núp'o (? uiuo) *B m. pr.*   dona *Lachmannus*
damna *codd.* (dampna *BOX b*)   feras *P Pet² m. pr.*
7. Hannc *B*   genetrix *B*   foetida *P*.
8. Fundit *B*   Fuderat et *O*   propriis *R* ⁱ   aquas *R* ⁱ   *Num* in
propriis ludere misit aquas?   ᵘ
10. rursus *RX*   russus *B*   rorsum *P*   littoris *CT et O m. pr.*
litoris *RX Pet²*   litoras *A*   quadrabis *P Vossianus L. O.* 15 *et*
Voss. L. Q. 86 *m. pr.*   ora dab//it *C*.
11, 12 *uncis inclusit Lachmannus.*
11. inmensi *TORX*   pastus per serula *B*   depastum *T*.
12. redibo *corrector O*.
13-15. *Verba post* nefas *usque ad* miserum est *uncis inclusit Lachmannus.*
13. nephas *BX*   refferens *B*   referrens *P*   pissem *B*.
14. Defficiles *B*   Deficiles *Pet²*   casibus *codd.*   cassibus
Froehnerus ualde probabiliter.
15. inquid *Pet²*.
16. est *BX Pet²*   inquit rursus *X*   rursuṣ *P* ᵐ   russus *B*.

XXI.

DE ALITE ET MESSIONE *A*   De alite et messore *R*   DE ALITE
ET RUSTICO *O*   DE LVSCINIA *C*   *Fabula extat in codice Sangallensi*
1396 *saec. XI (S).*
1. progeniēṣ *B*   mundauerat *C*.
2. Qui *P*   Quo *T*   cespite *CORSTX Pet²*.

Rusticus hanc fragili cupiens decerpere culmo
  Vicinam supplex forte petebat opem.
Sed uox inplumes turbauit, *a*credula, nidos,   5
  Suasit et e laribus continuare fugam.
Cautior hos remeans prohibet discedere mater,
  ' Nam quid ab externis proficietur ? ' ait.
Ille iterum caris operam mandauit amicis.
  At genitrix rursum tutior inde manet.   10
Sed postquam curuas dominum conprendere falces,
  Frugibus et ueram sensit adesse manum,
' Nunc,' ait, ' o miseri, dilecta relinquite rura,
  Cum spem de propriis uiribus ille petit.'

XXII.

DE CVPIDO ET INVIDO.

Iuppiter ambiguas hominum praediscere mentes
  Ad terras Phoebum misit ab arce poli.

4. suplex *B Pet*².
5. inplumes *BCORSTX Pet²*   implumes *A*   implumest *P*   turbabat *B*   credula *ACOPRSX Pet²*   crụdula *T*   pauida *B*
sedula *b*   credita *Withofius*   acredula *scripsi. Isid. XII.* 7. 37
Luscinia auis inde nomen sumpsit, quia cantu suo significare solet surgentis
exortum diei, quasi lucinia. Eadem et acredula. *Gloss. Balliolense* acredula luscinia auis modica. *An scribendum erat* stridula ?
  6. Suaserat *codd.*   et *codd. praeter X*   suaserat e *X*   suasit et e
laribus *ex coniectura scripsi.*
  7. Certior *B*   h/s *X*   Fuerat has   reuocans *Lachmannus.*
  8. Numquid *b*   extremis *AX Pet²*   perficietur *COPRTX Pet²*
proficietur *AS.*
  9, 10 *uncis seclusit Lachmannus.*
  9. cum *pro* iterum *B*   rerum *P*   opē'// *T*   mandarat *X.*
  10. Et *X Cabeliauii schedae*   genitrix *ABCORSTX Pet²*   genetrix *P.*
  11. pos quam *S*   conprendere *CRS*   comprehendere *A Pet²*
conprehendere *OPTX*   deprendere *Galeanus*   depandere *B.*
  12. ueram *codd. praeter O*   scuam *O*   fortasse scram   seruam
Withofius   sentit *B.X bb³.*
  13. delicta *B m. pr.*
  14 *non extat in S.*

XXII.

DE CVPIDO ET INVIDO *COR*   DE IOVE ET CVPIDO ET INVIDO *A*
Fabula extat in S.
  1. hom prodecere *B*   p̄dicere *X*   prenoscere *ed.* 1494.
  2. Id terras *B*   *Fuerat* In terras.

Tunc duo diuersis poscebant numina uotis
Namque alter cupidus, *l*iuidus alter erat.
His sese medium Titan, scrutatus utrumque,   5
Optulit, et precibus cum peteretur, ait,
'Praestant di facilis, quae namque rogauerit unus,
Protinus haec alter congeminata feret.'
Sed, cui longa iecur nequeat satiare cupido,
Distulit admotas in noua damna preces,   10
Spem sibi confidens alieno crescere uoto,
Seque ratus solum munera ferre duo.
Ille ubi captantem socium sua praemia uidit,   .
Supplicium proprii corporis optat ouans.
Nam petit extinctus *sic* lumine degeret uno,   15
Alter ut hoc duplicans uiuat utroque carens.
Tum sortem sapiens humanam risit Apollo,

3. Cum *Lachmannus* poscebat *B*   numina *ABCPRS*   munera *O.X.*
4. alius *B*   liuidus *Withofius*   inuidus *codd.*
5. His sese *RS Galeanus*   His se *P Vossianus L. Q.* 86 *m. pr.*   His
quoque se *ACOTX*   scrutandus *O.*
6. Obtulit *O*   conjiteretur *X* (ut peteretur above)   ut peteretur *cett.*   Iuppiter
aecus *Lachmannus*   quom peteretur *ego*   quod peteretur *ed.*
1494.
7. Prestandi facilis *ABOPRSX Pet²*   Praestabit facilis *C*   Praestandi facilist *Froehnerus*   Praestandist facilis *Baehrensius*   Praestant
di facilis *ego*   nam quaeque rogauerit *CORSTX*   namque rogauerat *B Pet²*   nam quaeque poposcerit *Galeanus*   namque
sperauerit *Vossiani duo*   sperauerit *etiam AP*   quae namque
rogauerit *ego.*
8. congemina *AP.*
9. nequeat (nequea *P*) *codd.*   nequit *cod. Campensis Nodelli*   nequiit
Cannegieterus   sociare *B.* (a above)
10. Postulit a/motas *T* (di above)   ammotas *O*   amotas *Galeanus*   dona
Lachmannus.
13. suum *B* (m with marks)   sibi *T*   uidet *B.* (i above)
15. extingtus *B*   Extincto sub lumine degat ut *Cannegieterus*   Extincto
sibi lumine degeret (degat ut *Withofius*) uno *Wopkensius et Withofius*   Extincto iam lumine d. ut uno *Baehrensius*   extincto cum lumine ut
aegreat uno *Huemerus Wien. Studien* II. p. 160   *Erat quom putarem scri-*
bendum esse Extinctus ut lumine duceret uno, *ut* extinctus *accusatiuus*
pluralis esset, sicut apud Prudentium reperiuntur excussus salis, incussus silicis
P. 5. 226, *C.* 5. 7   sic *ego*   ut *codd. praeter T Pet¹*   quo *T*
quod *Pet¹.*
16. dupplicans *B*   uterque *T.* (ro above)
17. Tunc *BORSX Galeanus Pet².*

Inuidiaeque malum ret*u*lit ipse Ioui,
Quae dum prouentis aliorum gaudet iniquis,
Laetior infelix et sua damna cupit.   20

XXIII.

DE VENDITORE ET MERCATORE.

Venditor insignem referens de marmore Bacchum
Expositum pretio fecerat esse deum.
Nobilis hunc quidam funesta in sede sepulchri
Mercari cupiens compositurus erat ;
Alter adoratis ut ferret numina templis,   5
Redderet et sacro debita uota loco.
'Nunc' ait 'ambiguum facies de mercibus omen,
Cum spes in pretium munera dispar agit,
Et me defunctis seu malis tradere diuis,
Siue decus busti seu uelis esse deum.   10
Subdita namque tibi est magni reuerentia sacri,

---

18. retulit *BCOPX Petrenses*   rettulit *RS*   ille *B Pet*[1]   inde
unus Pulmanni.

19. Quaedam *A*   Qui *BX b b*[2]*b*[3] *cod. Campensis*   malorum *Pet*[2].
    cupit
20. querit *T.*

XXIII.

DE VENDITORE ET MERCATORE *AR*   DE BACHO *C*   DE VENDI-
TORE ET BACHO *O.*
1. bachumi *P*   baumi *Vossianus L.Q.* 86 *m. pr.*
2. ipse *pro* esse *b*[2].
                                              h
3. hanc *R*   in *om. BX*   sepulcri *C*   sepulcri *Galeanus Pet*[2].
                                                        v
4. compositurus *CT*   composituros *R sic*   expositurus *Galeanus.*
5. adoratus *B*   ut oratis ciro ferret *b*   at ornatis *Lachmannus*
An ut auratis inferret ?   munera *BX cum Galeano et b*[2]   numina
ACPRTO m. pr.
6. ut *O b*[2] *Petrenses*   scacro *B.*
                            i
7. Tunc *X b*   Huc *b*[2]   Ht iñc *B h. e.* Hinc *in* tunc *mutatum*
ambiguo *Lachmannus*   omen *om. P.*
8, 9 del. *Guietus, uncis inclusit Lachmannus.*
8. agat *BX b Petrenses.*
9. Et *codd.*   Sei *Froehnerus*   Seu *Cabeliauii schedae*   mauis
BOTX b[2] *Petrenses*   uiuis *pro* diuis *Baehrensius.*
10. uelis esse *codd.*   seu posuisse *Withofius*   siue locasse *Froeh-*
nerus   seu deus esse uelis *Lachmannus, uersum* 7 *cum* 10 *mercatori*
tribuens, sicut 11, 12 *Baccho.*
11. neque tibi *A*   nequitiae *om.* est *P et Vossianus L.Q.* 86   neinpe

Atque eadem retines funera nostra manu.
[Conuenit hoc illis quibus est permissa potestas,
An praestare magis seu nocuisse uelint.]

XXIV.

DE VENATORE ET LEONE.

Certamen longa protractum lite gerebant
Venator quondam nobilis atque leo.
Hi cum perpetuum cuperent in iurgia finem
Edita continuo fronte sepulchra uident.
Illic docta manus flectentem colla leonem   5
Fecerat in gremio procubuisse uiri.
'Scilicet affirmas pictura teste superbum
Te fieri? extinctam nam docet esse feram.'
Ille graues oculos ad inania signa retorquens
Infremit et rabido pectore uerba dedit.   10
'Irrita te generis subiit fiducia uestri,

tibi *Lachmannus*   est *om.* *Pet*[2]   nostri *pro* magni *A*   referencia
B Pet[2] *m. pr.*   fati *BCRTX Pet*[1]   facti *AO m. pr. b Pet*[2]   sati *P*
Bacchi *paraphrastes*   sacri *ego*   Subdita nempe tibist m. r. Bacchi
Lachmannus.
   12. referes *B*   retinens *b*[2]   retine//s *X.*
13, 14 *uncis inclusit Lachmannus.*
   13. *om. b*[2]   premissa *T.*
   14. Aut *O m. pr. B Pet*[2]   prodesse *X et cod. Campensis Nodelli*
uelis *B m. pr.*

XXIV.

DE VENATORE ET LEONE *COR*   *In A titulus erasus est; ve tamen recentior manus superscripsit.*
   1. protectum *P.*
   2. quondam *ACPTO m. pr. R bb*[2] *Petrenses*   quidam *BX et cod. Campensis.*
   3. ad *pro* in *O Pet*[2].
   4. continuo forte *codd.*   contigue *Baehrensius*   continuo fronte
ego. Cf. Neue Formenlehre I. p. 687.   sepulcra *C*   sepulcra *X Pet*[2].
   5. leonjem *B.*
   6. gremiůo *B*   gremium *b.*
7–12 *suspectos habuit Guietus.*
   7. Silicet *Bb*[2]   Hic calet *Lachmannus*   Is calet *Froehnerus*
affirmans *codd. praeter B*   infirmans *B*   supernum *Lachmannus.*
   8. Se *codd.*   Te *ego*   ferri *B*   extinctum *C.*
   10. Ingemit *Galeanus*   Infremuit *X*   rapido *OPX Petrenses et cod. Campensis Nodelli.*
   11, 12 *uncis inclusit Lachmannus.*
   11. Irrita te *CORX*   inritat *P*   fidiscima *B*   nostri *X Pet*[2].

Artificis testem si cupis esse manum.

Quod si nostra nouum caperet sollertia sensum,
    Sculperet ut docili pollice saxa leo,
Tunc hominem aspiceres oppressum murmure magno,   15
    Conderet ut rabidis ultima fata genis.'

XXV.

DE PVERO ET FVRE.

Flens puer extremam putei consedit ad undam
    Vana superuacuis rictibus ora trahens.
Callidus hunc lacrimis postquam fur uidit obortis,
    Quaenam tristitiae sit modo causa rogat.
Ille sibi abrupti fingens discrimina funis   5
    Atque auri queritur desiluisse cadum.
Nec mora, sollicitam traxit manus improba uestem.
    Exutus putei protinus ima petit.
Paruulus exiguo circumdans pallia collo
    Sentibus inmersus delituisse datur.   10

---

13. Quid si *b*   Sed si *B*   Set si *b*[3]   O si *paraphrastes* solercia *X*   solertia *A*.

14. Scalperet *P Cabeliauii schedae*   indocili *B m. pr.*   police *PX Pet*[2].

15. expressum marmore *Lachmannus*.

16. rapidas *B*   rapidis *OX Petrenses et cod. Campensis Nodelli* genas *B*.

XXV.

DE PVERO ET FVRE *AR*   DE FVRE ET PARV *C*   DE PVERO ET LATRONE *O*.

1. extrema *Galeanus*   in undam *P*   ad oram *corrector X*   ad horam *paraphrastes*   in ora *Galeanus*.

2. Vara *Guietus*.

3. Hunc calidus *Lachmannus*   uidet *X*   abortis *BRX Petrenses*.

4. tristiae *P*.

5. abrumptae *Cabeliauii schedae*   fingend *C m. pr.*   fingens *A* fingit *Pet*[1] *Pet*[2].

6. Ac *C*   Atque *cett.*   Hac *Froehnerus*   desiluisse *PTX Pet*[2] *cum Vossianis*   dissiluisse *ACO b b*[2] *cum Galeano et Pet*[1]   dissoluisse *R* dilituisse *B*.

7. sollicitam *codd.*   sollicitans *Withofius*   inproba *X*   uestem *BX Pet*[1] *Pet*[2]   mentem *b*   mentem *ACPT*   In *OR nocabulum erasum est*.

9. tergo *B*.

10. immersus *C*   inmersus *RTX*   inmensis *AB b*[2]   dilucuisse *B*.

Sed post fallaci suscepta pericula uoto
Tristi*s ut* amissa ueste resedit humi,
Dicitur his so*l*lers uocem rupisse querc*l*lis
Et gemitu summos sollicitasse deos.
'Perdita, quisquis erit, post haec bene pallia credat,   15
Qui putat in liquidis quod natet urna uadis.'

XXVI.

DE CAPELLA ET LEONE.

Viderat excelsa pascentem rupe capellam,
Comminus esuriens cum leo ferret iter.
Et prior 'heus' inquit 'praeruptis ardua saxis
Linque, nec hirsutis pascua quaere iugis,
Sed cytisi croceum per prata uirentia florem   5
Et glaucas salices et thyma grata pete.
Illa gemens 'desiste precor fallaciter' inquit,
'Securam placidis ins*t*imulare dolis.

5. *Glossarium Phillippicum* 4626 Citisus est herba de qua Auianus
Florentem citisum carpe.

---

11. Fur *pro* Sed *Baehrensius*   postquam *Bb³b*   fallacis *R m. pr.*
facili *b³*   uotis *P*   uota *B*   uoto *R cum ceteris.*
12. Tristior *codd.*   Tristor *ed. Bodl.*   Tristis ut *Cannegieterus.*
Fortasse Sed quom post facili suscepta pericula uoto Tristior amissa u. r.
humi.
13. solers *ACX*   querelis *CRTX*   querclis *O*   querilis *B.*
14. gemitus *P*   solos *Pet¹*   solicitasse *X Pet¹*   solissitasse *B.*
                                    hac
15. posthac *CPT*   posthaec *R*   post haec *ABO.*
16. petat *Lachmannus*   quae *Lachmannus*   natet *OP Pet² T*
natat *CRX Pet¹.*

XXVI.

DE CAPELLA ET LEONE *AOR*   DE LEONE ET CAPELLA *C.*
1. idera *B*   pacentem *B.*
2. Cominus *X Pet¹ Pet².*
3. purior *P*   inquid *PX*   preruptus *B.*
                n
4. hec *R*   hyrsutis *AR*   uiis *O.*
5. cythisi *COR*   cithici *X*   scitici *Pet¹*   sticici *B*   florent *A.*
6. tima *BX*   thima *ACRT*   p/ete *R.*
7. Illa desiste gemens precor falliciter inquit *O*   Ille *P*   siste *X*
m. pr.   inquid *BPX.*
8. instimulare *b² et paraphrastes*   insimulare *ABCOPRTX cum*
Galeano   dissimulare *Pet¹*   insidiari *ed. Bodl.*   insinuare *Cabeliauius*
    i
dolos *R.*

Vera licet moneas, maiora pericula tollas,
  Tu tamen his dictis non facis esse fidem.   10
Nam quamuis rectis constet sententia uerbis,
  Suspectam hanc rabidus consiliator habes.'

XXVII.

DE CORNICE ET VRNA.

Ingentem sitiens cornix aspexerat urnam
  Quae minimam fundo continuisset aquam.
Hanc enisa diu planis effundere campis,
  Scilicet ut nimiam pelleret inde sitim,
Postquam nulla uiam uirtus dedit, admouet omnes   5
  Indignata noua calliditate dolos.
Nam breuis inmersis accrescens sponte lapillis
  Potandi facilem praebuit unda uiam.
Viribus haec docuit quam sit prudentia maior,
  Qua coeptum *cornix* explicuisset opus.   10

9, 10 *uncis inclusit Lachmannus.*
9. celas *Froehnerus.*
10. in his *P.*
11. constat *C b²*   constant *A*   contet sentia *P.*
12. hanc *erasum in R,* om. *bb²*   rabidus *Ashburnhamensis teste Baeh-*
rensio   radibus *ed. Bodl.*   grauidus *codices nostri omnes*   hēs *b⁹*
Lachmannus   habet *cett.*

XXVII.

DE CORNICE ET VRNA *ACOR.*
1. siens *P*   cisciens *B*   asperat *P*   aspexerit *B.*
2. nimiam *P et Vossianus L. Q.* 86   continuisset *CRT*   contenuisset *P*
continuasset *BX b².*
3. Hinc *P*   enisa *COT*   enixa *BX Petrenses*   ecfundere
schedae Cabeliauii   efundere *ed.* 1494.
4. Silicet *X*   *an* pelleret unda ?
5. admouet *CX*   admonet *P Petrenses R*   admoet *B*   ammouet *O*
ammonet *T.*
6. dolor *P.*
7. inmersis *CORT*   acrescens *B Pet²*   adcrescens *O*   lapellis *T.*
8. Portandi *P.*
9, 10 *uncis inclusit Lachmannus.*
10. Qua *ACPR bb² Petrenses*   Quae *OX Voss. L.Q.* 86   cornix *ego*
uolucris *codd. praeter T*   uolucri *T sed erasa post i littera, ut uidetur*
explicuisset *P.*

XXVIII.

DE RVSTICO ET IVVENCO.

Vincla recusanti dedignantique iuuenco
Aspera mordaci subdere colla iugo,
Rusticus obliqua succidens cornua falce
Credidit insanum defremuisse pecus.
Cautus et immenso ceruicem innectit aratro,　　5
(Namque erat hic cornu promptior atque pede)
Scilicet ut longus prohiberet uerbera temo,
Neue ictus faciles ungula saeua daret.
Sed postquam irato detractans uincula collo
Inmeritam uacuo calce fatigat humum,　　10
Continuo euersam pedibus dispergit harenam
†Quam ferus in domini ora sequentis agit.
Tum sic informi squalentes puluere crines
Discutiens, imo pectore uictus, ait,

XXVIII.

DE RVSTICO ET IVVENCO *CO*　　　DE IVVENCO ET ARATORE *AR*.
1. dedignante *om.* que *B.*
3. obloquia *A*　　succindens *X.*
　　　de
4. infremuisse *C.*
5. inmerso *B*　　immensae *P*　　nectat *O*　　nectit *X b b³ cod.*
Campensis Nodelli.
　　hic
6. in *C*　　hic *om. Bb*　　prumcior *P*　　*Fort.* Namque errat
cornu.
7. proiberet *B*　　uerberet *P omissis quae supererant uersui.*
8. uirgula *Bb*　　deret *P.*
9. inuito *Lachmannus*　　detrectans *OP*　　detractat *X.*
10. uacuo *B*　　uacuo *Cabeliauii schedae X Petrenses Ashburnhamensis cum Campensi idque tuitus est Guietus ex Pers. III.* 105. *Cf. Neue Formenlehre I.*
694　　uacua *cett. cum T.*
11. dispersit *X.*
　　　　　　　　　r
12. Quam (Qua *b*) ferus (ferus *T* fere *b³*) in domini (in *om. b*) ora *codd.*
hic ora *B*　　Num nare ?　　agit *BORX Galeanus cum Petrensibus*　　agat
ACPT b　　Quam feriens Boreas ora s. agit *Withofius*　　*Fort.* Quam
super os domini pone sequentis agit.
　　　　　　　　c
13. Tunc *BRX b*　　sis *B*　　qualentes *A*　　*Ante* squalentes *erasum
est in R* sordidos　　in puluere *B*　　*An* Tum sic informis squalenti
puluere crines.
14. Decutiens *R*　　immo *B.*

'Nimirum exemplum naturae derat iniquae,   15
Qua fieri posset cum ratione nocens.'

XXIX.

DE VIATORE ET SATYRO.

Horrida congestis cum staret bruma pruinis,
    Cunctaque durato stringeret arua gelu,
Haesit in aduersa nimborum mole uiator,
    Perdita nam prohibet semita ferre gradum.
Hunc nemorum custos fertur miseratus in antro   5
    Exceptum Satyrus continuisse suo.
Quem simul aspiciens ruris miratur alumnus,
    † Vimque homini tantam protinus esse pauet.
Nam gelidos artus uitae ut reuocaret in usum
    Afflatas calido soluerat ore manus.   10
Sed cum depulso coepisset frigore laetus
    Hospitis eximia sedulitate frui,
(Namque illi agrestem cupiens ostendere uitam

---

15. *ne pro* naturae *B*   derat *A m. pr. P Froehnerus*   praebet
Schenkelius paraphrasten sequens.
16. *Post* Qua *rasura in R*   Qui *P*   ferri *B*   possit *ACT*
Schenkelius.

XXIX.

DE VIATORE ET SATY(i R)RO *AOR*   DE VIATORE ET FAVNO *C.*
   1. Horida *BX*   coniestis *b²*   coniectis *B*   pruinas *P*   pruineis
Froehnerus.
   2. Vinctaque *Heinsius ad Trist. III.* 10. 25   gelou *X.*
   3. membrorum *B bb² Pet²*   menbrorum *X*   ueator *Cabeliauius*
ex meator *quod in uno ex codd. inuenerat.*
   4. nunc *Pet².*
   5. custus *P.*
   6. satirus *O*   saturus *b²*   continuasse *B bb² Pet¹*   continuisse *Pet².*
   7 *om. P*   accipiens *b*   alumnis *C.*
   8. *Versus corruptus*   Vsibus omi tantam *B m. pr.*   Vimque boni *b²*
hominis *Pet¹*   *Fort.* Vicinusque homini   tanta *P*   pectoris
Lachmannus   prouidus *Froehnerus*   frontis inesse *ego olim.*
   9. gelidus *P*   uitat *P*   uite reuocaret ut usum *X*   usus *O.*
  10. Afflatas *BCORTX Petrenses*   callido *PO m. pr.*   suerat *B*
solueret *AC*   fouerat *Lachmannus.*
  12. exigua *Pet²*   sed utilitate *P.*
  13. Nam *X*   Iamque *Lachmannus*   illi *codd. nostri omnes et sic*
Cabeliauius   agrestam *b²*   aggrestem *O num* aggestam   tendere *B.*

Siluarum referens optima quaeque dabat,
Optulit et calido plenum cratera Lyaco,   15
Laxet ut infusus frigida membra tepor)
Ille ubi feruentem labris contingere testam
Horruit, algenti rursus ab ore *re*flat.
Opstupuit duplici monstro perterritus hospes
Et pulsum siluis longius ire iubet.   20
'Nolo' ait 'ut nostris umquam successerit antris,
Tam diuersa duo qui semel ora ferat.'

XXX.

DE SVE ET ILLIVS DOMINO.

Vastantem segetes et pinguia culta ruentem
Liquerat abscisa rusticus aure suem.
Vt memor accepti referens monimenta doloris
Vlterius teneris parceret ille satis.
Rursus in †excepti deprensus crimine campi,   5
Perdidit indultae perfidus auris onus.

---

14. refferens *B*   dab*i̊*t *B*.
15. Obtulit *O*   callido *B*   crahera leo *B*   alreo *P*.
17. Illi *P*   labiis *B b*.
18. Orruit *P*   algente *R*   algentem *Neueletus*   suflat *BCPTX b Pet*[2]
su/flat *R*   sufflat *AO b*[2] *Pet*[1]   reflat *Schenkelius. Error ex repetito* re:
testis est uetus editio Bodl. in qua est ore flauit   gelat *Lachmannus.*
19. Ostupuit *C*   Obstupuit *BORT Pet*[1]   Opstupuit *X*   Ob-
stipuit *Pet*[2]   dupplici *BO*.
20. Expulsum *O bb*[2] *Petrenses*   Depulsum *B*.
21. succederet *T*.
22. ore *BX bb*[2]*b*[3] *Petrenses*   ora *R*   ore gerat *Lachmannus.*

XXX.

DE SVE ET ILLIVS DOMINO *AR*   DE APRO ET QVOQVO *C*   DE
SVE ET RVSTICO *O*.
2. Linquerat *B et Cabelianius*   absisa *B*   abscissa *OR m. pr.*
3. *num* retinens?   monimenta *ABCORT Petrenses.*
4. Alterius *P*   pasceret *C*.
5. inexcepti *CT*   et *pro* in *X*   exculpti *Galeanus et sic ex*
coni. Lachmannus   exempti *ed.* 1494   excerpti *Guietus*   *Num*
opsaepti *cf.* Νόμοι Γεωργικοί, *Tit.* 4. 6 *in Harmenopouli ed. Heimbachiana p.* 840
Ἐάν τις βοῦς ἢ ὄνος θέλων εἰσελθεῖν ἐν ἀμπελῶνι ἢ κήπῳ ἐμπαρῇ ἐν τοῖς τοῦ
φραγμοῦ πάλοις ἀζήμιος ἔστω ὁ τῆς ἀμπέλου καὶ τοῦ κήπου κύριος   depressus
PX   deprehensus *T*   gramine *Pet*[2].

D

Nec mora, prae*dator* segeti caput intulit horrens,
   Poena quod indignum congeminata facit.
Tunc domini captum mensis dedit ille superbis,
   In uarias epulas plurima frusta secans.   10
Sed cum consumpti dominus cor quaereret apri,
   Impatiens fertur quod rapuisse cocus,
Rusticus hoc iustam uerbo compescuit iram
   Affirmans stultum non habuisse suem.
'Nam cur membrorum demens in damna redisset,   15
   Atque uno totiens posset ab hoste capi?'
Haec illos descripta monent, qui saepius ausi
   Numquam peccatis abstinuere manus.

XXXI.

DE MVRE ET BOVE.

Ingentem fertur mus quondam paruus oberrans
   Ausus ab exiguo laedere dente bouem,

---

7. praedator *Lachmannus*   praedite *P l'ossianus L. Q.* 86 *m. pr.*
praedictae *cett.*
   8. quod *OR Pet²*   sed *ABCPTX b²b³ Pet¹*   indictum *Cabeliauii*
'*cod. Miioui.*'   congeminata *BCORX Pet²*   quod geminata *APT*
Poena sed insignem congeminata facit   *Lachmannus probabiliter*
   9. Tum *P Vossianus L.Q.* 86   dedi *P*   super his *P.*
           frusta
   10. facta *Pet²*   Inuentas e. p. frustra secant *P.*
   12. Inpat(c *Pet*)iens *O Pet²*   Impatiens *CR*   cor rapuisse
                                      c
BXb²b³ ed. 1494   cocus *AOPRX*   coqus *C*   corripuisse coquum
Wopkensius.
   13. cumpescuit *A.*
   14. Cor firmans *Pet¹*   Affirmans *CORTX Pet²*   stultam *B.*
   15. menbrorum *CX*   dāpna sedisset *C.*
   16. Ac *C*   totiens *CT*   totiens in d. r. Terque uno demens
Withofius.
   17, 18 *uncis inclusit Lachmannus.*
   17. discripta *BX*   disscripta *Pet¹*   monent *om. P.*
                    a
   18. a peccatis *X*   peccatis *Pet²*   abstinure *P*   abstinuisse
                                      ere
O (post rasuram), X Pet²   abstinuisse *R*   abstituisse *B.*

XXXI.

DE MVRE ET BOVE *AOR*   DE MVRE ET TAVRO *C.*
   1. obherrans *X*   aberrans *B*   aborrens *Pet².*
   2. exguo *P.*

Verum ubi mordaci confecit uulnera rostro,
  Tutus in amfractus conditur inde suos.
Ille licet uasta toruum ceruice minetur,   5
  Non tamen iratus, quem petat, esse uidet.
Tunc indignantem *lusor* sermone fatigans,
  Distulit hostiles calliditate minas.
'Non quia magna tibi tribuerunt membra parentes,
  Viribus effectum constituere tuis.   10
Disce tamen breuibus quae sit fiducia *r*ostris,
  Et facias quicquid paruula turba cupit.'

XXXII.

DE ARATORE ET BOBVS.

Haerentem luteo sub gurgite rusticus axem
  Liquerat et nexos ad iuga tarda boues,
Frustra depositis confidens numina uotis

3. mordacem *B m. pr.*   cumfecit *Pet²* et ed. 1494.
4. amfractus *C Pet¹ T*   anfractus *OR*   amfractis conditur ille
suis *X*   ampharactis̯ *Pet²*   ille *etiam b² et Petrenses*   suos *Pet²*.
5. uasto *Pet²*   torum *R*   torua uastum *P*   minatur *X et*
Cabeliauii schedae   monitur *B*.
6. quam *B*   petit *X b³*   ille *pro* esse *X b²*.
7. Hunc *O*   lusor *ego*   iusto *codd.*   mus hoc *Withofius*
An iuxta?
8. Dispulit *Lachmannus*   ostiles *P*.
9–11 *om. P*.
9. membra *CX*   phentes *X*.
10. contribuere *Lachmannus*.
11, 12 *uncis inclusit Lachmannus*.
11. rostris *Froehnerus egregie*   monstris *ACOPTX Petrenses*   stris *R*
erasis quae scripta fuerant ante stris   membris *B*.
12. Vt *Vossianus L. O.* 15 *Pet¹*   faciat *ACPRTB m. pr. Pet²*   facies
X b³   facias *paraphrastes, Pet¹ B m. sec.*   Vt faciat *Bachrensius*
quicquid *CRT*   quicquit *BX*   pusila turba *b*   *Fort.* turba pusilla.

XXXII.

DE ARATORE ET BOBVS (BOVE *A*) R*A*   DE PIGROYRINTI͞V FRVS-
TRA ORANTE *C*   DE RVSTICO ET AXE *O*.
1. iurgite *T*   liquerat axem Rusticus *X*.
2. Liqueat *B*   Linquerat *Cabeliauius*.
3, 4 *uncis inclusit Lachmannus*.
3. Frustraque (Frustaque *X*) *codd. praeter B Galeanum et Petrenses, quam-*
quam in CR erasum est que   Frustra est *B*   Frustra *Galeanus et*
Petrenses   dispositis *PRX b²*   *An* Frustra ex dep.

Ferre suis rebus, cum resideret, opem.
Cui rector summis Tirynthius infit ab astris   5
  (Nam uocat hunc supplex in sua uota deum)
'Perge laborantes stimulis agitare iuuencos,
  Et manibus pigras disce iuuare rotas.
Tunc quoque congressum maioraque uiribus ausum
  Fas superos animis conciliare tuis.   10
Disce tamen pigris non flecti numina uotis,
  Praesentesque adhibe, cum facis ipse, deos.'

XXXIII.

DE ANSERE OVA AVREA PARIENTE.

Anser erat cuidam pretioso germine feta,
  Ouaque quae nidis aurea saepe daret.
Fixerat hanc uolucri legem natura superbae,
  Ne liceat pariter munera ferre duo.
Sed dominus cupidum †sperans uanescere† uotum,   5

4. cum res desideret *b.*
5. uictor *B m. pr.*   tyrinthius *T*   terincius *B*   tiricintius *C*
fit *P*   inquid *B.*
7. iuuencus *P.*
8. tituare rotos *P.*
    r te
9. Tunc *R*   Tunc *ABCPT*   Tu *X b²*   congressus . . . ausus
BX b² Cabeliauii schedae.
10. Fas *ACPRT*   athlis *Baehrensius*   Fac . . . consiliare *BOX b²b³*
et Cabeliauii schedae.
11. prigris non fleti *P.*
12. adhibet um *P*   esse *pro* ipse *C Pet¹.*

XXXIII.

DE ANSERE OVA AVREA PARIENTE *CR, in quo tamen* OVA A. P. *paruis
litteris nec miniatis addita sunt*   DE ANSERE *A*   DE ANSERE
ET AVREIS OVIS *O.*
1. Ansera cuidam *P*   quondam *X*   condam *b²b³*   gemine *P*
foeta *R.*
2. Oua (Dona *Pet²*) quaeque *X Pet¹ Pet²*   cum uidis *P.*
3-6 *uncis inclusit Lachmannus.*
3. Finxerat *Pet²b²*   Finxserat *X*   Fuerat *B m. pr.*   Dixerat
Heinsius ad Ouid. Her. 12. 39.
4. Non *B.*
5. spirans *A*   spernans *B*   uanescere (suan. *B) codd.*   euanescere *X*   cupidus sperans augescere uotum *Hopkensius*   spectans
uanescere *Froehnerus*   Fuitne grandescere (*cf. Cic. de Diuin. I.* 9. 15
Lentiscus triplici solita grandescere fetu) *uel* inuadere ?

Non tulit exosas in sua lucra moras,

Grande ratus pretium uolucris de morte referre,

Quae tam continuo munere diues erat.

Postquam nuda minax egit per uiscera ferrum,

Et uacuam solitis fetibus esse uidet,   10

Ingemuit tantae deceptus crimine fraudis.

Nam poenam meritis rettulit inde suis.

Sic qui cuncta deos uno male tempore poscunt,

Iustius his etiam uota diurna negant.

XXXIV.

DE FORMICA ET CICADA.

Quisquis torpentem passus transisse iuuentam

Nec timuit uitae prouidus ante mala,

Confectus senio, postquam grauis affuit aetas,

Heu frustra alterius saepe rogabit opem.

Solibus ereptos hiemi formica labores   5

Distulit et breuibus condidit ante cauis.

6. ꞃ tulit *B*   *Fort.* Nec, *cf. XXXIV.* 2   lustra *B m. pr.*
7. *An* Fraude   de mor *P*   de more *B m. pr.*   referret *A.*
8. Qui *b*³   diuers *P.*
9. aegit *R*   transegit uiscera *X b*².
10. foetibus *R*   uidit *P et Vossianus L. Q.* 86 *m. pr. et sic Cabelianius ex codd.*
11. deceptū *A.*
12. meritus *B*   rettulit *T*   retulit *COP Pet*¹   rettulit *R* redderet *Pet*²   pertulit *X*   attulit *B.*
13, 14 *uncis inclusit Lachmannus.*
14. uita *P*   negat *B.*

XXXIV.

DE FORMICA ET CICADA *OR*   DE CYCADA ET FORMICA *C   Titulus deest in A.*
1. Quis^quis *R*   Quisqui *P*   torpente *P*   passust *Froehnerus* transisse *ACPT*   transire *OR Petrenses*   transcire *B*   transsire *X.*
2. Ne *Pet*²   uita *P.*
3. Collectus *ACPTO m. pr.*   Confecto/ *R*   Confectus *Galeanus X Pet*¹ *Pet*²   fuit *P*   affluit *b*³.
4. Heu *B ut uidetur*   se *P*   rogabat *R m. pr. O m. pr. BX*   rogabit *ACP Pet*¹ *Pet*²   rogauit *Cabeliauii schedae.*
5. Silj *pro* Solibus *B*   Aestibus *Withofius*   exceptos *B et sic Baehrensius*   obreptans *Cannegieterus*   erepens *Lachmannus* ereptans *Froehnerus*   ycmi *B*   hieme *P.*
6. casis *BX b*³ *Camp.*

Verum ubi candentes suscepit terra pruinas
  Aruaque sub rigido delituere gelu,
Pigra nimis tantos non aequans corpore nimbos
  In *l*aribus propriis umida grana legit.   10
Discolor hanc precibus supplex alimenta rogabat
  Quae quondam querulo ruperat arua sono,
'Se quoque maturas cum tunderet area messis,
  Cantibus aestiuos explicuisse dies.'
Paruula tunc ridens sic est affata cicadam,   15
  (Nam uitam pariter continuare solent)
'Mi quoniam summo substantia parta labore est,
  Frigoribus mediis otia longa traho.
At tibi saltandi nunc ultima tempora restant,
  Cantibus est quoniam uita peracta prior.'   20

XXXV.

DE SIMIAE GEMELLIS.

Fama est quod geminum profundens simia partum,
  Diuidat in uarias pignora nata uices.

7. candendes *X*.
8. *Incipit fr. Karoliruhense K*   sub gelido *B Pet*[1] *Pet*[2] *Etiam in R gelido erasum fuisse uidetur*   diliruere *PK.*

9. Pigranimis *CKT Barthius*   tanto non aequas *C*   tanto *RT Pet*[2] aequas *P*   nimbus *P*   corpora nimbo *R sed fuerat* corpore nimbos *Num* tanto n. ae. corpore nimbos, *ut* tanto *sit* tam pusillo?
10. In propriis laribus *codd. quod correxit Lachmannus*   humida *codd.* hunida (huuida?) *B*   tumida *cod. Milouianus Cabeliauii*   fumida *Cannegieterus.*
11. Decolor *AKPT*   Discolor *C*   summis precibus *R.*
13. naturas *R*   maturos *C m. pr. et fragm. Karoliruhense*   tonderet *ABO*   non tundere *Pet*[2]   erea *A m. pr.*   aera *B*   aurea *P* messis *Pet*[1]   messes *cett.*
14. estiuos *C.*
15. sit *pro* tunc *B*   cicada *B.*
17. Mi *codd. praeter C*   En *C solus, fortasse uere*   est om. *BX b*[2]*b*[3].
18. Frigoris *B m. pr.*   ocia *C*   ossia *B.*
19. Ast *X*   saltanti *BPX Pet*[1].
20 *om. P.*

XXXV.

DE SIMIAE GEMELLIS *C*   DE SIMIA ET DVOBVS NATIS EIVS (ILLIVS *R*)
OR   *Titulus deest in A.*
1. simila *B.*
2. Diuidit *BOX Pet*[2]   pignora *codd.*   cara *BX cum recentioribus.*

Namque unum caro genitrix educit amore,
Alterius*que* odiis exsaturata tumet.
Coeperit ut fetam grauior terrere tumultus, 5
Dissimili natos condicione rapit.
Dilectum manibus uel pectore gestat amico,
Contemptum dorso suscipiente leuat.
Sed cum lassatis nequeat consistere plantis,
Oppositum fugiens sponte remisit onus. 10
Alter ab hirsuto circumdans brachia collo
Haeret et inuita cum genitrice fugit.
[Mox quoque dilecti succedit in oscula fratris
Seruatus uetulis unicus heres auis.
Sic multos neglecta iuuant atque ordine uerso 15
Spes humiles rursus in meliora refert.]

XXXVI.

DE VITVLO ET BOVE.

Pulcher et intacta uitulus ceruice resultans
Scindentem assidue uiderat arua bouem.

3. raro *Cabeliauius*   caro *codd.*   educat *C et fragm. Karoliruhense*
l'e
producit *R*   eduxit *X.*
4. Alteriusque *bb³ codices non sinceri*   Alterius *cett.*   exsaturata
ORX Petrenses   exaturata *CT*   exturata *P*   insaturata *Cannegieterus*
uix saturata *Barthius Aduers. L.* 7.
5. C Seperat *B*   Ceperat *X b²b³ Petrenses*   fetam *CO*   grauior
fetam *O*   tumultis *C.*
7. gestit *P.*
8. concoeptum *P*   suspiciente *R*   locat *Pet².*
9. laxatis *X*   nequiat *b³*   nequiit *malim.*
10. Obpositum *OR*   Appositum *Heinsius ad Ouid. Her.* 9. 60   remisit
l'sit
t
KPTX Petrenses   remisit *C*   remittit *ABO m. pr. b²b³*   remittit *R.*
11. Alter *om. A*   ab *codd. praeter P Pet¹*   ad *P*   et *Pet¹*
at *uulgo et Lachmannus*   Codicum scripturam cum Cataldo Iannellio seruaui
circundans *C.*
12. inuenta *P.*
13–16 *uncis inclusit Lachmannus, quem secutus sum.*
13. delicti *B*   succidit *A*   patris *B m. pr.*
14. Scruatis *P*   heris *Heinsius*   cura superstes *Withofius.*
15. neclecte *P*   orde *P.*
16. *Fortasse* Rursus spes humiles   russus *B.*

XXXVI.

DE VITVLO ET BOVE *ACOR.*
2. adsidue *K*   uidera *Pet¹.*

'Non pudet heus,' inquit, ' longaeuo uincula collo
     Ferre nec *haec* positis otia nosse iugis?
Cum mihi subiectas pateat discursus in herbas   5
     Et nemorum liceat rursus opaca sequi.'
At senior, nullam uerbis compulsus in iram,
     Vertebat solitam uomere fessus humum,
Donec deposito per prata liceret aratro
     Molliter herboso procubuisse toro.   10
Mox uitulum sacris *ut* nexum respicit aris
     Admotum cultro comminus ire popae,
'Hanc tibi,' testis ait, ' dedit indulgentia mortem,
     Expertem nostri quae facit esse iugi.
Proderit ergo grauis quamuis perferre labores,   15
     Otia quam tenerum mox peritura pati.'
Est hominum sors ista, magis felicibus ut mors
     Sit cita, cum miseros uita diurna necat.

---

3. Nec *B*   longeuo *CORTX.*

4. Ferre (Ferrea *B*) nec (*om. P*) expositis otia (ēxpositis ostia *B*) nosse (ferre *C*) iugis *codd.*   inpositis *Lachmannus*   haec positis *ego* *Fortasse tamen ex B scribendum* Ferrea nec positis otia nosse iugis.

5. Cu mihi *P*   pateant *P*   decursus *Lachmannus.*

7. commotus *B.*

8. solidam *AT*   solida *K* *In C legi non potuit.*

10. exoso *Pet*[1].

11. sertis *pro* sacris *Cannegieterus*   innexum *codd.*   ut nexum *ego* conspicit *B.*

12. Admotā *B*   Admoto *b*[3] *et sic Heinsius ad Ouid. Met. XIII.* 589 popae *KORT cum Galeano. Idem ex coniectura reposuerat Guietus*   prope *ACP*   pauet *B*   Admoto et cultro comminus ire popam *Heinsius.*

13. testis *C et fragm. Karolirulcense*   tristis (tristris *X*) *T cum cett.*

14. nostris *Pet*[2]   iugis *Pet*[2].

15—18 *uncis inclusit Lachmannus.*

15. grauis *Pet*[2]   graues *cett.*   proferre *X.b*[2].

16. Ossia *B*   ox *pro* mox *P*   pati *om. P.*

17. felicius *C*   felicior *T*   morsi Fit *P*   ut sit Mors cita *malebat Neueletus refragantibus codd. nostris omnibus. Simili modo Orientius in uocabulis* et mors *claudit hexametrum I.* 295.

18. miseris *B m. pr.*   negat *B et b*[2] *m. sec.*   regat *cett. et b*[2] *m. pr.* terat *Nodellus*   necat *ego ex coniectura posui.*

XXXVII.

DE CANE ET LEONE.

Pinguior exhausto canis occurrisse leoni
  Fertur et insertis uerba dedisse iocis.
'Nonne uides duplici tendantur ut ilia tergo,
  Luxurietque toris nobile pectus?' ait.
'Proximus humanis ducor post otia mensis,   5
  Communem capiens largius ore cibum.'
'Sed quod crassa malum circumdat guttura ferrum?'
  'Ne custodita fas sit abire domo.
At tu magna diu moribundus lustra pererras,
  Donec se siluis obuia praeda ferat.   10
Perge igitur nostris tua subdere colla catenis,
  Dum liceat faciles promeruisse dapes.'
Protinus ille grauem gemitu collectus in iram
  Atque ferox animi nobile murmur agit.
'Vade' ait 'et meritis nodum ceruicibus infer,   15
  Compensentque tuam uincula dura famem.

At mea cum uacuis libertas redditur antris,
  Quamuis ieiunus quaelibet arua peto.'
Has illis epulas potius laudare memento
  Qui libertatem postposuere gulae.   20

XXXVIII.

DE PISCE ET PHOECIDE.

Dulcibus e stagnis fluuio torrente coactus
  Aequoreas praeceps piscis obibat aquas.
Illic squamigerum despectans improbus agmen
  Eximium sese nobilitate refert.
Non tulit expulsum patrio sub gurgite phoecis,   5
  Verbaque cum †salibus asperiora dedit.
Vana †laboratis aufer mendacia dictis,
  Quaeque refutari te quoque teste queant.
Nam quis eat potior populo spectante probabo,
  Si pariter captos umida lina trahant.   10
Tunc me nobilior magno mercabitur emptor,
  Te simul aere breui †debile uulgus emet.'

17. reditur *P*   redditor *Withofius.*
19. Vas *B*   illas *P.*
20. Qui libertati praeposuere gulam *R*   Qui libertatem praeposuere
gulae *C*   Qui libertati postposuere gulam *Pet*[1].

XXXVIII.

DE PISCE ET PHOCA (FOCA *O*) *AOR*   DE PISCE ET FOCIS *C.*
1. est agnis *BK*   e cm. *P*   ex *ed.* 1494   coactis *CK.*
2. Equor eas *B*   obbibat *B*   abibat aquis *P.*
3. squamigeras *B m. pr.*   despectus *CK*   iprobus *C*   improbus *OR.*
5. iurgite *T*   phoecis *CK*   phoetis *P*   phocis *A*   phocas
(focas *O*) *ORT Pet*[2]   phycis *Cannegieterus.*
6. com *A*   cum *om. codex Campensis*   cum sociis *Galeanus uitiose*
probris *uel* salibus liberiora *Withofius*   cum salsis *Lachmannus*   An
sannis ?   *cum reprehensionibus* Certe in *Pet*[2] salibus *inueni.*
7. Vna *P*   laborantis *cod. Campensis*   *Fortasse* uaporatis *nisi potius*
Martialem imitatus IV. 33. 1 *scripsit* Plena laboratis.
9. eat *Baehrensius*   erit *codd.*   sit *Lachmannus*   probabo popello *X.*
10. humida *codd.*   trahunt *BX.*
11. mercabitur auro *b*[2].
12. debile *codd.*   *Num* futtile ?   emit *APT*   emet *R.*

XXXIX.

DE MILITE ARMA CREMANTE.

Vouerat attritus quondam per proelia miles
  Omnia suppositis ignibus arma dare,
Vel quae uictori moriens sibi turba dedisset,
  Vel quicquid profugo posset ab hoste capi.
Interea uotis *fors* affuit et memor arma   5
  Coeperat accenso singula ferre rogo.
Tunc lituus rauco deflectens murmure culpam
  Inmeritum flammis se docet *isse* pyr*ae*.
'Nulla tuos, inquit, petierunt tela lacertos,
  Viribus affirmes quae tamen acta meis.   10
Sed tantum uentis et cantibus arma coegi,
  Hoc quoque summisso (testor et astra) sono.'
Ille resultantem flammis crepitantibus addens,
  'Nunc te maior,' ait, 'poena dolorque rapit.
Nam licet ipse nihil possis temptare nec ausis,   15
  Saeuior hoc, alios quod facis esse malos.'

XXXIX.

DE MILITE ARMA CREMANTE *AR*   DE MILITE VETERANO *C*   DE MILITE ET LITVO *O*.

1. prelia *OR*   milex *B*.
2. subpositis *ORX*   daret *Pet²*.
4. ab ęę oste *B*   rapi *Cannegieterus*.
5. sors *codd.*   fors *Wopkensius*   affuit *BCOX*   adfuit *R* Interea uotis et sors memor affuit arma *X*.
6. sigula *B*   iugo *CK*.
7. lituis *B*   runco *Pet² m. pr.*   de ferrens *Pet²*   defendens *BOX*.
8. flacmas *B*   esse prius *codd.*   esse piis *Cannegieterus*   esse cibum *Withofius*   ipse peti *Lachmannus*   in flammis se d. c. pyrae *Froehnerus*   isse *ego*   Fort. hisce frui.
9. inquid *T*.
10. Virribus *B*   affirmas *ORX*   affirmans *Pet²*   adfirmoes *A* mens *P*.
11. uenas *Pet¹*   uentis errantibus *Reg.* 15 A. *VII. Mus. Brit.*   uanis ego cantibus *Lachmannus*.
12. submisso *RX Petrenses*   summisso *COT*   ad *X b²b³ Petrenses* at *Lachmannus*   ut *Baehrensius*   arma *C*.
13. acdens *K*.
14. Hoc *pro* Nunc *Lachmannus*   te *om. B*   colorque *potius quam* dolorque *B*   Fort. calorque.
15. posse *P*   ausis *B*   ausus *cett. omnes*.
16. quo *b² m. pr.*   facit *C*   malum *P*.

XL.

DE PARDO ET VVLPE.

Distinctus maculis et pulchro pectore pardus
    Inter consimiles †ibat inira† feras.
Sed quia nulla graues uariarent terga leones,
    Protinus his miserum credidit esse genus.
Cetera sordenti damnans animalia uultu,   5
    Solus in exemplum nobilitatis erat.
Hunc arguta nouo gaudentem uulpis amictu
    Corripit et uanas approbat esse notas.
'Vade' ait 'et pictae nimium confide iuuentae,
    Dum mihi consilium pulchrius esse queat.   10
Miremurque magis quos munera mentis adornant,
    Quam qui corporeis enituere bonis.'

XL.

DE PARDO ET VVLPE *ACOR.*

  1. pulcro *C*   pectore *ABCOPRTX b²* cum Galeano et Vossiano *L. O.* 15 corpore *cod. Campensis et codex Iannellii.*
  2. ibat inira *C et fragm. Karoliruhense*   ibat in ira *A m. pr.*   ibat mira *P*   ibat inire *RT*   ibat in arua *A m. sec., BX Petrenses* respuit ire *Neueletus*   ibat honore *Withofius*   abnuit ire *Lachmannus* quod tuetur *Schenkelius ex Babrii fab.* 101. 3 τῶν δὲ συμφύλων Ἀποστατήσας τοῖς λέουσιν ὡμίλει   uitat itare *Froehnerus*   *Fort.* ibat in ora *cf.* XXXVII. 8 *ubi C* abore *exhibet.*
  3. que *B*   leonis *P.*
  4. reddidit *P.*
  5–12 *desunt in P.*
  5. clamans *A*   dampnans *ORX*   dampnas *B*   cultu *Lachmannus.*
  6. eat *Pet².*
  7. gädentem *B*   uulpis *C Pet² T*   uulpes *ORX Galeanus et Pet-.* renses   uulgus *B*   *Fort.* ludentem uulgus. *Vulpes enim ex solo epitheto arguta significari poterat, ut* paruula *formica XXXIV.* 15, auritulus *asinus,* laniger *agnus apud Phaedrum, dicuntur (I.* 11. 6, *I.* 1. 6).
  8. *om. B*   uarias *Pet² X m. pr.*   approbat *CORTX Petrenses*   adprobat *Vossiani duo Baehrensii*   inprobat *b².*
  9. et picte *B*   figurae *Cannegieterus.*
  10. Sed *X*   rear *Froehnerus*   puerius *B*   cluat *Baehrensius.* 11, 12 *uncis inclusit Lachmannus.*
  11. mentis *codd. omnes.*
  12. uiri *pro* bonis *B.*

XLI.

DE IMBRE ET FICTILIBVS VASIS.

Inpulsus uentis et pressa nube coactus
    Ruperat hibernis se grauis imber aquis.
Cumque per effusas stagnaret turbine terras,
    Expositum campis fictile pressit opus.
Mobile namque lutum tepidus prius instruit aer,   5
    Discat ut admoto rectius igne coqui.
Tunc nimbus fragilis perquirit nomina testae,
    Immemor illa sui†, 'Amphora dicor,' ait.
'Nunc me docta manus, rapiente uolumina gyro,
    Molliter obliquum iussit habere latus.   10
'Hactenus hac,' inquit, 'liceat constare figura,
    Nam te subiectam diluet imber aquis.'
Et simul accepto uiolentius amne fatiscens
    Pronior in tenues uicta cucurrit aquas.
Infelix, quae magna sibi cognomina sumens   15
    Ausa †pharetratis nubibus ista loqui.

XLI.

DE IMBRE (AE *A*) ET FICTILIBVS VASIS *AR*   DE IMBRE ET TESTA *O*
DE OLLA CRVDA A FLVVIO RAPTA *C*.
  1–14 *desunt in P.*
  1. Inpulsus *CORTX Pet²*.
  3. Quoque per fussas *A*   efusas *X*   infusas *Pet²*   effossas
Lachmannus.
  4. positum *A*   expulsum *Pet²*   prescit opis *B*.
  5. trepidus *O m. pr. Pet²*.
  7. nymbus *C*   perquirat *T*.
  8. Immemor *C*   Inmemor *T*   *Fort.* olla sui est   su amphora *b³*
frui *B*   sui est *cod. Iannellii*   situs *Withofius*   anphora *Pet²*.
  10. obliqum *Pet²*   obloqinum *B ut uidetur*.
  11. ac *B*   liceat inquid *B*.
  12. Nam *ACORX*   Iam *Vossianus L. O.* 15   te *om. X*   deluet *C*
diluit *B*   pelluet *Gabelianii schedae*   aquis *OX cum Voss. L. Q.* 86
ait *ACRT*   agens *Galeanus.*
  13–18 *cum XLII extant in Sangallensi* 1396 (*S*).
  14. tenues *AOSTX*   temues *R*   teneras *C*   cucurit *A*.
  15, 16 *uncis inclusit Lachmannus.*
  15. Infelixq: sibi magna *O*.
  16. *Fort.* Ausa erat iratis   Ausa foret atris *Wopkensius*   A. foret
tantis *Baehrensius.*

Haec poterunt miseros post hac exempla monere
Subdita nobilibus ne sua fata gemant.

XLII.

DE LVPO ET HAEDO.

Forte lupum melior cursu deluserat haedus
    Proxima uicinis dum petit arua casis.
Inde fugam recto tendens in moenia cursu
    Inter lanigeros astitit ille greges.
Inpiger hunc raptor mediamque secutus in urbem,   5
    Temptat compositis sollicitare dolis.
'Nonne uides,' inquit, 'cunctis ut uictima templis
    Inmitem regemens morte cruentet humum?'
Quod nisi securo ualeas te reddere campo,
    Ei mihi uittata tu quoque fronte cades.   10
Ille refert, 'Modo quam metuis, precor, exue curam,
    Et tecum uiles, improbe, tolle minas.

17. post hac *COT*   post haec *APR m. pr. SX.*
18. mouilibus *B m. pr.*   nobilius *C*   ne *B et sic ed.* 1494   ut *cett.*
Quod ego in B inueni, iam ex coniectura reposuerat Withofius   facta *P.*

XLII.

DE LVPO ET HEDO *ACR*   DE HEDO ET LVPO *O.*
1. haedus *CS*   hedus *ART*   aedus *P*   edus *O.*
2. aura *B*   casis *AOPRSTX*   cauis *C.*
3. menia *S.*
4. astit *B*   asstitit *T.*

5. Impinger *A*   /mpier *S*   medeam *om.* que *B*   sectatus
Guietus.
6. conpositas *P*   solicitare *X*   solisicitare *B.*
7. ut *om. P.*
8. Inmitem *C*   Inmitem *PST*   inmittere *A*   Inmeritam *BX*
regemens *RST*   regimens *P*   redimens *C*   reuomat *A*   generis *B*
pecudum *X*   *In O uerba erasa*   cruente dumum *C*   cruentat humum
R   cruente thimum *A*   cruentat hymum *P*   cruentet humum *O*
cruentat humum *BSX.*

9. si *S*   si *R.*
10. Ei *R*   Hei *O*   Heu *BCST*   Hen *X*   uitata *P*
fronde *C*   cadis *CPT*   cap is *S*   carens *B.*
11. mihi quod *Lachmannus*   exuc *BX*   exime *ACOPRST*   ura *A.*
12. uiles *ex* uires *S.*

Nam sat erit sacrum diuis fudisse cruorem,
  Quam rabido fauces exsaturare lupo.
Sic quotiens duplici subcuntur tristia casu   15
  Expedit insignem promeruisse necem.

i. melius
13. Satius *Withofius*   sat erit *R*   sat erit *ACOST*   fas erit *X*
poteris *P*   Namque ma$\bar{g}$ est *B*.
    14. rapido *BPSX*   fauces rapido *BX*   exaturare *C*   exsaciare
PSX   exsatiare *R*.
    15. subeunt discrimina *B*.
EXPLICIT LIBER AVIANI POETAE *C*   EXPLICIVNT FABVLAE AVIENI
POETAE AEGREGII *R*   EXPLICIT LIBER AVIANI *O*   *tum* Omnes fabulę aut
hęsopicae sunt aut libisticę.   H/esopice sunt quę de sensibilibus animalibus
feruntur libisticę quę de inuisibilibus dicuntur.   Explicit liber auiani *BX*.

Sed in B erasa priore subscriptione iterum rubrica scriptum est Explicet liber
auiani.

COMMENTARY.

PRAEFATIO.

1. **Theodosi.** Probably Macrobius Ambrosius Theodosius, the author of the *Saturnalia*, is meant. See the discussion in the Prolegomena. **litterarum titulo**, 'head of composition,' a sense into which *titulus* naturally passes from that of 'label.' 2. **nostri nominis memoriam mandaremus.** Veget. de re milit. i. Praef. *Antiquis temporibus mos fuit bonarum artium studia mandare litteris atque in libros redacta offerre principibus.* i. 28 *auctoribus qui rei militaris disciplinam litteris mandauerunt.* Mamertin. Grat. Actio Iuliano xxx *mandanda sunt litteris, inserenda monumentis.* Symmach. Epist. i. 46 *neque omnia mandanda sunt litteris.* Saluian. de Gub. Dei vii. 258 *de hac re et libros condidit et memoriae haec pudenda mandauit.* **textus** narrative. Quintilian ix. 4. 13 (if Spalding is right in so reading) opposes *in textu* to *in fine* as the connected series of words which form the main sentence to the close of the sentence. In the sense of 'narrative' (Gloss. Bodl. Auct. T. ii. 24 *textus narratio*) it is not uncommon in the History of Ammianus. xv. 7. 6 *breui textu percurram.* xv. 8. 1 *ut ostendit textus superior.* xxviii. 6. 1 *textus aperit absolutus.* So several times in the strange tessellated poems of Optatianus Porfirius, a contemporary of Constantine, iv. 9 *Quor textu scruposa siet mea pagina simplex* (see Lucian Müller's ed. 1877). 3. **urbane concepta falsitas deceat,** 'because fables possess the charm of a gracefully framed fiction.' Philostr. Vit. Apollon. 199 ὁ δ' (Αἴσωπος) ἐπαγγέλλων λόγον ὅς ἐστι ψευδής, πᾶς οἶδεν ὅτι αὐτὸ τὸ μὴ περὶ ἀληθινῶν ἐρεῖν ἀληθεύει. ib. ὁ δὲ εἰπὼν μὲν ψευδῆ λόγον, ἐπαγαγὼν δὲ νουθεσίαν, ὥσπερ ὁ Αἴσωπος, δείκνυσιν ὡς τὸ χρήσιμον τῆς ἀκροάσεως τῷ ψεύδει κέχρηται. 4. **incumbat necessitas,** 'it is incumbent.' This use is quoted by Cannegieter from the Digest, and so Veget. de r. m. iii. 2, *quibus necessitas et belli incumbit et morbi.* **ueritatis.** A fable-writer speaks freely, because he is not bound by the rules of strict truth. His vehicle is fiction, and he moves in it at will. This is the meaning, I believe, of the 'free Muse' which Babrius Praef. i. 15, 16 ascribes to Aesop, rather than 'prose' as opposed to 'poetry' (Rutherford). Lachmann's *seueritatis* is plausible, but not necessary. Cf. however Sen. Consol. ad Polyb. 8, where he is speaking of fable-writing as against graver literature, *si poterit a seuerioribus scriptis ad haec solutiora procedere.* 5. **poemate,** here and below, *poemati suo Flaccus aptauit,* 'poetry,' not 'a poem.' Capitolin. Vit. Maximi et Balbini vii *eloquentia clarus, poemate inter sui temporis poetas praecipuus.* In Quintil. i. 8, 16, *tropos omnes quibus praecipue non poema modo, sed etiam oratio ornatur,* the word of course has its proper sense of a single poem; but the age of Quintilian is removed by a long interval from the age of Avianus. **litterarum,** composition. 6. **latinitate.** Barth Aduersar. xix. 24 objected to this as not sufficiently antithetic to *Graeca eruditione,* and conjectured *latina arte.* His criticism finds some support in a Vienna MS quoted by Schenkl (Österr. Gymnas. xvi. p. 399) in which *latina* is written for *latinitate,* and this Schenkl would

E

retain constructing it with *eruditione*. Yet there seems to be nothing forced in saying that Theodosius was superior to the Athenians in knowledge of Greek, and to the Romans in command of pure Latin. *latinitas* is thus used by Cic. Att. vii. 3. 9, where Caecilius is called *malus auctor latinitatis*. 7. **Huius materiae.** This subject, fable-writing. **ducem** with **nobis**, a leader to us. **Aesopum.** Babr. Praef. i. 14 Μάθοις δ' ἂν οὕτω ταῦτ' ἔχοντα καὶ γνοίης, Ἐκ τοῦ σοφιστοῦ, τοῦ γέροντος Αἰσώπου. See Rutherford's History of Greek Fable (Babrius xxv–l.). Quintil. v. 11. 19 *Illae quoque fabellae quae, etiamsi originem non ab Aesopo acceperunt (nam uidetur eorum primus auctor Hesiodus), nomine tamen Aesopi maxime celebrantur.* 8. **noueris,** 'you are to know,' a polite imperative. Hor. S. i. 9. 7 *Noris nos*, where Acron paraphrases 'hoc uolo, ut scias nos.' **responso Delphici Apollinis monitus.** Whence is this statement? Possibly it was in the scazons of which a fragment is preserved in the Homeric lexicon of Apollonius s. v. "Αειδε. ταῦτα δ' Αἴσωπος Ὁ Σαρδιηνὸς εἶπεν, ὄντιν' οἱ Δελφοὶ "Αδοντα μῦθον οὐ καλῶς ἐδέξαντο. In the life of Aesop ascribed to Planudes (I in Eberhard's *Fabulae Romanenses*) Aesop on his way to be executed by the Delphians narrates four fables, (1) The Mouse and Frog, (2) The Hare, the Eagle, the Beetle, and Jupiter, (3) The Old Man and the Asses, (4) The Man and his Daughter; but nothing is said of this being the suggestion of the oracle. **ridicula,** droll or amusing stories, the Αἰσωπικὸν γελοῖον of Arist. Vesp. 1259, Αἰσώπου τι γελοῖον Vesp. 566. 9. **orsus est,** set on foot, started. Cic. de Orat. i. 21. 98 *princeps Crassus eius sermonis ordiendi fuit.* **legenda,** lessons or rules of virtue, which as set forth in written compositions would form a proper study for youthful readers. Macrobius' *seria et discenda* (S. ii. 5. 1) is somewhat parallel. **pro exemplo,** by way of example, παραδείγματος χάριν. Phaedr. Praef. ii. 1 *Exemplis continetur apologi genus.* Macrob. S. vii. 4. 4 *Quia plebeia ingenia magis exemplis quam ratione capiuntur, ammonuisse illum contentus forem institutionis pecudum.* 10. **Socrates.** In the Phaedo (60) Socrates says that at the suggestion of a haunting dream he had translated such of the Aesopian fables as he knew into verse; but Av. probably alludes to the apologues, in the style of fables, which from time to time are found in the Platonic dialogues, e. g. of Pain and Pleasure having two heads growing out of one stem (Phaed. 60), of the Grasshoppers (Phaedr. 259), of Plenty and Poverty (Symp. 203), of Prometheus and Epimetheus (Protag. 320). See Rutherford's Babrius, p. xxviii. **diuinis,** admirable, inimitable. Common in Cic. and subsequent writers. Macrob. S. i. 11. 41 *librum illum diuinum de immortalitate animae.* Cf. v. 1. 18, v. 14. 11, v. 15. 16, vii. 10. 1. **poemati.** Av. cannot mean a particular poem as Quintilian does v. 11. 20 *Et Horatius ne in poemate quidem humilem generis huius usum putauit in illis uersibus* Quod dixit uulpes aegroto cauta leoni (Epist. i. 1. 73). Horace introduces fables in his Satires and Epistles, and, by way of allusion, even in his Epodes (iv. 1 *Lupis et agnis*). 11. **iocorum communium,** also in the late Latin comedy Querolus. Prol. p. 5, ed. Peiper, *Nemo sibimet arbitretur dici quod nos populo dicimus neque propriam sibi causam constituat communi ex ioco,* which proves the meaning to be 'jests of general application.' Cp. Phaedr. iii. Praef. 45 *Suspicione si quis errabit sua Et rapiet ad se quod erit commune omnium* (Cannegieter). The only other sense it could have, 'open to the use of all,' i. e. which any fable-writer might use as common property, might be supported by Horace's *Difficile est proprie communia dicere* (A. P. 128). 12. **uitae argumenta.** Either (1) *stories* of real life, Quintil. ii. 4. 2 *argumentum quod falsum sed uero simile comoediae fingunt*, where Quintilian distinguishes such *argumenta* from *fabula quae uersatur in tragoediis atque carminibus, non a ueritate modo sed etiam a forma ueritatis remota*, and again from *historia, in qua est gestae rei* *expositio.* Macrob. Somn. Scip. i. 2. 9 *In quibusdam et argumentum ex ficto locatur et per mendacia ipse relationis ordo contexitur, ut sunt illae Aesopi fabulae elegantia fictionis inlustres* ; or (2) in a more general sense, 'subjects,' like Suetonius' *argumenta inferorum* Calig. 57. Macrobius says, S. v. 17. 5, the story of Dido is treated so wonderfully by Vergil that artists of all kinds, *tamquam unico argumento decoris utantur,* the one best subject in which they can exhibit their artistic powers. In this sense it nearly = our 'illustration.' **iambis,** choliambics or scazons. Babrius speaks of his own πικρῶν ἰάμβων, i. Praef. 19. **Babrius.** A Roman name, not a Greek, as Otto Crusius shows de Babrii aetate, pp. 189-191. It is found several times in inscriptions. The conclusion of Crusius that the author of two books, the latter imperfect, of fables in Greek scazons, which were first published by Boissonade in 1844 from a codex in the monastery of Laura on Mount Athos, discovered by a Greek named Minoides Menas (Rutherford, p. lxvii), was a Roman who wrote in Greek, modifying his diction by Latin idioms, is, if not demonstrated, at least very probable. **13. coartauit,** 'abridged' or 'reduced:' the opposite of *resoluit,* 'expanded.' **14. quinque.** This is the number as stated in the colophon at the end of the now destroyed Reims MS (Hervieux, Phaedrus p. xliv). The whole number of Phaedrus' fables is 93 (as given by Orelli and Hervieux), a smaller total than the Babrian collection even in its imperfect extant form. Hence *resoluit* would seem to refer more particularly to the distribution into a number of separate books which Phaedrus adopted. That the books were short is perhaps indicated by *libellos.* **15. in unum redactas.** In the same way as Varro and Vegetius use *in libros redigere.* Macrob. S. v. 2. 5 *uniuersas historias . . . in unam seriem coactas redegerat.* **dedi,** as we say 'have given,' meaning 'presented to the reader,' nearly = *edidi* or *in publicum dedi.* **rudi latinitate** need not be taken too literally. He speaks with the modesty of an unfledged author. To judge truly of the style of Avianus we have only to compare him with Ausonius' version of Babrius lxxv. (Auson. Epig. 75). I cannot agree with O. Crusius and Schwabe, who explain *rudi latinitate conpositas* of the prose version of Iulius Titianus (de Act. Babrii p. 238, Teuffel-Schwabe Geschichte d. Röm. Lit. § 450). **18. cautus,** on your guard against error. Phaedr. ii. Praef. 2. 3 *Nec aliud quicquam per fabellas quaeritur Quam corrigatur error ut mortalium Acuatque sese diligens industria.* Seren. Sammon. 856 *Vis et mirificos cautus praediscere odores.* **Loqui uero arbores.** Phaedr. i. Prol. 6, 7 *Quod arbores loquantur, non tantum ferae, Fictis iocari nos meminerit fabulis.* And so Babrius Praef. 6 sqq. Ἐπὶ τῆς δὲ χρυσῆς καὶ τὰ λοιπὰ τῶν ζῴων Φωνὴν ἔναρθρον εἶχε καὶ λόγους ᾔδει. Ἀγοραὶ δὲ τούτων ἦσαν ἐν μέσαις ὕλαις, Ἐλάλει δὲ πέτρη καὶ τὰ φύλλα τῆς πεύκης. Στρουθοὶ δὲ συνετὰ πρὸς γεωργὸν ὡμίλουν. Uncle Remus c. xxi. *In dem days de beastesses kyar'd on marters same ez fokes. Dey went into fahmin', en I specke, ef de troof wuz ter come out, dey kep' sto', en had der camp-meetin' times en der bobbycues wu'en de wedder wuz 'greeble.* **19. gemere,** growl in converse with mankind. Cannegieter shows that *gemere* is used not only of bulls (Aen. xii. 722), but also of bears (Hor. Epod. xvi. 51), lions (Val. Fl. i. 758), dogs (Stat. Theb. iv. 429). **uerbis certare,** carry on verbal disputes. **20. fecimus** = *finximus,* common in this sense with infin. and sometimes with participle. Dräger (Hist. Synt. ii. p. 394) quotes five instances from Cicero, and the whole usage is discussed at length by Thielmann in *Archiv für Latein. Lexicographie* iii. 177-206. **21. inanimis** for *animis* of MSS may be considered certain.

I.

Babr. i. 16, Aesop. 275, 275ᵇ, 275ᶜ.

BABR. i. 16.

Ἄγροικος ἠπείλησε νηπίῳ τίτθη
κλαίοντι 'παῦσαι, μή σε τῷ λύκῳ ῥίψω.'
ὁ λύκος δ' ἀκούσας τήν τε γραῦν ἀληθεύειν
νομίσας ἔμεινεν ὡς ἕτοιμα δειπνήσων,
ἕως ὁ παῖς μὲν ἑσπέρης ἐκοιμήθη,
αὐτὸς δὲ πεινῶν, καὶ λύκος χανὼν ὄντως,
ἀπῆλθε νωθραῖς ἐλπίσιν παρεδρεύσας.
λύκαινα δ' αὐτὸν ἡ σύνοικος ἠρώτα
'πῶς οὐδὲν ἄρας ἦλθες ὥσπερ εἰώθης;'
ὁ δ' εἶπε 'πῶς γάρ, ὃς γυναικὶ πιστεύω;'

Donatus on Ter. Adel. iv. 2. 21 alludes to this fable. *Lupus in fabula. Alii putant ex nutricum fabulis natum, pueros ludificantium terrore lupi, paulatim e cauea uenientis usque ad limen cubiculi.* Plaut. Stich. 577 *Atque eccum lupum in sermone: praesens esuriens adest:* cf. Cic. ad Att. xiii. 33.

1. deflentem paruum. I retain this, the reading of the Paris MSS *APG* against *deflenti paruo* of the rest as palpably the original and earlier tradition, of which the dative is a later alteration caused by the difficulty of finding a construction. The first form of the sentence would be *Rustica deflentem paruum iurauerat escam fore;* the intervening clause *Ni taceat* gives occasion for a change to the other construction of *iurare* with *quod* which is found in the Historia Augusta (Dräger ii. p. 225) and elsewhere, e.g. Macrob. S. vii. 3. 12 *iurauerat quod eum passurus esset.* So *polliceri quod* in the immediately following sentence of Macrobius. The construction would thus resemble that of *facere, efficere* with an accus. followed by an *ut* clause which is common enough in Plautus and belongs to the language of common life. *paruum=puerum* Prud. Perist. x. 716 *Sitire sese paruus exclamauerat* and elsewhere.   **iurauerat**=Babrius' ἠπείλησε. The emendation *iurgauerat,* cf. *iurgia* (v. 14), is tempting, but *iurgare* does not seem to be constructed with an accus.   **olim,** 'once on a time' = the recurring ποτέ of Babrius and the Aesopic fables.   **2. foret** for *futurus esset* would seem to be part of the Latinity of the Decadence. Amm. Marc. xxiv. 4. 24 *cum se ultro offerret, si miles fuisset memorabilis conscius facti=oblaturus esset;* xxii. 6. 2 *pollicitus quod ipse quoque protinus ueniret — uenturus esset.* In *foret* the form itself is future, cf. *fore.*   **3. ipsas Ante fores,** 'close before the door,' like Vergil's *Vestibulum ante ipsum.*   **4. irrita uota gerens,** 'disappointed in his hopes' — Babrius' νωθραῖς ἐλπίσιν παρεδρεύσας. *Vota gerere* like *curam gerere* and with little, if any, more special meaning.   **5. nimiae,** 'overpowering,' 'deep.' Very common in this sense in Ammianus Marcellinus and the writers of the Decadence. It seems to have belonged to the language of common life; hence its occurring in the uncouth Latin of the Christian Acts of Martyrs. Thus twice in the Passio Sanctorum Quattuor Coronatorum, p. 10 ed. Wattenbach *cum nimio desiderio requireret,* p. 13 *Diocletianus iratus est uehementer et nimio furore plenus dixit.* This seems to have lasted on from the time of Plautus: see Ramsay's Mostellaria Excursus xii.   **6.** Wopkens' emendation *Spem quoque raptoris sustulit inde fami* is accepted by Lachmann and does little violence to MSS 'and besides by so doing (inde) robbed the famishing plunderer of his last hope.' So Macrob. S. vii. 1. 13 *Hoc commento spem detraxit insidiantibus regnantis quieti.* The MS reading *Spem quoque raptori sustulit inde fames* may be defended, as a poetical transference by which the wolf's despair of satisfying his hunger is described as hunger making the wolf despair by not being satisfied. This is only an extension of a use common enough in Latin poetry. So Propertius says *aspergat tempora sudor* for *aspergantur tempora sudore* ii. 24. 3; *sinus condit murmura Ioniae aquae* for *sinu conduntur m. I. a.* (Postgate on Prop. iv. 6. 16). Valerius Flaccus *motis seu uos uia flatibus urguet* for *motis flatibus ad uiam urguemini* iii. 624. Vergil *ni cursus in altum Vela uocet* for *uela uocentur ut cursum faciant in altum* Aen. iii. 454. Claudian Laud. Stil. i. 3 *Conubii necdum festiuos regia cantus Sopierat.* **raptori,** Aen. ii. 355 *lupi ceu Raptores.* **9, 10.** The reading here is very doubtful. It is hardly probable that Avianus would have admitted *referis* as a form of *refers*, and impossible that *rēfers* should stand as a spondee, as Schenkl suggested. *Referes* the reading of *A* seems to point to *referens* which is actually found in the Galeanus. If this is adopted, *sed trahis* must be a corruption either of *sic trahis* (Bährens) or possibly of *attrahis.* Avianus is fond of this construction of participle in the hexameter followed by final verb in the pentameter, iii. 7, 8; v. 11, 12; vi. 3, 4; vii. 5, 6, and passim. **9. referens,** 'bringing home.' **10.** The emaciated checks draw in *.trahunt*) the features of the wolf, giving them a pinched and sickly appearance. **consumptis,** by starvation. **ora,** possibly 'jaws,' in the narrower sense of 'mouth,' rather than 'features.' **12. uix,** 'with difficulty skulked pitiably away and took nothing.' **uacua,** not the same as *uana*, but empty of prey: as Catullus speaks of Penios coming *non uacuos* lxiv. 288. **13. rogas,** 'Can you ask ?' as often in Plautus. *rogo* of some MSS might be supported by such passages as Salvian. de Gub. Dei i. § 10 *Et quae, rogo, insania est aut quae caecitas, ut egestuosa ac mendicante re publica diuitias posse credant stare priuatas?* vii. § 222 *Et quae nobis, rogo, spes ante Deum est ?* vii. § 260 *Et quae esse, rogo, Romano statui spes potest ?* Indeed the formula is of constant recurrence in this writer. **14. Iurgia,** the scolding words addrest by the nurse to the child. Ovid Met. iii. 261, 2 *tum linguam ad iurgia soluit. Profeci quid enim totiens per iurgia? dixit.* **uerba darent,** 'deceived.' Ovid Trist. ii. 500 *Verbaque dat stulto callida nupta uiro.* Elsewhere Av. uses *uerba dare = loqui*, in which sense it is hardly classical. **15. arte,** which Withof criticised as unmeaning, is probably here 'lesson,' 'teaching.' Manuals of instruction in Grammar, Rhetoric, etc. were called *Artes*, and from this sense the word would naturally come to mean 'primer,' so 'lesson.' This seems more probable than to explain *arte* of the artifice of the nurse, which is a censure on over credulity. *Arte* would thus nearly = *story of* the artifice. **notari,** 'is marked for reprobation.' Ovid Trist. ii. 7 *Carmina fecerunt ut me moresque notaret Iam pridem inuisa Caesar ab Arte meos.* **16. Femineam.** Av. here follows Babrius closely, πῶς γάρ, ὃς γυναικὶ πιστεύω ; Two of the prose versions given are more general ; the wolf says ἐν ταύτῃ τῇ ἐπαύλει ἄλλα μὲν λέγουσιν, ἄλλα δὲ πράττουσιν, and the moral is that men's words do not agree with their acts. This is perhaps the older application of the fable ; the special reference to women belongs to a period when their position was more established and gave them a formidable power in the world of intrigue. **esse,** 'has an existence.' Ovid Am. iii. 3. 1 *Esse deos, i crede.* Stat. S. i. 4. 1 *Estis io Superi.* Val. Fl. v. 645 *Est honor his etiam suus, est.*

II.

Babr. 115, Fab. Aesop. 419 Halm.

This fable existed in no less than three poetical Greek versions, the Babrian, an iambic version of which one line and a half are preserved by Suidas s. v. Νῦν σωθείην, and another in hexameters, of which four and a half lines are also extant in Suidas s. v. μεταχρονίην, στυφελῶν, οἴτῳ, σκῶλον. They are quoted at length by Rutherford, pp. xxi, xxii. The fact of the tortoise promising to repay the bird that lifted it into air with jewels from the Erythraean Sea points, I think, to India as the original home of the fable. Phaedrus has a somewhat similar fable II. 7 (6) in which an eagle that has carried off a tortoise into the sky is instructed by a crow to dash it down upon a rock in order to get at the flesh inside, and the meal is then shared between the two birds.

BABR. 115.

Νωθὴς χελώνη λιμνάσιν ποτ' αἰθυίαις
λάροις τε καὶ κήυξιν εἶπεν ἀγρώσταις·
'κάμέ πτερωτὴν εἴθε τις πεποιήκει.'
τῇ δ' ἐκ τύχης ἔλεξεν αἰετὸς †ταῦτα
'πόσον, χέλυμνα, μισθὸν αἰετῷ δώσεις,
ὅστις σ' ἐλαφρὴν καὶ μετάρσιον θήσω ;'
'τὰ τῆς Ἐρυθρῆς πάντα δῶρά σοι δώσω.'
'τοίγαρ διδάξω' φησίν. ὑπτίην δ' ἄρας
ἔκρυψε νέφεσιν, ἔνθεν εἰς ὄρος ῥίψας
ἤραξεν αὐτῆς οὖλον ὄστρακον νώτων.
ἡ δ' εἶπεν ἐκψύχουσα 'σὺν δίκῃ θνήσκω.
τίς γὰρ νεφῶν μοι καὶ τίς ἦν πτερῶν χρείη,
τῇ καὶ χαμᾶζε δυσκόλως προβαινούσῃ ;'

1. testudŏ, so *harundŏ*, xvi. 8. **2.** This line is full of perplexities : (1) *eam* where correct Latin required *se* ; (2) *uolucrum* after *quis* ; (3) the over compression of meaning in *constituisset humi*, which must signify 'had after a flight through air set her safe on the ground.' But (1) the change of the reflexive to the demonstrative pronoun, perhaps for clearness, is quite common even in Caesar, Livy, and Tacitus (Dräger i. pp. 58, 59), and cannot raise any difficulty in the later Latin of Avianus. (2) *Volucris* is masc. in the hexameter translation of the Homeric prodigy Il. ii. 299sqq. which Cicero has introduced in the second book of his *de Diuinatione* (ii. 30. 64) *tam teneros uolucris matremque peremit*, and in Corippus laud. Iustini i. 199 (Neue i. 634), but not elsewhere (Avianus himself expressly makes it fem. XV. 1, XXXIII. 3); and here the indeterminateness of the genitive, *si quis uolucrum* not *si qui uolucris*, as well as the fact of *quis* being sometimes used of feminines (Cannegieter) takes from the harshness of the combination. (3) might be got over by reading with the Galeanus and *B*, two good MSS, *destituisset*, 'had set firmly down,' cf. Plaut. Rud. iii. 5. 43, C. Gracchus ap. Gell. x. 3, Livy ii. 12, vii. 10, xxiii. 10, xxvii. 15, where *destituere* is an emphasized *statuere*, nearly = *defigere* : see Lipsius Epistol. Quaest. iv. 10 and cf. Hildebrand on Apul. M. ii. 25. Another possibility would be to read *uolucrem* with *P* and the corrector of *A*, which would express Babrius' ὅστις σ' ἐλαφρὴν καὶ μετάρσιον θήσω. **humi** might thus mean firm ground on some high elevation, as opposed to the low levels on which the tortoise ordinarily moved. For *uolucrem* thus used predicatively cf. Cic. Tusc. Disp. v. 13. 38 *alias bestias nantes aquarum incolas natura esse uoluit, alias uolucres caelo frui libero.* I do not think Lachmann is right in considering *uolucrem constituisset* a translation of Babrius' κάμέ πτερωτὴν εἴθε τις πεποιήκει. [Withof's ingenious *restituisset humo* has some support from one of the Oxford MSS which has *humo*.] **3.** Guiet and Wopkens rightly explain this as loose Latin (*genus loquendi barbarum*, Guiet), for *protinus se prolaturam esse conchas*, comparing IX. 2 *Securus, quodcumque malum fortuna tulisset, Robore collato posset uterque pati.* A close parallel is Plaut. Merc. iii. 1. 38 *Inter nos coniurauimus nisi cum illo ego et ille mecum, Neuter stupri causa caput limaret*, quoted by Dräger i. p. 242. **rubris**, of the Erythraean Sea. Tib. ii. 4. 30 *e rubro lucida concha mari.* iv. 2. 29 *Et quascumque niger rubro de litore conchas Proximus Eois colligit Indus aquis.* Prop. iii. 13. 6 *Et uenit e rubro concha Erycina salo.* **4.** **pretium**, 'value,' cf. *in pretio esse* and Ovid Pont. iv. 8. 68 *Iudicio pretium res habet ista tuo.* **cortice,**

the exterior coating or surface of the pearl. **baca** = *margarita* from its globulous bead-like shape. Cul. 67 *nec Indi Conchea baca maris pretio est.* Pers. ii. 66 *Haec bacam conchae rasisse . . . iussit.* **5. Indignum,** sc. *esse,* ' it was an outrage to her nature that with all her diligence her slow pace kept her from doing or effecting anything in the whole course of the day.' So I read with the earliest MSS. *Indignum* as an exclamation 'shame!' and *indignum est* are both Ovidian (Am. i. 6. 1, 10. 53). Most edd. prefer the other reading *Indignans,* which certainly gives more meaning to *sibimet.* **6.** ' Non praetulerim *proficeretque,* obtinente codicum parte maiori, in quibus *perficeretque.* Tali synonymia Salvian. G. D. p. 110 [iv. 42 Pauly] *nullus ad hoc tam hebes, qui ad hoc aliquid agat atque perficiat, ut perfecta non curet.* Sallustius in Cic. § 6 *Egeris, oro te, Cicero, perfeceris, quod libet.* Componatur Cicero Academ. ii. 7. 22 *quarum (artium) omne opus est in faciendo atque agendo.* Arnobius i. frag. 21 (c. 37) *quae fecerint egerint pertulerint actitarint.* Vopiscus in Aureliano cap. vi *si forte quaereretur, quis Aurelianus aliquid uel fecisset uel gessisset.*' WOPKENS. **7. promissis implet,** 'loads with promises,' much as Ovid uses *Hanc imple meritis,* load with services, ingratiate yourself by a multitude of services, Am. ii. 3. 11. **8.** Perhaps an imitation of Propertius iii. 13. 66 *Experta est ueros irrita lingua deos.* **similem fidem,** a return of treachery. **9. male mercatis,** 'ill-bought,' i.e. dearly. *mercatus* as a passive participle is not very common, Prop. i. 2. 5. **10. Occidit.** Bährens is perhaps right in conjecturing *Excidit,* for not only Babrius but the prose version represents the eagle as letting the tortoise fall upon a rock which broke its shell. MSS have *Occidit* which ought to mean that the eagle tore open the tortoise with its talons (*ungue fero*). If Av. meant simply that the tortoise was smashed to pieces by the eagle's cruelly dropping him, he would hardly have used words which suggest a different idea. **11. sublimis,** either nominative as Met. iv. 721 *modo se sublimis in auras Tollit* or, as is perhaps more probable from the variant *sublimes,* accus. plural. Hesiod has a similar line 'Ε. κ. 'Η. 204 ''Υψι μάλ' ἐν νεφέεσσι φέρων ὀνύχεσσι μεμαρπώς. **cum iam moreretur,** 'in the death agony,' ἐκψύχουσα. **in auras** with Ingemuit. **13. exosae quieti** does not mean that the tortoise chafed at its own enforced slowness of progression almost = 'discontented inaction,' but 'disagreeable,' or 'surly.' This agrees with the character of the tortoise as drawn by Rose's Physiognonomist p. 167 *Testudo animal quod neque sibi aliquid neque cuiquam alteri prodest,* as well as with Seneca's gibes at the *otiosus* and his witty comparison of him to a worm, Ep. 87. 19 *ne quietem quidem et molestia uacare bonum dicam : quid est otiosius uerme? Exosus* as a passive is very rare, but occurs in Macrob. S. i. 11. 45 *dis exosos,* and again *infra* XXXIII. 6. **post haec,** 'thenceforward,' so XXV. 15, XLI. 17. **14.** 'That only the supremest effort climbs to greatness.' **15, 16.** This epimythion is singularly flat after the former moral in 13, 14. It is found, however, in all the best MSS, and seems to be part of the earliest tradition we possess of the fables. As Cannegieter points out, *meliora* in Avianus has the special sense of something higher in position, XI. 10 *Et quia nulla breui est cum meliore fides,* of the uncertain friendship between the powerful and the weak.

III.

Babr. cix, Fab. Aes. 187 Halm, Bodl. 91 Kn.

BABR. CIX.

Μὴ λοξὰ βαίνειν ἔλεγε καρκίνῳ μήτηρ
ὑγρῇ τε πέτρῃ πλάγια κῶλα μὴ σύρειν.
ὁ δ᾽ εἶπε ʻμῆτερ ἡ διδάσκαλος, πρώτη
ὀρθὴν ἄπελθε καὶ βλέπων σε ποιήσω.᾽

Aristoph. Pax 1083 Οὔποτε ποιήσεις τὸν καρκίνον ὀρθὰ βαδίζειν. Skolion ap.
Athen. 695 ʻΟ καρκίνος ὧδ᾽ ἔφα τᾷ χαλᾷ τὸν ὄφιν λαβών, Εὐθὺν χρὴ τὸν ἑταῖρον
εἶμεν καὶ μὴ σκολιὰ φρονεῖν. The saying was proverbial. Apostol. ix. 50 (in
Leutsch's Paroemiographi Graeci ii. 472) καρκίνος ὀρθὰ βαδίζειν οὐ μεμάθηκεν·
ἐπὶ τῶν ἀεὶ ὡσαύτως ἐχόντων περί τι φαῦλον. Petron. S. 42 antiquus amor
cancer est i. e. retro cedit.
    1. **Curua** = λοξά of Babrius and the prose versions.   In better
Latin it would have been obliqua, cf. Macrob. S. i. 17. 63 Cancer animal
retro atque oblique cedit.   ib. 21. 23 Cancer obliquo gressu.   **retro
cedens.** Vegetius uses the word of rams iv. 14 more arietum retro
cedit. Macrobius expresses the same idea by retrorsum recedere Sat. vii.
9. 3.   2. **Hispida,** 'scaly.' Plin. ix. 9 squamis hispido corpore.   **saxosis
aquis,** a harsh expression for saxis quibus aquae abundabant.   **relisit,**
a rare word, used again IX. 10 sponte relisus humi, ' dashing on the ground.'
Here it=προστρίβειν (τὰς πλευράς) of the Bodleian Paraphrast.   Unrein,
p. 41, cites Prud. x. 47 inque ora tabellas Frangunt : relisa fronte lignum
dissilit, where the meaning is that the boy-pupils of Cassianus dash their
tablets in his face, and then the wood striking against the Martyr's forehead splits asunder.   3. **procedere** C, praecedere most of the other
MSS. The latter would not be without a meaning, as the mother-crab
would then be represented as trying to make her child take up the position
of guide which she herself would naturally assume, and is asked to assume
in v. 9. But procedere is simpler and more direct ; and the authority of C
is sufficient to outweigh the other MSS.   4. **praemonuisse** of MSS is suspicious, as the advice comes after the injury has been done. The form of
P (prae) is so close to one form of E as to suggest that Av. wrote **emonuisse,**
though this is a very rare word : and Cannegieter's statement that one of his
codices gave semonuisse is a practical confirmation of this view.   Cic. Fam.
i. 7. 9 Te uero emoneo tum beneficiis tuis, tum amore incitatus tuo.   **datur,**
' is said,' again XV. 10, XXV. 10. Da for dic is not uncommon : but the
passive use of datur = dicitur is rare ; Forc. quotes Ovid F. vi. 433, 4 Seu
genus Adrasti, seu furtis aptus Ulixes, Seu pius Aeneas eripuisse datur. Stat.
Theb. vii. 315 Asopos genuisse datur. Claud. Rapt. Pros. iii. 337 Captinamque
pater post proelia praedam Aduexisse datur.   5. **transuerso** = transuer-
sim eunti. Cannegieter quotes a line of Plautus' Pseudulus (iv. 1. 45), ap.
Varro L. L. vii. 81 It transuersus, non prouersus cedit quasi cancer solet.   **haec
deuia,** sidelong courses or swervings from the straight road.   6. ʻ And
think not to move backwards slantwise upon your feet.' There is no difficulty in the words **in obliquos pedes,** which well describe the drawing
of the body backwards upon the feet.   **Rursus** seems to be here for retror-
sus, a sense justified and determined by pro(r)so in 8 Rursum prorsum are
correlatives like sursum deorsum (Non. 384). **uelis** occurs again XXIII.
10 Seu uelis esse deum, and may, I think, be accepted as a licence Av. permitted himself. So in the poem addrest by Flavius Felix to Victorinianus
Master of the Rolls (primiseriniarius), probably a contemporary of Sidonius
(A. L. 254. 40 Riese) Clericus ut fiam, dum uelis ipse, potes.   7. ʻ But step-
ping vigorously on with a straightforward effort.'   **contenta** expresses the

effort which the crab must use to keep his feet from their natural sidelong direction, and make them move in a constrained attitude of advance in a straight line. Phaedr. i. 26 (24). 6 *rursus intendit cutem Maiore nisu*, of the frog swelling out its skin to an unnatural size. Incert. Paneg. Constantio viii (*terra*) *cedat ad nisum et hauriat pressa ue stigium*. **8. Innocuos.** Proleptic (see on X. 6) so as to be unharmed by coming into contact with hard objects. Ovid Fast. iv. 800 *Innocuum uicto cui dedit ignis iter*, of Aeneas making his way safely through the fires of Troy. Barth Aduers. xxxix. 7 prefers to explain 'qui tibi non noceant, ne iterum decidas.' proso =*prorso*. Paulus Diac. p. 223 M. *Prorsum ponebant pro recto*. Plautus in the passage of the Pseudulus cited on v. 5 uses *prouersus* (trisyllable) as the adjective form : except in the meaning ' prose,' the adj. is rare. **9. praecesseris.** Sen. Ep. 59. 3 *non ituros si nemo praccesserit, sed bene secuturos*. **10. Recta**, primarily 'the straight course' with a secondary suggestion of the right line of conduct. **certior**, ' with more assurance in my turn' (**ipse**). **11, 12.** Wopkens can hardly be right in explaining these verses as *a general* reflection ; they would then have been introduced by *Nam*, nor would *stultum* have been enforced by *nimis*, which gives the remark a sort of personal character. **11. tu**, the parent crab. **prauissima temptes** is an infelicitous piece of language, quite unworthy of Av. **12. censor**, 'critic.' Gloss. Sangallense ed. M. Warren *Censor index*. The lengthened *ō* before *ut* indicates a later hand : and *ut* would in Av. probably have been *si*.

IV.

Babr. xviii, Fab. Aesop. 82, 82^b Halm, Bodl. 17 Kn.

BABR. XVIII.

Βορέη λέγουσιν ἡλίῳ τε τοιαύτην
ἔριν γενέσθαι, πότερος ἀνδρὸς ἀγροίκου
ὁδοιπορῦντος τὴν σίσυραν ἐκδύσει.
βορέης δ' ἐφύσα πρῶτος οἷος ἐκ Θρᾴκης,
βίῃ νομίζων τὸν φοροῦντα συλήσειν·
ὁ δ' οὐ μεθῆκε μᾶλλον, ἀλλὰ ῥιγώσας
καὶ πάντα κύκλῳ χερσὶ κράσπεδα σφίγξας
καθῆστο, πέτρης νῶτον ἐξοχῇ κλίνας.
ὁ δ' ἥλιος τὸ πρῶτον ἡδὺς ἐκκύψας
ἀνῆκεν αὐτὸν τοῦ δυσηνέμου ψύχους,
ἔπειτα δ' αὖ προσῆγε τὴν ἀλὴν πλείω·
καὶ καῦμα τὸν γεωργὸν εἶχεν ἐξαίφνης,
αὐτὸς δὲ ῥίψας τὴν †τσισυραν ἐγυμνώθη.

There is a passage in the Saturnalia of Macrobius, to whom Avianus is believed to have dedicated his work, which is a curious parallel to the introduction in 1-2 of the stars in conjunction with Jupiter. After quoting the three lines of Il. i. in which Zeus is said to have gone to the blameless Aethiopians with all the gods following in his train (423-425), Macrobius adds: *Nam quod ait θεοὶ δ' ἅμα πάντες ἔποντο sidera intelleguntur, quae cum eo ad occasus ortusque cotidiano impetu caeli feruntur eodemque aluntur umore*. Θεοὺς enim dicunt sidera et stellas ἀπὸ τοῦ θέειν id est τρέχειν *quod semper in cursu sint*, ἢ ἀπὸ τοῦ θεωρεῖσθαι.

1, 2 are full of difficulty, perhaps corrupt. The general meaning is however clear. The north wind and the sun dispute before the assembled powers of the sky (*praesentia numina* 15) which is the more powerful, and decide the question by each attempting to make a traveller strip off his *pallium*. The tribunal consists of the stars (*ad sidera*) and Jupiter, who seems to be thought of as presiding judge. Possibly then *cum magno Ioue* in 2 is to be constructed closely with *ad sidera*, 'before the stars with supreme Jupiter as arbiter.' The order of the words however is against this ; and it seems safer to explain that the two claimants dispute *with* Jupiter *in presence* of the stars. Each contests with Jupiter the superiority of his claim. [G. Murray's conj. *Inmitis Boreas rapit usque ad sidera Phoebum : Iurgia cum magno conseruere Ioue* is ingenious, but *usque ad sidera*, a Vergilian expression, Ecl. v.43 *hinc usque ad sidera notus*, would be somewhat of an exaggeration, except perhaps as implying the violent determination of Boreas to settle the question.] **1. Inmitis.** Verg. G. i. 370 *Boreae de parte trucis.* **placidusque** is an antithesis to *inmitis:* the fable turns on the contrast of the two forces, violence and gentleness. **ad sidera,** a juristic use of *ad, ad censores dicere* Tusc. Disp. ii. 21. 51 *ad arbitrum, ad reciperatores, ad praetorem accusare* etc. Dräger i. 535. **2. Iurgia conserere,** which is found in Auson. Perioch. Odys. 18, like *iurgia nectere* Ovid Am. ii. 2. 35, followed by *cum* and abl. must mean to quarrel *with.* **3. Quis** = *uter,* as several times in Phaedrus, i. 26 (24). 8, iv. 24. 3 (Cannegieter). **inceptum peragat,** 'effect his purpose,' Vergilian, Aen. iv. 452. **mediumque.** 'And at the moment, a traveller happened to be wending his way along a plain.' *que* expresses the simultaneousness of the quarrel with the opportunity chance offered of deciding it by a practical trial. So in the well-known line of Ennius *Dono ducite, doque uolentibus cum magnis dis,* the actual making over of the thing given follows immediately on the promise to give it. Aen. x. 825 *Arma quibus laetatus habe tua, teque parentum Manibus et cineri siqua est ea cura remitto.* Veg. iv. 21 *Quemadmodum in cithara chordae sunt, ita in trabe ... funes sunt, qui pontem de superiore parte trochleis laxant, ut descendat ad murum, statimque de turri exeunt bellatores.* **aequor,** the first hand of *C* seems better than *orbem* of most MSS. A plain would be the most favourable locale for a trial of strength between wind and sun. **4. Carpebat iter.** C.I.L. iv. 558 TV QVI CARPIS ITER GRESSV PROPERANTE VIATOR. **5. Conuenit,** 'it is agreed.' Ovid F. iv. 811 *Contrahere agrestes et moenia ponere utrique Conuenit.* **potius.** Out of a selection of possibilities, they agree to select as the case for introducing the suit (or, under which the suit should be tried) the task of stripping the man bare and tearing his cloak from his back. **praefigere,** as it were to *preface* their contention. **causam,** the matter on which the case was tried. **6. Pallia decutienda,** object accus. in apposition with *causam.* 'The stripping off of the man's outer garment.' See Dräger ii. 794. **nudato** expresses the result of the stripping, viz. leaving him lightly clad. **7. inpulsus uentis,** 'with the shock of the winds' = *inpulsu uentorum.* Apuleius de Mundo xii *Procellosus flatus Cataegis dicitur, quem praefractum possumus dicere, uentus qui de superiore caeli parte summissus inferiora repentinis inpulsibus quatiat.* **8. depluere** with an accus. is found in our MSS of Prop. ii. 20. 8 *Sollicito lacrimas depluit a Sipylo,* but *lacrimans* is a plausible conjecture. **9. magis** is to be constructed closely with *quod,* 'the more that.' **duplicem** possibly expresses part of the man's action, as if it were *duplicatum,* 'folding his cloak double' as the wind increases in intensity. Against this is the Vergilian *duplicem ex umeris reiecit amictum* Aen. v. 421, and the words of Cornelius Nepos Datam. 3 *agresti duplici amiculo circumdatus,* from which it would seem that a double-folded *amictus* was a regular part of the countryman's equipment against foul weather. Fröhner's prose paraphrast has *quanto tempestas acrior insurrexit, tanto uiator circa se uestes suas attentius colligebat.* **10. summotos trahit,** 'pushes rudely aside and tugs at the folds.' **quod** *C,* **quo** *O* and *R,* my two best Bodleian MSS. This may be right, cf. Liv. i. 25. 13 *eo maiore cum gaudio, quo prope metum res fuerat* (Dräger ii. 627). **11.**

tenues, not 'slight' or 'feeble' as opposed to their subsequently increased heat, but 'penetrating' i. e. gradually pervading the pores of the body and making it by degrees warmer and warmer.　increscere, 'grew more powerful' nearly = *inualescere*, with which it is combined in the Digest. Macrob. S. i. 21. 17 *solis uis prima parte diei ad meridiem increscit . . . mox elanguescens deducitur.*　12. surgeret MSS, wh'ch Wopkens altered to *spargeret* from not understanding the force of iubar.　Isidor. Orig. iii. 70. 18 *Sed et splendor solis ac lunae et stellarum iubar uocatur, quod in modum iubae radii ipsorum extendantur.*　In the Treves MS of the Fables *iubar* is glossed by *splendor*.　Here then *iubar* is the full brightness of the sun which concentrating by degrees its rays is properly said to *rise* (*surgeret*), its orb having been before obscured and only now coming into view ; or we might explain *surgeret* in relation to *nimio igne* as Ovid says *ut solet adfuso surgere flamma mero* (Her. xiii. 114 quoted by Wopkens' Reviewer p. 428), cf. Auson. Mosel. 16, 17 *Sed liquidum iubar et rutilam uisentibus aethram Libera perspicui non inuidet aura diei.* Amm. Marc. xxviii. 4. 12 *nondum solis puro iubare* (*iuuare* Nissen's Fragm. Marburg. p. 5).　13. requiescere, active as in Verg. Ecl. viii. 4, Ciris 232, Prop. ii. 29. 75, and the fragm. of Calvus' Io quoted by Servius on Ecl. viii. 4.　15. praesentia, assembled to witness.　numina, the stars and Jupiter.　See the passage of Macrobius quoted in the introduction.　16. praemissis, a military word, used of despatching troops in advance.　Veg. iii. 22 *leuis armatura praemittebatur,* 79 *loca praemissis praesidiis occupanda,* hence uincere, as any army might.　It is useless for securing victory to open the campaign with threats.

V.

Fab. Aesop. 333 (＝99 Kn.), 333ᵇ, 336 Halm.

This fable is not in our Babrius. It is preserved however in three prose versions of which the nearest to the outline of Avianus is as follows. It will be found in Lucian's *Piscatores* c. 32.

332ᵇ Halm. Ὄνος ἐν Κύμῃ λεοντῆν περιβαλόμενος, ἠξίου λέων αὐτὸς εἶναι πρὸς ἀγνοοῦντας τοὺς Κυμαίους ὀγκώμενος μάλα τραχὺ καὶ καταπληκτικόν· ἄχρι δή τις αὐτὸν ξένος, καὶ λέοντα ἰδὼν πολλάκις καὶ ὄνον, ἤλεγξε παίων τοῖς ξύλοις.

1-4. The Promythion is not required, and is probably not by Av.　1. Modelled on Horace Epist. i. 7. 98 *Metiri se quemque suo modulo ac pede uerum est.*　The Christian writer Ennodius (fifth century) several times uses *metiri se* in his Epistles, as Hartel shows in his Index s. v. Ep. ix. 1 *Tu te ut metiaris imploro.* iii. 17 *Numquam se metitur quem stimulat caritatis imperium.*　iuuari, 'to find a satisfaction in,' nearly = to be contented. Barth Aduers. xxxix. 7.　In this sense the passive is not very common.　Cic. Orator xlviii. 159 *refer ad auris, probabunt : quaere cur ita sit : dicent iuuari : uoluptati autem aurium morigerari debet oratio,* where I cannot think *iuuare* is rightly introduced by Sandys from Gellius ii. 17.　Ovid Pont. ii. 7. 71 *Temperie caeli corpusque animusque iuuatur,* where *iuuatur* corresponds to *dulce est* 69, *uoluptas* 73.　2. ferre sibi, 'to claim as one's own.'　Barth illustrates from Ovid M. xiii. 383 *fortisque uiri tulit arma disertus.　Ferre* in the Latin of some writers of the Decadence so completely = *auferre* as to be constructed with a dat. of the person robbed : for which see Pauly's index to Salvianus, and cf. Roby Introd. to Digest p. 79.　3. miracula, 'finery,' 'gauds,' lit. objects of false admiration.　So in a letter of Symmachus to the Emperor Theodosius I in which he asks leave to return to the simpler conveyance which antiquity assigned to the Prefect of the

City, and deprecates the grander and more cumbrous vehicle which later fashion had introduced, he says : *Absit ut moderator urbis liberae atque adeo deuotae tamquam Salmoneus alius inuehatur. nihil moramur externa miracula* x. 24.   In Phaedrus i. 11. 6-9 *hic auritulus Clamorem subito totis tollit uiribus Nouoque turbat bestias miraculo*, the word is used of the prodigious or portentous noise raised by the ass imitating the lion.   And so here *miracula* might express the phenomenal look of the lion's skin on the ass's body, with which cf. Vergil's *Omnia transformat sese in miracula rerum* (G. iv. 441).   **faciant risum**, like the jackdaw stript of his borrowed plumes, Hor. Epist. i. 3. 19 *ne si repetitum uenerit olim Grex auium plumas, moueat cornicula risum Furtiuis nudata coloribus.*   **4.** 'When once he finds himself left in forlorn possession of his native deficiencies.'   **remanere** aptly expresses the poor residuum left behind when adventicious merits are stript away, and the individual is left *in puris naturalibus.* Sen. Ep. i. 5 *Non enim tantum minimum in imo sed pessimum remanet.*   **malis**, here 'defects,' 'imperfections,' opposite of *bona* as used in the Propertian *Nec sinere in propriis membra nitere bonis* i. 2. 6 (Cannegieter).   **5. Exuuias.**   Aen. ix. 306 *pellem horrentisque leonis Exuuias.*   **Gaetuli**, as Africa is the natural home of lions (*leonum arida nutrix* Hor. C. i. 22. 15).   **6. spoliis.**   Hor. ix. 113 *Falleris et nescis : non sunt spolia ista leonis, Sed tua ; tuque feri uictor es, illa tui*, of Omphale wearing the lion's skin of Hercules.   **7. incongrua**, ' ill-suited,' 'unsuitable.' Paucker Supplem. Lexic. Latinor. p. 365 quotes it from Apuleius, Symmachus, Vegetius, Jerome, Rufinus, Boethius and others. Veg. ii. 19 *incongruum uideretur imperatoris militem, qui ueste et annona publica pascebatur, utilitatibus uacare priuatis.*   **8. miserum**, 'sorry,' 'ignoble.'   **tanto honore**, of the majestic *appearance* of the lion.   Aen. viii. 617 *deae donis et tanto laetus honore*, as explained by Wagner.   **9. mimo**, Cannegieter's conj. for *animo* of MSS is more than probable, as the words are often confounded in MSS, and it was the special function of the *mimus* to *personate* characters, Amm. Marc. xxiii. 5 *cum Antiochiae scaenicis ludis mimus cum uxore inmissus e medio sumpta quaedam imitaretur.* Petron. S. 80 *Grex agit in scaena mimum . . . Mox . . . Vera redit facies, adsimulata perit.*   Besides, the *bare feet* of the mime-actor (Diomedes iii. 490 K. *Quarta est species planipedis, qui Graece dicitur μῖμος, ideo autem Latine planipes dictus, quod actores planis pedibus, id est nudis, in proscaenium introirent, non ut tragici actores cum cothurnis, neque ut comici cum soccis*) would excellently suit the ass of the fable, whose feet would not be covered by the lion's skin but be exposed to view.   Similarly Eur. Rhes. 255 τετράπουν | Μῖμον ἔχων ἐπὶ γαῖαν | θηρός of Dolon disguised in a wolf's skin to escape detection as a spy.   [*limbo*, my own conj., would refer to the mane of the lion which formed a fringe round the front of the ass's body, and would agree well with *horror*.]   **mimo with terribilis**, 'farcically terrible.'   **circum stetit**, Schenkl aptly compares Aen. ii. 559 *At me tum primum saeuus circum stetit horror.*   **horror** 'hic actiue sumitur' Guiet, like our 'fright.'   The word rather expresses the grim and forbidding look of the lion's mane on the ass's body, than the bristling and rugged appearance of the hair.   **10. praesumptus**, the courage with which the ass had armed himself in advance, viz. in assuming the externals of the lion.   This seems better than explaining with Barth (Aduers. xxxix. 7 'temere arrogatus'), and Wopkens from the later use of *praesumere*, 'to presume,' ' arrogate on false pretences,' as Pacatus uses *p. ueniam* Paneg. Theodos. 42.   This sense is very common in Salvianus, Ennodius and other 5th century writers (see the Excursus), but if I am right in holding that Av. wrote before 400, he would have been using unclassical Latin if he meant this.   Or is it a piece of his *rudis latinitas?*   **11. calcans** does not mean simply that the ass trod the same pasture-ground with other tame beasts (Wopkens), but that he *disdained* to share their food, considering

himself beyond them. So Cannegieter who compares Capitolin. Vit.
Maximi et Balbini xiv *Cum Balbinus Maximum quasi ignobilem contemneret,
Maximus Balbinum quasi debilem calcaret.* Symm. Epist. x. 32 *gaudia corporis ut caduca calcauit.* Of course in an animal that makes so much use
of its heels as the donkey (Phaedr. i. 23 (21). 9 *asinus calcibus frontem extudit*) calcans would suggest the *way* in which the ass showed his contempt viz. by spurning the ground *with his heels,* 'kicking his heels at the
pasture.' 12. 'Drove the scared cattle in confusion over their
fields.' 13. deprendit, 'caught by grasping (ab) his ear (*capistro prehendere* of an ass Apul. M. x. 21) and then hurried him off to confinement and
drubbing' (correptum u. u. domat). magna aure. So Ovid describing the donkey's ears of Midas Met. xi. 174-7 *Nec Delius aures Humanam
stolidas patitur retinere figuram, Sed trahit in spatium uillisque albentibus inplet
Instabilesque imas facit et dat posse moueri.* 14. uinclis all MSS ; he was
chained, to prevent any such escapades in future. *Vinclis uerberibusque* occurs
in Tib. ii. 3. 80 (Sittl) and is a favorite combination, as Wölfflin shows:
Prud. Perist. xi. 106 *uerbera uincla faces.* 15. tergo = *tergore,* as in
Aen. v. 351 *tergum Gaetuli inmane leonis* (Barth). 16. pecus, 'beast,'
of a single animal VIII. 5. So *Olenium pecus* Heroid. xviii. 188. 17.
ignotos, 'strangers.' Ovid A. A. iii. 300 *Allicit ignotos ille fugatque uiros.*
Phaedr. i. 11. 1 *Virtutis expers, uerbis iactans gloria Ignotos fallit, notis est
derisui,* a passage Av. may have been copying. imitato, passive, as in
the fragm. of the Timaeus ascribed to Cicero iii *imitata et efficta simulacra.*
There was an archaic verb *imitare,* Non. 473. Dräger ii. 768, 9 gives a
long list of past participles of deponents used passively. murmure,
'roar,' here and XXIV. 15 of a lion; XVII. 13 of a tiger. 18. qui
quondam, 'as of old.' Verg. Ecl. i. 53 *Hic tibi quae semper uicino ab limite
saepes.*

VI.

Babr. cxx, Fab. Aesop. 78, 78 ᵇ, Bodl. 113 Kn.

Halm's 78 ᵇ substitutes a worm for the frog of the other versions, and both 78
and 78 ᵇ have χωλόν for χλωρόν. The Bodleian Paraphrase (113 Kn.) which otherwise agrees exactly with 78 ᵇ retains the frog and the green colour of Babrius : for
though both MSS of Babrius give χωλόν, the conj. of Seidler χλωρόν is admitted
as certain by Rutherford and most editors.

BABR. CXX.

Ὁ τελμάτων ἔνοικος, ὁ σκιῇ χαίρων,
ὁ ζῶν ὀρυκτοῖς βάτραχος παρ᾽ εὐρίποις,
εἰς γῆν παρελθὼν ἔλεγε πᾶσι τοῖς ζῴοις
'ἰατρός εἰμι φαρμάκων ἐπιστήμων
οἵων τάχ᾽ οὐδεὶς οἶδεν, οὐδ᾽ ὁ Παιήων
ὡς Ὄλυμπον οἰκεῖ καὶ θεοὺς ἰατρεύει.'
'καὶ πῶς' ἀλώπηξ εἶπεν, 'ἄλλον ἰήσῃ,
ὃς σαυτὸν οὕτω χλωρὸν ὄντα μὴ σώζεις ;'

1. limoque for *olimque* of MSS, the conj. of Nevelet, is supported by the
Bodl. Paraphrase ὁ τῷ πηλῷ συζῶν βάτραχος, and Phaedrus' exactly corresponding *Immersae limo* (i. 2. 16). Liv. xxii. 2 *hausti paene limo immergentesque se.* 2. semper amica, modelled on Babrius' χαίρων. 3.
superos, *the open air of* the hills in the upper world (εἰς γῆν ἐξελθών
Bodl. Paraphr.) as opposed to the watery region in which the frog was
ordinarily plunged. Vergil's *superum lumen* the light of the upper world is
parallel. recurrens, 'revisiting,' i. e. visiting and revisiting, once and
again. *Recurrere* very early lost much of its full meaning and became nearly
= *redire,* in which sense it is found below XX. 12, Macrob. S. vii. 5. 11. 4.
Mulcebat ... quod, 'comforted with the assurance that.' *quod* here is not

'because' but belongs to the later construction by which it follows verbs like *dicere putare agnoscere sentire*, etc. **miseras... feras**, double rhyme. *miseras*, 'afflicted' by disease and want of care, and so ready to be *deluded* by a medical charlatan. **turgida**, a recurring idea in reference to toads or frogs : Propertius has *turgentis rubetae* iii. 6. 27, and Shakespere talks of the 'sweltered venom' of the toad, Macbeth iv. 1. **5. Callida**, 'by leech-craft.' **succurrere**, with a dat. of the *thing* relieved as in Frontin. de Aquaed. 119 *multa atque ampla opera* (repairs etc.) *subinde nascuntur, quibus ante s u c c u r r i debet quam magno auxilio egere incipiant.* **6. continuare**, 'prolong'=*porrigere.* Cf. Auson. Parent. i. (iii. Schenkl) 13, 14 *Praeditus et uitas hominum ratione medendi Porrigere et fatis amplificare moras* (Cannegieter). **7.** Lachmann's *Paeoni* seems unnecessary, as *Paeonius magister* is a common formula of Latin poetry for 'the Master Paeon,' and gives besides the extra notion of healing associated with the adj. by long tradition from Vergil (Aen. vii. 768, xii. 401) and Ovid (Met. xv. 535) onwards. **Nec se iactat cessisse**, a little forced for *et se non cessisse iactat.* **magistro**, master in the craft of healing, 'master-leech.' **8.** Av.'s way of translating ὃς "Ολυμπον οἰκεῖ καὶ θεοὺς ἰατρεύει. **perpetuos**, 'ever-living,' 'immortal.' The combination *perpetuos deos* suggests the cry addrest to the later Roman Emperors *Di te perpetuent*, Lamprid. Alex. 6. **in orbe**, one after another in rotation = *in orbem ;* which latter is found in Vegetius ii. 21 *postquam in orbem omnes cohortes per diuersas administrauerit scholas*, where Lang's Palatinus gives *orbe.* Sen. Dial. vi. 15 *it in orbem ista tempestas et sine delectu uastat omnia.* **9. uulpes**, all good MSS here, but *uulpis* has the last syllable is short in XL. 7 is given by both *C* and *T.* Neue Formenl. i. 180 states that *uulpis* is given by the twelfth cent. Pithoeanus as well as the coeval Rheims MS of Phaedrus, not only in passages like i. 7. 1, iv. 3. 1, iv. 20. 1, but also where the syllable must be long ; the Munich MS collated by Lütiohann of Apuleius de deo Socratis §§ 109-111 consistently gives *uulpis* five times ; in Petron. 58 *H* gives *bella res est uolpis uda* (Bücheler). The question therefore is not whether the *-is* form is correct, but whether in the classical period it was adopted for cases where a short syllable was required. **quietem**, 'the indifference,' or 'apathy': it was impossible to rouse them or make them angry. Compare the use of *quiesce*, 'don't ruffle yourself' in Ter. Phorm. iv. 3. 64. **10. uacuam**, all MSS 'unreliable.' The idea is of something hollow, which gives way when tested. **prodidit**, 'disclosed'; another word which has come to lose much of its significance. It nearly = ἀπέφηνε, 'intimated.' **12. caeruleus**, 'a livid hue marks the sickly (Pallida) features of the frog.' A line of Maximianus is very like this, perhaps imitated from it, El. ii. 26 *Et iam caeruleus* (? *-is*) *inficit ora color :* on which see American Journal of Philology for 1884, p. 155.

VII.

Babr. civ, Fab. Aesop. 224 Halm, Bodl. 71 Kn.

It is to be regretted that the last two lines of Babrius' version of this fable are corrupt in the Athoan MS which alone contains them. It cannot, I think, have ended with the abrupt question ὦ τάλαν, τί σεμνύνῃ ; (so Rutherford), as there is a close agreement in the general sense of these two verses, not only with the words of the prose version τί φαντάζῃ ; οὐ δι' ἀρετὴν τοῦτον φορεῖς, ἀλλὰ δι' ἔλεγχον τῆς κεκρυμμένης σου κακίας, but with the four last lines of Avianus. I have accordingly printed them, not indeed believing that they are genuine in their present form, but as necessary to complete the sense of Babrius, and not perhaps wholly beyond restoration.

The fable of Avianus is itself full of perplexity. In 2 *Muneribus* seems to mean 'requital' in the bad sense, i. e. punishment. In 8 *nolam* of most MSS is to my ears inconceivable; yet it seems early to have become the accepted reading, as it is quoted without variation in the Grammatical treatise printed by Hagen in his Anecdota Heluetica, p. 182, the MS of which was written in the tenth century. In 14 *singula*, if genuine, is weak, and unexampled in Avianus' other fables; *cupis* in 16 is harsh, if indeed explicable. It is little to the point to say that these anomalous uses are part of the *rudis latinitas* which the fabulist avows in his preface; for the style of the rest of the fable is as carefully elaborated as usual, and the words in question stand out in marked relief to the generally correct flow of the language. I accept this fable then as a sufficient proof that Avianus' text underwent considerable depravation before the time when it was redacted in its present form. In any case the Promythion stands on a level with the others and cannot be from Av.

BABR. CIV.

Λάθρη κύων ἔδακνε· τῷ δὲ χαλκεύσας
ὁ δεσπότης κώδωνα καὶ προσαρτήσας
πρόδηλον εἶναι μακρόθεν πεποίηκε.
ὁ κύων δὲ τὸν κώδωνα δι' ἀγορῆς σείων
ἠλαζονεύετ'. ἀλλὰ δὴ κίων γραίη
πρὸς αὐτὸν εἶπεν ' ὦ τάλαν, τί σεμνύνῃ ;
οὐ κόσμον ἀρετῆς τοῦτον οὐδ' †ἐπιεικείης (ἐπεικείης Boissonade),
σαυτοῦ δ' ἔλεγχον τῆς πονηρίης κρούεις.'

1. **est** with **innatum** might seem nearly = *innascitur*, much as *natum esse* is used in Cat. x. 15, the neuter participle in each case individualizing more distinctly the quality or thing grown. 'It is a rare quality for a vicious nature to grow.' Yet as *facile* and *difficile* have a sympathetic attraction to the perfect, it is perhaps safer, to interpret it so. Veg. iv. 10 *difficile sitis uicit*, 'rarely has thirst overcome'; iv. 38 *difficile naufragium pertulit qui uentorum rationem diligenter inspexit*, 'a careful observer of the winds has rarely been wrecked.' **2. Muneribus** (for which neither Withof's conj. *Verberibus* nor Fröhner's *Vulneribus* satisfy) I had understood in a general sense : ' vicious natures can rarely be brought to think themselves rewarded as they should be or punished (only) as they deserve.' Then *dignas* = ' adequate to' the reward or punishment they get, cf. ἄξιος in Thuc. But I now accept Sittl's view that *Muneribus* is simply 'requitals,' 'retaliations' in a bad sense. That Av. would so have written I cannot believe : but in a promythiast all things are possible. **3. nullis latratibus horrens,** 'with no gruff bark.' This use of *nullus* where we should use an adverb 'never' or 'nowhere' is much affected by Av. cf. XXXVI. 7 *nullam uerbis compulsus in iram*; XL. 3 *nulla graues uariarent terga leones*. Sil. ix. 550 *diesque Qua nullas umquam transisse optauerit Alpes*. Cf. the use of οὔτις in Ag. 186 μάντιν οὔτινα ψέγων. **4.** ' And that gave no first sign of mischief by opening his mouth in wide grins.' So I interpret **primum** ; generally a snappish dog *begins by* showing some token of his intended bite, and *then* bites. This dog gave every sign of good temper and then bit suddenly. Such an animal was called by the Greeks λαίθαργος. Possibly *primum* is corrupt ; *simum* would be a plausible conj., constructed adverbially with *trahens*, cf. σιμὰ σεσηρώς in Meleager. This use of neuter adjectives, singular or plural, is frequent in Ammianus Marcellinus, e. g. *insanum loquentis et ferum* xxiii. 6. 80, cf. Mamertin. Grat. Act. Iuliano xiv *serenum renidens*. Symm. Epist. i. 7 *Bauli magnum silentes*. Prud. Perist. v. 416 *malignum murmurans*. **trahens,** 'i. pandens' Guiet. **5.** ' But set his softly-patting tail fearfully beneath him ' i. e. under his belly. **Mollia uerbera caudae** is on the analogy of *stuppea uerbera fundae* Verg. G. i. 309. **pauidae** recalls Vergil's *Caudamque remulcens Subiecit pauitantem utero* Aen. xi. 812 (Cannegieter). **6.** ' Would fly into a rage and snap about him recklessly.' **Concitus** = *concitus ira* of Ovid Met. vii. 413 spoken

of Cerberus. **7. dominus.** It was a law of Solon's that a dog which had bitten anyone should have a three-cubit collar fastened to him and be delivered up to the sufferer (Plut. Solon xxiv, Xen. Hell. ii. 4. 41). **8. nolam,** 'bell' of most MSS is suspicious, as (1) the *o* ought to be long ; (2) *Faucibus innexis crepitantia subligat aera* immediately following, makes a distressing tautology. Lachmann and Fröhner read *notam*, perhaps rightly ; *uolam* which I have found in one of the Peterhouse MSS would more easily explain the corruptions *nolam, mollam*, and from its rarity might be misunderstood. The St. Gallen Glossary recently edited by Prof. Minton Warren of Baltimore has *uola : manus caua in medio unde inuolare dicimus.* It was also applied to the sole of the *foot*. Hence the proverb *nec uola nec uestigium*, 'neither track nor trace' Non. 416 ; and in this sense it might possibly be used here. By belling his dog, the master made him carry his trail wherever he went. Yet as Prudentius has *Nŏlanus* short Perist. xi. 208, I have not ventured to alter *nŏlam* here : and I see that Bährens retains it also. **9. innexis** is part of the same action as *subligat*, which is here used in its strict sense of tying *beneath* the dog's throat. **crepitantia aera.** Verg. G. iv. 151, tinkling bell of bronze. Barth Aduers. xxxix. 13 quotes a gloss of Albinus : 'Crepitacula dicit : ea uero domini etiam furtiuis appendebant ut quaqua irent a uillico audiri possent.' Bells for oxen, sheep, and other animals are mentioned in the νόμοι γεωργικοί based on the code of Justinian. Tit. ii. 2, p. 836 in Heimbach's Harmenopoulus Ἐάν τις κώδωνα ἐκ βοὸς ἢ προβάτου ἢ ἐξ ἄλλου οἱουδήποτε ζῴου κλέψῃ καὶ γνωσθῇ, ὡς κλεπτὸς μαστιγωθήτω· εἰ δὲ καὶ τὸ ζῷον ἀφανὲς γένηται, δότω αὐτὸ ὁ κλέπτης τοῦ κώδωνος. **10. facili,** 'ready,' i. e. shaking and ringing spontaneously every time the dog moved. **signa cauenda,** 'signs of alarm;' *signa cauendi* would be plainer, but Av. transfers the alarm which the bell was to produce towards the dog wearing it to the bell itself: 'signals to be guarded against' for 'signals to be on one's guard.' **11. praemia ferri,** 'was brought him as a reward of conduct.' *Praemia* of a single reward, Ovid Met. viii. 503 *cape praemia facti.* **12. similem,** 'of his peers,' i. e. dog-companions: XL. 2 *consimiles feras.* **ouans.** So Merobaudes ii. 10 Niebuhr *Cuius sacra petit munera mundus ouans.* **13. insultantem** XV. 10. **senior** XXXVI.7. It is the κύων γραίη of Babrius. **de plebe** is Avianus' own addition. The contrast of the aristocrat with the plebeian is a point much affected in these fables. See XI. 10, XVI. 19, 20, XXXI. 11, 12, XXXVIII. 11, 12, XL. 1–4. **superbum,** here a substantive, τὸν ὑπερήφανον, 'the swaggerer.' **14. Tali,** 'what, so loud in shaking your collar ?' **cingula** is my conj. for *singula* of MSS; Varro R. R. ii. 9. 15 *Ne uulnerentur a bestiis, inponuntur his collaria, quae uocantur melium, id est cingulum circum collum ex corio firmo cum clauulis capitatis, quae (? quare) intra capita insuitur pellis mollis, ne noceat collo duritia ferri.* This proves that *cingulum* was used (against Serv. on Aen. ix. 357 *cingulum hominum generis neutri est. Nam animalium genere feminino dicimus has cingulas*) of a dog's collar. Here it would be the neck-strap to which the bell was attached. *Cingula* is written *singula* in Jeep's codex Ambrosianus of Claudian, Deprec. ad Hadrian. 51. **15. Infelix,** a word of abuse (Wopkens), like our 'wretch.' The line is slightly altered from Aen. v. 465 *Infelix, quae tanta animum dementia cepit ?* (Cannegieter). **sensum,** 'understanding.' **16. si cupis.** 'If you would have your bell to be a reward of merit ' = ' if you would like to make out your bell to be a reward of merit.' This is the obvious meaning, and, though not classical, intelligible. It doubtless belonged to the language of the people. See infra XXIV. 12 *Artificis testem si cupis esse manum.* Very parallel is the construction of *animum inducere* in a speech of Scipio Africanus ap. Macrob. S. iii. 14. 7 *non poteram animum inducere ea liberos suos homines nobiles docere*, 'I could not bring myself to believe.' **17.** ' This is no ornament of merit you flourish in its setting of bronze.' **in**, in bronze fittings or fixtures. **18. inde**, hardly with **sonum**, 'sound from it,' cf. *In Persas tetulere, suo post inde reuentu* in the passage of Sueius' *Moretum* ap. Macrob. S. iii. 18. 12, but more vaguely 'thereby,' 'by carrying it :' so XXI. 10, XXVII. 4.

VIII.

Fab. Aesop. 184 Halm, Bodl. 104 Kn.

AESOP. 184.

Κάμηλος, θεασαμένη ταῦρον ἐπὶ τοῖς κέρασιν ἀγαλλόμενον, φθονήσασα αὐτῷ ἠβουλήθη καὶ αὐτὴ τῶν ἴσων ἐφικέσθαι. Διὸ καὶ παραγενομένη πρὸς τὸν Δία τούτον ἐδέετο, ὅπως αὐτῇ κέρατα προσνείμῃ· καὶ ὁ Ζεὺς ἀγανακτήσας κατ᾽ αὐτῆς, εἴγε μὴ ἀρκοῖτο τῷ μεγέθει τοῦ σώματος καὶ τῇ ἰσχύϊ, ἀλλὰ καὶ περισσοτέρων ἐπιθυμοῖ, οὐ μόνον αὐτῇ κέρατα οὐ προσέθηκεν, ἀλλὰ καὶ μέρος τι τῶν ὤτων ἀφείλετο.

Οὕτω πολλοὶ διὰ πλεονεξίαν τοῖς ἄλλους ἐποφθαλμίζοντες λανθάνουσι καὶ τῶν ἰδίων στερούμενοι.

Furia observes that a similar apologue of a kite that wished to neigh and lost its original power of voice is mentioned by the Emperor Julian, Misopog. ad fin. Λέγεται καὶ τὸν ἴκτινα φωνὴν ἔχοντα παραπλησίαν τοῖς ἄλλοις ὄρνισιν ἐπιθέσθαι τῷ χρεμετίζειν, ὥσπερ οἱ γενναῖοι τῶν ἵππων· εἶτα τοῦ μὲν ἐπιλαθόμενον, τὸ δὲ μὴ δυνηθέντα ἐλεῖν ἱκανῶς, ἀμφοῖν στέρεσθαι καὶ φαυλότερον εἶναι τῶν ἄλλων ὀρνίθων τὴν φωνήν.

1. propriis rebus, 'his own possessions.' Cic. de Leg. Agrar. ii. 21. 55 *Venire nostras res proprias et in perpetuum ab nobis abalienari.* **2. fabula nostra** for *nostra fabella* of MSS is to some extent supported by *C*, in which the former is written as a correction over the ordinary reading. The Paraphrast too, who quotes vv. 13, 14 followed by 1–4, read *fabula nostra*. Yet this may be a mere correction of a learned scribe posterior to the time when the 4 vv. of the promythion were written. I have in the Introduction stated my belief that none of these promythia are from Av. At any rate it is inconceivable that a poet so familiar not only with Latin poetry as a whole, but with Phaedrus in particular, should give in to the licence of his time in so common a word as *fabella*. Both words are used for ' fable :' for though Phaedrus once distinguishes *fabula* from *fabella* as play from fable (iv. 7. 22 *Si nec fabellae te iuuant nec fabulae*), his general practice is to treat them indifferently : *fabula* i. 1. 14, *fabellam* i. 2. 9, *fabella* i. 5. 2, *fabula* i. 10. 3, *fabella* i. 17. 3, *fabella* i. 28. 2. **3, 4** seem modelled on Horace C. iii. 10. 10 *Ne currente retro funis eat rota*. ' Lest fortune in anger run quickly back to a stand-still, and the very wheel which at first brought her bounties (*dedit*), end with humbling its owner.' In this however **dedit**, whether we supply *fortunam* or suppose it used absolutely (cf. XXIII. 14) is hardly a well-defined antithesis to *minuat*. Possibly here, as in some other passages (Val. Fl. ii. 29, 30, Aegrit. Perdicae 97, 98 in Bährens' P. L. M. v. pp. 112–125) a word really belonging to the second of the verses has got into the first, and a word belonging to the first into the second. Hence I would write *Indignata citos ne det Fortuna recursus Atque eadem minuat, qua* (so Paris *A*) *stetit ante, rota.* Cf. Uncle Remus xvi *Good-by, Brer Fox, take keer yo' cloze, Fer dis is de way de worril gees. Some goes up en some goes down, You'll git ter de bottom all safe en soun'.* **5. Corporis inmensi**, a somewhat bare genitive of quality, 'huge-bodied,' like *Cernicis rigidae equo* Trist. i. 4. 14. The remarks which

F

Servius ap. Macrob. S. vi. 8. 1-6 addresses to Avienus on the similarly bare Vergilian *ablative* of quality are very pertinent to this passage. **pecus.** See on V. 16. **isse per auras** is the reading of most MSS and might be supported by XIV. 1-4 in which all the beasts present themselves before Jupiter, and XXII. 2 in which Jupiter sends Phoebus from heaven (*ab arce poli*) to decide between two petitioners, and Phoebus returns to Jupiter with the result; on this view Jupiter might be supposed to have his seat in heaven, and the camel would therefore make his way to him *per auras*. The grotesqueness of thus representing a camel mounting to the sky was indeed felt by Nevelet, and perhaps may have given rise to the corrected reading of *R*, *per aras*, which I have found also in a Brit. Mus. codex (*b*). On this latter view the camel goes from altar to altar in its eagerness to make Jupiter attend, much as Dido in Aen. iv. 56 paces by the altars of the gods to secure, if possible, their good will. But Lucian Icaromenipp. x 'Ο λογοποιὸς Αἴσωπος ἀετοῖς καὶ κανθάροις ἐνίοτε καὶ καμήλοις βάσιμον ὑποφαίνων τὸν οὐρανόν seems decisive in favour of *per auras*. **7-10.** 'All alike held it an outrageous scandal and a matter for scorn, that while oxen went their way in the pride of double horns, the camel should alone walk entirely undefended, a laughing-stock open to the gibes of the whole beast-world.' **7. irridendum,** rare. Ausonius has *Deridendasque Camenas* Epist. iv. 66. **9. Et solum ... camelum,** sc. *ire.* Et adversative = *et tamen* (Dräger ii. 20-22). **nulla munitum parte,** language of siege operations, but also of bodies Veg. i. 20 *Dimicandi acriorem sumat audaciam qui munito capite uel pectore non timet uulnus.* **10. Obiectum and expositum** are combined as in Aen. x. 694 *obuius* and *expostus.* Merobaudes Carm. iv. 43 Niebuhr *Obiectus Geticis puer caternis.* **11. arridens.** Macrob. S. iii. 17. 17 of Cleopatra dissolving the pearl *Tunc regina adridens fialam poposcit, cui aceti nonnihil acris infudit atque illuc unionem demptum ex aure altera festinabunda demisit.* **sperata,** 'his petition.' **12. magnae auris.** The shortness of the camel's ears is noticed by Buffon Hist. Naturelle xi. p. 244. It is probably the want of proportion between these and the long neck of the animal that suggested the idea of their having lost part of their natural size in that pre-historic period when beasts and birds 'conversed as well as sung.' **13. minor merito,** 'beneath your merit' i.e. on humbler conditions than you might naturally claim. Ovid Pont. ii. 6. 6 *Et mala me meritis ferre minora doces.* Wopkens however explains 'mutilated as you deserve to be,' 'with the loss of a limb as you deserve.' Cf. Juv. viii. 4 *umeroque minorem Coruinum.* **cui non sufficit,** '*since* you are discontented.' XXXIII. 8, XXXVI. 14, Dräger ii. 507. **14. gome,** 'deplore.' My Brit. Mus. codex *B* gives *tene* which avoids the short concluding syllable, a rare occurrence in these fables.

IX.

FAB. AESOP. 311.

Δύο φίλοι τὴν αὐτὴν ὁδὸν ἐβάδιζον. "Ἄρκτου δὲ αὐτοῖς ἐπιφανείσης, ὁ μὲν εἰς φθάσας ἀνέβη ἐπί τι δένδρον καὶ ἐνταῦθα ἐκρύπτετο· ὁ δὲ ἕτερος μέλλων περικατάληπτος γίνεσθαι, πεσὼν ἐπὶ τοῦ ἐδάφους ἑαυτὸν νεκρὸν προσεποιεῖτο. Τῆς δὲ ἄρκτου προσενεγκούσης αὐτῷ τὸ ῥύγχος καὶ περιοσφραινομένης, τὰς ἀναπνοὰς συνεῖχε· φασὶ γὰρ νεκροῦ μὴ ἅπτεσθαι τὸ ζῶον. Ἀπαλλαγείσης δέ, ὁ ἀπὸ τοῦ δένδρου καταβὰς ἐπυνθάνετο τοῦ ἑτέρου, τί ἡ ἄρκτος πρὸς τὸ οὖς εἰρήκει. Ὁ δὲ εἶπε, τοῦ λοιποῦ τοιούτοις μὴ συνοδοιπορεῖν φίλοις, οἳ ἐν κινδύνοις οὐ παραμένουσιν.

Ὁ λόγος δηλοῖ, ὅτι τοὺς γνησίους τῶν φίλων αἱ συμφοραὶ δοκιμάζουσιν.

Phaedrus v. 2 has a parallel fable, in which two travellers meeting a
robber, one shows fight, the other runs away. The robber is killed, and
the coward immediately runs up to his friend, draws his sword and promises
to assist him to the death. The other replies in words partly resembling
Avianus *Ego qui sum expertus quantis fugias uiribus, Scio quam uirtuti non sit
credendum tuae.*

1. The road led them sometimes over high mountain-ground, sometimes
through winding valleys. The expression is a little like Vegetius iii. 22
Oportunis uallibus uel siluosis montibus. **artum** with **iter** as Tacitus Ann.
xv. 38 *Artis itineribus bueque et illuc flexis,* but in a different sense, not of
narrow *roads,* but a *journey* through close ground. 2. **Cum socio
quidam,** 'two comrades.' 3. **Securus, quodcumque malum fortuna
dedisset ... posset uterque pati.** This construction is like II. 3. If
any change is to be introduced, perhaps *quoicumque,* suggested by *quocumque*
of *B,* may seem to anticipate *uterque* somewhat more effectively and clearly
than *quodcumque* of most MSS. It will mean 'to whichever *of the two,*' as
Quis is used for *uter* in IV. 3. 4. **posset,** a lively change from the
oratio obliqua in which the protasis is couched to an apodosis stated directly.
From **securus** to **tulisset** the sentence begins as if *posse utrumque pati* were
to complete it; but with the new line, the form of the apodosis is suddenly
altered 'Feeling safe, whatever misfortune chance should bring,—why, each
would be able to combine their strength and endure it.' Wopkens quotes
Hyg. Fab. cxxxix *Quod sciret, si quis ex eo natus esset, se regno priuaret.* Guiet
explained *securus (ut) posset = certus posse utrumque pati quodcumque robore
collato :* but this can hardly be right. 5. **per inseptum,** 'through a piece
of unenclosed ground,' where they could converse with more freedom, and
where the bear's attack would be less apprehended and from the want of
means of escape more dangerous. MSS have *inceptum,* which Guiet retains,
explaining *iter inceptum.* **uario sermone,** a Vergilian phrase, Aen. i. 748,
vi. 160, viii. 309. 6. **praeceps conuenit,** 'rushes to meet them.'
XVII. 15 *Nulla quidem medio conuenit in aggere forma.* 7. **facili ...
cursu,** 'grasping an oak stem with an easy run.' A lively picture of the
traveller's frightened agility in swarming up the tree. 8. Modelled on
a favourite pentameter ending of Ovid's. Her. ix. 98 *Fauce pependit onus.*
Rem. 18 *Triste pependit onus.* Fast. ii. 760 *Dulce pependit onus* (Cannegieter). 9. **trahens nullo iacuit uestigia gressu,** interlacing of
clauses as in XXIII. 3, 4, not common in Av., see my note on Cat.
xliv. 9. 10. **Exanimem fingens,** 'counterfeiting dead,' i.e. counterfeiting a dead man. **sponte relisus humi,** 'dashing himself purposely to
the ground.' **relisus** suggests the rebound caused by the body dashing
heavily on the earth. 12. **ante,** 'first,' i.e. before making him her prey
and eating him. **leuat,** 'lifts,' XXXV. 8, to see whether he was alive.
Veg. iv. 18 *Depositi quoque homines funibus ... rursum leuantur in murum.* 13.
concreto timore, as Ovid has *concreto dolore,* Pont. ii. 11. 10. Translate
'icy fear.' 14. **mentis calor,** nearly = 'vital warmth.' Verg. Aen. ix.
475 *At subito miserae calor ossa reliquit.* Ovid Her. xiv. 37 *Sanguis abit,
mentemque calor corpusque reliquit* (Cannegieter). 15. **olidum,** 'rank,'
not an otiose epithet, but suggesting the reason why the she-bear retired
in disgust from a corpse: her sense of smell was offended. 17. **in uerba redissent,** 'they began to talk again.' 18. **Liberior iusto,** 'over
gay, or jocose,' after he had shown his cowardice by leaving his friend in
the lurch. The joke is contained in 20. For the adj. used adverbially see
Dräger i. 325. **fugax** may have been suggested by the last line in Phaedrus' parallel fable v. 2. 15 *Qui re secunda fortis est, dubia fugax.* 19.
Dic, sodes, 'pray, tell me.' Fronto Epist. i. 1 *Dic sodes hec mihi.* **rettulit,** 'told, related.' Ovid Her. i. 39 *Rettulit et ferro Rhesumque Dolonaque
caesos.* 20. 'For she spoke much with you in private and long.' **diu**

F 2

with **multa** following is slightly tautologous, but the language of fables is supposed to be natural, and tautology is the commonest vice of natural talk. Uncle Remus is an exaggerated example. **21, 22** are rightly suspected by Lachmann : **quoque** in 21 is weak, and **dixit** in 23, which where it stands is effective if 21, 22 are omitted, becomes tautologous after **iussit** in 21. **21. quoque** of MSS would mean that grave as were the warnings of the bear, they included one more serious than all the rest, viz. to be chary of making friends. The old English Translation may be quoted here. 'He taught me many faire secrets, but among all other things he said to me, that I should never trust him which hath once decived mee.' **22. sunt** of MSS is perhaps meant to break off the connexion of the clause with **haec maxima iussit**. 'And I, poor wretch, must needs carry out her warning uniformly.' This seems to be supported by the repetition of **dixit** in 23, as if after an interruption. But it would be wrong to argue this from Av. writing **sunt**, not *sint :* for in writers of this age the fact of the clause **Quae misero ... mihi** belonging to the reported speech of the bear would not determine the choice of *sint* rather than *sunt*. So in Veg. iv. 35 *Obseruandum praecipue, ut a quintadecima luna usque ad uicesimam secundam arbores praecidantur, ex quibus liburnae contexendae sunt,* none of Lang's MSS give *sint*, yet the sense is obviously that during the days from the 15th to the 22nd the wood is to be felled for making Liburnian galleys. This lax use of the indic. where correct Latin requires the subj. is common in law Latin, Roby Introduct. to Digest p. ccxvi. **23. facile,** 'lightly,' 'without consideration.' Veg. ii. 17 *Legionis ius est facile nec fugere nec sequi.* **repetas** repeats *alterius*, 'return again to partnership with a new friend,' now you have had experience of the first. **24. insana,** 'rabid,' here of a voracious animal : in XXVIII. 4 of a restive bullock.

X.

Fab. Aes. 410 Halm, Bodl. 141 Kn.

The Bodleian Paraphrast seems here to come nearer to what must have been a Babrian original than the version printed by Halm. I give it accordingly, omitting the promythion.

Φαλακρός τις τρίχας ξένας τῇ ἑαυτοῦ κορυφῇ περιθεὶς ἵππευεν, ἄνεμος δὲ φυσήσας ἀφείλετο ταύτας. γέλως πλατὺς δὲ τοὺς παρεστῶτας εἶχεν. κἀκεῖνος εἶπε τοῦ δρόμου παύσας· τὰς οὐκ ἐμὰς τρίχας τί ξένον φεύγειν με, αἳ καὶ τὸν ἔχοντα ταύτας, μεθ' οὗ καὶ ἐγεννήθησαν, κατέλιπον.

Haupt reduced this to an original by no means worthy of Babrius. The latest scazontic attempt is Gitlbauer's (179).

Avianus has nowhere repeated himself so often as in this short twelve-line fable. *Capillos, comas* of 1, 2 = *capillos, comae* of 11, 12 ; *capiti* of 1 = *caput* of 6 ; *nudo* of 2 = *nudo* of 7 ; *nitidis conspectus* of 4 = *nituit* of 7, *conspiciente* of 6 ; *Ridiculum* 6 = *risus* 9 ; *adposita* 8 = *positos* 11.

1. capiti, probably dative, and so I think Ovid M. xiv. 735 *Cum foribus laquei religaret uincula summis*. **2.** A mere expansion of 1. **alias,** 'strange,' ξένας of the prose versions. In ordinary Latin it would be *alienas*. Ovid A. A. iii. 165, 6 may have suggested the expression *Femina procedit densissima crinibus emptis, Proque suis alios efficit aere suos*. **uertice,** 'crown.' Apuleius M. xi. 10 *hi capillum derasi funditus uertice praenitente,* of priests of Isis. **3.** Cannegieter wrote *Ad Campum,* supposing the *eques* to be displaying his horsemanship in the favorite exercising-ground of the Roman youth. But Av. throughout avoids localizing his fables ; and as an open piece of ground is at once necessary for cavalry evolutions and particularly exposed to wind, it seems unnecessary to understand anything more special. Paneg. ii. 6 *A tribunali temet in campum, a curuli in equum transtulisti.* **conspectus,** 'conspicuous,' a common use from Vergil onwards. See Servius on Aen. viii. 588. Apul. x. 17 *Conspectum atque famigerabilem meis uiris artibus effeceram dominum.* So *acceptus.* **4.** Observe the alliteration **facilem frenis flectere. facilem.** Nemesian. Cyn. 266 *Nam flecti facilis lasciuaque colla secutus,* of a Moorish horse. **flectere,** as in Hor. C. iii. 7. 25 *Quamuis non alius flectere equum sciens Aeque conspicitur gramine Martio,* a passage which might seem to favour the view that **campum** in 3 is the Campus Martius. **5. Huius** might possibly be constructed with **ab aduerso,** as Wopkens suggested; for a genitive is found not only after *ex aduerso* (Plin. iv. 11) but *ex contrario* (Ampel. Memor. vi *Ex contrario harum*). This however is unnecessary here, as **caput** follows in 6. **spiramina.** Amm. Marc. xvii. 7. 11 *l'entorum apud nos spiramina nulla sentiri.* Veg. iv. 38 *Secundo spiramine optatos classis inuenit portus.* **praeflant** seems at least a possible correction of the MSS *praestant,* as the wind blew in the man's face. *praestant* of MSS must =*faciunt,* a sense very frequent in the Decadence: and found as early as Serenus Sammonicus (second century) e.g. 49 *Iuuenem praestant rediuiuo flore capillum.* Veg. iii. 8 *Tutum iter commeantibus praestant.* Auson. Grat. Act. 3 *Non palatium, quod tu, cum terribile acceperis, amabile praestitisti.* Eutrop. x. 7 *Nihil occasionum praetermittens, quo opulentiores eos clarioresque praestaret.* Symmach. Epist. i. 14 *Ita me dis probabilem praestem ut ego hoc tuum carmen* (Ausonius' Mosella) *libris Marouis adiungo.* Prud. Perist. x. 779 *Me partus unus ut feracem gloriae, Mea uita, praestet, in tua situm est manu.* **6. Ridiculum** if **praeflant** (or, as most edd. give, *perflant*) is read, must be used predicatively, the wind blew upon the front of the knight's head, making it look laughable in the eyes of the bystanders. With this cf. Symm. Epp. i. 50 *Quaeso ut nos plenos gaudii quam primum reuisas,* 'revisit and make us full of joy.' **7. galero,** 'a wig of artificial hair sewn on to a scalp, in order to fit the head in the same manner as still practised.' Rich, Companion to the Latin Dictionary, p. 313, who quotes Juv. vi. 120 *Et nigrum flauo crinem abscondente galero.* Cornelius Severus ap. Charis. 80 Keil *Flauo protexerat ora galero.* **8. Discolor,** 'tinged by its accompaniment of false hair.' **adposita** expresses the Greek πρόσθετον, 'wig.' Manilius similarly v. 146 *Illis cura sui cultus, frontique decorae Semper erit : totos in fluctum ponere crines, Aut uinclis reuocare comas, et uertice denso Fingere et adpositis caput emutare capillis.* Cannegieter (who cites this passage) thought Avianus' knight wore what remained of his natural hair surmounted by a wig on the crown; then **discolor** would express the distinct colours of the natural hair and the wig. There is nothing to support this view : the knight's head becomes a ridiculous sight simply because the wig gets loose and exposes the forehead in its bald nudity. **9. sagax,** 'shrewd' or 'discerning.' He was equal to the emergency. **tantis** nearly = *tot.* So often in Vegetius Macrobius and other writers of this period. Veg. iv. 44 *Inter tanta mortium genera.* Macrob. S. iii. 18. 1 *Vellem ex te audire, Serui, tanta uccibus nomina quae causa uel origo uariauerit.* Hildebrand on Apuleius M. vii. 9 considers this use *African,* and quotes many passages from Tertullian. **10. Distulit,** all MSS, not 'put off' to another time,' but as in XXXI. 8 *Distulit hostiles calliditate minas,* 'dispersed,' 'routed.' So Paneg. iii. 16 *Omnem illam rabiem extra terminos huius imperii in terras hostium distulistis,* where Bährens records no v.l. **ammota,** 'by calling in.' Ovid Pont. i. 3. 90 *Neu iuuer admota perditus aeger ope.* **11. referens** simply = *dicens.* **positos,** all MSS, 'assumed' as θετός = πρόσθετος. '*Postici* Italice i. e. supposititii,' Guiet. **12. aequaeuae,** a word used twice by Vergil (Aen. ii. 561, v. 452), seven times by Claudian, twice by Ausonius Parent. xxvi. 5, xxxi. 3, and by Symmachus Laudat. in Gratianum *Pro liberis nostris aequaeuus insudas.*

XI.

Fab. Aesop. 422 Halm = Bodl. 147 Kn.

Χύτραν ὀστρακίνην καὶ χαλκῆν ποταμὸς κατέφερεν. Ἡ δὲ ὀστρακίνη τῇ χαλκῇ ἔλεγεν· ʼμακρόθεν μου κολύμβα, καὶ μὴ πλησίον· ἐὰν γάρ μοι σὺ προσψαύσῃς, κατακλῶμαι, κἂν (τε) ἐγὼ μὴ θέλω σοι προσψαῦσαι.ʼ

Ὅτι ἐπισφαλής ἐστι βίος πένητι, δυναστοῦ ἄρχοντος πλησίον παροικοῦντος.

This fable is alluded to in the Son of Sirach xiii. 2, as Mr. Margoliouth has pointed out to me.

1. **Eripiens**, snatching away from their position. on the bank by the sudden falling in of the earth at the edge.   **cedentibus** virtually = *sidentibus*.   2. **Insanis**, ʻviolent,ʼ XXVIII. 4.   **pariter**, ʻside by side.ʼ   3. **ars et natura**. Not only were the materials different to start with (**natura**), but the way in which they were worked up (**ars**); one was of earth fashioned by the potter, the other of bronze, fused by the smith.   5. **Dispar concordia motus**, ʻan uneven (discordant) uniformity of motion.ʼ Oxymoron.   **Dispăr** like **impăr** XVIII. 10, a licence which may readily be condoned from the *ă* of the other cases.   **fragili**, ʻthe brittle,ʼ **solidae**, ʻthe solid,ʼ are opposed here as in Hor. S. ii. 1. 77 *Fragili quaerens illidere dentem Offendet solido.* Most MSS give **fragili et solidae**, a very rare deviation from the strict rules of elision generally followed by Av. There is no other instance in the fables of the last syllable of the second foot being elided. It is therefore possible that et should be omitted as it is in my Bodleian MS X. Some of the earliest MSS too give *solido*. Possibly Av. wrote *Dispar erat fragili solido concordia motu, solido motu* depending on *concordia* and representing a poetical variation on *solidae motu*. ʻThe brittle pot kept even but irregular pace with the movement of the solid.ʼ The two pots move on together (**concordia**) but not evenly (**dispar**): each is borne on by the stream, but with an irregular motion, sometimes approaching, sometimes drifting away from each other.   6. I follow here without hesitation my Brit. Museum MS *B* which has **uagans**, against *uagus* of most MSS. The steps of error probably were *uagās uagas uagus*. The river had flooded its banks and was running irregularly (**incertum iter**), its currents drifting unsteadily.   7. **elisam confringeret** = *elideret et confringeret*, ʻshould smash and shatter.ʼ The two words are not synonymous; **elisam** expresses the previous bruising, **confringeret** the final breaking up. Schenkl's *illisam* is tempting.   **aerea testa**, which I venture to write on the authority of *P*, may be supported by Pliny's *aereo testo* H. N. xxxii. 81.   8. **solitam** of MSS can hardly be right, as the pots were on a quite exceptional journey. **solidam** seems an easy conjecture, and would aptly express the course taken by the more *solid* of the companion travellers, at the same time that it suggests the *brittleness* of the other (*fragili et solidae* 5). [Sittl writes the two vv. thus, *Ne tamen elisam confringeret, aerea testa Iurabat solitam longius ire uiam,* and explains ʻAerea testa fictili, quae longius ire uiam solebat, iurabat se non elisam confringere eam.ʼ On this view **iurabat ne confringeret** = ʻswore not to break,ʼ with which Sittl compares I. 2.]   **ire** = *se ituram esse*, see on I. 1. ʻSwore to pursue its metallic course at a distanceʼ from its frailer brother. Prop. iii. 6. 40 *Iurabo et bis sex integer esse dies,* ʻwill swear to remain chaste.ʼ   9. ʻFearing it might prove *a case of* light damaged by heavy.ʼ Such, I think, is the force of the neuters. A good instance of Av.'s occasional felicitousness.   10. ʻAnd because confidence cannot exist between the humble and the exalted.ʼ Phaedr. i. 5

Numquam est fidelis cum petente societas. Varro ap. Macrob. S. ii. 8. 3 *dulcibus cum πέψει societas infida.* **breui,** τῷ βραχεῖ, 'the small and insignificant.' Forcellini quotes Claudian de Bello Gildon. 107 *Breuior duxi securius aeuum. Ipsa nocet moles,* words supposed to be spoken by Rome: but there the sense is rather 'less in *extent.*' **meliore,** see on II. 16. Here it = τῷ βελτίονι, Phaedrus' *potente.* 'Robustiore, ualentiore,' Guiet. **11. uerbis,** in implied opposition to *facts,* 'so far as words go.' **12. decutiendus,** *AC* and virtually both the Vossian MSS, *discutiendus BO* and the second Peterhouse MS, which would be Lucretian vi. 38–40. The participle in *-dus* from the third century onwards was increasingly used as a future passive participle. In Ammianus Marcellinus it is very frequent, see Dräger ii. p. 791. 'I shall not be able to shake my soul rid of its fear :' the pot has a *soul,* as the fish has tears in XX. 5. **13. conferat,** 'bring into collision,' lit. 'bring close.' **14.** 'I alone shall always be the victim of either misfortune.' **ambobus** seems here to mean each disaster in succession or indifferently, i.e. of myself knocking against you, or your knocking against me. Whereas the bronze *olla* would be uninjured in either case.

XII.

Fab. Aesop. 101.

Γεωργός τις σκάπτων χρυσίῳ περιέτυχε. Καθ' ἑκάστην οὖν τὴν Γῆν, ὡς ὑπ' αὐτῆς εὐεργετηθείς, ἔστεφε. Τῷ δὲ ἡ Τύχη ἐπιστᾶσά φησιν· ' ὦ οὗτος, τί τῇ Γῇ τὰ ἐμὰ δῶρα προσανατίθης, ἅπερ ἐγώ σοι δέδωκα, πλουτίσαι σε βουλομένη ; Εἰ γὰρ ὁ καιρὸς μεταβάλοι, καὶ πρὸς ἑτέρας χεῖρας τοῦτό σοι τὸ χρυσίον ἔλθοι, οἶδ' ὅτι τηνικαῦτα ἐμέ, τὴν Τύχην, μέμψῃ.'

Ὁ μῦθος δηλοῖ, ὅτι χρὴ τὸν εὐεργέτην ἐπιγινώσκειν καὶ τούτῳ χάριτας ἀποδιδόναι.

Suarez (Praeneste Antiqua c. xiv. 1655) speaking of the famous Inscription to Fortune at Praeneste (Anth. Lat. i. 622 Meyer) thought it belonged to the age of Valentinian and Gratian, and asserts that Fortuna was still worshipped at that time, as the letters of Symmachus show. The inscription must certainly be late, as Rome is called in it *urbs sacra.*

1. molitus, 'after breaking up.' Colum. vi. 2. 10 *Aratro iniuneto terram moliri cogitur (iuuencus).* **2. Thensaurum.** It was a common thing to find treasure in digging or ploughing. Hor. S. ii. 6. 10 *O si urnam argenti fors quae mihi monstret !* Pers. ii. 10 *O si Sub rastro erepet argenti mihi seria dextro Hercule !* Calp. iv. 116–120 *Iam neque damnatos metuit iactare ligones Fossor et inuento, si fors dedit, utitur auro. Nec timet, ut nuper, dum ingera uersat arator Ne sonet offenso contraria uomere massa : Iamque palam presso magis et magis instat aratro,* a passage which shows that at some time before Calpurnius wrote treasure discovered in this way was appropriated by the state. See Wernsdorf Poet. Minor. ii. p. 338. Petron. S. 38 *quom Incuboni pilleum rapuisset, thesaurum inuenit.* In the Digest xli. 1. 63 various questions are raised as to the different claims which the discoverer of such treasure (presumably a slave), the owner of the land where it was found, etc., might make to take part or all. **3. indigna,** 'disesteemed,' 'despised.' Phaedr. iii. 12. 3 *Iaces indigno quanta res, inquit, loco,* not 'innocent,' as if the plough deserved better treatment. **aratra,** of a single plough, as in Ovid Her. ix. 29 *Quam male inaequales ueniunt ad aratra iuuenci.* **4.** 'Driving his oxen to a better feed,' as a kind of recognition of the good service they had done him in turning up the treasure. **Semina** seems here to be used in one of its Vergilian senses for 'plants,' G. ii. 268, 301 : or possibly for herbs like cytisus which spring from seed sown. Plin. H. N. xiii. 132, Colum. v. 12. 3, viii. 4. 2. Avienus, the translator of Aratus, 398, 9 has a similarly vague use of the word, *Tunc suc-cisa Ceres statim cum mergite culmi Construitur, flauos tondentur semina crines Omnia et aduectas late coquit area messes*, where it nearly = 'crops.'   **meliora**, than barley, for instance (Plin. xiii. 130).   **con-pellens.** Verg. Ecl. ii. 30 *Haedorumque gregem uiridi conpellere hibisco.* In Av. the preposition has lost much of its force, as a poor countryman would only have enough oxen for the purpose of his plough, not a drove.   **5. supplex**, not in its ordinary sense of imploring favours, but as Apuleius uses *supplicue gratiis persolutis* M. xi. 24 fin. Macrobius tells us that vows were made to Earth *in a sitting posture*, and her worshippers carefully touched the ground (S. i. 10. 21).   **telluri.** Varro R. R. i. 1. 4 *Et quoniam dei facientes adiuuant, prius inuocabo eos . . . primum, qui omnes fructus agriculturae caelo et terra continent, Iouem et Tellurem.* Macrobius S. i. 10. 20, 21 says Tellus was by some identified with Ops, *cuius ope humanae uitae alimenta quaeruntur, uel ab opere per quod fructus frugesque nascuntur.* Av. probably alludes to this identification in 6 *depositas opes.*   **aras**, plur. to show his gratitude. They would doubtless be made of grass. Hor. C. i. 19. 13 *Hic uiuum mihi caespitem, hic l'erbenas, pueri, ponite turaque.* Prud. Perist. v. 50 *Aut ara ture et caespite Precanda iam nunc est tibi.*   **6. sibi**, to the rustic.   **depositas**, 'committed to her charge.' *Depositum, depositor* are frequent in the Digest.   **7. fortuna.** Treasure found accidentally, as by digging or strolling near the spot (Dig. xli. i. 63 *Finge terram fodien-tem inuenisse—quod uero subito in abdito loco positum nihil agens, sed aliter ambulans inuenit*) was looked upon as a gift of fortune. Dig. l. c. *Thensaurus donum fortunae creditur.*   **prouida**, 'with an eye to the future,' when the treasure would be exhausted, and its owner reduced to poverty. So XXXIV. 2 *Nec timuit uitae prouidus ante mala.* According to Macrobius S. v. 16. 8 *Philosophi qui eam (Fortunam) nominant, nihil sua ui posse sed de-creti siue prouidentiae ministram esse noluerunt.*   **8. indignam ... dolens,** 'complaining that she in her turn was *not thought* worthy of incense.' But the form of the sentence is unusual as (1) indignam = *indig-nam haberi* ; (2) quoque would more naturally follow a non-negative word. Hence there is plausibility in my conj. *indiguam se quoque ture docens* (*docens* Lachm.). *Indiguus* was used by Paulinus of Nola twice in his poems on S. Felix (xx. 4, xvi. 195 Migne) but with a genitive : Hildebrand has restored it from some MSS in Apul. M. iv. 12 *Refectione uirium uehementer indiguus*, where other MSS give *indignus*, and again in Apul. de Deo Socrat. § 11 (see Lütjohann's Greifswald Progr. for 1878) *alienae lucis indigua* (MSS *indicia*). The abl. would be justified by Lucretius' *indi-gus omni l'itali auxilio* v. 225.   **9. Nunc**, 'at present' as opposed to the coming future *Sed cum subrepto fueris tristissimus auro.*   **in-uenta**, Calp. iv. 117 quoted above.   **non prodis munera** MSS, except that *P* has *predi*, and the oldest Vossianus as quoted by Bährens, *pro.* The verb *prodere* in the sense of handing on, transmitting is not un-common, especially with *memoriae* or *litteris*, each of which is found in Vegetius (iii. 1, iii. 26), more rarely of passing on a personal or concrete object, as in Macrob. S. iii. 9. 8 the gods who leave a captured city are im-plored *proditi Romam ad me meosque ueniatis.* Here, then, Fortune would complain that the countryman kept his treasure to himself, instead of making it over to some one of her temples. In being so committed to Fortune's charge, it would not of course pass out of its owner's hands; but be stored up in reserve to be removed as occasion required. The other sense of 'announcing,' 'making public statement of' any-thing, which is more common in the Latin of this period (Mamert. Paneg. xv *proditio futuri*, xviii *nondum cuncta prodidimus.* Symm. i. 31 *libelli tui arguis proditorem*, in each of which last two passages it is opposed to *secre-*

tum) seems to me not to suit the passage.   **templis**, a vague plural, not implying more than ' to temple of mine.'   **10. participare** = *participes facere*, the more classical use of the verb in Plautus and other early writers, and common in Symmachus and other writers of the Decadence, as Parcus' ind. to Symm. and Schenkl's to Ausonius show.   Symm. v. 91 *Me sermonis tui honore participas.*   Auson. Epist. xxi *Vt me participes.*   **12. inops**, the rare adjective ending of the pentameter is here very effective.   Compare Propertius' *Ante fores dominae condar oportet iners*, the last line of the Elegy on Paetus (iii. 7. 72).

XIII.

Babr. xci, Fab. Aesop. 396, 396ᵇ Halm, Bodl. 72 Kn.

BABR. XCI.

Λέοντα φεύγων ταῦρος εἰς ἐρημαίην
σπήλυγγα κατέδυ ποιμένων ὀρεσφοίτων,
ὅποι τράγος τις χωρὶς αἰπόλου μείνας
τὸν ταῦρον ἄντα τοῖς κέρασιν ἐξώθει.
ὁ δ' εἶπεν ' οὐ σέ, τὸν λέοντα δ' ἐκκλίνω.
ἀνέξομαί σου μικρὰ τῆς ἐπηρείης·
ἐπεὶ παρελθέτω με, καὶ τότε γνώσῃ
πόσον τράγου μεταξὺ καὶ πόσον ταύρου.'

2. Tuta antra, ' the safety of a cavern.'   Another plural used singularly.   **desertis**, 'leaving the open road-ways.'   **uiis** is here opposed to the seclusion of the forests.   If *iugis* is read, *desertis iugis* will be local abl.   This agrees better with Babrius, but has little MS support.   **3. Speluncam.** Babrius' ἐρημαίην σπήλυγγα.   *repetit* of *C* and the first hand of *R* may be right ' returns to ' the cavern he had been familiar with before.   It is noticeable too that **rĕperit** as a present is rare, though found in Vergil G. iv. 443, where *R* (the Roman MS) gives REPPERIT (see Ribbeck), Ovid Rem. 95; whereas *repperit* perf. is of constant occurrence; Burman's Index to Ovid gives twelve instances.   **hirsutus.** Verg. G. iii. 311 *Barbas incananque menta Cinyphii tondent hirci, saetasque comantes*, ' a hairy brute.'   **4. Cinyphii ... gregis**, ' goats.'   The long-haired goats bred in the Mauritanian territory washed by the Cinyps from the time of Vergil (G. iii. 312), became typical of the whole race, and the adj. *Cinyphius* almost connoted goats.   See the passages collected in my edition of Ovid's *Ibis* p. xxvi.   **solet**, historic present for *solitus est.*   **5. Post**, rather more significant than *Ast.*   The bull only gradually discovered that the cavern was already occupied.   A slight pause is supposed to intervene—then after some time he retires.   [Sittl reading *Hunc post* explains *post* as = *postquam*, on the analogy of *mox = mox ut*, which Hartel and Petschenig prove for late Latin poets (Wiener Studien i. 210, 247, iii. 306).   But though a parallel might perhaps be thought to exist in XXV. 11, this barbarism is not proved for Av.]   **summissa** *C* and the earliest MSS, not *submissa*, as **irrumpere** not *inrumpere.*   The bull's stature would oblige him to bend his head downwards to enter the mouth of the cavern.   **6. obliquo.**   Babrius says the goat τὸν ταῖρον ἄντα τοῖς κέρασιν ἐξώθει, where ἄντα corresponds to **Obuius**, but the pushing with horns is changed by Av. to frightening with a sidelong look.   Verg. E. iii. 8 *transuersa tuentibus hircis.*   **terruit**, partly by the surprise, partly by the grotesqueness of the goat's physiognomy.   **7. longumque,** my conj. from *longamque* of a MS in the British Museum (*b*), I construct with **locutus**, ' sending a long-drawn reply ' of course in reference to the peculiarly protracted sound of a bull's bellow coming from a distance. Cf. Ecl. iii. 79 *Et longum formose, uale, uale, inquit, Iola.* Symm. Epist. i. 7 *quousque longum loquor?* 63 *longum loquantur pro incognitis aut alienis uerba faeturi.* 73 *ne longum loquar* all = 'to make a long talk.' Most MSS give *longaque,* 'the *long reaches* of the valley.' The sound of the bull's voice would be carried along these upwards to the goat's cavern. So *aetkere longo,* 'far along the sky,' Val. Fl. iii. 43. **8. Nam** gives the reason why the bull did not make his reply on the spot. **expulsum.** My conjecture *expulsans,* suggested by the Brit. Mus. MS *B,* which in many ways is unique and not interpolated, might be supported by the usage of Martial and Ammianus. **iurgia ferre,** 'to quarrel,' is a mere variation on *iurgare,* not classical, as Nevelet rightly observed, but justified by many similar combinations, *f. iudicium, bella* (Sil. iii. 365) etc. (Cannegieter). **9, 10.** 'It is not a noisome creature like you that I fear, with your beard sweeping the ground, and your thick hair—it is the other who has still to come and follows in my track.' A rather lengthy paraphrase of οὐ σέ, τὸν λέοντα δ' ἐκκλίνω. ἀνέξομαί σου μικρὰ τῆς ἐπηρείης. **9.** The MSS vary here considerably. *C* m. sec. virtually gives *demissum saetosis,* which would not be impossible, 'with your shaggy beard sweeping the ground.' **barbis,** in strict conformity with the rule that *barba* was to be used of men, *barbae* (plural) of animals. Servius on G. iii. 311 BARDAS. *sic de quadrupedibus. Nam hominum barbam uccamus.* Caper Orthographia Gramm. Lat. vii. 99 Keil. *Barbam hominum, barbas pecudum dicimus.* Add Probi Append. iv. p. 201 Keil. **10. Illum,** i. e. *sed illum.* **super est,** 'still remains to come.' Stat. Theb. ix. 167 *Imus? an hi retinent manes, et uilior ille Qui super est?* The MSS agree in consequiturque. Nothing indicates that the lion was close upon the bull's heels (*insequitur*). **11. Nam si discedat** = ἐπεὶ παρελθέτω με. **12.** A weak translation of Babrius' πόσον τράγου μεταξὺ καὶ πόσον ταύρου. Otto Crusius points out (de Babrii Aetate p. 180) that Babrius has here adopted a Latin construction. Cic. Lael. xxv. 95 *Quid intersit inter popularem . . . et inter constantem?* Hor. S. i. 7. 11 *Inter Hectora Priamiden animosum atque inter Atriden.* By some curious accident Av. has not availed himself of this opportunity of introducing a choice Latin idiom. **a tauri uiribus hircus olens** = *hirci olentis uires a tauri uiribus* (Wopkens).

XIV.

Εὐτεκνίης ἔπαθλα πᾶσι τοῖς ζῴοις
ὁ Ζεὺς ἔθηκε, πάντα δ' ἔβλεπεν κρίνων.
ἦλθεν δὲ καὶ πίθηκος ὡς καλὴ μήτηρ,
πίθωνα γυμνὸν σιμὸν ἠρμένη κόλποις.
γέλως δ' ἐπ' αὐτῷ τοῖς θεοῖς ἐκινήθη·
ὁ δ' εἶπεν οὕτω 'Ζεὺς μὲν οἶδε τὴν νίκην,
ἐμοὶ δὲ πάντων οὗτός ἐστι καλλίων.'

The ape in Greek was nicknamed Καλλίας, and the nickname may have suggested this fable. Pindar, in a well-known passage, Pyth. ii. 73 Καλός τοι πίθων παρὰ παισὶν αἰεὶ καλός, introduces the not too common word πίθων, 'a young ape,' and Babrius seems to have remembered both the passage and the word. Gildersleeve Comm. on Pindar, p. 264, quotes from Galen: 'The ape was a favorite in the nursery then as he is now. Galen de Usu Part. i. 22 Καλός τοι πίθηκος παρὰ παισὶν αἰεί, φησί τις τῶν παλαιῶν ἀναμιμνήσκων ὑμᾶς ὡς ἔστιν ἄθυρμα γελοῖον παιζόντων παίδων τοῦτο τὸ ζῷον.'

This fable does not seem to exist in the prose versions. But in one of the fables published by Halm (200, 200ᵇ) Jupiter assembles the birds with the view of electing the handsomest of them to be king : the jackdaw decks himself in borrowed plumes and is on the point of being chosen king, when the other birds strip him of his finery. To this extent the two fables agree.

1. in toto orbe =πᾶσι τοῖς ζῴοις.   **2.** 'Which gave the finest child as an offering.'   **natorum** is an epexegetic or appositional genitive, like *praemia pecuniae* Caes. B. C. iii. 83, Gell. x. 18. 5 ; *praemium missionis* Caes. B. C. i. 85 (Dräger i. pp. 429, 430).   **meliora,** 'better than the rest,' an inaccuracy natural and not necessarily belonging to debased Latin, as Unrein would make out, p. 53.   **3. Certatim,** 'eagerly.' Glossar. Sangallense ed. Minton Warren p. 148 *Certatim : studiosim (studiosim).*   **genus omne ferarum.** Calp. Ecl. ii. 10, 11 *Affuit omne genus pecudum, genus omne ferarum Et quodcumque uagis altum ferit aethera pennis,* where H. Schenkl shows the original is Verg. G. iii. 480, iv. 223.   **4.** The first suggestion of this v. is that cattle and men were forced to appear together, as well as wild beasts (*permixtos rusticis seruos haurire* Macrob. S. vii. 7. 14), before the tribunal of Jupiter. (So Schenkl.)   This is not impossible, as there would be a reason for the civilized animals appearing together; man and the beasts tamed by man.   But it seems unlikely, if this is the meaning, that the Babrian original should make no allusion to man, or that one of the principal actors in the piece should be introduced casually by Av. In the similar bird-story too (Halm 200, 200ᵇ) man is wholly omitted. I prefer then to explain **Permixtum homini pecus** as *tame* animals living promiscuously with mankind, as contradistinguished from wild creatures (**ferarum**). So Pliny speaks of two races intermarrying as *Aethiopia Trogodytis conubio permixta* xii. 86. (Bährens conj. *Permixtumque cieur.*)   **cogitur ire,** 'needs must go :' the words mean no more than that all were to present themselves without exception.   Somewhat similarly Uncle Remus xx *Brer wolf he up'n say he bleedzd fer b'leeve Brer Rabbit got dem fishes.*   **5. Sed nec,** like *Sed et,* belongs to the Latin of the Silver and subsequent periods.   Dräger ii. p. 106 quotes instances from Justin Lactantius and the Historia Augusta.   Add Macrob. S. vi. 7. 6.   **ad iurgia,** 'to contest their claim.'   Varro de L. L. vii. 93 (Spengel 1885) *Quod ait (Plautus) iurgio id est litibus ; itaque quibus res erat in controuersia, ea uocabatur lis ; ideo in actionibus uidemus dici : Quam rem siue me litem dicere oportet.   Ex quo licet uidere, iurgare esse ab iure dictum, cum quis iure litigaret.* (Cannegieter.)   **6. purior,** 'clearer' than the watery medium in which fishes live.   Ovid M. xv. 243 *Aer atque aere purior ignis.* Lucret. v. 448, 9 *Et seorsum mare uti secreto umore puteret, Seorsus item puri secretique aetheris ignes.*   Macrob. S. i. 22. 5 *Quidquid ex omni materia de qua facta sunt omnia purissimum ac liquidissimum fuit, id tenuit summitatem et aether uocatus est.*   **7.** Bährens' conj. *In tergo* is too grotesque to be admitted against all MSS. And at any rate the ape did not so introduce her child (**traheret** 9).   **Inter quos** seems to mean that in the general assembly of congregated animals the mother representative of each species led up her offspring to be inspected by Jupiter.   Somewhat more precisely Wopkens 'Nihil uetat intelligi affuisse etiam matribus suos coniuges.'   **trepidae,** 'in fluttering haste,' each hoping to be the lucky competitor.   **pignera,** 'children,' a sense found as early as Ovid M. xi. 542, 3 *Subeunt illi fraterque parensque, Huic cum pigneribus domus et quodcumque relictum est,* and increasingly frequent in the second and following centuries.   **8. discutienda,** 'to be examined, scrutinized :' properly *sifted.*   Ennod. Vit. Epiphanii p. 374 Hartel *animae meae et regni utilitate discussa.*   It is commoner in the substantives *discussor discussio* used of revising accounts.   Symmachus v. 76 uses the words of examining the costs

of a public building and forming estimates thereon. **9. breuis,**
'dwarfish.' Ovid F. ii. 574 *Qua breuis occultum mus sibi fecit iter.* Macrob.
S. v. 19. 19 *Lacus breues sed in immensum profundi. Breuis = paruus, breui-
tas = paruitas* are tolerably common in the writers of this period. See Iahn
on Macrob. S. v. 19. 19, Hildebrand on Apul. M. i. 23. **traheret,** as the
child cannot keep pace with the mother. Aen. ii. 457, Paneg. iii. 10. **natum** i. e. *simiolum,* a word used by Cicero. **10. ire in risum,** like
ire in lacrimas Verg. Aen. iv. 413. (Schenkl.) **11. Hanc** seems
preferable to *Haec* as the latter would require ante alias. **tamen** and
turpissima are in relation to each other. 'For all that, ugly as she
was.' **ante alios,** 'before anyone else could get in a word:' not with
turpissima. rupit uocem, Vergilian, e. g. Aen. ii. 129, 'breaks into speech.'
Mackail. **12. crimen,** 'the scandal,' 'reproach' (viz. ugliness) is more
naturally constructed with **generis** than with *genetrix,* which however is
found in *P* and other good MSS. **generis,** 'of her race,' the ape-tribe:
genetrix, 'as became the mother of a deformed progeny.' **13, 14.**
'Whether there be any for whom the victory is in store it is for Jupiter to
know: I maintain that my child has the advantage over all.' **13.
norit,** like *uiderit, uideris* (Dräger i. 261). **si quem** ends the hexameter
as in Trist. i. 1. 77 *Nec procul a stabulis audet secedere si qua.* **14. super
est,** as the Greek proves, 'Εμοὶ δὲ πάντων οὗτός ἐστι καλλίων, here = *superat,* 'is
superior,' 'has the advantage.' A. Gell. i. 22. 7 Hertz *M. autem Cicero in
libro qui inscriptus est de iure ciuili in artem redigendo, uerba haec
posuit: Nec uero scientia iuris maioribus suis Q. Aelius Tubero
defuit, doctrina etiam superfuit. In quo loco superfuit significare uidetur
supra fuit et praestitit superauitque maiores suos doctrina sua, superfluenti tamen
et nimis abundanti.* This use is not common.

XV.

Babr. lxv, Fab. Aesop. 397, 397ᵇ Halm, Bodl. 47 Kn.

BABR. LXV.

Ἤριζε τεφρῇ γέρανος εὐφυεῖ ταῷ
σείωντι χρυσᾶς πτέρυγας 'ἀλλ' ἐγὼ ταύταις'
ἡ γέρανος εἶπεν 'ὧν σὺ τὴν χρόην σκώπτεις,
ἄστρων σύνεγγυς ἵπταμαί τε καὶ κράζω.
σὺ δ' ὡς ἀλέκτωρ ταῖσδε ταῖς καταχρύσοις
χαμαὶ πτερύσσῃ φησίν 'οὐδ' ἄνω φαίνῃ.'

Suidas s. v. *γέρανος* quotes two verses which seem to belong to a fable on
the same subject:

Λίβυσσα γέρανος ἠδὲ ταὼς εὐπήληξ
χλωρὴν ἀεὶ 'βόσκωντο λείμακος ποίην.

Corrupt as these are, they show that the extant version of Babrius, given
above, is a poor and weak curtailment of the original (Rutherford). This
is proved also by the longer of Halm's prose versions (397ᵇ), from which it
appears that the complete Babrian fable made the peacock contrast his own
gold and purple with the crane's dull and colourless plumage, as Avianus
has also done. It seems probable then that the Latin poet's version is here
not so much an expansion as a paraphrase, from which we may try to reconstruct the complete Babrian original.

1. Threiciam uolucrem, 'the crane.' Ovid A. A. iii. 182 *Threiciamue
gruem.* Verg. Aen. x. 265 *Strymoniae grues.* Stat. S. iv. 6. 9 *hiberna
Rhodopes grue.* **Iunonius ales,** 'the peacock,' a bird sacred to Juno.

Ovid A. A. i. 627 *Laudatas ostentat auis Iunonia pennas.* Juno, when
Argus was slain, placed his hundred eyes in the peacock's tail. Ovid M.
i. 722 *Excipit hos (oculos) uoluerisque suae Saturnia pennis Collocat et gem-
mis caudam stellantibus inplet.* Hence there is a *motif* for the bird being here
called Iunonius. **2. Communi sociam . . . cibo.** This agrees with
the two lines, probably of the original Babrian fable, cited above from
Suidas. The two birds shared the same pasture-ground (V. 11, XXXVII. 6),
and the peacock took offence at the implied equality. **detinuisse** is my
conj. for *continuisse* or *continuasse* of MSS. Hor. Ep. i. 3. 27 *Nisi ceua prior
potiorque puella Sabinum Detinet*, 'engages' Wilkins there. I cannot
believe with Barth Aduers. xxxix. 13 that *continuasse* could mean as explained in a glossographer cited by him 'perpetuo colere atque amare :'
and if it could, this meaning would not suit the passage, any more than the
other and indubitable sense of 'following closely,' 'attending' which Scioppius
Suspect. Lect. iv. 16 established for both *continuari* and *continuare* from
Apuleius and Symmachus. The only Glossarial evidence I have found for
a meaning that would apply to our fable is from Auct. T. ii. 22 *Continuatus
congressus contestatus*, i. e. joining issue or impleading: this would be the participle of *continuari*, and it is just possible that *continuare* might have been used
in a similar sense. Among the various other emendations proposed, *conter-
uisse*, 'disparaged' (Ellis), or *conripuisse*, 'reproved' (Fröhner), are as plausible as any. **3.** ' For a quarrel had arisen to decide on diversities of
beauty, and they were protracting a keen contention on a point of easy
decision.' **inter**, 'to *decide between* different kinds of beauty.' Hand
Tursellin. iii. p. 395. **5. multimodo**, 'manifold,' a word used by
Apuleius, from whom Koziol Stil des Apuleius p. 275, quotes also *omnimo-
dus unimodus*. In MSS it is often confused with *multinōdis*. **decore.**
Cannegieter aptly quotes Columella viii. 11 *Harum autem decor auium
etiam exteros, nedum dominos oblectat*. Rose's Physiognomist Anecd. Graec.
p. 168, describing the character of the peacock, says *Pauus animal est
pulcritudini studens, stultum, posteriores partes sui corporis referens (? effer-
ens).* **6. Caeruleam . . . liuida**, 'the crane's dingy back gave her
an ashy hue.' Both Aristotle H. A. iii. 77 and Babrius called the crane
τεφρά. **C. facerent**, a construction much affected by Ovid, and necessary in Latin from the want of verbs formed from adjectives : it generally
has a prosaic effect. Ibis 390 *iacto canas puluere fecit aquas*. Pont. iv. 7.
20 *Puniceam Getico sanguine fecit aquam.* **7.** *tegmina* MSS which I
change to **agmina**, 'train,' 'lifting his sweeping tail into a circle about him.'
Verg. G. iii. 423 *Extremaeque agmina caudae Soluuntur.* Auson. Mosell. 138
Longi uix corporis agmina soluis (Zingerle *Zu späteren Latein. Dichtern* i.
p. 40). The Latin Paraphrast has *rota superbiens*, and similarly Phaedrus
iii. 18. 8 *Pictisque plumis gemmeam caudam e x p l i c a s*. [Colum. viii. 11. 8
*Semetipsum ueluti mirantem caudae gemmantibus pennis p r o t e g i t, idque cum
facit, r o t a r e dicitur*, might perhaps be thought to support the MS reading
tegmina.] **8. Sparserat** continues in orat. recta the past time of
detinuisse. **arcatum sursus** is the combined emendation of Barth
and Lachmann for *arcanum rursus* of MSS. 'A similitudine arcus
caelestis sic appellat : cuius fulgor ex aduerso sole tot colores trahit.'
Barth. ' Had scattered a rainbow lustre upwards to the sky.' Lucian
says the eyes at the top of a peacock's feather have a kind of *iris* running
round them. De Domo xi Πάσχει δὲ αὐτὸ μάλιστα ἐπὶ τῶν κύκλων οὓς ἐπ'
ἄκροις ἔχει τοῖς πτεροῖς, ἴριδός τινος ἕκαστον πεπιθεούσης. (Cannegieter.) **sursus** is often spelt wrongly by copyists. Thus in the Fragments of
Early Versions of the Gospels published by Wordsworth and Sanday
(Oxford 1886) *in duas partes acutu usque deorsu* for *a susu* Cata Marcum
xv. 38. **8. nullo . . . certet honore**, ' can never claim to vie in beauty
of plumage.' For this use of *nullus* like οὖτις see on VII. 3. The use of

nullus in the nom. *nullus respondit, nullus desinebat, nulli scitis* (all in Apuleius,
see Hildebrand on Met. ix. 30) is parallel. **honore,** 'beauty.' Symm.
Epist. i. 7 *arbusti honore.* **10. datur.** See on III. 4. **11.**
'Countless as is the array of painted hues upon your feathers, yet that gaudy
tail keeps ever close on the ground.' A very forced inversion of *quamuis
innumero ordine plumae uariatae sint*, not unlike Propertius' (ii. 13. 23)
Desit odoriferis ordo mihi lancibus, where the relation of *ordo* to *lancibus* (the
perfume-dishes to the array they make) is much the same as of Av.'s *ordo*
to **plumas** (the feathers to their grouping). The construction is very
parallel to l. 6 *Spem quoque raptori sustulit inde fames.* **innumerus** most
MSS. It is tempting to read *in numerum*, 'symmetrically.' **12.**
Mersus humi. Sil. x. 78 *mersa Nare tegit*, of a dog snuffing with his nose
close to the ground. Prud. c. Symm. ii. 326 *bibes inter Primitias, mersum-
que solo, ceu quadrupes, egit.* The peacock can fly into a tree, but not to any
height in the air. Colum. viii. 11. 1 *Nec sublimiter potest nec per longa spatia
uolitare.* **florida,** 'gay or bright-hued,' a specially apt word (1) to
colour, Plin. H. N. xxxv. 30 *Sunt colores austeri aut floridi* ; (2) to the bright
hues of the *peacock*, Lucian de Domo xi τὴν οὐρὰν ἐπάρας καὶ πάντοθεν αὐτῷ
περιστήσας ἐπιδείκνυται τὰ ἄνθη τὰ αὑτοῦ καὶ τὸ ἔαρ τῶν πτερῶν. **13.**
Several good MSS point to *deformis . . . pennis*, a not impossible variety
of inflexion like *sublimus sublimis, inermus inermis, inbecillus inbecillis*
etc. **14.** An excellent line, suggesting by its rapid and sweeping
rhythm the free motion of the crane in high air.

XVI.

Babr. xxxvi, Fab. Aesop. (Halm) 179 = Bodl. 29 Kn., 179ʰ, 179ᶜ.

BABR. XXXVI.

Δρῦν αὐτόριζον ἄνεμος ἐξ ὄρους ἄρας
ἔδωκε ποταμῷ· τὴν δ' ἔσυρε κυμαίνων,
πελώριον φύτευμα τῶν πρὶν ἀνθρώπων.
πολὺς δὲ κάλαμος ἑκατέρωθεν εἰστήκει
ἐλαφρὸν ὄχθης ποταμίης ὕδωρ πίνων.
θάμβος δὲ τὴν δρῦν εἶχε πῶς ὁ μὲν λίην
λεπτός τ' ἐὼν καὶ βληχρὸς οὐκ ἐπεπτώκει,
αὐτὴ δὲ τόσση φηγὸς ἐξεριζώθη.
σοφῶς δὲ κάλαμος εἶπε ' μηδὲν ἐκπλήσσου.
σὺ μὲν μαχομένη ταῖς πνοιαῖς ἐνικήθης,
ἡμεῖς δὲ καμπτύμεσθα μαλθακῇ γνώμῃ,
κἂν βαιὸν ἡμῶν ἄνεμος ἄκρα κινήσῃ.'

The popularity of this fable is proved by the numerous prose versions. Shakespere probably alludes to it in his Dirge (Cymbeline iv. 2) *To
thee the reed is as the oak.* Wordsworth, in his poem The Oak and the
Broom, has drawn out the rival pleadings at much length and with great
felicity of expression. Macrobius S. vii. 8. 6 has a passage which in its
wording looks as if Avianus' fable might have been known to him. *Habes
et hoc exemplum non dissonum, quod potentior mola ampliora grana confringit,
integra illa quae sunt minutiora transmittit : uento nimio abies aut quercus
auellitur, cannam nulla facile frangit procella.* Claudian Deprecatio ad
Hadrianum 37 *Incubuit numquam caelestis flamma salictis, Nec parui frutices
iram meruere Tonantis. Ingentes quercus, annosas fulminat ornos.*

1. **radicitus oruta.** Vergilian, Aen. v. 449, where Ribbeck gives
radicibus with the Medicean : the Roman (R) has *radicitus*. **quercus,**
the oak swept along by the swoln river is as old as Homer. Il. xi. 492 'Ως δ'
ὁπότε πλήθων ποταμὸς πεδίονδε κάτεισι Χειμάρρους κατ' ὄρεσφιν, ὀπαζόμενος

Διὸς ὄμβρῳ, Πολλὰς δὲ δρῦς ἀζαλέας, πολλὰς δέ τε πεύκας Ἐσφέρεται. **3.**
subter, 'below the tree.'   **decurrens,** 'flowing down,' and therefore
carrying with it in its current anything that falls in.   **alueus** is somewhat harsh with **et fluuio** following. Vergil's familiar *Atque illum in prae-*
ceps prono rapit alueus amni seems to be the suggesting outline.   **4.**
Suscipit = ἔδωκε ποταμῷ, as **rapit** = ἔσυρε.   **praecipitante,** intransitive
as in Cic. de Orat. iii. 48. 186 *in amni praecipitante.*   **5.** ' But when its
tall length was pushed by either bank from side to side.'   **diuersis.**
The oak struck against one bank and was then repelled by it to the other,
its height causing it to strike each with either end alternately, until it ended
with stranding on a bed of reeds.   **6. residit,** 'rests after drifting.'
residit P with one of Voss's MSS and my Brit. Mus. *B.* These I have
followed against *resedit* of *C* and most other MSS, as throughout this
fable there is a noticeable recurrence of the present, a marked avoid-
ance of past, tenses. [It is however to be noted that Seeck's MSS of
Symmachus' Epistles i. 19 give *residi* for *resedi.*]   **grande onus**
introduces the Babrian πελώριον φύτευμα.   **7.** ' Thereupon the
oak marvelled that a reed fastening as it does its stalks together with
only a slender tuft of roots stands firm in the flowing water.' So
Cannegieter, referring **conectens** to **harundo,** though the first impression of the passage is that **conectens** is said of the *oak* interlacing its boughs
with the slender tufts of the reeds, and so feeling their weakness and
expressing surprise at their power of resistance.   **exiguo caespite** seems to
mean the slender bunch of roots from which the reed with its branching
stalks rises: and so Philargyrius, whom Conington follows, interprets in
G. iv. 273 *uno ingentem tollit de caespite siluam.* Canneg. quotes besides
Claud. de R. Pros. iii. 371, Prud. Cath. x. 123, but both passages are doubtful. See below on XXI. 2.   **ramos,** properly the thin rods which surmount and sprout from the knotted or geniculated stem of the reed, Plin.
xvi. 163. Av. perhaps does not speak with such particularity.   **8.**
Babr. 5 ἐλαφρὸν ὄχθης ποταμίης ὕδωρ πίνων.   **harundŏ,** like **testudŏ**
II. 1.   **9.** I believe I have restored intelligibility to this line by reading **rectam non sistere** for *needum (rectum C) consistere* of MSS. The objection is not to *needum* being used for *nondum,* which Iahn (Introd. to Macrobius p. xli) shows to have been common in that writer (see Sat. vii. 4. 7,
vii. 7. 17 *Mustum cum needum suaue est, sed tantummodo dulce,* and cf. Symn.
Laud. in Gratianum *Qui needum nouerant felicius iudicarent.* Epist. i. 1 *Sed*
te Baulorum needum lenta otia quaerunt. Claud. Laud. Stilic. i. 3 *Conubii nec-*
dum festiuos regia cantus Sopierat), but to its being the exact reverse of what
we should expect, *non iam :* for all attempts to force the meaning of ' not
yet ' into the passage are futile.   **rectam non sistere** = Babrius' ἐξεριζώθη, as **tam uasto . . . trunco** = Babrius' τόσσην φηγός.   **Se quoque,**
' even he.' Macrob. S. vii. 5. 4 *Nec abnego potuisse me quoque tamquam palino-*
diam canere.   **10. tenui cortice** expresses λεπτός τ' ἐὼν καὶ βληχρός of
Babrius.   **ferre,** 'supported without falling.' Babr. has οὐκ ἐπεπτώκει.   **11. blando,** ' submissive,' 'deferential,' as became its character
of safe weakness (**tutam debilitate**).   **12.** *docens* Lachmann for *docet*
of MSS. This cannot be considered certain, as Av. has some undoubted
deviations from the normal use of *que, atque.* XVII. 13 *Illa gemens fracto-*
que loqui uix murmure cœpit, Lachm. *cœptans.* XXV. 5 *Ille sibi abrupti fingens*
discrimina funis Atque auri queritur desiluisse cadum (where *C* alone has *Ac,*
whence Fröhner *Hac*). It seems possible that the peculiar combination
of participle in the first clause followed by *Atque (que)* and a final verb in
the second which marks both XVI. 12 and XXV. 5 is a designed affectation
framed on similar anomalies of Greek syntax, e.g. Aesch. Ag. 99 Τούτων λέξασ'
ὅ,τι καὶ δυνατὸν Καὶ θέμις αἰνεῖν, Παιών τε γενοῦ τῆσδε μερίμνης. Thuc. ii. 29. 3
Τήρης δὲ οὔτε τὸ αὐτὸ ὄνομα ἔχων, βασιλεύς τε πρῶτος ἐν κράτει Ὀδρυσῶν

ἐγένετο. In Lucan Phars. vi. 400, 1 *Prima fretum scindens Pagasaeo litore pinus Terrenumque nouas hominem proiecit in undas* is a well-supported reading. **14. totis uiribus.** Claud. Rapt. Pros. iii. 378 *Alternasque ferit totisque obnixa trementes Viribus inpellit.* **acta.** Ovid M. ii. 184 *Vt acta Praecipiti pinus Borea.* **15.** Verg. Aen. iii. 481 *Fando surgentes demoror* ('keep dallying') *austros*, a line which Av. has applied very felicitously in a quite different way, to the wind playing gently in the reed-tops before it becomes boisterous. **surgentes paulatim,** 'gradually rising,' when they begin to make themselves heard, but only faintly. **16. quamuis leuibus,** 'however lightly-blowing,' the lightest breath of the south winds. XXXVI. 15 *Proderit ergo graues quamuis perferre labores.* Lucian Hermotim. 68 Ἐοικὼς καλάμῳ τινὶ ἐπ' ὄχθῃ παραποταμίᾳ πεφυκότι καὶ πρὸς πᾶν τὸ πνέον καμπτομένῳ, κἂν μικρά τις αὔρα διαφυσήσασα διασαλεύῃ αὐτόν. **prouida,** as in XII. 7. **17.** 'Against your sturdy stem the rain-cloud bursts in fury.' The reading is very doubtful, but **praeruptus** not *proruptus* is tolerably certain. **se fundit** for *offendit* of MSS might express the same idea as Lachmann's *se effundit* without the improbable elision. Ovid M. i. 269 has *Densi funduntur ab aethere nimbi.* **praeruptus,** 'furious,' 'violent.' Amm. Marc. xxii. 8. 40 *praeruptis undarum uerticibus.* Lachm.'s *proruptus* is however very tempting: cf. *eruptus* in Amm. Marc. xxx. 4. 20 *Erupta maledicendi ferocia multos offendunt.* **18. Motibus,** a word very much affected by the Panegyrici, vii. 5 *Vt oceanus ille tanto uectore stupefactus caruisse suis motibus uideretur.* vi. 7 *Vt enim ille qui omnes aquas caelo et terris praebet oceanus semper tamen in motibus suis totus est.* **ludificata,** 'mocked' or 'baffled,' a Plautine and Terentian word, almost invariably used of *persons.* Gloss. Sangall. *ludificat inludit.* Babrius has Ἡμεῖς δὲ καμπτόμεσθα μαλθακῇ γνώμῃ Κἂν βαιὸν ἡμῶν ἄνεμος ἄκρα κινήσῃ. **19, 20.** On the ordinary reading of these vv. they contain the moral which is summed up in the Hesiodic hexameter ap. Macrob. S. v. 16. Ὤφρων δ' ὅς κ' ἐθέλοι πρὸς κρείσσονας ἀντιφερίζειν, and more at large in the epimythion of Halm's prose fable 179ᵇ Ὁ μῦθος δηλοῖ, ὅτι οὕτω καὶ οἱ πρὸς τὸν καιρὸν καὶ τοὺς κρείττονας αὐτῶν μὴ ἀνθιστάμενοι κρείττονές εἰσι τῶν πρὸς μείζονας φιλονεικούντων. 'These words warn us that it is in vain we resist the great, and that it is by slow degrees that we surmount their fierce threats.' But one of my best MSS (*B*) has a remarkable variant *lustra* which seems to point to a different reading, possibly **fluxa** = *inbecilla* (Plin. Paneg. 33 *non enerue nec fluxum*). With this *subsistere* of the Bodleian MS *O* would well agree, whereas it could not have been admitted as a variant if *frustra* had stood in the text originally. I would suggest, then, to write the vv.—

Haec nos dicta monent magnis subsistere fluxa,
Paulatimque truces exsuperare minas.

'This fable teaches us that weak things hold out against strong, and by slow degrees surmount their menace and fury.'

XVII.

Babr. i, Fab. Aesop. 403 Halm, 11 Kn.

BABR. I.

Ἄνθρωπος ἦλθεν εἰς ὄρος κυνηγήσων,
τόξου βολῆς ἔμπειρος· ἦν δὲ τῶν ζώων
φυγή τε πάντων καὶ φόβου δρόμος πλήρης.
λέων δὲ τοῦτον προὐκαλεῖτο θαρσήσας
αὐτῷ μάχεσθαι. 'μεῖνον' εἶπε 'μὴ σπεύσῃς,'
ἄνθρωπος αὐτῷ 'μηδ' ἐπελπίσῃς νίκην·

τῷ δ' ἀγγέλῳ μου πρῶτον ἐντυχὼν γνώσῃ
τί σοι ποιητέ' ἐστίν.' εἶτα τοξεύει
μικρὸν διαστάς. χὠ μὲν οἰστὸς ἐκρύφθη
λέοντος ὑγραῖς χολάσιν· ὁ δὲ λέων δείσας
ὥρμησε φεύγειν εἰς νάπας ἐρημαίας.
τούτου δ' ἀλώπηξ οὐκ ἄπωθεν εἰστήκει.
ταύτης δὲ θαρσεῖν καὶ μένειν κελευούσης
'οὔ με πλανήσεις,' φησιν, 'οὐδ' ἐνεδρεύσεις·
ὅπου γὰρ οὕτω πικρὸν ἄγγελον πέμπει,
πῶς αὐτὸς ἤδη φοβερός ἐστι γινώσκω.'

1. **iaculis uulnera torquens**, condensed for *uulnera edens iacula tor-
quendo*. The original is Statius, Theb. x. 744 *Nunc spargit torquens uolucri
noua uulnera plumbo.* **haud irrita**, for he was an expert huntsman, τόξου
βολῆς ἔμπειρος. 2. **trepidas** Lachmann for *pauidas* or *rabidas* of
MSS. Babr. has ἦν δὲ τῶν ζώων Φυγή τε πάντων καὶ φάβου δρόμος
πλήρης. **per sua lustra feras.** Vergil has *lustra ferarum* G. ii. 471,
Aen. iii. 647, and so Nemesianus Cyneg. 98. Cf. Macrob. vii. 2. 13 *Qui
uenatibus gaudet, interrogetur de siluae ambitu, de ambage lustro-
rum.* 3. **pauidis audax,** an effective juxtaposition of *antitheta*. 4.
Verbere commoto, 'lashing about with his tail,' partly to show his
anger, partly to call the huntsman's attention. See my note on Cat.
lxiii. 81. **adesse,** 'to present himself,' 'come up and fight.' A free
translation of προύκαλεῖτο αὐτῷ μάχεσθαι. 5. **solito**, though gram-
matically constructed with **lacerto**, really refers to the action expressed in
contorquens, 'brandishing a dart as usual with his shoulder.' So Val. Fl.
iii. 45 *Hostis habet portus, soliti rediere Pelasgi,* 'the Pelasgi have come back
as usual,' and perhaps Vergil Aen. ix. 214 *Solita aut si qua id fortuna uetabit.*
Ovid Her. iii. 131 *Est aliquid collum solitis tetigisse lacertis* may have suggested Avianus' somewhat bolder variation. 6. Fröhner's **qualis
eam** for *qualis eram* of MSS is more than probable. There is, perhaps, a
touch of over-grandiloquence in **eam**, 'how I go on my way,' not quite
suited to the plain directness of the rest of the speech, unless indeed Av.
consciously imitates the heroic style of Mezentius, Aen. x. 881 (quoted
by Barth) *Venio moriturus et haec tibi porto Dona prius.* **nuntius iste,**
'this messenger,' the arrow. **refert,** 'announces,' twice used by Vergil
of a messenger, Aen. ii. 547 *Refere s ergo haec et nuntius ibis Pelidae genitori,*
xii. 75 *Nuntius haec Idmon Phrygio mea dicta tyranno Haud placitura refer*
(Cannegieter). 7. **emissum ... ferrum,** nominative as in Luc.
iv. 545 *Viscera non unus iamdudum transigit ensis.* More commonly the subject of *transigit* (the present is the usual tense) is the striker, not the weapon,
e.g. Stat. Theb. vii. 594, 5, viii. 477, 8. *uulnera* most MSS, including, I
think, *C.* But *transigere uulnus,* 'to deal a blow through,' is a construction
of which I have found no example, and I therefore follow *A,* one of the
earliest MSS, in writing **uulnere.** Such an ablative is frequent after *transigere.* 8. **Praestrinxit,** 'grazed,' and so Nonius cites Cic. Phil. ii.
40. 102 *Cuius quidem (aratri) nomere portam Capuae paene praestrinxisti,* where
however the ninth century Vatican MS has m. pr. *perstrixisti.* Some of the
best MSS of Avianus give here *Perstrinxit,* one, the remarkable Brit. Mus.
B, pertinxit, a spelling which perhaps points to a perf. form *stinxit,* cf.
praestigiae, and see Bücheler in Fleckeisen's Iahrbücher for 1872, p. 109 sqq.
In Amm. Marc. xxxi. 3. 7 *A superciliis Gerasi fluminis ad usque Danubium
Taifalorum terras praestringens muros altius erigebat* the sense seems to be
'skirting.' 9. **Molliter** with **traheret,** 'drew out gently,' to lighten
the pain and diminish the flow of blood. Cf. the medical use of *mollis
manus* Quintil. ii. 4. 12 *Ut remedia quae alicqui natura sunt aspera molli manu
leniantur.* So Cannegieter; but the Greek words χὠ μὲν οἰστὸς ἐκρύφθη

G

Λέοντος ὑγραῖς χολάσιν rather point to *molliter fixum* being taken together; the arrow had sunk gently into the yielding flesh of the beast. **10. A trepida ... uulpe retenta.** Quintil. vii. 2. 26 *Clusinium Figulum filium Vrbiniae acie uicta in qua steterat, fugisse, iactatumque casibus uariis, retentum etiam a rege, tandem in Italiam ac patriam suam uenisse.* **trepida,** 'dismayed' from seeing what had befallen the tiger. **retenta diu.** The fox keeps the tiger talking a long time because he is anxious to learn whence comes the danger which in its turn will threaten himself. Very similarly Terence Phorm. v. 6. 23 *Pone adprehendit pallio, resupinat : respicio, rogo Quam ob rem retineat me : ait esse uetitum intro ad eram accedere.* Av. here deserts Babrius, who makes his fox *encourage* the lion (θαρσεῖν καὶ μένειν κελευούσης), the very opposite of the *trepida uulpes* of our fable. **11.** I have written **Nempe quis** for *Dum quis* of *ACP*, *Dumque quis* of B. Among the other emendations of this v. Withof's *Ecquis et* for *Dic quis et* which is found in my Bodl. MS *X* would be very like the ἐπυνθάνετο τίς ἐστι καὶ πόθεν ἦλθεν of Halm's Fab. Aesop. 423 (Weasel and Parrot). Fröhner's *Vnde, quis* has the same meaning and is nearer to the best MSS. **uulnera ferret,** here of *dealing* blows, and so Ovid Rem. 44, Trist. ii. 20, both in the combination *uulnus opemque ferre.* More often of receiving them, Ibis 256, Her. vi. 82, Met. ii. 286, xii. 313. **12. ubinam,** rare. Stat. S. ii. 1. 45, and in the verse of Bibaculus ap. Suet. Gramm. ix *Orbilius ubinam est, litterarum obliuio?* **13.** See on XVI. 12. It is possible that **que** connects the participle clause with the final verb **coepit**, as it connects *respondens* with *decet* there, if the MSS are to be followed. Cf. Aen. ix. 402, 3 *Ocius adducto torquens hastile lacerto Suspiciens altam Lunam et sic uoce precatur.* Or again it might be compared with Aen. x. 874 *Aeneas agnouit enim laetusque precatur,* where *agnouit enim* introduces *laetusque precatur* much as *gemens* introduces *fractoque loqui m. coepit* here. But it is not to be denied that at any rate in the present instance a simpler explanation is possible, namely, that **que** connects **gemens** with **fracto murmure** : 'the tiger groaning and with a faltering growl at last spoke.' So Wopkens, comparing XLII. 5 *Inpiger hunc raptor mediamque secutus in urbem.* **fracto.** Lucretius, describing the effect of fear iii. 153 *Videmus Sudoresque ita palloremque existere toto Corpore et infringi linguam uocemque aboriri,* where Munro translates 'the tongue falter, the voice die away.' **14. solitas uoces,** a somewhat strained plural, 'his wonted utterance,' or 'power of utterance.' **dolor,** 'pain of the wound.' **15. medio in aggere,** 'confronted me on the road.' Aen. v. 273 *Saepe uiae deprensus in aggere serpens,* where Servius explains *agger est media uiae eminentia, coaggeratis lapidibus strata.* (Canneg.) **conuenit.** IX. 6. **16.** The combination *Nulla ... forma ... Quaeque ... sit repetenda* recurs XXXIII. 1, 2 *Anser ... feta, Ouaque quae ... daret.* XXXVIII. 9, 10 *Vana ... mendacia Quaeque refutari ... queant,* and is common in other authors of the period as well as in the Satires of Juvenal. See on XXXIII. 2. **oculis olim repetenda,** 'to be afterwards recalled by my eyes.' An Ovidianism, Pont. ii. 10. 5, 6 *An tibi notitiam mora temporis eripit horum? Nec repetunt oculi signa uetusta tui?* The gerundive has here the form of a simple fut. pass. participle. See above on XI. 12. **18. uirum,** emphasized, 'strong man,' 'man of might,' as in Sen. Epist. 98. 14 *Cum uiro tibi negotium est.*

XVIII.

Babr. xliv, Fab. Aesop. 394, 394ᵇ Halm, 36 Kn.

BABR. XLIV.

Ἐνέμοντο ταῦροι τρεῖς ἀεὶ μετ' ἀλλήλων,
λέων δὲ τούτους συλλαβεῖν ἐφεδρεύων
ὁμοῦ μὲν αὐτοὺς οὐκ ἔδοξε νικήσειν,
λόγοις δ' ὑπούλοις διαβολαῖς τε συγκρούων
ἐχθροὺς ἐποίει, χωρίσας δ' ἀπ' ἀλλήλων
ἕκαστον αὐτῶν ἔσχε ῥαδίην θοίνην.

2. **amicitiae tanta fides,** ' a friendship so firm.' **3. simul emissos,** sc. *stabulis,* as Vergil G. iv. 22 says of bees that have left the hive *fauis
emissa inuentus.* Colum. vi. 9. 2 *Quae medicina sub tecto fieri debet nec ante
sanitatem bos emitti* where Vegetius has *dimittatur in pastum* (Schneider
ad loc.). error is rightly explained by Wopkens 'numquam aberrantes
a se inuicem diuulsos fuisse.' Columella well illustrates the passage vi. 23. 3
*Nam id quoque semper crepusculo fieri debet, ut ad sonum bucinae pecus, si quod
in siluis substiterit, septa repetere consuescat. Sic enim recognosci grex poterit numerusque constare si uelut ex militari disciplina intra stabulariorum castra
manserint. Sed non eadem in tauros exercentur imperia, qui freti uiribus per
nemora uagantur, liberosque egressus et reditus habent.* **4. Rursus,**
not here otiose, but 'and then again.' *a pastu* all MSS, against the
practice of Vergil who has e **pastu** four times (G. i. 381, iv. 186, 434, Aen.
vii. 700). **amans,** 'still friends,' ' loving as before.' *ouans,* though it is
found in *B* and the second Peterhouse MS, and is a word elsewhere used
by Av. VII. 12, has comparatively little point. **5. quoque,** 'besides,'
transitional. Versus de xii Ventis in Reyfferscheid's Sueton. Fragm.
p. 305 *Hunc quoque Daedaleae Noton expressere Micenae* (44), Aegritudo
Perdicae 18 (Bährens Poet. Lat. Min. v. 112) *Hinc quoque partus amor
redeunti ad tecta parentum* where *Hinc quoque* is not ' Hence even,' but
' Hence too.' See on IX. 21. **collatis inter se cornibus** would
more naturally mean 'joining horns in an *encounter.*' Here it is used of
the four bullocks standing close to each other and presenting a formidable
array of eight horn power. So *collatis uiribus* Plin. Ep. viii. 14. 17. Varro
R. R. ii. 9. 2 (*cum sciam*) *tauros solere diuersos assistere clunibus continuatos,
et cornibus facile propulsare lupos.* **6. pertimuisse** is not merely
'feared,' but 'fought shy of' or ' refused to face.' Ovid M. xiv. 440 of
Macareus refusing to face a new voyage *Pertimui fateor nactusque hoc litus
adhaesi.* **8. coniuratos,** 'leagued.' **9. Sed,** all MSS, perhaps
rightly, as there is an opposition to the negative implied in **horret.** So
Colum. vi. 2. 14 of bullocks *Qui sunt uerentes plagarum et acclamationum,
sed fiducia uirium nec auditu nec uisu pauidi.* **factisque inmanior,**
'more savage in what he did,' not only reckless in spirit and purpose
(**audax**). **10. Tantorum,** hardly for *tot* (Canneg.) for which cf.
Maxim. El. i. 282 (Bährens Poet. Lat. Min. v. 313 sqq.) *Nec quisquam ex
tantis praebet amicus opem,* but 'of such mighty beasts,' *immensis inuencis* 1.
Nevelet's conjecture *Taurorum* in itself is not unlikely, but is unsupported
by any of the early MSS. **impăr.** See on XI. 5. **erat,** notice the
change from present (**prohibet, horret**) to imperfect. **11. uerbis,**
dative after **insistere,** 'to urge evil counsels.' **12. Collisum dissociare,** ' to make them quarrel and so divide them.' Canneg. quotes
Vell. Paterc. ii. 52 *Collisa inter se duo rei publicae capita.* Av. translates
συγκρούων of Babrius. **13. acerbis,** Babrius' λόγοις ὑπούλοις διαβολαῖς
τε. Nearly 'embittering,' 'exasperating,' like Vergil's *formidine crimen
acerbat* Aen. xi. 407 'gives sting to his charge' (Conington). **14.**

Inuasit of *BX Pet*[2] for *Inuadit* of most MSS seems necessary.　**diripuitque,** 'tore in pieces.' Ovid Ibis 599 *Diripiantque tuos insanis unguibus artus Strymoniae matres, Orpheos esse ratae.*　**15. seruare,** as Claudian Epigr. 35. 5 *placidam discit seruare quietem.*　**16. cupit ex** *BX Pet*[2] and the Treves MS for *cupiet* of *CR.* The two presents are slightly more pointed and neater.　**17. cito,** 'in a hurry.' Sen. de Ira ii. 29 *De eis quae narrata sunt, non debemus cito credere.*　**admotas.** Sen. Ep. x. 5 *Si quis admonerit aurem, conticescent.*　**18. ante** is probably to be combined with **fidem,** as Servius on Aen. i. 198 says ANTE MALORVM *ὑφ' ἑν est, id est antiquorum malorum.* Hand Tursellinus i. p. 389 quotes from the Hist. Augusta Capitolin. Vit. Gordiani xxiv *Cum inter se de bonis pessimi quique haberent ante consilia tibi suggerenda.* Dräger i. 111, 112 shows that this use of adverbs as attributes is found in every period of the language. Plaut. Pers. iii. 1. 57 *Non tu nunc hominum mores uides?* i.e. τῶν νῦν ἀνθρώπων. Cic. Pis. ix. 21 *discessu tum meo.* De Nat. Deor. ii. 66 *deorum saepe praesentiae.* From the writers of the Decadence he cites amongst others Apul. de Mag. 74 *illa tum mutatio* (ἡ τότε). Fronto ad Caes. ii. 18 *illa cotidie tua Lorium uentio.* Lamprid. Vit. Alex. Seueri 35 *meliorum retro principum.* Symm. Epist. i. 27 *tanta retro familiaritate* is very like our passage. This view is supported by a gloss in the Treves MS *ante fidem,* marg. *ante conditam.* Otherwise *ante* might be explained of the *preliminary* distrust which involves and is contrasted with the ruin that comes of listening to evil suggestions.

XIX.

Babr. lxiv, Fab. Aesop. 125 Halm, 48 Kn.

BABR. LXIV.

Ἥριζον ἐλάτη καὶ βάτος πρὸς ἀλλήλας.
ἐλάτης δ' ἑαυτὴν πολλαχῶς ἐπαινούσης
'καλὴ μέν εἰμι καὶ τὸ μέτρον εὐμήκης,
καὶ τῶν νεφῶν σύνοικος ὀρθίη φύω,
στέγη τε μελάθρων εἰμὶ καὶ τρόπις πλοίων,
δένδρων τοσούτων ἐκπρεπεστάτη πάντων.'
βάτος πρὸς αὐτὴν εἶπεν 'ἢν λάβῃς μνήμην
καὶ τῶν πελύκων τῶν ἀεί σε τεμνόντων,
βάτος γενέσθαι καὶ σὺ μᾶλλον αἱρήσῃ.'

1. Horrentes dumos introduces as a plural what afterwards figures as a singular 9 *tibi,* 11 *Ille refert.* The same change in a different form appears in *locamur* in 7 followed by *In me* in 8.　**pulcherrima.** Verg. Ecl. vii. 65 *Fraxinus in siluis pulcherrima, pinus in hortis, Populus in fluuiis, abies in montibus altis.*　**3.** 'Saying it was a pitiful strife that was waged with bushes, that had no title that equalized them on the ground of merit.' **dumis** is my correction of the MS reading *cunctis,* which written *cuntis* would easily be mistaken for it. Wopkens' defence of the MS reading 'quoscumque nullus ob merita consociaret honor, inter hos indigne de meritis certari' is slightly awkward, though in a writer of this period certainly possible. If *Quod* is retained (it is found in *ACP*) we must with Schenkl explain *cunctis haberi* as *ab omnibus iudicari* and *Quod* as *quia,* a poor meaning quite unworthy of Avianus.　**certamen haberi,** as in Ovid M. xiii. 159 *Ergo operum quoniam nudum certamen habetur.* Val. Max. viii. 7. Ext. 12 *Sophocles gloriosum cum rerum natura certamen habuit.*　**dumis,** dative, depends immediately on **certamen.**　**4.** *meriti* is a very seductive emendation.　**5.** Change from indirect to direct speech, with no connecting *ait* or *dixit.* So XXIV. 7, and cf. XXXI. 9.　**deductum,**

'tapering,' a sense into which it naturally passes from that of 'attenuated.'
See Spalding's Lexicon to Quintilian s.v. and cf. Ter. Eun. ii. 3. 23. But
though *deducta uox, deductum carmen* in the sense of 'thin' are found several
times (see Macrob. S. vi. 4. 12), it is not often that the word is applied to
the body, as here. ' Slim' perhaps is our nearest equivalent. In Avianus'
time *deductus* was inflected regularly as an adjective: e.g. *deductior paulo
numerus* in a Rescript of the Emperors Valens Gratianus and Valentinian
cod. Theodos. xiii. Tit. iii. § 11.   7. 'And when I am set amidships
on the barque's open floor, on me is hung the canvas that the breeze un-
furls.'   **Puppibus,** in the general sense of ships, as is shown by **patulis**
which of course refers to the open deck.   **media cum sede locamur.**
A reminiscence of Claudian, De Sext. Cons. Honorii 23 *Imperii sidus pro-
pria cum sede locauit.*   8. **explicat sinus.** Sen. de Ira ii. 30. 5 *Totos
sinus securus explicuit (gubernator).*   9. **spineta.** Verg. Ecl. ii.
9.   **figuram.** The unsightliness of a bush is its shapelessness. Its
form is ill-defined among the surrounding bushes.   10. **praeteriere,**
aoristic, 'are wont to pass unheeded.' So *remisit* XXXV. 10.   11.
refert, ' replies.'   **Nunc laeta quidem,** in opposition to **Sed cum** 13,
as in XII. 9, 11. ' Now, it is true, you are happy, and all you profess is
fair.'   **laeta,** fem.   **fateris,** in a general sense ' avow,' ' profess,' nearly
= *praedicas.* So Claudian Laus Serenae 94 *Omina non audet genitrix tam
magna fateri.*   12. **frueris,** i.q. *delectaris.* Claudian In Rufin. i. 234 *Nec
celeri mittit leto, crudelibus ante Suppliciis fruitur.* De Sext. Cons. Honorii
112 *Supplicio fruitur natoque ultore triumphat.*   **imperiosa,** 'insulting.'
Coniunx imperiosa Lyci Ibis 536 will illustrate the meaning. See my note
there. The Treves MS glosses *imperiosa gloriosa.*   13. **minax** transfers to the axe which is constantly dealing new blows to fell the tree, the
very idea of *threatening* which Vergil applies to the tree while it is still
being felled (Aen. ii. 628) but has not yet fallen.   **membra,** of the
stem and boughs of a tree. Washietl de Similitudinibus Imaginibusque
Ouidianis p. 177: ' Met. i. 555 narratur Daphnen Apollinem fugientem
in laurum conuersam esse. cuius arboris ramos ut "membra" amplexus
est deus bracchiis et oscula dedit ligno. atque eadem similitudo paulo
post v. 567 continuatur, ubi cacumen huius arboris se mouisse dicitur
"tamquam caput." '   14. **Quam uelles,** of a useless wish. Donatus
on Ter. Adel. iv. 16 *Vah quam uellem etiam noctu amicis operam mos esset dari*
remarks *Quam uellem proprie dicimus in his quae non uidemus fieri.* Verg.
Aen. vi. 436 of suicides *Quam uellent aethere in alto Nunc et pauperiem et duros
perferre labores.* Here the future contingency **cum succidet membra
securis** is mentally realized as a fact accomplished, and **Quam uelles**
= ' how glad you would have been.' *Quam uellem* is common in the letters
of Symmachus, e. g. i. 5.   **tunc,** ' at the moment' of being felled. The v.
is a close imitation of Mart. Spect. viii. 2 *Quam cuperes pinnas nunc habuisse
tuas.*

XX.

Babr. vi, Fab. Aesop. 28 Halm : cf. Fab. Aesop. 231.

BABR. VI.

Ἁλιεὺς θαλάσσης πᾶσαν ἠόνα ξύων
λεπτῷ τε καλάμῳ τὸν γλυκὺν βίον σώζων
μικρόν ποτ' ἰχθὺν ὁρμίης ἀφ' ἱππείης
ἤγρευσεν, οὐ τῶν εἰς τάγηνον ὡραίων.
ὁ δ' αὐτὸν οὕτως ἱκέτευεν ἀσπαίρων·
'τί σοι τὸ κέρδος, ἢ τίν' ὦνον εὑρήσεις;
οὐκ εἰμὶ γὰρ τέλειος, ἀλλά με πρῴην
πρὸς τῇδε πέτρῃ φυκὶς ἔπτυσ' ἡ μήτηρ.

νῦν οὖν ἄφες με, μὴ μάτην μ' ἀποκτείνῃς.
ἐπὴν δὲ πλησθεὶς φυκίων θαλασσαίων
μέγας γένωμαι, πλουσίοις πρέπων δείπνοις,
τότ' ἐνθάδ' ἐλθὼν ὕστερόν με συλλήψῃ.'
τοιαῦτα μύζων ἱκέτευε κἀσπαίρων,
ἀλλ' οὐκ ἔμελλε τὸν γέροντα θωπεύσειν·
ἔφη δὲ πείρων αὐτὸν ὀξέῃ σχοίνῳ
'ὁ μὴ τὰ μικρά, πλὴν βέβαια, τηρήσας
μάταιός ἐστιν ἣν ἄδηλα θηρεύῃ.'

This fable has its double in another of the Aesopian collection 231 Halm. There a dog lying asleep in front of a house, and on the point of being eaten by a wolf, begs for mercy, on the plea that whereas at present he is thin and lean, he will soon get fatter with the good things at his master's wedding. The wolf spares him, and after a few days returns and finds the dog sleeping on the top of the house. He reminds him of his promise; and the dog taunts him with his folly in believing he can be simple enough to sleep again in front of the house after his former danger. Cf. Otto Crusius de Babrii aetate p. 204.

The Bodleian Paraphrast does not include Babr. vi.

1. **praedam** might be the bait, as it seems to be in Ovid Hal. 34, 5 *Atque ubi praedam Pendentem saetis auidus rapit* (*Polypus*). But the words of Babrius μικρόν ποτ' ἰχθὺν ὁρμῆς ἀφ' ἱππείης Ἡγρευσεν point to the other sense of prey taken by the fisher, cf. 15 and Auson. Mosell. 254 *Nec mora et excussam stridenti uerbere praedam, Dexter in obliquum raptat puer*, where it is used of a fish which has just taken the hook. So Ovid Met. xiii. 936. From the same point of view the fisherman is called *praedo* Auson. Mosell. 282. **saeta**, 'a horse-hair line.' Ovid Hal. 35, Mart. i. 55. 9, x. 30. 16, Auson. Mosell. 253 *crispoque tremori Vibrantis saetae nutans consentit harundo.* 2. **Exigui**. Babrius is equally indefinite: the prose version has μαινίδη, 'a sprat.' As early as the Odyssey (xii. 252) the fisherman is described ἰχθύσι τοῖς ὀλίγοισι δόλον κατὰ εἴδατα βάλλων. 3. **superas ad auras**, where it could not breathe. Auson. Mosell. 261 *Quoique sub amne suo mansit uigor, aere nostro Segnis anhelatis uitam consumit in auris.* 265 *haustas sed hiatibus auras Reddit mortiferos exspirans branchia flatus.* **captum perduxit.** Lucian Piscator 48 ἔψαυσεν, εἴληπται, ἀνασπάσωμεν. 49 κατέπιεν ἔχεται ἀνεσπάσθω. 50 ἔχανεν εἴληπται ἀνιμήσθω. 4. **auido.** Ovid Hal. 35 *praedam Pendentem saetis auidus rapit.* **fixum uulnus tulit**, 'the fish had been pierced with a wound.' *Figere uulnus* is found in Mart. i. 60. 4 of a lion *biting* bullocks; *f. mortem* in Seneca Herc. Oet. 519 of an arrow *piercing* mortally. It is in this latter sense it is used here; the wound is pierced, i. e. made by the piercing of the hook. **ab ore,** 'from,' i. e. 'through the mouth ' as in Ovid Her. vi. 82 *Non exspectato uulnus ab hoste tulit.* **tulit,** sc. *piscis*, a change of subject. 5. **lacrimis,** a grotesque touch all Avianus' own. 6. **quanta**, 'how small.' Hor. S. ii. 4. 81 *Vilibus in scopis, in mappis, in scobe quantus Consistit sumptus,* where A. Palmer quotes Prop. iv. 6. 65 *Di melius! quantus mulier foret una triumphus.* **dona,** Lachmann for *damna* of MSS. The line of Babrius is cited by Suidas τί σοι τὸ κέρδος; ἢ τίν' ὄνον εὑρήσεις; for the last word of which the Athoan codex substitutes ἢ πόσου με πωλήσεις; Either seems to require **dona**, as *damna* can hardly mean 'costs,' and so 'damage' or 'price.' Wopkens' view that **ex nostro corpore** = 'from *the loss* of my body,' i. e. by giving me up and restoring me to freedom, is harsh, but not impossible. 7. **Nunc,** 'as it is.' Catull. xxi. 10 *Nunc ipsum id doleo, quod esurire Mellitus puer et sitire discet.* The Brit. Mus. codex *B* has *Hanne,* possibly a mistake for *Hunc.* 'Such as you see me here my mother bore me under rocky caverns,' i. e. in contradistinction from the full-grown

fish it would afterwards become. This certainly agrees well with Babrius'
οὐκ εἰμὶ γὰρ τέλειος, ἀλλά με πρώην Πρὸς τῇδε πέτρῃ φυκὶς ἔπτυσ' ἡ
μήτηρ. **saxosis.** Lucian Piscator 48 εἴληψαι λιχνεύων περὶ τὰς πέτρας,
ἔνθα λήσειν ἤλπισας ὑποδεδυκώς (sub antris). In his Halieutica Ovid gives
rules for fishing in rocky, sandy or open waters (85 sqq.), distinguishing the
kinds of fish which haunt each. Fish that haunt rocky water were called
saxatiles. Colum. viii. 16. 8 *Optime saxosum mare nominis sui pisces nutrit,
qui scilicet, quod in petris stabulentur, saxatiles dicti sunt, ut merulae turdique
nec minus melanuri.* **8. Fudit,** 'spawned,' Babrius' ἔπτυσ'. **9.
tuis mensis,** 'for your table.' Symm. Ep. i. 14 *In tuis mensis saepe uersa-
tus ... numquam hoc genus piscium deprehendi* in a letter to Ausonius prais-
ing his description of the fish in his Mosella. The plural probably expresses
the general idea of dining; the dinner recurs and the dining-table is
renewed. Or, as A. Palmer suggests on Hor. S. ii. 2. 122, several tables
were used, and hence the plural. **11. Protinus** softens down to a
minimum the interval which must elapse before the young fish can grow
big and fat. 'A moment and I shall have gorged on the waters of the
vasty deep and be returning of my own accord all the fatter to your
rod.' **depastus,** deponent, as in Claud. de Sext. Cons. Honorii 239 *frondes-
que licet depastus amaras.* **caerula.** Canneg. quotes Auson. Epist. iii.
13 *Remipedes* (ducks) *late populantes caerula rostro.* **12. Pinguior.**
Babrius' ἐπὴν δὲ πλησθεὶς φυκίων θαλασσαίων Μέγας γένωμαι. Cf. Fab. Aesop.
231 κἀγὼ τηνικαῦτα πολλὰ φαγὼν πιμελέστερος γενήσομαι. **sponte,** an
exaggeration as absurd as the springing tears of the fish in 3. The word is
used with similar laxity in XII. 6 where the earth turned up by the plough
is said *sponte dedisse.* **recurro,** pres. for future, a use as old as Ennius.
Macrob. S. vi. 1. 15 *Non pol homo quisquam faciet inpune animatus Hoc nisi tu,
nam mi calido das sanguine poenas.* Roby L. Grammar 1461 cites Caesar
B. C. iii. 94 *Tuemini castra et defendite diligenter si quid durius acciderit : ego
relicuas portas circumeo et castrorum praesidia confirmo.* In the Greek Acta S.
Christophori edited by Usener (1886 Bonn) it occurs several times : p. 61 εἰ
δὲ μή, ἡμεῖς ἀπελθόντες λέγομεν τῷ βασιλεῖ ὅτι οὐχ εὕρομεν αὐτόν. p. 64 εἰς τὸ
πρόσωπόν μου βλέπε καὶ μανθάνεις τὸ ἔθνος μου. Δέκιος εἶπεν· "Ακουσόν μου,
'Ρέπρεβε, καὶ θῦσον τοῖς θεοῖς, καὶ γράφω τοῖς πᾶσιν, ἵνα ἱερέα σε κατα-
στήσω. **13. nefas (esse) referens,** 'saying it was a crime.' **14.**
All MSS *casibus* which Fröhner changes to **cassibus.** I follow the
learned editor in holding this to be true; and it is recommended by its
simplicity. Yet Av. *may* mean merely that accidents are variable and
difficult to count upon or manage, 'intractable,' as Seneca speaks Epist.
101. 9 of *uarietas mobilitasque casuum.* Withof paraphrases 'uices uocat
difficiles quod sint periculosae et incertae, quibus difficulter aliquis possit
confidere quarumque exitum nemo sibi facile polliceatur.' Ammianus
Marcellinus xxv. 8. 4 *discrimine per difficiles casus extracti* uses *diff. casus*
to mean 'arduous casualties'; and again xxxi. 15. 7 *reputantes difficiles
Martis euentus.* **15. miserum,** 'a wretched folly': as we say *pitiable.*
Iahn on Pers. iii. 15 '*Miser* de eo qui praua stultitia laborat, ut 66, 107,
v. 65 (?); Graecis τύλας e. g. Arrian diss. iii. 2. 9, 16.' [Sittl compares
IX. 22 and Greek δυστυχής e. g. in Soph. O. C. 800, where however Jebb
explains of Creon's failure to win Oedipus.] **amittere,** 'let go,' 'allow
to escape.' Plaut. Mil. ii. 5. 47 *Manibus amisisti praedam.* **16.
Stultius,** 'yet more foolish.' **rursum,** with **sequi,** 'to pursue again,'
'make a fresh pursuit of.' **futura,** 'in the uncertain future.' Fab.
Aesop. 28 ἀλλ' ἔγωγε εὐηθέστατος ἂν εἴην, εἰ τὸ πάρον κέρδος ἀφεὶς ἄδηλον
ἐλπίδα διώκοιμι.

XXI.

BABR. LXXXVIII.

Κορυδαλλὸς ἦν τις ἐν χλόῃ νεοσσεύων,
[ὁ τῷ χαραδριῷ πρὸς τὸν ὄρθρον ἀντᾴδων]
καὶ παῖδας εἶχε ληίου κόμῃ θρέψας,
λοφῶντας ἤδη καὶ πτεροῖσιν ἀκμαίους.
ὁ δὲ τῆς ἀρούρης δεσπότης ἐποπτεύων
ὡς ξηρὸν εἶδε τὸ θέρος, εἶπε 'νῦν ὥρη
πάντας καλεῖν μοι τοὺς φίλους ἵν' ἀμήσω.'
καί τις δὲ κορυδοῦ τῶν λοφηφόρων παίδων
ἤκουσεν αὐτοῦ τῷ τε πατρὶ μηνύει,
σκοπεῖν κελεύων ποῦ σφέας μεταστήσει.
ὁ δ' εἶπεν 'οὔπω καιρὸς – ⏑ – – –
ὃς γὰρ φίλοις πέποιθεν οὐκ ἄγαν σπεύδει.'
ὡς δ' αὖτις ἦλθεν, ἡλίου δ' ὑπ' ἀκτίνων
ἤδη ῥέοντα τὸν στάχυν θεωρήσας
μισθὸν μὲν ἀμητῆρσιν αὔριον δώσειν
μισθὸν δέ φησι δριγματηφόροις δώσειν,
κορυδαλλὸς εἶπε παισὶ νηπίοις 'ὥρη
νῦν ἐστὶν ὄντως, παῖδες, ἀλλαχοῦ φεύγειν,
ὅτ' αὐτὸς αὐτῷ κοὐ φίλοισι πιστεύει.'

A. Gellius N. A. ii. 29 gives a version of this 'apologue of the Phrygian Aesop' in Latin, the language of which perhaps retains some of the words used by the poet Ennius in his translation into trochaic septenarii, of which Gellius quotes two lines (see below on 14). As it differs considerably from the Babrian version I give it entire from the new edition of Martin Hertz 1883:

Auicula est parua, nomen est cassita. Habitat nidulaturque in segetibus, id ferme temporis, ut appetat messis pullis iam iam plumantibus. Ea cassita in sementibus forte congesserat tempestiuiores : propterea frumentis flauescentibus pulli etiam tunc inuolucres erant. Dum igitur ipsa iret cibum pullis quaesitum, monet eos, ut, si quid ibi rei nouae fieret diceretur ue, animaduerterent idque uti sibi, ubi redisset, nuntiarent. Dominus postea segetum illarum filium adulescentem uocat, et 'uidesne' inquit 'haec ematuruisse et manus iam postulare? idcirco die crastini, ubi primum diluculabit, fac amicos eas et roges, ueniant, operamque mutuam dent et messim hanc nobis adiuuent.' Haec ubi ille dixit, et discessit. Atque ubi redit cassita, pulli tremibundi, trepiduli circumstrepere orareque matrem, ut iam statim properet, inque alium locum sese asportet : 'nam dominus,' inquiunt, 'misit qui amicos roget, uti luce oriente ueniant et metant.' Mater iubet eos otioso animo esse : 'si enim dominus' inquit, 'messim ad amicos reicit[1], crastino seges non metetur, neque necessum est, hodie uti uos auferam.' 'Die' inquit 'postero mater in pabulum uolat. Dominus, quos rogauerat, opperitur. Sol feruit et fit nihil; it dies, et amici nulli eunt. Tum ille rursum ad filium : "amici isti magnam partem" inquit, "cessatores sunt. Quin potius imus et cognatos adfinesque nostros oramus, ut assint cras temperi ad metendum?"' Itidem hoc pulli pauefacti matri nuntiant. Mater hortatur, ut tum quoque sine metu ac sine cura

---

[1] Here we seem to have a relic of the Ennian original—
Crastino seges
Non metetur, neque necessumst hodie uti uos auferam.

sint, cognatos adfinesque nullos ferme tam esse obsequibiles ait, ut ad laborem capessendum nihil cunctentur et statim dicto oboediant : ' uos modo,' inquit, ' aduertite, si modo quid denuo dicetur.' Alia luce orta, auis in pastum profecta est. Cognati et adfines operam, quam dare rogati sunt, supersederunt. Ad postremum igitur dominus filio : ' ualeant,' inquit, ' amici cum propinquis. Afferes primo luci falces duas ; unam egomet mihi et tu tibi capies alteram et frumentum nosmetipsi manibus nostris cras metemus.' Id ubi ex pullis dixisse dominum mater audiuit : ' tempus,' inquit, ' est cedendi et abeundi ; fiet nunc dubio procul quod futurum dixit. In ipso enim iam uertitur cuia res est, non in alio unde petitur.' Atque ita cassita nidum migrauit, seges a domino demessa est.

Crusius (de Babrii aetate p. 204) well observes that the Ennian version is superior to the Babrian in its dramatic grouping into three acts.

There is considerable difference of opinion as to the bird which figures as protagonist in the fable. Babrius makes it a lark[1], and describes its young as crested. Gellius calls it *cassita*, a word seemingly ἅπ. εἰρημ. but identified rightly it would seem with *galerita*, which Pliny, H. N. xi. 121 *In capite paucis animalium nec nisi uolucribus apices ... praeterea paruae aui quae ab illo galerita[2] appellata quondam, postea Gallico uocabulo etiam legioni nomen dedit alaudae,* describes as a crested or tufted lark. The words of Pliny *paruae aui* coincide closely with Avianus' **Paruula ales,** and it might seem that this settled the question. But one of the earliest and most reliable MSS, the Paris C, prefixes to the fable the words DE LVSCINIA ; and Isidorus xii. 7. 37 describes this bird in words which suit Babrius' ὁ τῷ χαραδριῷ πρὸς τὸν ὄρθρον ἀντᾴδων exactly : *Luscinia auis inde nomen sumpsit, quia cantu suo significare solet surgentis exortum diei, quasi lucinia. Eadem et acredula.* Similarly the Balliol Glossary *Acredula luscinia auis modica.* Now this looks as if it might be the word disguised in the MSS as *credula* in 5 ; **acredula** is written *credula* in Reyfferscheid's Brussels MS of the Carmen de Philomela 15 *Vere calente nouos componit acredula cantus, Matutinali tempore rurirulans[3]* ; and if so we may perhaps suppose that in Avianus' time the word *luscinia* or **acredula** was no longer identified with the nightingale (*philomela,* see de Philom. 45), but meant a bird which sang at daybreak and heralded morning.

1. **mandauerat,** ' had consigned.' Ovid Her. v. 215 *Quid harenae semina mandas ?* The word is very common in Claudian. 2. It is not easy to pronounce whether **caespite** is the ground on which the corn-crop rises, or the lower part of the stalk, which, as near the root and close to the ground, would remain green after the upper part, including the ear, was ripe and yellow (**flaua**). In the former case **caespite** would be a local ablative ' rose on the green soil ' ; in the latter an abl. of circumstance ' the yellow corn-crop rose erect with a green root-stem.' The question is not decided by Babrius, for ἐν χλόῃ νεοσσεύων might as easily mean in the green corn, as in the green grass. *Caespes* is perpetually used in Ennodius (A. D. 473-521) of the young blade just risen from the root, as the passages cited in Hartel's Index prove. Dict. viii. p. 448 H. *Nouellum caespitem fotu quo cuncta fructificare soles adtolle.* ix. p. 453 *Disce iam nunc uerborum luxuriem artis falce truncare, ut nouellus caespes sub ferri disciplina proficiat.* xiii. p.

---

[1] The Vatican codex has in 1 χαραδριός and in 2 ὁ τῷ κορυδαλλῷ πρὸς τὸν ὄρθρον ἀντᾴδων ; but erroneously, as not only metre, but the subsequent mention of the lark in 8, 17 show. Besides the χαραδριός was a water-bird. Aristoph. Av. 1141 οἱ χαραδριοὶ καὶ τἄλλα ποτάμι᾽ ὄρνεα.

[2] This must be the *galeritus, quod in capite habet plumam elatam* of Varro L. L. v. 76, cf. Seren. Sammon. 575 *Man.le galeritam uolucrem quam nomine dicunt.*

[3] Cf. our ' ritooralooral.'

466 *Habeat caespes radici obsecundans poma quae tribuat.* Av. himself in XVI. 7 applies the word to the lower extremity of a reed, from which the stalks rise: and so Vergil G. iv. 273. The difficulty is perhaps due to the same straining after antithetic effect which is seen in Merobaudes' *nigro caudentes aethere terras*, of snowy ground under a dark sky (v. 2 of the hexameter fragment on Aetius' victories). **3. fragili culmo**, abl. after **decerpere**, as in Met. v. 536. **5. Sed** as in XXII. 9 introduces a new stage in the narrative. 'But, you must know.' If it has any adversative force, it is in relation to the clause commencing at 7, as if the construction were contracted from *Sed—nam uox turbauit nidos—hos mater uetuit d.* **inplumes nidos**, 'unfledged nestlings.' Verg. G. iv. 512 of a nightingale's nest robbed by a countryman, *fetus, quos durus arator Obseruans nido inplumis detraxit.* As here **nidos**, Vergil Aen. xii. 475 *Pabula parua legens nidisque loquacibus escas.* *credula* MSS is either **acredula**, in which case Av. apostrophises the bird, see my note on Cat. liv. 2 or an epithet agreeing with **uox** possibly *sedula*, which is found in a Brit. Mus. MS (*b*) and would well suit the business-like diligence of the farmer (*sedulus agricola* Plin. H. N. xvii. 101). **6. Suasit et e** is my conj. for *Suaserat et* for which *X* gives *Suaserat e.* The preposition seems absolutely required, though *fugere* is sometimes constructed with the simple abl. See on Cat. xxxvii. 11. **continuare fugam**, 'to take to flight without a moment's delay.' Sen. de Ira ii. 36. 5 *Multi continuauerunt irae furorem*, 'have carried on their anger into madness,' 'passed immediately from anger into madness.' Pacat. Paneg. xxxix *Exercitus spatio lucis unius Illyrico continuauit Aquileiam*, 'marched from Illyricum to Aquileia without stopping.' *continuare accelerare* is a gloss in the Treves MS. **7. Cautior**, 'more wary than her young.' **8.** 'Why, what good will come of strangers' help?' **9. operam mandauit.** Stat. Theb. ix. 168 *Miserum sociis opus et sua mandat Proelia.* x. 81 *Orbibus accingi solitis iubet Irin et omne Maudat opus.* Sen. Controv. xvi. 1 Bursian *Nec satis memineram tale ministerium mihi pater an nouerca mandasset.* Merobaudes Paneg. Actii 98 Nieb. *Non proelia maudet, Sed gerat*, 'not commit to others, but conduct himself,' a good illustration of our fable. **10. inde**, all the safer *in consequence.* See on VII. 18. **12. ueram**, the true hand of the master, not the false hands of the recusant friends. *saeuam*, the reading of *O* and some of Cannegieter's MSS, points I think rather to *seram* than *seruam.* But it is in every way weaker than **ueram**. **13. o miseri**, compassionately, in reference to their enforced migration. **14. de propriis uiribus.** Babr. ὅτ' αὐτὸς αὑτῷ κοὐ φίλοισι πιστεύει. It is remarkable that this fable has no epimythion or moral. Gellius has preserved the Ennian epimythion: *Hoc erit tibi argumentum semper in promptu situm.* *Ne quid exspectes amicos quod tute agere possies.* There was a rustic proverb, *Frons occipitio prior*, 'things go better in the master's presence than behind his back,' Cato R. R. 4, Plin. H. N. xviii. 31.

XXII.

This fable is not in our Babrius nor in any of Halm's prose versions.

1. ambiguas, 'uncertain,' and which he therefore wished to ascertain in advance (**praediscere**) to guide him in answering their prayers. **praediscere**, infin. of purpose after **misit**, 'sent Phoebus to learn.' Common from the earliest Latin to the latest, especially in Plautus, Terence, Lucretius (Roby) and writers that approach the language of common life ; not unfrequent in Augustan and post-Augustan poetry. Plaut. Pseud. ii. 2. 47 *Reddere hoc, non perdere crus me misit.* Curc. i. 3. 50 *Parasitum misi nudius-*

quartus Cariam Petere argentum. Cas. iii. 5. 48 *Ego huc missa sum ludere.*
Ter. Eun. iii. 3. 22 *Misit porro orare.* Prop. ii. 16. 17 *Semper in Oceanum
mittit me quaerere gemmas.* Ovid Her. i. 39 *Te quaerere misso.* Stat. Ach.
i. 209 *Laxantem Aegaeona nexus Missa sequi.* Apul. M. iii. 13 *Quod alterius
rei causa facere missa sum.* Rutil. Namat. i. 210 *Missus Romani discere iura
fori.* Maxim. El. v. 1, 2 *Missus ad Eoas legati munere partes Tranquillum
cunctis nectere pacis opus.* Ennod. C. ii. 109. 11 *Mitteris ad laicum locupletem
poscere parua.* (Heinsius on Ovid Met. v. 660, cf. Hildebrand on Apul. M.
v. 31, Roby L. G. 1116, 1362, W. Wagner on Trin. iv. 3. 8, Sonnenschein
on Most. i. 1. 64, Hartel Index to Ennodius, p. 676).   **3. diuersis,**
'imploring the gods' help for opposite vows.' **uotis** is better explained
as dative if **numina**, the reading of the best MSS, is kept.   It seems doubtful whether *poscere numen* can mean 'to beseech a god,' though Conington
on Aen. i. 666 *Ad te confugio et supplex tua numina posco* appears to favour
that view.   Even in so late a poet as Claudian, Rapt. Pros. i. 66 *Posce Iouem,
dabitur coniunx,* a second accusative of the thing asked for is easily supplied
from the accompanying clause *dabitur coniunx.*   Two of my Bodleian MSS
have *munera* which is certainly easier, and may be right, as *numen munus*
are constantly confused.   **4. liuidus,** 'jealous,' for *inuidus* of MSS
is Withof's excellent conj. accepted by Lachm.   Mamertinus Paneg.
Iuliani xv *Si quis hoc liuidus iactitat, ipso tempore refutatur.* Seren. Samm.
1054 *Vel quicumque tuo carpetur liuidus auctu.*   **5.** If *His quoque se* is
read, *quoque* merely carries on the story as in XVIII. 5, 'And so to
them.'   I have preferred to follow the S. Gallen fragm. **His sese.   medium,** as mediator.   Verg. Aen. vii. 536 *Dum paci medium se offert*
(Optulit).   **6.** I have followed the suggestion of my Bodleian *X,*
which has *precibus confiteretur* written by the first hand, with the reading
of the other MSS *ut peteretur* superscribed.   If I mistake not, I have
cleared up the difficulty by my conj. **precibus cum peteretur, ait, Praestant di facilis,** 'when he was assailed by their prayers, replied, The gods
are kind and grant fulfilment.'   Lachmann's *et 'precibus Iuppiter aecus' ait
'Praestandi facilis'* though at first sight brilliant, does not seem to me right.
It is not in Av.'s manner to accumulate two adjectives both predicates
without a verb expressed: and *Praestandi facilis* is a construction more in the
style of Prudentius.   **7. Praestant.**   Ovid F. iv. 149 *Vt tegat hoc celet-
que uiros Fortuna uirilis Praestat et hoc paruo ture rogata facit.*   **quae
namque** seems preferable to *nam quaeque,* although the use of *quisque* for
quicumque in writers of this period and in the Digest is indubitable (Dräger
i. 84).   Even Symmachus has it Ep. i. 58 *quisque bonae frugis est = quicumque,* and cf. Wölfflin *Gemination im Lateinischen* p. 450.   **8. congeminata,** 'doubled,' or rather 'dupled.'   Apul. de Dogm. Plat. ix *Substantiam
mentis huius numeris et modis confici congeminatis ac multiplicatis.*   **9.
longa,** 'far-reaching.'   Somewhat similar is Catullus' *longa poena* xl.
8.   **iecur,** which Horace makes the seat of lust, is here the seat of
cupidity.   Cannegieter aptly quotes Claud. de iv Cons. Honorii 248 *At sibi
cuncta petens, nil conlatura Cupido, In iecur et tractus imos conpulsa reces-
sit.*   **nequeat** MSS, justifiably, as **cupido** suggests the subject *cupidus.*
'But since far-reaching greed cannot be contented, he (i. e. the covetous
man) put off his vow.'   **10. Distulit,** 'Put off (realizing) the prayer
which, when addressed to the gods, brought only new loss,' i. e. which
ultimately involved the loss of both his eyes.   Lachmann's *dona* is
simpler and very probable; *in noua dona* would mean the additional
bounty which the gods would have to pay to the second petitioner,
viz. twice as much as the first had received.   **admotas preces,** always
in the sense of *addressing* a prayer.   Ovid Met. vi. 689 *Admouique
preces quarum me dedecet usus?*   Pont. iii. 7. 36 *Quas admorint non ualuisse
preces* (quoted by Schenkl).   Curt. v. 10. 14 *Preces deinde suppliciter admotae*

Dareum . . . flere coegerunt. noua, of which he had no experience before. The word is in opposition to the expected *gain.* 11. 'Not doubting that his hopes would rise by what the other wished.' confi- dens, followed by pres. infin. as in Caesar B. G. ii. 30 *Quibusnam manibus tanti oneris turrim in muro sese collccare confiderent?* which is nearly the same as B. C. ii. 31 *Qua fiducia et opere et natura loci munitissima castra expugnari posse confidimus?* So *fretus* in the hexameters inscribed on the basis of the Obelisk dug up in the Circus Maximus and erected by Pope Sixtus V in front of the Lateran Basilica, v. 10 in Castalio's edition (Var. Lect. p. 44, ed. Rom. 1594) AT. DOMINVS. MVNDI. CONSTANTIVS. OMNIA. FRETVS. CEDERE. VIRTVTI. 13. Ille, 'the other,' the *inuidus.* cap- tantem, 'grasping' at the reward that was meant for himself: for the jealous man would in the natural course of things get twice the amount of the covetous man's desire. He was *bidding for* something he could not be sure of. 14. Supplicium, 'to be mulcted in his own body.' ouans, 'triumphant' in the opportunity of turning the tables on the other, and making him *lose* twice as much as himself. 15. 'He asked to live with one eye put out, on condition the other should double the punishment and lose both.' extinctus lumine uno, a variation on the ordinary construction, *lumen extinctum* which Ovid has Met. i. 721 of an eye put out. sic for *ut* of MSS seems to satisfy metre and give more point to v. 16. Orientius i. 311 *Sic miseros uindex semper populabitur ignis, Vt sem- per seruet pabula laeta sibi.* degeret is perhaps an error for *degat ut,* though there is something harsh in the sound of the repeated ut in the next v. In a writer so late as Av. a change from historic present (petit) to imperf. and then back again to present is not very surprising. Even Pro- pertius v. 5. 11, 12 has *Quippe et Collinas ad fossam mouerit herbas, Stan- tia currenti diluereutur aqua.* 16. hoc, 'this amount,' viz. of one eye. 17. sapiens, 'taught wisdom' (Canneg.). 18. Inuidiae malum, 'the curse of jealousy,' i. e. what an accursed thing jealousy was. So Claudian Epig. 40 *Esuriens pauper telis incendor amoris Inter utrumque malum deligo pauperiem,* 'the curse of Poverty, the curse of Love.' Fab. Perottin. ix. 11 *Fassa est naturae malum,* the hen's irresistible tendency to scratch up earth. The opposite *bonum* 'blessing' in Symm. Ep. i. 59 *Amicitiae bonum.* ipse, 'himself' announced, as he had himself wit- nessed. 19. prouentis iniquis. Non. 521 *Prouentum etiam malarum rerum dici ueteres uoluerunt.* Lucilius lib. xxvi dein (l. deinde) *quae adeo male me accipiunt decimae et proueniunt male.* The masc. *prouentus* is com- mon, especially in such combinations as *prosperiorem prouentum, lucrosum prosperumque prouentum* (Apul. xi. 20, iv. 27, see Hildebrand on x. 26) : the neuter *prouentum* is rather rare. Here iniquis determines the character of prouentis, 'luckless issues ' = 'miscarriages,' 'disappointments.' 20. ' In its exultation is unhappy enough to long for its own harm.'

XXIII.

BABR. XXX.

Γλύψας ἐπώλει λυγδινόν τις Ἑρμείην.
τὸν δ' ἠγόραζον ἄνδρες, ὃς μὲν εἰς στήλην
(υἱὸς γὰρ αὐτῷ προσφάτως ἐτεθνήκει).
ὁ δὲ χειροτέχνης ὡς θεὸν καθιδρύσων.
ἦν δ' ὀψέ, χὠ λιθουργὸς οὐκ ἐπεπράκει,
συνθέμενος αὐτοῖς εἰς τὸν ὄρθρον αὖ δείξειν
ἐλθοῦσιν. ὁ δὲ λιθουργὸς εἶδεν ὑπνώσας
αὐτὸν τὸν Ἑρμῆν ἐν πύλαις ὀνειρείαις
' εἶεν ' λέγοντα ' τἀμὰ νῦν ταλαντεύῃ·
ἐν γάρ με, νεκρὸν ἢ θεόν, σὺ ποιήσεις.'

This fable forms a curious contrast to the proverb *Non ex omni ligno debet Mercurius exsculpi* Apul. de Magia xliii; perhaps, pointing to a time when the worship of images was in growing disrepute, as indeed it was forbidden by Christianity.

There is no prose version of this fable; but the last verse of it recurs in another and less known fable 55 Halm. There a man wishing to test the Delphian oracle hides a young sparrow in his robe and asks 'is the thing I have in my hands alive or dead'? intending to kill the sparrow, if the oracle answered 'alive,' and expose it to view, if the answer were 'dead.' Then the god, detecting his malicious purpose, replies: 'Have done. It is for yourself to determine whether the thing is living or dead' (ἐν σοὶ γὰρ ἔστι, τοῦτο ὃ ἔχεις ἢ νεκρὸν εἶναι ἢ ἔμψυχον).

This is, I think, the most difficult of the Avianianian collection, if indeed it is by Avianus. It is also one of the least finished in point of diction, e.g. 2 **fecerat expositum esse**, 3, 4 the awkward interlacing of clauses, 6–10 the extreme obscurity of the language, which induced Lachmann to doubt the genuineness of 8, 9, and led Bährens to one of his most infelicitous attempts at restoration: lastly, the difficulty of connecting the epimythion 13, 14 with the fable.

1. **referens,** all MSS rightly, whether the word means 'representing,' 'modelling,' a sense of which I have found no exact example, for *referre uultum, ora, parentem* etc., are only approximately similar, or, as is more likely, 'conveying from the marble-block the new form of a Bacchus,' 'converting a marble-block into a handsome Bacchus.' The idea of change which is here assigned to *referre* seems to exist elsewhere e. g. Pacat. Paneg. xxix *Cum damnatorum frena tractassent, pollutas pœnali manus contactu ad sacra referebant,* i. e. transferred.   2. 'Had put up the god for sale.' A most awkward circumlocution for *exposuerat.* Cic. de Off. iii. 12. 51 *Aduexi exposui uendo meum non pluris quam ceteri.* Mart. ix. 59. 8 *Expositumique alte pingue poposcit ebur.* **Expositum fecerat esse,** i. e. *fecerat expositum esse. Facio,* followed by the *present* infin. is shown by Dräger ii. p. 393 to be common in late Latin, but he quotes no instance of the *perfect.* Thielmann however (Archiv für Latein. Lexicographie iii. p. 178) shows that the perfect infin. after *facere* is found, though much more rarely, in good writers. Verg. Aen. viii. 630 *Fecerat... Procubuisse lupam.* Ovid Met. vi. 75 *Fecit... stare... ferire... exiluisse.* xiii. 69 *Facit... dare... cecidisse ... ferri... cremari... exire... ducere.*   3. **Nobilis.** Such men would be likely to have elaborate funeral monuments (Canneg.).   **funesta in sede** with compositurus erat. The tomb is called *sedes* as the place where the body rests. Hence in inscriptions it is commonly i. q. *sepulchrum.* Auson. Prof. xii. 6 Schenkl *Esto placidus et quietis manibus sedem foue.* xxvii. 11 *Sedem sepulchri seruat innotus cinis.* Epitaph. Heroum xxiv. 1 *Hic Priami non est tumulus, nec condor in illa Sede.* (Hildebrand on Apul. M. iv. 18.)   4. **Mercari cupiens** is not only out of its place, but awkward in itself as an expression. The writer, perhaps *not* Avianus, meant *mercari uoluit ut componeret in s. sepulchri,* which would otherwise be *mercari uoluit compositurus.* The form of the fut. participle seems to have suggested **erat** and the change to **Mercari cupiens** followed. The declining sense of Latin syntax is particularly perceptible in the use of the pres. participle. Thus in 1 *referens = qui rettulerat.*   **compositurus,** 'intended to arrange.'   5. The sentence is loosely attached to v. 4. Formally ut seems determined by **compositurus,** but the meaning is not so much that the man intended to arrange the statue with a view of making an offering of it to some temple, as that he wished to purchase it with that purpose.   **adoratis,** most MSS, perhaps rightly. Verg. Aen. iii. 84 *Templa dei saxo uenerabar structa uetusto.* Inscript. ap. Muratori iii. p. 1638, quoted by van Goens de Cepotaphiis

p. 107 QVOD. CREDIS. TEMPLVM. QVOD. FORTE. VIATOR. ADORAS. POMPTIL-
LAE. CINERES. OSSAQVE. PARVA. TEGIT. Rutilius Namatianus, addressing
Rome, says, i. 50 *Non procul a caelo per tua templa sumus.* Apul. de Magia
lvi *Si fanum aliquod praetereat, nefas habet adorandi gratia manum labris
admouere.* numina, of a single god, as in Verg. Aen. i. 666. See Dräger i.
p. 7. [My conj. *Alter ut auratis inferret* might be defended by Ovid's
words F. i. 77 *Flamma uitore suo templorum uerberat aurum.*] 6.
He had made a vow to place an image in a temple. Redderet, correlative to debita, 'pay the debt of a vow.' 7. ait, the statue. 'It is for
you now to make a two-fold forecast of the future of your wares, when
two unequal offers put a price upon your gift; and to forecast, it may
be, consigning me to the dead, it may be, if you prefer, to the gods;
perhaps converting me into an ornament on a tomb, perhaps into a
divinity.' omen, if the fable has come down to us entire here = 'forecast,'
i. e. little beyond a mere balancing of two possibilities still equally uncertain. Possibly a sense somewhat like this is to be found in And. i. 2. 29
Ea lege atque omine, 'on these terms and with this forecast of the future.'
But the Babrian version makes it probable that one or perhaps more
distichs have been lost, in which the god appeared in a dream to the maker
of the statue, and then spoke vv. 7–12. The St. Gallen Glossary recently
edited by Prof. M. Warren, has *omen quod homo somniatur, aus-
picium, auguria maiora.* Then Nunc instead of referring to Cum spes,
etc., will mean 'after my thus appearing to you in a dream.' 8.
spes, here of opposite 'bids.' dispar with spes rather than with
pretium. 9. Et MSS. The construction is *facies omen de mercibus
et (seu) malis me defunctis seu diuis tradere.* From seu malis another
seu is to be supplied to the former clause. A second, but harsher, possibility would be to supply *trades* out of seu malis tradere. 10. seu
uelis is too favorite a commonplace to be changed arbitrarily into *seu
posuisse* (Withof), or *siue locasse* (Fröhner). Veget. i. 4 *Siue equitem siue
peditem sagittarium uelis imbuere siue scutatum.* 11. sacri for *facti*
(*fati*) of MSS seems more probable than *Bacchi,* which is found in the
Paraphrast. Indeed one of the earliest MSS, Fröhner's *P,* has *sati,* and
the change of *f* and *s* is one of the commonest. Moreover the Treves MS
glosses the words *magni reuerentia fati* by *honor diuini cultus.* By sacri I
understand a religious observance, here the cultus of Bacchus 'in your
disposal lies the respect paid to a solemn act of religion.' Bährens' *fani*
hardly accounts for the variants *facti fati sati.* 12 eadem. The
synizesis of *ea, eo, eas, eos,* in the cases of *idem* is proved by Ramsay (Latin
Prosody p. 122) for Lucretius, Vergil, Propertius, but it does not seem to
occur in Ausonius, Claudian, or Prudentius. funera nostra, 'my death-
warrant'; to consign me to a tomb. The erection of statues is constantly
mentioned in Inscriptions in connexion with sepulchral monuments. C.I.L.
iv. 1130 *Locum sepulturae statuam ponendam.* 1286 *Locum sepulturae impen-
sam funeris clupeum statuam pedestrem.* Av. is very far from the happy con-
ciseness of his original ἐν γάρ με, νεκρὸν ἢ θεόν, σὺ ποιήσεις. 13, 14.
This epimythion is quite on a par in its obscurity with the rest of the fable.
The best MSS agree in praestare, not *prodesse,* and as the fable turns on
the doubts of a seller, it seems probable that the word is used in its technical meaning of securing a buyer against loss. Cic. de Off. iii. 16. 65 *Ac
de iure quidem praediorum sanctum apud nos est iure ciuili, ut in iis uendendis
uitia dicerentur, quae nota essent uenditori. Nam cum ex duodecim tabulis satis
esset ea praestari* ('should be made good,' i. e. the buyer should be secured
against loss, Holden *ad loc.*) *quae essent lingua nuncupata, quae qui infitiatus
esset, dupli poenam subiret, a iuris consultis etiam reticentiae poena est constituta.
Quidquid enim esset in praedio uitii, id statuerunt, si uenditor sciret, nisi nomina-
tim dictum esset, praestari oportere.* Cf. Roby on Justinian p. 156, where the

legal uses of *praestare* are classified. If this is the sense of **praestare**, it fixes that of **nocuisse**, to be injuring a buyer by selling something without mentioning its defects or the liabilities which make it less valuable. The point of the fable, on this view, lies in the absolute control which the seller has over the thing sold: he can make a god of his article or condemn it to the service of the tomb at pleasure. The moral of which is that vendors would do well to utilize their opportunity and turn their goods to the best advantage. Yet it is also possible that the writer of the distich may mean ‘I address this fable to those who have it in their power to be generous or to injure indifferently. Let them weigh well beforehand which they intend to do, and what will come of either line.’ This is simpler; but **praestare**, though frequently used of giving a bounty (Mart. v. 52. 1 *Quae mihi praestiteris memini, semperque tenebo*, 3 *tua dona*, 7 *quamuis ingentia dona*) is in that meaning almost necessarily followed by an accusative expressed or implied.   **14. An ... seu.** Auson. Epitaph. 31. 5 Schenkl *Nec quisquam Marius seu Marcius anne Metellus Hic iaceat, certis nouerit indiciis.* **nocuisse** after *uelit* is quite regular. Dräger, who reviews the instances i. 230, 231, says no case of this so-called aoristic infin. is found in Cicero, Caesar, Sallust, Tacitus. The combination of it with the *present* infin. (**praestare**) is probably due, partly to metre, partly to the fact that in the legal sense found in this passage *praesto*, *praestare* not *praestiti*, *praestitisse* is the almost invariable form.

XXIV.

Fab. Aesop. 63, 63^b Halm, 148 Kn.

FAB. AESOP. HALM 63.

Ποτὲ συνώδευσε λέων ἀνθρώπῳ. Ἐκαυχῶντο οὖν πρὸς ἀλλήλους τοῖς λόγοις. Εὗρον δὲ ἐν τῇ ὁδῷ πετρίνην στήλην ὁμοίαν ἀνδρί, ἑτέραν στήλην λέοντος συμπνίγουσαν. Καὶ ὁ ἄνθρωπος ὑποδείξας πρὸς αὐτήν, ταῦτα ἔφη· "Ἴδε πῶς ἐσμεν κρείττονες ὑμῶν πάντων, καὶ ῥωμαλέοι ὑπερ ἅπαν θηρίον.’ Ὑπολαβὼν δὲ ὁ λέων ἔφη· ‘Ὑφ’ ὑμῶν εἰσιν οὕτω ταῦτα γινόμενα καὶ πραττόμενα· εἰ γὰρ ᾔδεσαν λέοντες γλύφειν λίθους, πολλοὺς ἂν εἶδες ὑποκάτω λεόντων.’

Ὁ μῦθος δηλοῖ ὅτι πολλοὶ καυχώμενοι πειρῶνται ἐν λόγοις ἑαυτοὺς ἐπιφημίζειν, καίπερ μὴ ὄντες τοιοῦτοι.

2. nobilis with **Venator,** ‘a huntsman of fame,’ who might fairly contend with a lion of the finest breed. Cannegieter’s lengthy citation of passages showing that the lion is often called *noble* or *generous* (XXXVII. 14 *nobile murmur*, Plin. H. N. viii. 50 *Illa nobilior animi significatio*, Ovid Trist. iii. 5. 33–6, Mart. i. 48. 4, Claud. de Mallii Consul. 305, to which add Plin. viii. 48 *Animalis omnium generosissimi.* 50 *Generositas in periculis maxime deprehenditur*), cannot outweigh the counter-arguments of metre and Avianian usage. In the eleven instances where Av. uses atque there is not one in which it stands second word in the sentence; it invariably *begins* the sentence or clause to which it belongs; in nine of the eleven instances is the first word of a pentameter. The rhythm is equally decisive in joining **nobilis** with the first half of the line, not the last.   **3. perpetuum,** ‘lasting,’ as the quarrel was of long-standing.   **4. continuo fronte,** for *continuo forte* of MSS seems justified as an archaism by the passages cited in Gell. xv. 9 from the comic writer Caecilius and M. Cato, in Festus p. 286 M. from Cato, in Nonius 204 from Titinius Pacuvius Cato Caecilius; as a technical word Forcellini quotes Vitruv. x. 17. 7 *Quod autem est ad axona quod appellatur frons transuersarius.* Here it would be specially appropriate, as the continuous frontage of the tomb would give room for a sculptured group of some size. Auson. Parent. 2. 12 *Frontibus hoc scrip-*

tis et monumenta iubent. Epitaph. 21. 3, 4 *Nec satis est titulum saxo incidisse sepulchri. Insuper et frontem mole onerant statuae.* Schenkl defends the MS reading, translating 'they came on the instant to a high tomb.' But the juxtaposition *continuo forte* is very weak, and the sense given to *continuo* not supported by Av.'s use of the word elsewhere. **sepulchra,** here of a single monument. Catull. lxiv. 368 *Alta Polyxenia madefient caede sepulchra.* **5. docta manus,** 'an artist hand.' Stat. S. iii. 3. 200 *Te lucida saxa, Te similem doctae referet mihi linea cerae : Nunc ebur et fuluum uultus imitabitur aurum.* **flectentem colla,** 'bowing or drooping his neck submissively,' here used of the vanquished beast. So *flectere poplitem,* of a kneeler, Pacat. Paneg. xlii. More usually *flectere colla (equi)* is said of a rider managing his horse with bit or rein. Verg. Aen. i. 156, Ovid Pont. ii. 9. 58. **6. Fecerat ... procubuisse** from Vergil. Aen. viii. 630 *Fecerat et uiridi fetam Mauortis in antro Procubuisse lupam,* 'had represented lying prostrate.' **7, 8.** MSS give *Scilicet affirmans (infirmans B) pictura teste superbum Se fieri ?* Two readings seem to be suggested by this, according as *affirmans* or *infirmans* is adopted. (1) **Scilicet affirmas pictura teste superbum Te fieri ?** 'Can you really assert, when there is a picture to give evidence, that you have a right to be elated ? Why, it shows the lion dead.' (2) *S. infirmas p.t. s. Defieri ?* 'I suppose, you deny, when there is a painting to prove it, that pride (lit. the proud one) may fail ' ? **Scilicet** is, I think, to be retained at all risks, as introducing with no need of further preliminaries an ironical question. *affirmans* MSS for **affirmas** reverses the more usual substitution of *-as -es* for *-ans -ens.* If *infirmas* is read, cf. Rosc. Com. xv. 45 *testis fidem infirmare* which agrees very well with **pictura teste.** But there is some harshness in constructing *infirmare* with an infinitive. **superbum.** Lachm.'s conj. *supernum* is possible, though not a very good word in the sense required. **8.** If *Defieri* is read, De Vit's Forcellini will supply parallels, e. g. Gell. xx. 8. 4 *Eadem autem ipsa, quae crescente luna gliscunt, deficiente contra luna defiunt* (of oysters losing flesh). **nam** I consider to be part of the hunter's speech. It might also be explained (less well) as a parenthetical remark by the poet. **9. Ille,** 'the lion.' **graues,** probably 'downcast,' from shame. Thus Statius S. ii. 5. 14, 15 speaking of lions ashamed by the defeat of Domitian's *leo mansuetus* in the Amphitheatre says *Tunc cunctis cecidere iubae, puduitque relatum Aspicere et totas duxere in lumina frontes.* The words *graues oculi* are found elsewhere in various senses (1) of eyes heavy with sleep, Prop. ii. 29. 16, Val. Fl. iv. 18 ; (2) heavy with the approach of death, sinking, Verg. Aen. iv. 688 *Illa graues oculos conata attollere.* Stat. Theb. i. 546 *graues oculos languentiaque ora* of the cut off head of Medusa, and again v. 502 of a tired child falling asleep : xi. 558 *Cerno graues oculos atque ora natantia leto* ; (3) with the heavy look of debauchery Cic. Cum Senatui Grat. Egit vi. 13 ; (4) seemingly = 'serious,' though the passage is disputed, Apul. vi. 15 *Nec Prouidentiae bonae graues oculos innocentis animae latuit aerumna.* In the passage of Av. **graues** seems to be partly determined by **retorquens ;** the eyes are turned heavily earthwards and only lifted from their position by an effort to the pictured counterfeit on the tomb. The Bodl. Paraphrase strangely has κἀκεῖνος (the lion) εἶπεν ὑπομειδιάσας. **inania** gives a slight notion of contempt for the unreality of the presentation, Ovid M. iii. 668 *Quem circa tigres simulacraque inania lyncum Pictarumque iacent fera corpora pantherarum.* **retorquens.** Claud. Rapt. Pros. i. 191 *quoties oculos ad tecta retorsit.* **11.** From Vergil Aen. i. 136 *Tantane uos generis tenuit fiducia uestri ?* which same passage, as Castalio long ago remarked (Var. Lect. p. 75, ed. 1594) has been twice imitated by Claudian, Bell. Gild. 330, B. Get. 122. **generis uestri** 'of your *human* origin' : **uestri** of course includes mankind in general. 'Your origin as man.' **12. si cupis,** see on VII. 16, and cf. the use of *pugnare* with an infin. in Cic.

Acad. ii. 21. 68 where see Reid. **13. caperet,** 'admitted of,' 'were
equal to.' So Cannegieter, quoting Claud. Laud. Stil. iii. 132 *Cuius nec
spatium uisus, nec corda decorem, Nec laudem uox ulla capit.* **sollertia,**
'ingenuity,' 'natural cleverness.' Ian's Index to Pliny's N. H. shows that
the word is constantly used by Pliny of the instinctive dexterity with which
animals avoid danger, secure their food, etc.: *dogs* viii. 147, *dog-fishes* ix.
153, *she-goats* viii. 201, *apes* viii. 215, *foxes* viii. 103, *crocodiles* xi. 226, *birds*
x. 92, *shell-fish* ix. 111. **14. Sculperet** MSS generally, and so I
think Av. wrote, comparing Prudentius c. Symm. ii. 779 *Exta litant sculptis qui tabida saxis* where a Saxon MS in the Bodl. Auct. F. 3. 6 has
sculptis, MS Trin. xii. m. pr. *scultis.* **docili pollice** is like Claudian's
pollice docto Prob. et Olyb. Cons. 177 used of a clever embroideress. **15,
16.** A Greek construction in Latin comparable with Babrius' constructions
in Greek. (Rutherford p. xii.) 'Then you would see how the man, stifled
by a deep growl, closed his day of doom in ravening jaws.' **15.
oppressum murmure magno** MSS oddly but intelligibly. Lachmann's
expressum marmore magno is clever, and that is as much as can be said for
it. It is very doubtful whether *magnum marmor* would have been used by
Av. = 'a great block of marble.' **16. Condere fata,** which Vergil Aen.
x. 35 and Lucan vii. 131 use for *framing* a destiny, here = 'to *close* a destiny.'

XXV.

This fable is not in Babrius nor in any of the prose versions. But the associa-
tion of the well and the boy who loses something in it, is also found in the Greek
Joe Miller Philogelos 33 Eberhard.

'A boy sat crying at the edge of the water in a well, drawing his mouth
wide asunder as he blubbered helplessly. A knave of a thief seeing him with
the tears standing in his eyes asked "What was the reason he was in the
dumps *now*"? The child makes up a story how his rope had broken and
parted in two pieces, complaining withal that a crock of gold had leapt
down the well. Without more ado, the thief's hand tugged at the robe
that got in his way; a moment and he is stript and on his way to the well's
bottom. Our little fellow, drawing the thief's mantle round his own small
throat, plunged, they say, into the brambles, and lay lurking there. The
other seeing how his purpose had betrayed him and only brought him face
to face with danger, no sooner took his seat on the ground a saddened
and discoated man, than with imploring groans to the high gods he gave
vent to his sad experience, they say, in these indignant words: "From
this time forward, if anyone is fool enough to fancy a jar can swim on
flowing water, let him be sure, whoever he may be, that he has no right
to complain if he finds his coat is gone."'

1. ad undam (for which some MSS give *ad oram*) implies that the
water came sufficiently far up the well for the boy to be described as sitting
by its edge. **2. Vana** seems a mere expansion of **superuacuis,**
though from XXXVIII. 7, XL. 8 it might also be explained as 'hypo-
critical.' The boy is described throughout as sly. *Vara,* the conj. of
Guiet, would more properly be said of the *legs* than the mouth. But Av.
here imitates Juvenal xiii. 137, xvi. 41 *Vana superuacui dicunt chiro-
grapha ligni.* **rictibus,** open-mouthed and demonstrative blubbering is
meant. **4. modo,** of something which has just happened and is still
fresh. Ter. Hec. iii. 5. 8 *Aduenis modo?* **5, 6.** The MSS (except *C*
which has *Ac*) give **Atque** in 6, thereby introducing another anacoluthic
construction like XVI. 12 *respondens canna Seque docet,* perhaps like XVII.
13 *gemens fractoque loqui uix murmure coepit.* In the present instance **Atque,**

which is specially used by Plautus *in apodosi* = 'on the instant,' e. g.
Bacch. ii. 3. 44 *Forte ut adsedi in stega Dum circumspecto me atque ego lem-*
bum conspicor, Most. v. 1. 9 *Quom eum connoeaui, atque illi se ex senatu segre-*
gant (Dräger ii. 57, Sonnenschein on Most. l. c.) makes the unlogical
character of the construction less marked and glaring. I have therefore
retained **Atque,** but with hesitation, as Fröhner's *Hac* is not only an easy,
but a highly probable, solution of the difficulty, and the weight of *C* as
evidence on a question of readings is very great.   **discrimina,** 'the
parting asunder.'   So Gratius Cyn. 486 *Medio in discrimine luci* where the
forest parts off, Columella vi. 15. 2 *Discrimen ipsum quo diuisa est bouis*
ungula, Ovid A. A. ii. 302 *discrimina lauda,* partings in the hair.   **6.**
dilituisse, a variant found in *B* 'had disappeared,' ἀφανισθῆναι, is noticeable.   **7. sollicitam,** if not as in the translation, must mean the resistance which the mantle made in being pulled off. So I interpret Mart. xii. 60.
9 *Turbida sollicito transmittere Caecuba sacco,* of a strainer, through which
the wine passes slowly and with resistance.   **improba,** either 'greedy,'
'bent on lucre,' here the crock of gold: or 'thievish,' Guiet, nearly =
'furis.'   **uestem** has the respectable support of *BX,* and seems absolutely required by the sense.   *mentem ACP,* and Schenkl defends this ' die
freche (an das Stehlen gewöhnte) Hand riss den versaglichen, argwöhnis-
chen Sinn mit sich fort.'   But **traxit** can scarcely mean this.   The sense
is obviously as I have expressed it in my translation.   **8. ima petit,** a
Macrobian expression.   S. vii. 8. 11 *Frigus ima petens uitium radicibus inual-*
uitur.   vii. 11. 4 *Natura imum petendo penetrat sanguinem.*   **9. Paruu-**
lus, 'the boy.'   So *paruolae* several times in Fronto = 'little girls,' v. 19,
35 ed. Naber.   **11. fallaci.** Inscript. Orell. 4845, 4846 *Decipimur*
uotis.   **uoto** I explain of the thief's engaging to recover the lost crock,
which *uotum* is *fallax* as betraying him into the danger (1) of drowning,
(2) of losing his clothes.   To this I think **suscepta** points: for the word
is obviously chosen with a double significance, the *actual,* of encountering
danger (**suscepta pericula**), the *suggested,* of taking on oneself a vow
(*suscipere uota* technical in the best Latin e. g. Prop. ii. 9. 25, cf. Mamertin.
Paneg. Maximiani vi *Et uota suscipere et soluta reddere,* Eumen. Paneg. Con-
stantii v *uota suscipio*).   Otherwise **fallaci** uoto might naturally be explained
of the *boy's* wish to recover the crock: and so Guiet.   **suscepta pericula,**
like *tantum laboris uigiliarumque suscipere* Mamert. Grat. Act. xx, *geminatum*
itineris laborem susceperas Incerti Paneg. Constantin. xxi Bährens.   **13.**
sollers is explained by Cannegieter as 'taught wisdom.'   He quotes Avienus
Aratea 673 *Tum quoque si piceam spectaris surgere noctem, Informem taetris*
tellurem ut uestiat alis, Litus ama, sollers fuge caerula tegmina noctis, where
however Breysig's best MS *V* gives *fuge sollers.*   But the connexion of *sollers*
with dexterity in thieving (Ovid Met. iv. 776 *Id se sollerti furtim, dum*
traditur, astu Supposita cepisse manu) makes it possible that Av. has used
the word here as little more than a variant for *fur,* 'the shrewd
knave.'   **uocem rupisse,** Vergilian.   Aen. ii. 129 *Composito rumpit uocem.*
iii. 246 *Celaeno Infelix uates, rumpitque hanc pectore uocem.*   xi. 377 *Exarsit*
dictis uiolentia Turni Dat gemitum, rumpitque has imo pectore uoces.   Servius
on Aen. iii. 246 *Rumpit uocem cum indignatione loquitur.*   **15. bene**
with **Perdita,** as we might say 'well lost,' meaning that there is nothing
surprising or unreasonable in the loss.   It is hardly likely that bene can
here = 'cheaply' as in *bene emere,* though the sense would well suit, as the
descent into the well might have cost the man his life.

XXVI.

This fable is not found in our Babrius, but it exists in a slightly altered form in several prose versions. The lion in these has become a wolf.

FAB. AESOP. HALM 270.

Λύκος θεασάμενος αἶγα ἐπί τινος κρημνοῦ νεμομένην, ἐπειδὴ οὐκ ἠδύνατο αὐτῆς ἐφικέσθαι, παρῄνει αὐτῇ κατωτέρω καταβῆναι, μὴ καὶ πέσῃ λαθοῦσα, λέγων, ὡς καὶ λειμῶνές εἰσι παρ' αὐτῷ, καὶ ἡ πόα φαιδροτέρα. Ἡ δὲ πρὸς αὐτὸν ἔφη ''Ἀλλ' οὐκ ἐμὲ ἐπὶ νομὴν καλεῖς, αὐτὸς δὲ τροφῆς ἀπορεῖς.'

Οὕτω καὶ τῶν ἀνθρώπων οἱ πονηροί, ὅταν παρὰ τοῖς εἰδόσι πονηρεύωνται, ἀνόνητοι τῶν τεχνασμάτων γίνονται.

The valuable Latin Glossary 4626 in Sir Thomas Phillipps' library at Cheltenham contains an extract from Avianus' version of this fable. *Citisus est herba de qua Auianus florentem citisum carpe.*

2. **Comminus**, 'near,' 'close at hand,' as in Mamert. Genethl. Maxim. xii *Ad intuendum comminus quantum potuit accessit.* This use which Hand Tursellin. ii. p. 97 dates from the Augustan era, but which Servius more generally ascribes to the *ueteres* on Geor. i. 104 *Veteres enim non in tempore sed in loco comminus ponebant*, a passage which seems to justify the retention of the word in Catull. lxiv. 109. 3. From Vergil Aen. i. 321 *Ac prior, heus, inquit, iuuenes* ('Ha! my men,' Mackail) *monstrate*, where Servius notes *Heus nunc aduerbium uocantis est.* **prior**, 'first,' before he was accosted by the she-goat. **ardua** with **praeruptis saxis**, 'the ground steep with precipitous crags.' 4. **hirsutis**, 'the prickly slopes,' mainly in reference to the briars and hairy shrubs with which they bristle. Propertius has *hirsuti rubi* (iv. 4. 28), Vergil *hirsuti uepres, hirsutae frondes* (G. iii. 444, 231), Calpurnius *hirsuta genista* (i. 5). 5. **cytisi**. Keightley (Flora Vergiliana pp. 381, 2) states that this is the arborescent lucerne, a view first put forward by a Candian physician, Vicentini, and now generally followed. It has a yellow flower of which bees are fond, and cows as well as goats eat its leaves with avidity. In the Αἶγες of Eupolis a chorus of she-goats enumerating the various shrubs on which they feed mention cytisus, a kind of willow named πρόμαλος, and thyme (Eupol. Αἶγες fr. 14 Kock): and Theocritus x. 31 'Ἁ αἲξ τὸν κύτισον, ὁ λύκος τὰν αἶγα διώκει seems to imply that the goats' fondness for cytisus was proverbial. Cf. Hehn Kulturpflanzen p. 299 ed. 1870. 6. **glaucas salices** from Verg. G. iv. 182. Vergil calls the leaves of the willow pale-green, G. ii. 13 *glauca canentia fronde salicta.* **thyma grata**, from Horace C. iv. 2. 29. 7. **gemens**, 'with a groan'; a rather strong word for the occasion. Av. probably implies the goat's consciousness of perpetual danger from the lion, which is too strong to be put out of mind by flattering words. This is why 'heavily she answers with a groan.' Shakespere Sonnet 50. 8. *insimulare* MSS, perhaps rightly in the sense of 'pretend.' In Plaut. Amph. iii. 2. 21 *Nisi etiam hoc falso dici insimulaturus es*, Verr. ii. 2. 24, 59 *Aduersarii non audebant contra dicere: exitus nullus reperiebatur. Insimulant hominem fraudandi causa discessisse: postulant ut bona possidere iubeat*, the word has been thought to have this meaning; and so certainly in Apul. M. vii. 11 *Insimulatione promendi quae poscebat usus, ad puellam commeabat assidue.* See Hildebrand l.c. Cf. the S. Gallen Glossary edited by Minton Warren *insimulat accusat fingit.* The construction however (with which cf. *arguitur nimosus* Hor. Epp. i. 29. 6 Wiikins, *sperate deos memores* Aen. i. 543) is peculiar, *insim. securam me* for *ins. secur. me esse:* and it is better either (1) to read *insinuare* whether as active 'take to your bosom,' or as neuter, in which sense both *insinuare* and *insinuari* are constructed by Lucretius

H 2

with an accus. dependent on the *in* (Munro on Lucr. i. 116, cf. iv. 1030) 'steal over my security,' or (2) as the Paraphrast read, and as Wopkens suggested, **instimulare**, Ov. Fast. vi. 508. This I have adopted as perhaps the least objectionable view, and as accepted by Lachmann, Fröhner, and Bährens. In Plaut. Pers. i. 3. 48 most of Ritschl's MSS give *instimulas* for *insimulas*: conversely in Orientius Common. i. 220 Delrio's MS gives *instimulare* for *insimulare*.　　　**9.** 'Though the dangers you urge are true, and though you suppress the greater dangers (of following your advice), after all you cannot make me believe what you say.'　　**Vera** makes a better antithesis to **maiora** if taken with **pericula**. But it is of course possible that Av. meant merely 'though what you urge is true.'　　**tollas** MSS. 'Withdraw' or 'keep out of view' seems to be the idea. Quintilian v. 10. 65 '*ut sit ciuis, aut natus sit oportet, aut factus*': *utrumque tollendum est*, '*nec natus nec factus est*' uses *tollere = refellere*, 'to deny': but this the lion in our fable did not do, except by implication.　　**10.** The position of **Tu** at the beginning of the clause, as well as of the line, makes the statement more marked and positive: 'be sure you cannot get your words believed.'　　**non facis esse fidem** *= non facis credi*. Av. is fond of the combination *facis, facit, esse*, so XXXIX. 16 *alios quod facis esse malos*, XXXVI. 14 *Expertem nostri quae facit esse iugi*, XXIII. 2 *fecerat esse deum*, no doubt determined by its metrical convenience. Thielmann (Archiv für Latein. Lexicog. iii. p. 188) traces this construction in the Early Latin versions of the Bible and in Tertullian, Cyprian, etc. Infin. after *facere* is especially frequent in the Christian poets from Prudentius to Venantius Fortunatus. The former has two instances, Perist. xiii. 45, c. Symm. ii. 220; the latter more than sixty. The tendency was an increasing one from the first century onwards.　　**11.** 'Though your words are honest and have a sound drift.'　　**constet sententia** is like *constat mens*, 'the mind is sane,' Cels. iii. 19. 1; *constat lingua*, 'the tongue does not falter,' Sen. Epist. 83. fin. [For **constet** C and virtually *A* give *constat*, and both *quamuis* and *licet* are sometimes followed by indic. in the Digest (Roby Introd. to Digest p. ccxvi)].　　**12. Suspectam.** Quintil. v. 14. 35 *Quoque quid est natura magis asperum, hoc pluribus condiendum est uoluptatibus: et minus suspecta argumentatio dissimulatione, et multum ad fidem adiuuat audientis uoluptas.*　　**rabidus**, 'hungry' or 'famished.' Aen. vi. 421 *Ille fame rabida tria guttura pandens.* ix. 63 *collecta fatigat edendi Ex longo rabies* (Canneg.).　　**consiliator**, a word used by Phaedrus ii. 7. 6 *Si uero accessit consiliator maleficus* (Canneg.) as well as Ausonius Grat. Act. x *Habes ergo consiliatorem et non metuis proditorem*, which looks as if it might be a reference to our fable. These nouns in *-tor -ator* are much affected by writers of this period. Symm. Epist. i. 90 *Fit plerumque ut leuia rerum portator festinus exornet*, a sentence which in form is exactly like Av.'s line. ii. 1 *Hic ille est Paralius cui accusator pater quantum discriminis mouit, tantum laudis parauit.*　　**habes**, though only found in one MS (*b³*) is approved by Wopkens and adds immensely to the point. As Wopkens points out, *suspectam habes sententiam* = 'sententiae fidem ab aliis non impetras.'

XXVII.

This fable is not in our Babrius, nor in any of Halm's versions. It exists however in the short collection of eighteen fables ascribed to Dositheus (ed. Böcking, 1834).

If Aelian may be trusted, the ingenuity here ascribed to the crow, properly belongs to the Libyan species of the bird. It seems a fair inference that this is one of the Λιβυστικοὶ λόγοι.

DOSITHEI FAB. VIII.

Κορώνη διψῶσα προσῆλθεν ἐπὶ ὑδρίαν καὶ ταύτην ἐβιάζετο ἀνατρέψαι· ἀλλ' ὅτι ἰσχυρῶς ἐστήκει, οὐκ ἠδύνατο αὐτὴν καταβάλλειν, ἀλλὰ μεθόδῳ ἐπέτυχεν ὃ ἠθέλησεν· ἔπεμπε γὰρ ψήφους εἰς τὴν ὑδρίαν καὶ τούτων τὸ πλῆθος ἀπὸ κάτωθεν τὸ ὕδωρ ἄνω ὑπερέχεεν, καὶ οὕτως ἡ κορώνη τὴν ἰδίαν δίψαν κατέπαυσεν.
Οὕτως οὖν φρόνησις ἀνδρότητα πλανᾷ.

1. urnam, 'a jar' = ὑδρίαν.   **2. minimam**, 'a very small amount of water.'   **fundo**, 'in bodome' Treves MS, 'the water did not rise above the bottom of the jar.'   **continuisset** is probably a mere attraction into the tense of **aspexerat**, cf. Dräger i. 291 sqq., though the pluperf. might have its proper meaning 'which the crow had found on examining to hold only a very little water.' The subjunctive carries on the definition of the jar as observed by the bird.   **3. enisa** C and so I think Av. wrote. Cannegieter quotes Serv. on Aen. i. 144 *Adnixus antiquum est, ut 'conixus,' quibus hodie non utimur; dicimus enim 'adnisus' et 'conisus.'* Charisius p. 374 Keil *nitor niteris, perfecto nisus sum : sed ueteres inmutantes nixus declinant, ut Vergilius* (then four quotations from Verg. of *conixus adnixus obnixus adnixus*) *melius autem dicimus nisus et nisa a nitendo, enixa enim appellatio est et ad partum refertur, cum dicimus geminos enixa est, ut apud Vergilium Triginta capitum fetus enixa: ut sit enisa uiribus conata, enixa in genua.*   **effundere**, 'to spill.' None of my MSS support the spelling *ecfundere*, which Fröhner has ventured to introduce on the very doubtful evidence of Cabeljau.   **5. uiam uirtus** is a combination found in Claudian B. Gild. 318 *Neui consilium, noui Stilichonis in omnes Aequalem casus animum : penetrabit harenas : Inueniet uirtute uiam.*   Here **uiam** answers to μεθόδῳ of Dositheus' fable, 'system' or 'plan,' 'way of effecting:' just as **uirtus** expresses ἀνδρότητα, 'resolution,' 'stout effort.' Canneg. compares Phaedr. i. 13. 13 *Virtute semper praeualet sapientia.*   **admouet**, a soldiers' word, used by Vegetius and the Panegyrici of moving up (προσάγειν) military engines, ladders, towers, rams, etc.   Veg. iv. 2 *adm. scalas uel machinas,* iv. 13 *admouentur testudines arietes falces uineae plutei musculi turres,* cf. iv. 21.   Translate, 'brings to bear all the appliances (engines) of his craft.'   **6. noua calliditate.** Aelian confines this ingenuity to the *African* crows. H. N. ii. 48 Λίβυες δὲ κόρακες, ὅταν οἱ ἄνθρωποι φόβῳ δίψους ὑδρευσάμενοι πληρώσωσι τὰ ὑγεῖα ὕδατος, καὶ κατὰ τῶν τεγῶν θέντες ἐάσωσι τῷ ἀέρι τὸ ὕδωρ φυλάττειν ἄσηπτον, ἐνταῦθα ἐς ὅσον μὲν αὐτοῖς τὰ ῥάμφη κάτεισιν ἐγκίπτοντες, χρῶνται τῷ ποτῷ· ὅταν δὲ ὑπολήξῃ, ψήφους κομίζουσι καὶ τῷ στόματι καὶ τοῖς ὄνυξι, καὶ ἐμβάλλουσιν ἐς τὸν κέραμον· καὶ αἱ μὲν ἐκ τοῦ βάρους ὠθοῦνται καὶ ὑφιζάνουσι, τό γε μὴν ὕδωρ θλιβόμενον ἀναπλεῖ. καὶ πίνουσιν εὖ μάλα εὐμηχάνως οἱ κόρακες, εἰδότες φύσει τινὶ ἀποῤῥήτῳ δύο σώματα μίαν χώραν μὴ δέχεσθαι.   **7. accrescens.** Cicero similarly, speaking of a river rising suddenly under a storm, *flumen subito accreuit* De Inuent. ii. 31. 97.   **9.** Cf. the Epimythion of Phaedr. i. 13. 13, 14 *Hac re probatur ingenium quantum ualet. Virtute semper praeualet sapientia,* if indeed it is genuine.   Nevelet cites a line of Titinius ap. Non. 186 *Sapientia gubernator nauem torquet, non ualentia.*   **10. cornix** for *uolueris* of MSS restores metre so easily and naturally that I have not scrupled to introduce it.   **explicuisset** is the correlative of **coeptum**, 'as by it the crow had despatched the task it had undertaken,' i.e. had got at the water at last by the mechanical and dilatory process of dropping stones into the jar.   So Pomponius in the Digest xxvii. 7. 1 *Quamuis heres tutoris tutor non est, tamen ea quae per defunctum inchoata sunt per heredem, si legitimae aetatis et masculus sit, explicari debent.*   Apuleius M. x. 6 has *sepulturam explicare,* Florus i. 17 *bellum periculosissimum exp.*   Frontin. de Aquaed. 121 *Ideoque haec opera sollicita festinatione explicanda sunt.*   Sulpicius Severus Chron. i. 40 *Coeptum templi* *opus uigesimo anno explicuit.* The word always gives the idea of something to be evolved or got through with difficulty.

XXVIII.

I have been unable to find this fable either in Babrius or any prose version.

1. Vincla. Columella ii. 6 gives directions for breaking in young bullocks (*domitura*). The horns were to be fastened with ropes of hemp; headstalls wound round with wool to prevent wounding the forehead to be placed beneath the horns. When taken to the stall they were to be tied to stakes (*stipites*) or to the manger (*praesepe*).   **recusanti,** 'shirking.' So Val. Fl. vii. 589 *Ille* (the fire-breathing bull) *nirum atque ipsam tunc te, Medea, recusans.* Col. ii. 2, 26 *Vltima sint opus recusantibus remedia plagae.*   **2. Aspera,** 'fierce,' 'ill-tempered.' Pallad. iv. 12 *Si nimia fuerit asperitas, uno die ac nocte inter uincula mitigentur atque ieiunia;* ib. *Asperum bouem mansueto et ualido boui coniungas.* In Digest. ix. 1 it is used of a *dog, si canis asperitate sua euaserit.*   **mordaci,** 'griping' or 'pinching.'   **3. obliqua** might be explained of the zig-zag or notched indentations of the *falx*, if we suppose the countryman to have used such an implement as is figured by Rich Companion p. 273 No. 3, in which such a notched blade (*denticulata*), is represented. It is more likely that **obliqua** refers to the slanting *position* in which the knife was held by the countryman, perhaps to cut the horns away with more effect, or to make the task easier.   **4. insanum,** 'ferocious,' IX. 24.   **defremuisse** = *desaeuisse* of Columella vi. 2. 4. *Defremere* is found in the younger Pliny ix. 13. 4 of anger, and several times in Apollinaris Sidonius. (Unrein p. 39.)   **5. immenso.** Av. like Merobaudes Paneg. Aetii 73 *Pace sub immensa,* uses the word *immense* in a sense considerably short of our word, of large bullocks XVIII. 1, of a full-grown lion XIII. 1. Here then it need mean no more than 'ponderous,' such as would keep in check the outbreaks of temper in an untamed steer. Yet it is noticeable that one of the earliest MSS *P* has *immensae,* possibly a relic of a variant *immensam,* which would well suit the thick neck which often is found in vicious beasts.   **aratro.** Columella directs (vi. 2. 7) that on the seventh day of the *domitura,* a yoke with a bough attached to it to serve as a pole (*temo*) was to be put on unbroken steers, and after this they are, as the next step, to draw an empty wagon: thus at last to be yoked to the plough.   **6. cornu promptior** atque pede, 'over-ready to butt or kick.' Col. vi. 2. 8 *Curandum ne in domitura bos calce aut cornu quemquam contingat, nam nisi haec caueantur, numquam eiusmodi uitia quamuis subacto eximi poterunt.*   **promptior,** a favorite word in Symmachus' Letters.   **7. uerbera** in good Latin is so regularly used of lashes from a whip that Av. might seem to mean that the pole of the plough-share was meant to prevent any necessity of whipping the animal, e.g. if it turned fractious and lay down, cf. Pallad. iv. 12. 4 *Si post domituram decumbit in sulco, non afficiatur igne, uel uerbere.* Colum. vi. 2. 10 *Seu conatur decumbere . . . ad patientiam laboris paucissimis uerberibus producitur.* Stat. Theb. v. 231 *Vt fera quae placido rabiem desueta magistro Tardius arma mouet, stimulisque et uerbere crebro In mores negat ire suas.* But the two vv. can hardly be separated from each other, and as in 8 Av. speaks of the steer using his hoof, he probably meant in 7 that he tried to use his horns, 'uerbera, capitis et pedum' Guiet. Elsewhere he applies the word to the strokes of a dog's or tiger's tail VII. 5, XVII. 4.   **8. saeua,** 'angry.'   **9. irato,** as Ovid speaks of *irati ocelli, irata manus* Am. ii. 8. 15, iii. 6. 76. Here the epithet suggests the convulsive plungings of the animal to get rid of the neck-straps by which the plough is attached.   **detractans** the best MSS, not *detrectans,* and so Jeep writes the word in Claud.

Rapt. Pros. i. 156 : *retractare* is, I believe, invariable. **10. In-meritam**, the unoffending ground, which the bullock kicks in impotent rage. So Catullus *Irascere iterum meis iambis Inmerentibus*, and Propertius more than once, ii. 4. 3 *Et saepe inmeritos corrumpas dentibus ungues*, iv. 5. 16. Hor. S. ii. 3. 8 *Inmeritusque laborat Iratis natus paries dis atque poetis.* uacuo is found in *BX* and the two Peterhouse MSS as well as in the Treves MS (Saec. x) and Bährens' Ashburnamensis (Saec. xi–xii). To *B* I incline to give great weight, perhaps the more so that the dot added beneath the *o* shows *uacuo* to have been the *m. pr. Calx* was used masc. by Lucilius (Charis. 93. 2 Keil), Plautus and Varro (Non. 199), Gratius (Cyn. 278), and in the Excerpta Charisii 551 K. is included among nouns which are fem. in Greek, masc. in Latin. The seeming preponderance of antiquity in favour of *uacua*, which is found in all Fröhner's Paris MSS, is rather diminished by the testimony of the Trevirensis; but in a case of this kind the abnormal gender, even though supported by evidence on the whole inferior, seems likely to be right *as* abnormal. The meaning seems to be ' ineffectual.' Wopkens cites Claud. in Rufin. i. 16 *Vacuo quae currere semina motu Adfirmat*. Apul. M. ix. 14 *Confictis obseruationibus uacuis* (unreal). **fatigat**, ' worries.' **11. euersam** is glossed in the Treves MS by the word *emotam*. **12.** A verse not yet satisfactorily emended. **sequentis**, to guide the plough. **agit**. This use of the hind feet to kick up earth or stones in the face of a pursuer is ascribed by Amm. Marcellinus xxiii. 4. 7 to *onagri*. His words well illustrate Av. *Ita eminus lapides post terga calcitrando emittunt, ut perforent pectora sequentium aut perfractis ossibus capita ipsa displodant.* **14. Discutiens**, ' shaking ' about him to get rid of the dust. Not a common use. **imo pectore uictus**, he felt he was utterly beaten. Ovid Trist. i. 4. 11, 12 *Nauita confessus gelido pallore timorem Iam sequitur uictus, non regit arte, ratem.* **15, 16.** ' Sure enough I needed to learn what a vicious temper can be : how it can have *a method* in its mischief.' **15. derat**, the imperf. of *reflection*. The mind goes back to its past experiences, and returns with the conclusion which results from comparing them with the present. This use of the imperf. is common in Plato. **iniquae**, ' vicious ' or ' intractable.' Hor. S. i. 9. 20 *iniquae mentis asellus*. **16. Qua**, ' how.' Verg. Aen. i. 676 *Qua facere id possis nostram nunc accipe mentem*, where Servius notes *Qua id est quomodo*. **cum ratione**, ' on system,' ' methodically.' Veget. i. 15 *Vt dextra* (of the archer) *cum ratione ducatur*, where it seems to mean, with the *proper* method. A different, but I think less correct, interpretation is suggested by Colum. vi. 2. 11 *Eum* (an ox that lies down instead of drawing the plough) *non saeuitia, sed ratione* (by methodical *treatment*) *censeo emendandum.* Then **cum ratione** will be ' under methodical treatment ' which was meant to cure vice, and ends with producing it. In Orientius i. 603, 4 *Hinc cohibet totum pacis concordia mundum, Quae brutis etiam cum ratione datur* the meaning is doubtful. Guiet notes : ' ita libere recusans iugum i.e. hominum more, non brutorum,' which seems to be virtually my first suggestion.

XXIX.

Fab. Aesop. 64 Halm, 145 Kn.

ΦΑΒ. AESOP. 64.

Ἄνθρωπόν ποτε λέγεται πρὸς Σάτυρον φιλίαν σπείσασθαι. καὶ δὴ χειμῶνος καταλαβόντος καὶ ψύχους γενομένου ὁ ἄνθρωπος τὰς χεῖρας τῷ στόματι ἐπέπνει. Τοῦ δὲ Σατύρου τὴν αἰτίαν ἐρομένου, δι' ἣν τοῦτο πράττει, ἔλεγεν, ὅτι θερμαίνει τὰς χεῖρας διὰ τὸ κρύος. Ὕστερον δὲ παρατεθείσης αὐτοῖς τραπέζης καὶ προσ-φαγήματος θερμοῦ σφόδρα ὄντος, ὁ ἄνθρωπος ἀναιρούμενος κατὰ μικρὸν τῷ στό-

ματι προσέφερε καὶ ἐφύσα· πυνθανομένου δὲ πάλιν τοῦ Σατύρου, 'τί τοῦτο ποιεῖ;
ἔφασκε καταψύχειν τὸ ἔδεσμα, ἐπεὶ λίαν θερμόν ἐστι. Κἀκεῖνος ἔφη πρὸς αὐτόν·
ἀλλ' ἀποτάσσομαι σου τῇ φιλίᾳ, ὦ οὗτος, ὅτι ἐκ τοῦ αὐτοῦ στόματος τὸ θερμὸν
καὶ τὸ ψυχρὸν ἐξιεῖς.'
   Ἀταρ .οὖν καὶ ἡμᾶς περιφεύγειν δεῖ τὴν φιλίαν ὧν ἀμφίβολός ἐστιν ἡ
διάθεσις.
   There is a passage in Symmachus' Letters which might seem to allude to
vv. 21, 22 in a different application, Epp. i. 101 *Qui fieri potest ut os unum
contrariis adfectionibus induamus?*

   1. congestis. Av. seems to have in his mind Vergil's description of a
Siberian winter G. iii. 353 sqq., especially 354, 5 *Sed iacet aggeribus niueis
deformis et alto Terra gelu late septemque adsurgit in ulnas.* See again
on 5.   **2. Cunctaque** well expresses the universal veil of whiteness
that lay on the frozen fields. *Vinctaque*, though conjectured by Heinsius
and said to be found in some MSS (it is not in any of mine), introduces a
tautology that Av. would have avoided.   **durato stringeret arua gelu.**
Orientius Common. ii. 279 *Illos constringet . . . dura gelu glacies.*   **3.
Haesit,** 'was stopt or arrested,' 'brought up suddenly in his course.' Cic.
Mil. xxi. 56 *In quos incensos ira uitamque domini desperantes cum incidisset,
haesit in iis poenis quas ab eo serui fideles pro domini uita expetiuerunt.* Verg.
Aen. xi. 289 *Hectoris Aeneaeque manu uictoria Graium Haesit.*   **nimborum
mole** may have been suggested, as Cannegieter thought, by Vergil's *torpent
mole noua* G. iii. 370, said of stags numbed by an unusual weight of snow.
But **nimborum** (for which *B* and the second Peterhouse MS absurdly
substitute *membrorum*) can only apply to snow so far as it is still unfallen
and while descending with rain or in the form of sleet. This however
is not the meaning; Av. obviously refers to the heavy and thick *mists*
which often supervene after severe frost, and in which it is easy to be
lost.   **4. Perdita,** 'obscured,' 'lost to sight.' Val. Fl. i. 466 *Cumque
aethera Iuppiter umbra Perdiderit, solus transibit nubila Lynceus.* (Cannegieter.)   **6. continuisse,** 'to have given shelter to.' There is no
idea of *confining* indoors, as Cannegieter supposed, though in Geor. i. 259,
Amphit. ii. 2. 58 the rain (*imber*) and the weather (*tempestas*) are said to
detain the farmer and the intending traveller (*continere*).   **7.** 'Construe
Quem ruris alumnus aspiciens, simul (*dum nempe aspicit*) *miratur'* Wopkens.
Cf. Aen. x. 856 *Simul hoc dicens attollit in aegrum se femur,* where Conington quotes Liv. xxii. 3 *Haec simul increpans cum ocius signa conuelli iuberet,*
and compares the Greek construction ἅμα λέγων or ἅμα εἰπών.   **8.**
The reading of this v. is very doubtful. The MSS generally give *Vimque
homini tantam protinus esse pauet,* which cannot be right, as (1) *Vim tantam*
is a ludicrous exaggeration ; (2) *protinus,* unlike the instances compared by
Schenkl from the other fables, is pointless and flat. Believing with
Lachmann and Fröhner that the v. is corrupt, I think it possible that for
this should be read *frontis in esse :* the Satyr is frightened at the man's un-
blushing use of his mouth for two purposes so wholly different, warming
and cooling. The *effrontery* lies in the *contradiction* of the two uses ; the
alarm which follows it, springs from the dangerous character naturally
attributable to such perverse inconsistency. This use of *frons* is common :
Pers. v. 103-104 *Nauem si poscat sibi peronatus arator Luciferi rudis, excla-
met Melicerta perisse Frontem de rebus.* Juv. xiii. 242 *Eiectum semel attrita
de fronte ruborem.* Mart. xi. 27. 7 *At cum perfricuit frontem posuitque ruborem.* Sen. N. Q. iv Praef. 9 *Quo magis frontem suam perfricuit.* A
passage from Symmachus' Letters (i. 90) well illustrates my conj. *Vereor
protelare testimonium meum, ne magis laudi eius obsecutus iudicer quam pudori :
nam quorum mens honesta est, eorum inbecilla frons est.* It is however true, as Wilkins has observed on Hor. Epist. i. 9. 11, that in this sense

of assurance *frons* is ordinarily combined with some adjective like *inuere-cunda proterua* etc. **pauet.** Anecd. Fulgentianum ed. Reyfferscheid p. 7 *Flamma etiam pluere didicit atque in suis incendiis guttas habere se repentinas expauit.* **9. uitae in usum,** like Vergil's *usum in castrorum, usum agrestem* G. iii. 313, 163. **10. calido ore,** 'with the hot breath of his mouth.' **soluerat,** 'had thawed.' Hor. C. i. 4. 1 *Soluitur acris hiemps.* The transference from snow and winter to the frozen limbs is so natural as to make any change like Lachmann's *fouerat* unnecessary. **12. Hospitis sedulitate,** 'attentions of his host.' Canneg. crowds his columns with illustrations of this well-known use. I have found a typical instance which is better than any of his. Ovid F. vi. 529–534 *Hospita Carmentis fidos intrasse penates Diceris et longam deposuisse famem. Liba sua properata manu Tegeaea sacerdos Traditur et subito cocta dedisse foco. Nunc quoque liba iuuant festis Matralibus illam. Rustica sedulitas gratior arte fuit.* **13. agrestem uitam,** 'how they lived in the country.' **14. referens,** 'bringing *from his stores*,' i.e. from the place where they were stowed away, or possibly 'one after the other,' *optima quaeque.* But in the time of Av. *referre* had lost much of its original distinction of meaning, as may be seen in a passage of the Panegyrici, Gratiarum Actio Constantin. x *Tu fructus meritorum tuorum statim nos metere et in conditis referre iussisti.* **dabat,** of successive offers : whereas the **optulit** refers to the single offer of the goblet. **18. algenti,** the natural opposite of *calidus.* Plin. H. N. xx. 117 *Sucus (olusatri) algentis calefacit potus.* **rursus,** 'now again,' in reference to his blowing on his hands before to *warm* them. **reflat,** Schenkl's conj. for *suflat* of MSS satisfies all requirements. Lucretius iv. 938 *Cum ducitur atque reflatur (aer)* 'as it is inhaled or exhaled.' Munro. Apul. M. ix. 25 *Hominem crebros anhelitus aegre reflantem.* This sense 'breathes out, exhales' would suffice ; but it is possible that Av. has a more direct antithesis in view, viz. to *Adflatas calido soluerat ore manus ;* as there the mouth breathes on the hands to thaw them, so here it breathes a *counter* breath on the goblet to cool it : **reflat** would then be 'blows the other way.' **19. monstro,** 'prodigy.' It was strange to the Satyr to see the mouth used for either purpose, warming or cooling. This is the natural interpretation : but it is possible Av. meant not a *double*, but a *two-sided* prodigy, i.e. one which was equally surprising from either point of view ; if the breath could warm, how could it cool ? if it cooled, how could it warm ? **21.** 'Nolo with *ut* has no existence, though *prohibere* and *cohibere* with *ut* are found.' Dräger ii. p. 249. The present instance is therefore a rare exception. Of *uolo ut* Dräger quotes eight instances from Plautus, several from Cicero. **successerit,** from Verg. Aen. iv. 10 *Quis nouus hic nostris successit sedibus hospes ?* and Ecl. v. 6 *Siue antro potius succedimus,* 19 *successimus antro.* **22. duō.** Krenkel (De Aurel. Prudentii Clementis Re Metrica 1884) quotes a similar *duō* before *fluxerunt* from Prud. Hamart. 122, Lucian Müller de R. M. p. 335 *duō cogunt* in a hexameter from Perist. xi. 89, to which add *duō uariarum* Hamart. 13.

XXX.

This also is not in our Babrius, nor in any prose version. The joke, however, with which it ends, the pig's want of *heart*, i.e. intelligence, a Roman not a Greek play of words (see on 14), is found in the ninety-fifth fable of the Babrian Collection.

Λέων δ' ἕκαστον ἐγκάτων ἀριθμήσας
μάτην ἀπ' ἄλλων καρδίην ἐπεζήτει,
καὶ πᾶσαν εὐνὴν πάντα δ' οἶκον ἤρεύνα.
κερδὼ δ' ἀπαιολῶσα τῆς ἀληθείης
'οὐκ εἶχε πάντως' φησί· 'μὴ μάτην ζήτει.

ποίην δ' ἔμελλε καρδίην ἔχειν, ἥτις
ἐκ δευτέρου λέοντος ἦλθεν εἰς οἴκους;᾽

The last two verses, rejected no doubt rightly by Rutherford, are retained
here, as they correspond closely with Avianus' closing distich :

Nam cur membrorum demens in damna redisset,
    Atque uno totiens possit ab hoste capi?

Similarly in the Aesopic fable of the Dog and the Cook (Halm 232),
when the dog has run off with a heart, the cook tells him : ' You have given
me heart, not taken my heart away : for henceforward I shall be taught
wisdom and be on my guard against you.' This joke about the pig's want
of heart may be compared with Cleanthes' dictum that, as pigs were only
good for eating, their soul (ψυχή anima Cic. de Nat. Deor. ii. 64, 164) was
given them to keep the flesh from putrifying. See the learned note of Jos.
Mayor on the passage of Cic.

Hartung (Thesaur. Critic. ii. 8. 5 in Gruter's Lampas ii. p. 726) cites a
passage from Eustathius on Odys. xviii. 29 which states that there was an
alleged law in Cyprus that a pig found eating the crop of any one not its
master, should lose its teeth. Σῦς ληϊβότειρα ἢ διαβοσκομένη ἀλλότριον λήϊον,
ἣν ἐξωδόντιζον οἱ δεσπόται τοῦ χωρίου· ὁ νόμος δέ, φασι, παρὰ Κυπρίοις. Cf.
Dindorf's Scholia in Odyss. vol. ii. p. 655.

Damage done by an animal was called *pauperies*, and the animal was said
pauperiem fecisse. Dig. ix. i. 1 *Si quadrupes pauperiem fecisse dicetur, actio ex
lege duodecim tabularum descendit ; quae lex uoluit aut dari id quod nocuit, id est
animal quod noxiam commisit, aut aestimationem noxiae offerre.* The title
mentions a variety of such cases with the legal compensations.

Mr. H. A. Pottinger, of Worcester College, kindly sent me the following
notes on this subject : —

' The law did not allow owners of land to detain beasts trespassing, if
the owner were known.

' There were numerous actions for damage done by animals, and therefore
the law would not allow mutilation.

' Anyone who blinded an ox or cut off his ears or tail (for trespassing),
had to give the owner a sound animal of equal value.

' A pig, sheep, or dog might be deprived of his tail for a third offence.

' Besides the leges agrariae the sources of information about the rural
population and their laws are—

Theodosian Code.

Justinian's Code, Bk. ii.

Some of the Novels.

Letters of Gregory the Great.'

1. **Vastantem.** Hyg. Fab. 173 *Aprum (σῦν ἄγριον) immani magnitudine
qui agrum Calydonium uastaret.* **pinguia culta.** Vergilian, G. iv. 372,
Aen. x. 141. **ruentem,** 'trampling down.' Donatus on Adelph. iii. 2. 21
*Ruere est toto corpore uti ad impellendum, quod faciunt qui ipsi praecipites alios
prosternunt. Vnde proprie sues ruere dicuntur. Vergilius* Ipse ruit, dentesque
Sabellicus exacuit sus *et Horatius* Hac rabiosa fugit canis, hac lutulenta
ruit sus: from which he would seem to connect the neuter sense of *ruere*
with the active, the headlong course of the boar with the reckless knocking down of the crops produced by it. 'fodientem' Guiet, wrongly, I
think. 2. The MSS are in favour of **abscisa,** 'cut off,' rather than
abscissa, 'slit off.' The latter suggests more distinctly the instrument,
perhaps a pair of scissors, with which the ear was removed. **aure.** As
here the pig loses an ear, so in the Odyssey he loses his teeth, and again
in the Νόμοι Γεωργικοί said to be based on Justinian (p. 840 in Heimbach's
Harmenopoulus) he loses his tail. 'Εάν τις εὕρῃ χοῖρον ἐν πραίδᾳ (*praedan-
tem*) ἢ πρόβατον ἢ κύνα καὶ παραδώσῃ αὐτὸν ἐν πρώτοις τῷ κυρίῳ αὐτοῦ, εἴτα

δευτερώσας, καὶ παραγγείλας τὸ τρίτον οὐροκοπήσῃ ἢ τοξεύσῃ, ἀζήμιος ἔστω.
(Cannegieter.) **3. referens,** 'carrying home' the reminder of his
pain. **4. Vlterius,** 'from that time forward,' 'for the future.' Pacat.
Paneg. xxx *Vlterius se negare supplicio non poterat.* **teneris satis.** Verg.
G. i. 112, 113 *Luxuriem segetum tenera depascit in herba, Cum primum
sulcos aequant sata.* **5. in excepti** most MSS. The gloss in one
of my Bodl. MSS *R, excepti* ^{uetiti} seems substantially right. The field was
'reserved' perhaps under a special stipulation (*exceptio*) which forbade it to
be used for any ordinary purpose, e.g. a field used for burial (see van Goens
de Cepotaphiis); or, in a more general sense, set apart and reserved for
crops of a particular and valuable kind, which would make the invasion of
them by the pig a more heinous offence (**crimine**). It is however true that
the participle agreeing with **campi** would more naturally express *the nature*
of the offence; then *exsculpti,* 'grubbed up,' which was conjectured by
Lachmann, and has since been found in the Gale MS, would seem better
than *excerpti* of Guiet and Fröhner, though this has the support of Wopkens, who notes p. 41 'Proprie quidem non campi excerpebantur, sed illa
quae de campis proueniebant, atque inde a sue auferebantur.' **crimine
campi,** 'offence of grubbing up a field.' Juv. vi. 493 *flexi crimen facinus-
que capilli,* 'the offence and crime of spoiling a ringlet.' **6. indultae,**
'spared.' Sil. xiv. 672 *Indulgens templa uetustis Incolere atque habitare deis.*
Indulgere followed by an accus. of the thing conceded is common in the
Digest, e.g. xlii. 6. 1 § 14 *Praetoris erit uel praesidis notio, nullius alterius, hoc
est eius qui separationem indulturus est.* The passive participle which is found
in some MSS of Nux 39 hardly belongs to classical Latin. **perfidus,**
'by his treachery.' **auris onus,** the one ear he was still allowed to
bear. **7. praedictae** of MSS is not impossible, as it might well mean
'the before,' i.e. 'first-mentioned' crop, viz. that in v. 1, and the *pig-headed*
violation a second time of a field which had cost him the first of his two
lost ears, would be an aggravation of a signal kind. In the natural sense of
'the field aforesaid,' i.e. in 5, the word is a little flat, though common
enough in writers of an even early period. Colum. Praef. lib. i. 1 *Saepenu-
mero cinitatis nostrae principes audio culpantes modo agrorum infecunditatem,
modo caeli per multa iam tempora noxiam frugibus intemperiem : quosdam etiam
praedictas querimonias uelut ratione certa mitigantes.* vi. 5. 4 *Facto foramini
praedicta radicula inseritur.* vi. 7. 4 *Nec minus cacumina praedictarum arbo-
rum obiciunt,* 'the aforesaid trees,' 18 *quod si praedictum uitium inhaeserit* sc.
coriago (skin-disease), 19 *post fomenta praedicta.* Quintil. viii. 3. 83 *Vicina
praedictae sed amplior uirtus est* and so often, see Spalding's Index. Auson.
Parent. v. 2 *praedicto Arborio* mentioned in Parent. iv; Tetrast. Caesarum
i. 1 *Nunc et praedictos et regni sorte sequentes,* 'those I have spoken of already
and those who succeeded them.' Ennod. Epist. ix. 2 *Praedictum iuuenem,* 'the
aforesaid young man.' Exactly similar is the use of προειρημένος in Polybius.
Thus in two consecutive sections of the same chapter xv. 31. 9, 10 τὴν
εἰκόνα τοῦ προειρημένου = the image of the said Agathocles, λαβὼν τὰς προειρη-
μένας ἐντολάς, 'the commands I mentioned above': the former referring to
what had *immediately* preceded, the latter to what had been mentioned
some sections above. If Av. meant this, he was guilty of a prosaism not
usual in the fables; if the other, of a reprehensible ambiguity. Hence Lachmann may have been right in his conj. **praedator;** for *praeda* was, at least
in its Greek form, technically used of the damage done by an animal in grubbing up or in other ways injuring a piece of ground: seen on 2. **horrens**
is glossed in the Treves MS *truncatum.* Rightly. **8.** *Poena sed indignum*
the best MSS, **Poena quod indignum** two Bodleian and the second
Peterhouse. If **indignum** was written by Av. it can only mean that the
loss of an ear which the pig had twice successively suffered made the third
offence *an outrage :* which outrage was instantly followed by the death of

the guilty animal (Tunc 9). In this case quod is neater than *sed*, which indeed introduces an abruptness alien to our author's style. Hence there is high probability in Lachmann's conj. *Poena sed insignem*[1], 'but the double repetition of the punishment (cutting off both ears) makes him a *marked* pig,' and therefore easily detected. Cf. Lucil. xxvii. ap. Non. 331 *Cocus non curat cauda insignem esse illam (hillam) dum pinguis siet.* **congeminata,** XXII. 8. **9. superbis,** 'sumptuous dinner.' Pork in various forms would hardly now figure at a grand dinner ; since Av.'s time Jewish scruples have been reinforced by Mahommedan ; European tastes have succumbed to Oriental. **10. epulas,** 'dishes' or 'entrees.' Cic. Tusc. Disp. v. 21. 62 *Aderant unguenta, coronae, incendebantur odores, mensae conquisitissimis epulis exstruebantur.* **11. consumpti,** 'eaten up,' one dish after another. Verg. Aen. vii. 125 *Accisis cogat dapibus consumere mensas.* **12. Impatiens,** 'ravenous.' His hunger could not brook delay. **rapuisse,** 'to have appropriated.' **14. stultum non habuisse,** 'the pig was a fool and had no such thing.' Cic. Tusc. Disp. i. 9. 18 *Aliis cor ipsum animus uidetur, ex quo excordes uecordes concordesque dicuntur, et Nasica ille prudens bis consul Corculum et Egregie cordatus homo catus Aelius Sextus.* Plin. H. N. xi. 182 *Ibi (in corde) mens habitat.* Hence the combinations *cor sapientiae* Plaut. Epid. iii. 3. 3 ; *cor sapiens habere* Pers. iv. 4. 71 ; *cor habere*, 'to be of understanding,' Cic. de Fin. ii. 28. 91 ; Petron. 59 *Et tu cum esses capo, cocococo, atque cor non habebas* ; Mart. ii. 8. 6, iii. 27. 4 *mihi cor non est*, vii. 78. 4, xi. 84. 17 *Vnus de cunctis animalibus hircus habet cor*, 'has sense' (Paley and Stone). **15. membrorum in damna redisset,** 'had lost one limb after another.' Juv. x. 233 *Sed omni Membrorum damno maior dementia.* **redisset,** orat. obliqua, 'why, he asked, had he'? **16. posset** here nearly = 'allowed himself.' In **XXXIX.** 4 *Vel quicquid profugo posset ab hoste capi* the meaning is simply 'could be.' **17. descripta,** 'marked out,' 'drawn up on rules.' Hor. S. ii. 3. 34 *Si quid Stertinius ueri crepat, unde ego mira Descripsi docilis praecepta haec.* It is tempting to believe that **descripta** might = 'rules,' cf. *optata disposita dictata*, etc. **ausi,** sc. *peccare.* **18. abstinuere,** 'have never *learnt* to keep their hands from offending.'

XXXI.

BABR. CXII.

Μῦς ταῦρον ἔδακεν. ὁ δ' ἐδίωκεν ἀλγήσας
τὸν μῦν· φθάσαντος δ' εἰς μυχὸν φυγεῖν τρώγλης
ὤρυσσεν ἑστὼς τοῖς κέρασι τοὺς τοίχους,
ἕως κοπωθεὶς ὀκλάσας ἐκοιμήθη
παρὰ τὴν ὀπὴν ὁ ταῦρος. ἔνθεν ἐκκύψας
ὁ μῦς ἐφέρπει καὶ πάλιν δακὼν φεύγει.
ὁ δ' ἐξαναστὰς οὐκ ἔχων ὁ ποιήσει
διηπορεῖτο· τῷ δ' ὁ μῦς ἐπιτρύξας
'οὐχ ὁ μέγας ἀεὶ δυνατός· ἔσθ' ὅπου μᾶλλον
τὸ μικρὸν εἶναι καὶ ταπεινὸν ἰσχύει.'

1. oberrans, 'as he went his rounds,' 'roamed to and fro.' Vegetius twice uses the word of *a spy* wandering about an enemy's camp unobserved (iii. 26), of an enemy wandering about *carelessly* in quest of plunder (iii. 10). **2. The use of ab** here may be compared with **XX.** 4 *Atque*

---

[1] It is noteworthy that the Brit. Mus. XIIIth century MS of Avianus 21, 213 has *Insignem* for *Ingentem* in XXXI. 1. Possibly a v. l. *Insignem* was transferred from the margin of XXX. 8 to XXXI. 1.

auido fixum uulnus ab ore tulit. In both *ab* accentuates and brings into relief the source through which the wound comes. But in the present v. **ab** is used where ordinary Latin would use a simple abl., as very often in Ovid, e.g. M. viii. 513 *Inuitis correptus ab ignibus arsit.* A.A. i. 763 *Hi iaculo pisces, illi capiuntur ab hamis.* Pont. iv. 7. 9 *Qui semel est laesus fallaci piscis ab hamo.* (From Dräger i. p. 508, cf. my note on Ibis 145.)   **3.** *conficere uulnera* is very rare and somewhat doubtful in meaning. Dr. K. E. Georges thinks it is merely a stronger *facere ;* Ovid Quintilian Martial use *uulnus facere* = to wound, and so **confecit uulnera** might here be simply 'had well wounded him.' On the other hand, the far commoner use of *conficere* for despatching or effecting anything thoroughly, makes it possible that Av. meant ' *to make an end of* wounding.' And this agrees better with the natural sequel of completing so super-murine a task, viz. the *safe* retirement of the mouse to his hole, which follows in 4 *Tutus in amfractus conditur.*   **4.** *anfractus* most MSS, *amfractis* my Bodl. *X* and virtually the second Peterhouse, in which the first hand wrote *ampharactis.* The word is ordinarily masc., sometimes neuter ; Nonius 192 quotes *anfracta* from Accius and the Parmeno of Varro (*cauata aurium anfractu*). Cf. Varro de L. L. vii. 15 M. *Quod est Terrarum anfracta reuisam ; anfractum est flexum, ab origine duplici dictum, ab ambitu et frangendo ; ab eo leges iubent in directo pedum viii esse, in anfracto xvi, id est in flexu.* Professor Key considers *anfractus* to be 'a compression of *amberactus,* so that the second part of the word comes from *ago.* This agrees with the use of it for the sun's revolution in his orbit in Cic. de Rep. vi. 12. 12, and in the religious ceremony of the *ambarualia, in annuis amfractibus* Leg. ii. 8. 19.' Language p. 385. Here the word is applied to the winding hole in which the mouse lived.   **inde,** 'thereupon.'   **5. uasta ceruice minetur,** cf. XXVIII. 5.   *minatur* is given by some MSS, and so *certat* XV. 9.   '*Licet* is generally used with the subjunctive in law Latin as well as in other: but occasionally we have the indicative.' Roby, Justinian, p. 78.   **6.** 'For all his rage sees nowhere the foe he must attack.'   **esse** most MSS, which is slightly accentuated 'exists,' not merely 'is.' *X* and my Brit. Mus. *b²* (a good one) give an interesting and lively v.l. *ille* which well expresses the complete and decided defeat of the enraged ox, spite of all his attempts, 'not for an instant can he see.'   **7.** *iusto* of MSS is weak, even if interpreted 'fitting,' 'suitable,' as in Aegritudo Perdicae 68 ed. Bährens *O socii uestro iustum si corde uidetur.* Withof saw this, but his conj. *mus hoc* is improbable. I have written **lusor** which would explain **sermone.** Amphit. ii. 2. 62 *Quid enim censes? te ut deludam contra lusorem meum?* **fatigans** is interpreted by Savaron on Sidon. Ep. v. 17 in the sense of 'joking,' 'bantering,' which is common in Sidonius' Letters and quoted by Savaron from Sulpicius Severus, Acron the commentator on Horace, Victor in his Life of Carus, Cassianus, the author of the treatise de Vita Contemplatiua, ascribed to Prosper, and the Scholiast on Juv. ix.   Sid. i. 8 *Facete et fatigationum salibus admixtis.* iii. 13 *Si fatiget, in contumelias, si fatigetur in furias (fertur),* where the Bodleian Glosses edited by me in Anecd. Oxoniens. i. 5, p. 40 note *Si fatiget s. alios conuicia dicendo, si fatigetur ab aliis .s. quasi diceret, si alii derideant eum.* Sid. iv. 10 *Dicere solebas quamquam fatigans quod meam quasi facundiam uererere ;* and hence the substantive *fatigatio,* 'banter,' adj. *fatigatorius,* 'bantering.' There can be little doubt that this was Av.'s meaning ; for what force could there be in representing the mouse, after his successful attack on the bull, going on to *worry* him with a *lengthy* admonition on the text Pride has a fall? The Treves MS however glosses **fatigans** by the word *prouocans.*   **8.** Almost a repetition of X. 10 *Distulit ammota calliditate iocum,* where see note.   **9. tribuerunt.** Very similarly Fab. Perottin. ii. 3 *Nam cuncta nobis (natura) attribuisset commoda*

Quaecumque indulgens Fortuna animali dedit. **10. effectum,** 'efficiency,'
'potency.' The combination **Viribus effectum** is Propertian. El. iii. 9.
27 *Et tibi ad effectum uires det Caesar,* which A. Palmer, following Beroaldus,
wrongly alters to *affectum.* **constituere,** 'assigned,' MSS. Lachmann's
conj. *contribuere,* 'have given with the limbs' is very seductive: cf.
Mamertin. Paneg. Maximiani xi *Pulcherrimis rebus tu tribuis effectum.* **11. breuibus,** 'little' as in XIV. 9, XXXIV. 6. **rostris,**
the admirable conj. of Fröhner removes all difficulties. The MSS have
monstris which is meaningless. **fiducia** as in XXIV. 11 *subjectively*
of the mouse, 'what self-reliance pigmy snouts possess.' **12.** *Et
faciat* MSS, to which Guiet supplied *ut* from the relative in 11 'et disce
ut paruula turba faciat quidquid cupit.' Wopkens also retained *faciat,*
making the subject **paruula turba** referred backwards. But the construction Wopkens quotes from Tusc. Disp. iv. 4. 7 *Defendat quod quisque
sentit,* cf. *Cantet amat quod quisque* Nemes. Ecl. iv, is peculiar to *quisque* or
quis, and therefore not parallel. See Madvig on Fin. iii. 20. 67. I prefer
to follow the first Peterhouse, the *m. secunda* of *B,* and the Paraphrast
in reading **facias.** **quicquid paruula turba cupit,** 'act on the suggestion of the mouse-population.' Av. here follows in the track of Phaedrus
iv. 6. 13 *minuta plebes,* in the Epilogue to the Fable of the Mice and the
Weasels. But possibly Av. wrote *sapit.*

XXXII.

Babr. xx, Fab. Aesop. 81 Halm.

BABR. XX.

Βυηλάτης ἄμαξαν ἦγεν ἐκ κώμης.
τῆς δ' ἐμπεσούσης εἰς φάραγγα κοιλώδη,
δέον βοηθεῖν αὐτὸς ἀργὸς εἱστήκει.
τῷ δ' ' Ἡρακλεῖ προσηύχεθ,' ὃν μόνον πάντων
θεῶν ἀληθῶς προσεκύνει τε κάτιμα.
ὁ θεὸς δ' ἐπιστὰς εἶπε 'τῶν τροχῶν ἅπτου,
καὶ τοὺς βόας κέντριζε. τοῖς θεοῖς δ' εὔχου,
ὅταν τι ποιῇς καυτός, ἢ μάτην εὔξῃ.'

1. gurgite, 'pool.' **3. depositis** seems to be used here not in the
classical sense of giving up (Juv. i. 133, where Mayor cites Sen. Suas. v.
1 *Quae male expertus est uota deponit*) but of placing or depositing for security,
as in *deponere aurum, d. pecuniam,* etc. Cf. Horace's *quidquid babes age
Depone tutis auribus,* a sense to which the common use of *depositum* as a
legal term would naturally lead the way. The reading of some MSS
dispositis is preferred by Cannegieter, and would bear a good sense, as the
prayers are offered to the gods (**numina**) generally, and might thus be
said to be distributed. But in the age of Avianus *disponere* had lost much
of its original meaning, as the recurring use of *disposita* = 'arrangements'
in Symmachus' Letters shows: and though in 3 he uses the plural numina,
he specifies the single god Hercules in 6, as indeed Babrius had done even
more clearly Τῷ δ' ' Ἡρακλεῖ προσηύχεθ,' ὃν μόνον πάντων Θεῶν ἀληθῶς
προσεκύνει τε κάτιμα. Hence I follow the earlier MSS in retaining **depositis** which is to be constructed with **Frustra,** 'feeling sure that the vows
he did but lodge in vain would move the gods to help his fortunes, despite
his own inactivity.' **4. Ferre.** See on XXII. 11. **resideret** (cf.
reses), 'remained idle,' a sense as old as Plautus. Capt. iii. 1. 8 *Ita uenter
gutturque resident esuriales ferias,* 'keep an idle holiday-time of hunger.'
Capitolin. Vit. Maximi et Balbini xvi *residisse apud Rauennam.* Babrius has

δέον βοηθεῖν αὐτὸς ἀργὸς εἰστήκει. **5. rector Tirynthius**, 'the Lord of Tiryns,' Hercules, like *rector Tartareus*, 'the Lord of Tartarus,' Pluto, Stat. Theb. xi. 421. Hercules was not only born at Tiryns (Serv. on Aen. vii. 662 *Tirynthius a Tirynthi ciuitate Argis uicina in qua nutritus est*) where Electryon, the father of his mother Alcmena, had reigned, but, after his father Amphitryon's expulsion from thence by Sthenelus (Apollod. ii. 4. 6), being ordered by the Delphian oracle, which he had consulted after his frenzied murder of his children, to dwell in Tiryns, returned there, and from it started to perform the XII *athla* imposed by Eurystheus. Thus Hesiod (Theog. 291) speaks of his driving the oxen of Geryon into sacred Tiryns, and Pindar (Isthm. v. (vi.) 40) states that he went σὺν Τιρυνθίοισι to Troy. The fact that already in the Telephus of Euripides fr. 697 Nauck he is styled τῷ Τιρυνθίῳ Ἡρακλεῖ, and that the Latin poets from Vergil onwards use *Tirynthius* to connote Hercules, is perhaps due to the legend mentioned by Apollodorus (ii. 4. 12) that the name Herakles was given him *for the first time* by the oracle which ordered his return to Tiryns, after the murder of his children as stated above. For **rector** of most MSS, which I believe to be a reminiscence of Statius, with whom the word is a favorite, Cannegieter conjectured *uictor*, which he shows in a learned note to be constantly applied to Hercules. It is interesting to confirm this conj. by the more than respectable testimony of my Brit. Mus. *B*, in which it is the *m. prima*. Cf. my note on Ibis 500 *inuicto deo*. **infit**, like **summis ab astris**, is a grandiose touch. **6. uocat in sua uota.** Conington on Aen. v. 234 shows Vergil to have used *in uota uocare* four times, Aen. v. 234, 514, vii. 471, xii. 780. He is wrong, I think, in explaining the meaning to be 'summoning to be a party to a vow'; the idea is rather summoning to help a vow. **7. stimulis.** To use the goad was an extreme remedy only to be applied in cases of desperation. Colum. ii. 2. 26 *Numquam stimulo lacessat iuuencum*. **9. Tunc quoque.** 'Then also,' *after* you have struggled and used your own utmost efforts, not only *before* any such effort and as a requisite *preliminary*. Symm. vi. 88 *Auditorem quondam popularis tui* (a pupil of your countryman) *aut silentio tuere aut tu quoque rursus institue*, 'you in your turn' might be cited in support of the v.l. *Te quoque*, 'you like others': but the weight of MSS is against this. **congressum**, 'when you have grappled with the task.' A very rare usage: somewhat similar is Cic. pro Sulla xvi. 47 *Nondum statuo te uirium satis habere, ut ego tecum luctari et congredi debeam*, where however it is a *personal* encounter. **10. animis**, either (1) your wishes, a meaning common enough in the singular from Terence onwards, cf. *ex animo, animo indulgere*, etc.; or (2) your determination, resolution, Val. Fl. iii. 519 *Verum animis insiste tuis astumque per omnem Teude pudor*. Eumen. Grat. Act. xiii *Desinunt odisse agrorum suorum sterilitatem, resumunt animos operi, praeparant culturam, melioribus annituntur auspiciis*, 'take fresh resolution for the task.' **conciliare**, 'win over to.' Ovid Fast. i. 337 *Ante, deos homini quod conciliare ualeret, Far erat*. **11. pigris uotis**, 'vows without action.' **12.** 'And call in the present help of the gods by acting yourself.' The sentiment is Aeschylean, Pers. 742 Ἀλλ' ὅταν σπεύδη τις αὐτός, χὠ θεὸς ξυνάπτεται. Nevelet quotes from Suidas (s.v. Αὐτός) αὐτός τι νῦν δρῶν εἶτα τοὺς θεοὺς κάλει, which Suidas compares with another proverb, σὺν Ἀθηνᾷ καὶ χεῖρας κίνει. Ἐπὶ τοῦ μὴ χρῆναι ἐπὶ ταῖς τῶν θεῶν ἐλπίσι καθημένους ἀργεῖν. **facis.** Wopkens cites Cato R.R. ii *Dicit uilicus sedulo se fecisse, seruos non ualuisse*. Varro R.R. i. 1 *Et quoniam ut aiunt dei facientes adiuuant* (assist those who act), *prius inuocabo eos*. **Praesentes deos.** Phorm. ii. 2. 31 *Ea qui praebet, non tu hunc habeas plane praesentem deum?*

XXXIII.

Of this fable the Athoan codex of Babrius possesses the first verse—

Ὄρνιθος ἀγαθῆς χρύσε' ὠὰ τικτούσης

and then stops.   It is preserved however in several prose versions, Halm 343, 343ᵇ, Kn. 112.

BODL. PARAPHR. 112 KN.

Ὅτι τοῖς παροῦσιν ἀρκείσθω τις καὶ τὴν ἀπληστίαν φευγέτω. Ὄρνιν τις εἶχε καλὴν χρυσᾶ ὠὰ τίκτουσαν. νομίσας δὲ ἔνδον αὐτῆς ὄγκον χρυσίου εἶναι καὶ θύσας εὗρεν οὖσαν ὁμοίαν τῶν λοιπῶν ὀρνίθων. ὁ δὲ ἀθρόον πλοῦτον ἐλπίσας¹ εὑρεῖν καὶ τοῦ μικροῦ κέρδους ἐστέρητο.

1. **pretioso germine**, 'a seed of price,' viz. golden eggs. *Germen* is here used nearly=*proles*, as in Nemes. Cyneg. 153, quoted by Canneg., *Nam postquam conclusa uidet sua germina flammis* of a dog and her puppies, and in numerous passages of Ennodius as Hartel's Index shows.   2. **Ouaque quae,** 'one of a kind to present her roosting-place with successive eggs of gold.' Cf. XXXVIII. 7, 8 *l'ana . . . mendacia Quaeque refutari . . . queant.* Macrob. S. vii. 9. 17 *Partem in homine et altam et sphaeralem tenuit et quae sensu careat,* and with an indicative in the relative clause, Aegrit. Perdicae 152 *Hippocrates illic fuerat qui forte uetustus Ac uitae spatio longum qui ceperat usum.* Eutrop. ix. 26 *Diocletianus moratus callide fuit, sagax praeterea et admodum subtilis ingenio et qui seueritatem suam aliena inuidia uellet explere.*   3. **Fixerat.** Cannegieter aptly quotes Apul. de Mundo xxii *Distinxit genera, species separauit, fixitque leges uiuendi atque moriendi.*   **uolucri superbae,** 'the sumptuous bird,' here as the producer of golden eggs. A comparison of Prop. iv. 5. 22 *Et quae sub Tyria concha superbit aqua,* Mart. vi. 55. 2, ix. 11. 4 *alitis superbae* (Phoenix), xiv. 67. 2 *Alitis eximiae cauda superba fuit* (fly-flap of peacock's feathers), proves that *superbus* sometimes very nearly = our 'superb,' 'gorgeous,' 'sumptuous.'   4. **munera ferre,** not in its proper sense of *proffering* gifts, but *producing.*   5. **cupidum,** 'greedy,' transfers to the vow the feeling of the man who made it. His cupidity was over-hasty.   **sperans uanescere** most of the MSS, which is not impossible, as *sperare* even in Vergil has the sense of apprehending or anticipating evil. Servius on Aen. i. 543 *At sperate deos abusiue* 'timete' *ut alibi Hunc ego si potui tantum sperare dolorem* (iv. 419) *cum speremus bona, timeamus aduersa.* Cf. Val. Fl. iii. 295, Stat. Theb. vi. 137, and the use of ἐλπίζειν, e.g. ἐλπίζω νοσῆσαι Hierocles 34 ed. Eberhard.   But we retain enough of the Babrian original to see that in it ἐλπίσας meant 'hoping,' and the variations of the MSS seem to indicate something wrong: *A* gives *spirans*, *B spernans*, *X euanescere*, *B suanescere.* Hence I follow Wopkens in considering **uanescere** corrupt, though what the word was which it has ousted is very doubtful. [Interesting, but perhaps hardly probable, is *B*'s *spernans*, 'disdaining that his covetous aspiration should vanish before him,' i.e. when he thought to realize a gold-harvest, his hopes proved illusory by the goose laying only one egg. *Spernans* from *spernari* may be paralleled by Juv. iv. 4 where the Pithoeanus gives *spernatur*, and Fronto p. 144 Naber *spernabere.* Both Mayor and Bücheler retain *spernatur* in Juv. iv. 4.]   6. **exosas in sua lucra moras** is like *admotas in noua damna preces*, 'delays hateful for the purposes of his gains,' i.e. which he disliked as retarding his gains. *Exosa nauigatio,* 'the voyage we hate' is found in Ennod. Dict. xxiv. fin.,

---

¹ The original may have been ὁ δ' ἐλπίσας τὸν πλοῦτον ἀθρόον εὑρήσειν.

but this passive sense is rare, cf. II. 13. Unrein p. 40 cites Eutrop. vii.
24. 3 *Ob scelera uniuersis exosus.* Macrob. S. i. 11. 45 *Omni modo dis exosos.* **7. ratus referre**=*ratus se relaturum,* with a notion of extra
certainty, as in XXII. 12 *Seque ratus solum munera ferre duo.* **8.
tam continuo munere,** 'so unfailing a bounty.' **erat,** not *esset,* in
spite of the orat. obliqua. The indicative distinctly assigns the *reason.*
Pacat. Paneg. Theodos. xvii *Sibi humilitatem et tenebras suas inputet iacens
uirtus, quae non obtulit se probandam.* **9. nuda,** probably 'stript of
its feathers' to make the opening with more dexterity. **minax,** the
knife was flourished in the bird's eyes and then plunged in the flesh. **11.
tautae crimine fraudis. crimine** is doubtful: possibly 'by the fault,'
or 'wrong,' as *crimine fati* Mart. x. 61. 2 ; more probably 'by a fraud so
gross and *culpable,*' 'the *scandal* of such a cheat.' Verg. Aen. x. 668
Tauton me crimine dignum Duxisti, et talis uoluisti expendere poenas, cf.
12. **12. meritis,** dative. **rettulit with poenam** as *referre praemium.* **inde,** as the consequence of the delusion. **13. male,**
'wrongly.' **14. diurna** is the opposite of **cuncta uno tempore,**
'the prayers of any single day :' an approach to the meaning of *quotidianus.*
Claud. de B. Gildon. 71 *Gaudetque diurnos, Vt famulae, praebere cibos.* Guiet
explained καθημερινά, τὰ καθ' ἡμέραν.

XXXIV.

Babr. cxxxvi, Fab. Aesop. 401, 401[b] Halm.

BABR. CXXXVI.

Χειμῶνος ὥρῃ σῖτον ἐκ μυχοῦ σύρων
ἔψυχε μύρμηξ ὃν θέρους σεσωρεύκει.
τέττιξ δὲ τοῦτον ἱκέτευσε λιμώττων
δοῦναί τι καυτῷ τῆς τροφῆς ὅπως ζήσῃ.
'τί οὖν ἐποίεις' φησί, 'τῷ θέρει τούτῳ ; '
οὐκ ἐσχόλαζον, ἀλλὰ διετέλουν ᾄδων.
γελάσας δ' ὁ μύρμηξ τόν τε πυρὸν ἐγκλείων
'χειμῶνος ὀρχοῦ' φησίν 'εἰ θέρους ᾄδεις.'

There is much in this fable which is common to Avianus and Phaedrus.
The fable of the Ant and the Fly (Phaedr. iv. 24) contains the following
verses, 15 sqq. :—

Ego granum in hiemem cum studiose congero,
Te circa murum pasci uideo stercore.
Aras frequentas : nempe abigeris quo uenis.
Nihil laboras : ideo cum opus est, nihil habes.
Aestate me lacessis ; cum bruma est, siles :
Mori contractam cum te cogunt frigora,
Me copiosa recipit incolumem domus.

Saluianus de Gub. Dei iv. 43 *Formicae in subterraneis latibulis uaria fru-
gum genera condentes ad hoc cuncta contrahunt ac reponunt, quia affectu uitae suae
diligunt quae recondunt.*

1-2. 'The man that has allowed his youth to slip by him without
action and never feared life's misfortunes or made provision for them
in advance.' **1. torpentem,** 'in sloth,' Inc. Paneg. Constantini xvi
*Vt ex inueterato illo torpore ac foedissimis latebris subito prorumperet et con-
sumpto per desidias sexennio ipsum diem natalis sui ultima sua caede signa-
ret.* **passus** all MSS. Fröhner's *passus* is inadmissible for Avianus.
It is probably a mere participle, though the omission of *est* is found in other
writers of the period, e. g. Claud. Epist. iii. 23 *Dignatus tenui Caesar scrip-*

I

sisse Maroni.   **transisse**, a strict perfect 'to be past and over.' Lucretius' use of the perf. inf. in iii. 69, 70 *Dum se falso terrore coacti Effugisse uolunt longe, longeque remosse* is very similar. I do not consider any of these perfects to be aoristic.   **2. Nec**, where *Non* would be expected, falls under the same class of anomalous constructions as XVII. 13, XXV. 5, in each of which a nominative participle is followed by a finite verb, but the verb clause is introduced by a *que* or *atque; respondens seque docet, fingens discrimine Atque ... queritur.* It is certain that **Nec** cannot here = *ne quidem;* and I cannot believe Av. meant it as a mere variation of *Non.* A very similar anacoluthon is found in Prop. ii. 32. 33, 34 *Ipsa Venus quamuis corrupta libidine Martis, Nec minus in caelo semper honesta fuit.*   **uitae** is possibly *dative,* 'apprehended *for* his life.' Juv. vi. 17 *Cum furem nemo timeret Caulibus aut pomis et aperto uiueret horto.*   **3. Confectus senio.** Val. Max. v. i. 1 Ext. *Senio iam confectum militem Macedonem* (Canneg.). The best MSS give *collectus,* which the Trèves codex glosses by *contractus.*   **senio** is not only age, but *senility,* i.e. the infirmities of age. In Symmachus' Letters *senio esse* = 'to be tiresome,' e.g. ii. 17.   **grauis aetas,** 'the decline of life,' when a man begins to be elderly.   **affuit,** 'is before him.' *Affluit,* 'is setting in,' the conj. of Heinsius, has the support of my Brit. Mus. *b³.*   **4. Heu frustra,** Vergilian. G. i. 158 *Heu magnum alterius frustra spectabis aceruum.*   **5. Solibus ereptos.** Cf. Seren. Sammon. 218 *Anguibus ereptos adipes aerugine misce.* It may be doubted whether **ereptos** is to be constructed with **Solibus,** 'rescued from the days of midsummer' (Withof), or **hiemi,** 'rescued from the winter.' The balance of the clauses **Solibus ereptos hiemi Distulit** as well as the use of **Distulit,** which is somewhat bare if it stands alone, is in favour of the former view. 'aestati praereptos distulit consumendos in hiemem.' (Withof.) On the latter **Solibus** must = 'at midsummer,' 'in summer days.'   **hiemi,** if constructed with **Distulit,** 'put off,' or 'reserved for winter' (so Guiet), may be compared with Stat. Theb. viii. 687 *Crudelis Erinnys Obstat et infando differt Eteoclea fratri,* and with Phaedrus' *Ego granum in hiemem cum studiose congero* quoted above.   **labores,** 'fruits of its toil,' Vergilian. G. i. 325 *Sata laeta boumque labores.*   **6. cauis.** Prud. c. Symm. ii. 1052, 3 *Nec metuit ne congestum populetur aceruum Curculio, uel nigra cauis formica recondat.*   **7. suscepit,** ἀνεδέξατο, 'assumed its winter robe of white hoar-frost.'   **candentes pruinas.** Minutius Vita Donati ap. Hagen Anecd. Heluet. p. cclx *Hiemis autem tempore solo canente pruina.*   **8. gelu** all MSS, where we might expect *niue* as in Mamert. Genethl. Maxim. ix *Cum agros glacies, glaciem niues premerent.*   **9.** Barth, whom Bährens follows, wished to write *Pigranimis,* which he called *uox noua quidem sed elegantissima.* It is so written in *C* and the Carlsruhe fragment, as reported by Fröhner, cf. *exanimis unanimis magnanimis semanimis louganimis pusillanimis.* Yet it seems hazardous to ascribe to Av. a word which is not known to exist elsewhere, and the balance of clauses is better preserved by reading **Pigra nimis,** to which **non aequans** stands parallel. As Schenkl observes, two reasons are given for the ant's remaining at home, (1) she is numbed with the cold; (2) her body is too small and feeble to face the stormy weather.   *tanto* of some MSS may be right = 'so little.' Trèves MS *tanto modico.*   **10. umida,** 'damp from the moisture sinking through.' Plin. H. N. xi. 109 *Semina adrosa condunt, ne rursus in frugem exeant e terra. maiora ad introitum diuidunt, madefacta imbre proferunt atque siccant.*   **legit.** The Paraphrast has *frumentum quod aestate collegerat, exsiccabat,* which agrees with the words of Babrius Χειμῶνος ὥρῃ σῖτον ἐκ μυχοῦ σύρων Ἔψυχε μύρμηξ ὅν θέρους σεσωρεύκει. On this view **legit** is 'picks' or 'sorts' for drying. This is not the ordinary sense of *legere* with *semina, grana,* etc. Cf. Ovid's *frugilegae formicae* Met. vii. 624, and *auidaeque uolucres Semina iacta legunt* M. v.

484, in both of which the idea is of picking up grain or seed for consumption. And so I think Av. meant here; the ant picks from her store of grain some for the need of the moment. Guiet explained 'edit uescitur.'　　11. It is hard to choose between Discolor of *ORX* and *Decolor* of *AP* and the Carlsruhe fragm. Though there is some confusion of the two words in MSS, their meanings are on the whole distinct. (1) Discolor is applied to objects which present a *mixture* of colours, as *a tiger's skin* (Stat. Theb. ix. 685), *a poplar-leaf* (S. ii. 3. 51), the *rainbow* (Theb. x. 119); and a cicala would be so called as not uniform in colour, but presenting in its body different hues crossing and intermingling with each other. This would be true of our grass-hoppers, which sometimes combine brown with green or yellow; and it may be equally so of Italian species. (Av. perhaps meant to contrast the motley colours of the cicala with the black hue of the ant, cf. Horace's *It matrona meretrici dispar erit atque Discolor* Epp. i. 18. 4). (2) *Decolor* is used of things which have changed or impaired their colour, whether by assuming a darker and dingier tinge, as *decolor Indus* (of which Passerat on Prop. iv. 3. 10 quotes 4 instances), 'the swarthy Oriental,' who has lost the fresh colour of the West, or by losing their healthy hue and turning pale, as in Prudentius' *decolor inuidia* Ham. 286. Here Av. might use the word somewhat less particularly, 'dingy' or 'sombre,' to suit the reversed circumstances of the insect now experiencing the shady side of its days.　　12. querulo ruperat arua sono, 'had made the fields split.' Vergilian, G. iii. 328 *Et cantu querulae rumpent arbusta cicadae.*　　querulo, a word not peculiar to the *cicada*, but expressing the 'noises' which each animal severally makes, the frog's *croak*, the she-goat's *bleat.* Apuleius uses the extraordinary adj. *obstreporus* to express the noise of the cicala (Flor. ii. 13).　　sono. Hence the Greek names for the τέττιξ mentioned by Aelian H. A. x. 44 λακέτας ἀχέτας. Cf. Plin. H. N. xi. 92. Aristophon Comicus fr. 10 Kock Πνῖγος ὑπομεῖναι καὶ μεσημβρίας λαλεῖν Τέττιξ.　　13. tunderet. The threshing-floor is personified as in Verg. G. i. 192, 298.　　Se quoque, 'she for her part,' i.e. she had had her own occupation like the ant. Verg. E. ix. 51 *saepe ego longos Cantando puerum memini me condere soles.*　　14. explicuisse, 'had worked out or finished off,' 'carried to their end': with some notion, as above XXVII. 10, where see note, of a lengthy and tiresome task: 'extendisse' Guiet.　　15. Paruula, 'the tiny one' *formica.* From Horace S. i. 2. 33 *Paruula nam exemplo est magni formica laboris.* So 'hardshell' for tortoise in Uncle Remus xxvi.　　16. A parenthesis exactly like XV. 3, 4.　　continuare, 'to prolong' from year to year, neither of them dying in the winter. (Cannegieter.)　　17. *En* which *C* alone of my MSS gives is hardly so good as Mi of the rest. The emphatic position of the word at the beginning of the v. is determined by the opposition of At tibi in 19; but instead of the nominative which might be expected, the pronoun is (doubtless for metrical reasons) constructed as part of the protatic clause, just as in Verg. Aen. iv. 340-2 *Me si fata meis paterentur ducere uitam Auspiciis et sponte mea componere curas, Vrbem Troianam primum dulcesque meorum Reliquias colerem,* the prose order *ego or equidem* gives way to *Me* constructed with the hypothetical clause.　　substantia, 'subsistence,' 'means,' a sense in which it is found in the Dialogus de Oratoribus viii *Sine commendatione natalium, sine substantia facultatum.* 'Sane est posterioris Latinitatis, uerum imprimis frequens apud ICtos,' Orelli there : but would Tacitus, or whoever wrote this dialogue, have used *substantia* by itself? At any rate neither Symmachus' Letters nor the Panegyrici nor Prudentius give any instance ; but Wopkens quotes it from Fulgentius (Myth. iii. 3), Sulpicius Severus (Chron. i. 76), Salvianus, and Aurelius Victor; Hartel's Index to Ennodius shows it was then quite established, and S. Jerome has the diminutive *substantiola* = 'a little property.'　　20.

Cantibus for *in cantibus* is noticeable. Manilius iv. 157 ed. Bentley *Otia et aeternam peragunt in amore iuuentam;* in ii. 205 *Non tenebris aut luce suam peragentia sortem (Signa)* is justified by the locative sense of the ablatives.

XXXV.

Babr. xxxv, Fab. Aesop. 366, 366ᵇ, 30 Kn.

BABR. XXXV.

Δύω μὲν υἱοὺς ἡ πίθηκος ὠδίνει,
τεκοῦσα δ' αὐτοῖς ἐστὶν οὐκ ἴση μήτηρ,
ἀλλ' ὃν μὲν αὐτῶν ἀθλίης ὑπ' εὐνοίης
θάλπουσα κόλποις ἀγρίοις ἀποπνίγει,
τὸν δ' ὡς περισσὸν καὶ μάταιον ἐκβάλλει.
κἀκεῖνος ἐλθὼν εἰς ἐρημίην ζώει.

Avianus has here deviated considerably from Babrius. In the Greek fable the mother ape stifles her favorite child by over-caressing; the less favored and discarded child escapes to the desert and comes to maturity. Babrius' version is identical with Oppian's, Cyneg. ii. 605 sqq. Schneider :—

Λείπω τρισσὰ γένεθλα, κακὸν μίμημα, πιθήκων.
τίς γὰρ ἂν οὐ στυγέοι τοῖον γένος, αἰσχρὸν ἰδέσθαι,
ἀβληχρὸν στυγερὸν δυσδέρκετον αἰολόβουλον;
κεῖνοι καὶ φίλα τέκνα δυσειδέα δοιὰ τεκάντες
οὐκ ἀμφοῖν ἀτάλαντον ἐὴν μερίσαντο ποθητύν·
ἀλλὰ τὸ μὲν φιλέουσι, τὸ δ' ἐχθαίρουσι λόχευμα,
αὐταῖς δ' ἀγκαλίδεσσιν ἑῶν τέθνηκε τοκήων.

1. **prōfundens** as in Catullus lxiv. 202; and in the hexameters on the Nile ascribed to Claudian xlvii. 12 (xxvii. 12 Jeep). The instance alleged by L. Müller from Lucan vii. 159 is not certain. He shows that in Christian poets the long *o* is of frequent occurrence. (De R. M. p. 363.) 2. 'Allots her children each to a separate destiny.' An inversion of the ordinary construction *diuidere uices in pignera* (Pers. v. 49 *Diuidit in geminos concordia fata duorum*). **pignera nata.** Canneg. quotes from Gruter DCCCVII. 12 *P. Memisianae uxori castiss. Q. Herculanius maritus cum pignerib. de ea natis locum consecrauit.* Claud. Laus Seren. 111 *non ante suis inpendit amorem Pigneribus.* Prud. Cath. x. 119 *Nullus sua pignera plangat.* The two oldest MSS of Prudentius are very clear for *e*, not *o*, in the oblique cases of *pignus.* Paris 8084 (in capitals, and perhaps of fifth century) gives PIGNERA P. ii. 523, C. x. 119, PIGNERE P. iv. 52, PIGNERIBVS Ps. 479. Bodl. Auct. T. 2. 22 (of eighth century) gives Cath. x. 119 *pignera*, Perist. ii. 523 *pignera*, xi. 210 *pigneribus*, v. 491 *pigneris*, all except the last in the sense of 'child': in Perist. iv. 52 alone *pignore*, not in the sense of child. 3. **caro,** 'fond' as an epithet of *amore* is unusual, but there is no evidence for *raro*. 4. **Alteriusque.** It is not true that when *unus (alter)* is followed by *alter*, the second *alter* is always without a copula. Vitruv. iv. 4. 3 *E quibus una sit non striata et altera striata.* iii. 5. 7 *Vnum cum sit positum ... et alterum diducatur.* **odiis exsaturata** from Vergil Aen. vii. 298. Cannegieter's conj. *insaturata* is plausible; but the word is very rare, though found twice in the Aratea of Avienus, *insaturatae odiis* Phaen. 183, *i. cibi* Progn. 513. **tumet,** 'rankles with excess of hate.' 5. **fetam,** here of an animal which has recently produced young ones. So Verg. Aen. viii. 630 *Fecerat et uiridi fetam Mauortis in antro Procubuisse lupam; geminos huic ubera circum Lambere.* **grauior,** 'serious' or 'threatening,' as *graue*

periculum Macrob. S. ii. 8. 6.   tumultus, 'sudden outbreak of war,' 'alarm of attack.' Verg. G. i. 464. It is noticeable that *tumultus tumescere* are there found in consecutive vv. as here tumet tumultus.   **6. Dissimili** condicione of unequal treatment like *dispar condicio* Cic. de Prouin. Consul. vii. 16.   **7. manibus,** here of the prehensile extremities of a monkey's fore-feet. Plin. H. N. xi. 246 (*Simiae habent*) *mammas in pectore et bracchia et crura in contrarium similiter flexa, in manibus unguis digitos longioremque medium.* So χεῖρες of apes in Aelian H. N. v. 7.   **pectore.** Fab. Aesop. 366ᵇ ἀεὶ ἐν τοῖς κόλποις περιφέρουσα,   **8. dorso suscipi-ente leuat.** Av.'s way of expressing *dorso susceptos leuat*, 'takes up and lifts on her back.'   **9. nequeat** of MSS need not be altered. Munro on Lucret. iii. 736 '*Cum subeant* and v. 62 and 680, as well as Cato de Re Rust. 90 *Cum far incipiat puriter facito*; in these cases *cum* with the pres. subj. or potent. seems to denote repetition; as *cum* seems to be clearly temporal in them all.'   **consistere,** 'stand,' i. e. maintain an erect post-ure. The ape is tired out with the combined effort of escaping and carrying her young, one on her back, the other supported in her front paws.   **10. Oppositum,** the burden at her breast, i.e. in front. (Guiet.) Heinsius' *Appositum* is comparatively weak and without any MS support.   **remisit** is not only given by *P*, the Trèves MS (*T*), and the Carlsruhe fragm. but was the *m. pr.* of *C*. It is an aoristic perfect.   **11.** Almost all MSS here agree in giving ab, which with Cataldo Iannelli I retain. It must be constructed with **Haeret,** 'hangs clinging to the neck.' Yet as *P* and the first Peterhouse MS give *ad*, the reading of most edd. *at* may be right; and the construction circumdans collo is certainly more simple, Ovid M. ix. 459, 605, vi. 479.   **12.** 'Shares the flight of his dam against her will.'   **13. quoque.** See on XVIII. 5.   **14.** unicus heres. Prud. Cath. xii. 82.   Symm. Epist. i. 3 *Solus hausisti ius-tus heres ueterum litterarum.* herĕs, as Ausonius Griph. 2. 39 writes *bipĕs* and *tripĕs*, Parent. 29. 4 *celeripĕs*, Maximianus *I'lixĕs* v. 20. Prudentius, as Krenkel shows p. 8, uses the nominatives *cautis famis prolis luis stipis Ioan-nis* and perhaps *pubis*, for the ordinary forms in *-es*. Vegetius i. 11 and 12 uses *cratis* as nom. for *crates*; and Av. himself seems to have written *uulpis* for *uulpes* in XL. 7. The Paris MS of Prudentius, which I examined for this purpose, gives PVBIS OMNIS LIQVERAT C. vii. 162, LVIS INCENTIVA FATIGAT H. 249, LVIS INPROBA Ps. 508, FAMIS INPIA NATOS Ps. 479; and it is a reasonable conclusion that where metre required a short syllable, the *-is* form was preferred. None of these however increase in the geni-tive, and as Priscian i. p. 156 Hertz ranks *quadrupes inquies* with *diues super-stes* as all ending in ĕs, it is clear that the earlier sense of quantity in these final syllables had then been lost, and Av. may have written *herĕs* as Ausonius wrote *bipĕs tripĕs celeripĕs.* auis, probably more after heres (Cic. Fam. xiii. 26 *Heres est M. Mindio fratri suo*) than Seruatus, though *seruare* with a dat. is common enough, e. g. in Symmachus' Letters (x. 12 (32)).   Titul. Sepulchr. Nicomachi Flauiani C. I. L. vi. 1783 SI EVM QVEM VIVERE NOBIS SERVARIQ VOBIS QVAE VERBA EIVS APVT VOS (of the Emperor Theodosius to the Senate) FVISSE PLERIQ. MEMINISTIS OPTAVIT. The less favored apeling is left the sole survivor of the name and fortunes of the family, by the death of his over-caressed brother.   **15, 16.** Hardly by Av. The Latinity wants clearness and point : rursūs before in is less likely to have been introduced as a corruption of something written by Av., than as a prosodial licence common in writers subsequent to him. Yet the fable would end very abruptly with v. 14 : and Lachmann's conclusion that the whole of vv. 13–16 is a later addition is critically very probable.   **15.** 'So it is that many find a pleasure in what they disparaged, and hope, reversing the order of things, brings men of mean estate back to a happier fortune.'   **16. rursus,** though it is tempting to alter its position and write *Rursus spes humiles,* is right where it stands before **in meliora.**

XXXVI.

Babr. xxxvii, Fab. Aesop. 113 Halm, 24 Kn.

BABR. XXXVII.

Δαμάλης ἐν ἀγροῖς ἄφετος, ἀτριβὴς ζεύγλης,
κάμνοντι καὶ σύροντι τὴν ὗνιν ταύρῳ
'τάλας' ἐφώνει 'μόχθον οἷον ὀτλεύεις.'
ὁ βοῦς δ' ἐσίγα χὐπέτεμνε τὴν χώρην.
ἐπεὶ δ' ἔμελλον ἀγρόται θεοῖς θύειν,
ὁ βοῦς μὲν ὁ γέρων εἰς νομὰς ἀπεζεύχθη,
ὁ δὲ μόσχος ἀδμὴς κεῖνος εἵλκετο σχοίνῳ
δεθεὶς κέρατα, βωμὸν αἵματος πλήσων.
κἀκεῖνος αὐτῷ τοιάδ' εἶπε φωνήσας·
εἰς ταῦτα μέντοι μὴ πονῶν ἐτηρήθης·
ὁ νέος παρέρπεις τὸν γέροντα καὶ θύῃ,
καί σου τένοντα πέλεκυς, οὐ ζυγὸς τρίψει.

1. **resultans** seems to mean 'bounding to and fro,' or 'backwards and forwards.' This sense is post-classical. There is nothing in Babrius corresponding, nor in Halm's prose version.   **4.** *Ferre nec expositis* MSS mostly. Withof explained *expositis* as ' open.' ' Exposita iuga uocat montes seu colles herbosos et apricos, et quod maxime uim epitheti exprimit, tales colles qui armentis libere patent, et unde non prohibentur,' p. 281. Cf. Stat. S. i. 2. 34 *Licet expositum per limen aperto Ire, redire gradu.* Most edd. however, including Guiet, who notes 'i. e. depositis, barbare,' have found the word objectionable : and *Ferrea* of *B,* with the omission of *nec* in *P,* perhaps points to a corruption. I have written **Ferre nec haec positis,** ' and never to get rid of the yoke and taste the sweets of repose like mine.'   **haec,** ' such as you see.' So *haec deuia,* ' your present sidling gait,' III. 5.   **5. subiectas** seems to suit *iugis* in the sense of *hills.* The calf might descend to the grassy ground on the lower part of the slopes, or mount to the woods higher up.   **discursus** all my MSS, ' to range freely over the grass.'   **6. rursus,** 'and then again, if I am so inclined.' Cf. XXIX. 18. Lachm. preferred *sursus* as in XV. 8, and Canneg. found *sursus* in two MSS. But here the antithesis to **subiectas** is somewhat flat ; **rursus** is more natural and quite in Av.'s manner.   **opaca,** if I need shade.   **sequi,** ' push into the dark depths of the woods.' Vergilian, Aen. ii. 737 *auia cursu Dum sequor,* v. 629 *pelagique extrema sequentem.*   **7. nullam,** ' not for a moment angered by what he said.'   **8. solitam,** XVII. 5.   **fessus.** Av. is here closer than usual to his original, κάμνοντι καὶ σύροντι τὴν ὗνιν ταύρῳ.   **9. per prata** with **procubuisse.** The ox is removed from the ploughing-field to the meadow.   **11.** I retain the MS reading, but for *innexum* write **ut nexum.**   **sacris aris,** ' sacrificial altars,' or ' altars of divine worship,' to be connected with **Admotum** as in Luc. i. 608 *sacris tunc admouet aris Electa ceruice marem.* Verg. Aen. xii. 171 *admouitque pecus flagrantibus aris.* Ovid M. xiii. 454 *postquam crudelibus aris Admota est.* Cannegieter's conj. (accepted by Lachm.) *sertis,* though well according with *innexum* (Ovid Trist. v. 3. 3) heaps up the successive clauses *sertis innexum, aris admotum,* very awkwardly, and could hardly be what Av. wrote. Besides, it only loosely expresses the Babrian εἵλκετο σχοίνῳ Δεθεὶς κέρατα.   **nexum,** ' tied with a cord.'   **12. popae,** genitive on which **cultro** depends,

'grapple with the knife of the priest's attendant.' Properly the *popa* seems to have been distinguished from the *cultrarius*, Suet. Gaius Caesar 32 : here the functions are blended. Both Suetonius and Propertius (iv. 3. 62) apply the word *succinctus* to the *popa* : see the illustration in Rich.   1C. It is difficult to decide between *tristis* of most MSS and **testis** of *C* and the Carlsruhe fragm. If we argue from Babrius, the words κἀκεῖνος αὐτῷ τουίδ' εἶπε φωνήσας (9) as well as ὁ νέος παρέρπεις τὸν γέροντα (11) which implies that the calf passed the ox on his way to be sacrificed, are somewhat in favour of **testis**. Rhythm on the other hand rather supports *tristis*, which itself well expresses the *disastrous* consequences of the forbearance (**indulgentia**) which has left the calf its freedom only to sacrifice it in the end.   16. **grauis quamuis**, 'however severe.' *Quamuis* with adjectives almost always precedes, here follows its adj. as *licet* does even in the polished Merobaudes Paneg. Aetii 70 N. *tali residem licet excitat orsu.*   16. **quam**, as if *magis* preceded : so XLII. 14.   **tenerum**, 'in childhood.' Verg. G. ii. 343 *in teneris*, Ecl. i. 8 *tener agnus.*   **mox peritura**, 'idleness doomed after a time to end.'   **pati.** Though used elsewhere *in re bona* as Forcellini shows from Asin. ii. 2. 58 *Fortiter malum qui patitur, idem post patitur* (Goetz *potitur*) *bonum*. Poen. iii. 3. 83 *Siquidem potes pati esse te in lepido loco.* Rutil. i. 446 *Dum mala formides, nec bona posse pati* is here at least half in a bad sense, 'be sentenced or condemned to.'   17, 18. If with most MSS *regat* is retained in 18, translate, 'This is the lot of men, that the happier die soon, whereas the poor are governed by the uncertainties of a life shifting from day to day.'· The two vv. are peculiar and, spite of Lachmann's condemnation, not unworthy of Av. Nevelet's reading *m. fel. ut sit Mors cita* is against all my MSS ; yet it certainly balances the sounds more effectively **sors ista—mors cita.** 'Vita diurna est ἐφημέριος, nullum diem secura aut certa sui,' Caspar Barth Aduers. L. 7, rightly, though as both Guiet and Wopkens thought, there may be in **diurna** some idea of *prolongation* from day to day.   A. Gellius xvii. 2 and Nonius 100 both quote the annalist Claudius Quadrigarius as using *diurnare = diu uiuere* : an inscript. in Gruter has *diurno parasito Apollinis* = 'qui quotidie epulabatur in synhodo Apollinis' (Forc.) ; and *diurnis diebus* in the medical writer Caelius Aurelianus = 'every day.' Cf. XXXIII. 16 *uota diurna*. But *regat* is, to say the least, somewhat forced ; and if we remember the close resemblance in some of the earlier forms of writing between *n* and *r* is very likely to be a corruption of *negat*, which is actually given by two Brit. Mus. MSS, *B* and *b²*. *B* had also as m. pr. *miseris*, and this gives a good sense, 'whilst the life they lead day after day (prolonged from day to day) says no (*Nulli negare soleo* Plaut. Stich. i. 3. 28) to the wretched,' i.e. will not permit them to die. Or again, *regat* may be a corruption of **necat**, the sense being 'the happy die soonest, whereas the wretched are slain day after day by the unhappy lives they lead.' This would agree with the common use of *enecare* in Plaut. and Terence for plaguing to death. [This conj. of my own I have decided to admit as more direct and intelligible than either of the other readings.]

XXXVII.

Babr. c, Fab. Aesop. 278.

The leading idea of this fable, the contrast of pampered slavery that hugs its chains with hungry independence, is presented in more than one form in the Aesopian collection. Here and in Fab. Aesop. 278 we have a dog and lion ; Aesop. 321 brings before us a tame ass which feeds well and becomes sleek, but is beaten severely by its master, and a wild ass which at first discontented with its rough life is consoled by seeing the rigorous treatment its domesticated brother has to endure.

Phaedrus has a long fable identical with this, except that a wolf takes the place of Av.'s lion (iii. 7). He prefaces it with the words *Quam dulcis sit libertas, breuiter proloquar*, a line which to the degenerate Romans of the declining Empire would have had little meaning, but in the age of Tiberius was very significant.

BABR. C.

Λύκῳ συνήντα πιμελῆς κύων λίην.
ὁ δ' αὐτὸν ἐξήταζε ποῦ τριφεὶς οὕτως
μέγης κύων ἐγένετο καὶ λίπους πλήρης.
'ἄνθρωπος' εἶπε 'δαψιλής με σιτεύει.'
ὁ δέ σοι τράχηλος, εἶπε, πῶς ἐλειικώθη;
'κλοιῷ τέτριπται σάρκα τῷ σιδηρείῳ,
ὃν ὁ τροφεύς μοι περιτέθεικε χαλκεύσας.'
λύκος δ' ἐπ' αὐτῷ καγχάσας 'ἐγὼ τοίνυν
χαίρειν κελεύω' φησί 'τῇ τρυφῇ ταύτῃ
δι' ἣν σίδηρος τὸν ἐμὸν αὐχένα τρίψει.'

1. **exhausto** = *exhaustis uiribus*, 'worn out,' as Lucan says iv. 622 *Exhausitque uirum*. Juv. ix. 59.   2. **insertis.** Quintilian ii. 10. 9 uses *inserere iocos* of introducing jests into rhetorical language. Ovid Trist. ii. 444 *Historiae turpes inseruisse iocos*, of weaving jokes into the texture of history. Av. means scarcely more than 'adding gibes' nearly = *iocans*. Possibly we should read *intertis* like *intorquere contumelias* Cic. Tusc. Disp. iv. 36. 77.   **uerba dedisse** like **insertis iocis** shows how the correct feeling of language had declined. As in IX. 20 it *locutus esse*, but without the epithets which there take from the strangeness of the expression. In classical Latin *uerba dare* = 'to deceive': Ter. Eun. Prol. 24 is a *double entendre* which proves nothing. Cf. the definition of Symmachus in the Explanat. in Donat. Grammat. Lat. Keil iv. 488 *Symmachus sic : uerba dare captiui est, argentum dare satellitis*.   3. **duplici tergo** was explained by Heinsius Advers. p. 611 as *lato tergo*, like Vergil's *duplex agitur per lumbos spina*, which Servius interprets *lata* and Oppian's Διπλὰ δὲ οἱ μετόπισθε μετάφρενα, πίονα δημῷ. If this is so, the abl. can only loosely be constructed with **tendantur**, 'how my flanks dilate (swell) and my back rises in a double ridge.' It seems more likely that **tergo** is here used more indefinitely of the ridge or projecting surface of the skin covering the dog's flanks, which is called double from the inequalities produced by the outstanding muscle or fat : for it can hardly be simply = *tergore* or *cute*, as explained in some of the mediaeval glosses. Another view has been suggested to me by my friend Mr. C. N. Eliot, viz. that **duplici tergo** means the point where the spine *parts off* into the haunches ; but Av. seems to be imitating Vergil here as in 4.   **tendantur,** 'dilate,' 'are distended,' Col. vi. 14. 4 *Intumescit collum, neruique tenduntur.*   4. Verg. G. iii. 87 *Luxuriatque toris animosum pectus*, where *animosum* corresponds to Av.'s *nobile.*   5. **Proximus** with **humanis mensis.** The dog is most in the confidence of man and is admitted to the nearest place at his table.   **post otia** is obviously modelled on Phaedr. iii. 7. 13, 14, where the dog says to the wolf *Quanto est facilius mihi sub tecto uiuere, Et otiosum largo satiari cibo*. It is true that in Amm. Marc. xvi. 12. 9 *post otium cibique refectionem*, Paneg. Maxim. et Constantin. xii *Bährens multo magis mirum est te imperium ferre post otium*, the words mean 'after resting,' whereas here they must mean 'when resting-time has set in.' But this is scarcely reason enough for altering them.   6. **Communem,** 'shared with my master.' Phaedr. iii. 7. 21 *Adfertur ultro panis ; de mensa sua Dat ossa dominus, frusta iactat familia Et quod fastidit quisque pulmentarium.* Poseidonius ap. Athen. 152 F τὸ παραβληθὲν κυνιστὶ σιτεῖται.   7. **crassa,** 'brawny' with

good fare. Lachmann's *rasa* is however very plausible, for Babrius has
κλοιῷ τέτριπται σάρκα, Phaedrus iii. 7. 16 *adspicit Lupus a catena collum
detritum cani.* **malum,** hardly the interjection (see Munro, Elucid. of
Catullus, xxix. 21, p. 102), but mockingly 'what is that villainous chain
round your throat?' Catullus' *mala tussis* is somewhat similar, xliv.
7. **8.** 'That when I have guarded the house (by night) I may not
be free to leave it (by day).' Phaedr. iii. 7. 18 *Quia uideor acer, adligant
me interdiu, Luce ut quiescam, et uigilem nox cum uenerit.* **9. moribundus,** 'ready to die' with hunger: Phaedr. iii. 7. 6 *Ego qui sum longe fortior,
pereo fame.* **lustra,** 'wilds,' where no food is to be got. **12. Dum,**
'till,' i. e. with the prospect of eventually being fed for your services. **faciles,** 'easily won,' opp. to the difficulty of getting food in the woods. **13.
collectus in iram** = *se colligens in i.* Lucan uses *colligere iram* of a lion,
i. 205 *Sic cum squalentibus aruis Aestiferae Libyes uiso leo comminus hoste
Subsedit dubius, totam dum colligit iram, Mox ubi se saeuae stimulauit uerbere
caudae Erexitque iubam et uasto graue murmur hiatu Infremuit:* and
so Val. Fl. vii. 335 *morituraque conligit iras,* where Burmann quotes Stat. Theb.
xii. 759 *extrema se conligit ira.* **14.** It is hard to decide whether
this is anacoluthon like XXV. 5, 6, or **collectus** and **Atque ferox animi**
are both nominatives to **agit.** The former is perhaps more in Av.'s manner. See XVI. 12, XVII. 13. **ferox animi,** 'in pride of soul.' **nobile,**
'a generous' growl. **agit,** 'heaves' or 'gasps forth': on the analogy
of *animam agere.* **15. meritis,** 'as it deserves': see on XVII.
5. **16.** 'And let your hunger be a set-off to the galling of your chain,'
i.e. an excuse which may be alleged on the other side. With a similar
inversion Horace says S. i. 3. 70 *mea compenset uitiis bona,* meaning 'counterbalance my vices by my virtues,' 'set my virtues against my vices,' see A.
Palmer in loc. The sense can hardly be 'let your chains counterbalance
(i.e. be set in the scale against) the *gratification of* your hunger,' which
forces **famem** over-much. *Conpescant* is not found in any of the earliest
MSS, and is in any case 'durius dictum' as Wopkens remarked. **dura,**
MSS, like Prud. Psych. Praef. 21, c. Symm. i. 473. Wopkens preferred
dira, 'quod nonnisi horum gestandorum pretio acquireret cibos de quibus
gloriabatur.' **17.** 'When I return in freedom to my solitary cavern,
famished as I am I start for any field I wish.' **mea libertas** = *ego
liber.* **redditur** of MSS must not be altered to *redditor* (Withof), which
would necessitate changing **peto** to *petam.* In itself the emendation is a
good and likely one: in Orientius Common. i. 52 *propriis cousequitor
meritis* is a certain restoration of Delrio's for the MS *consequitur.* **19.**
'Remember to commend this rich living, not to the lovers of independence,
but to those who have renounced freedom for gluttony.' **Has,** this
good feeding of yours, like *haec otia* in XXXVI. 4. **potius,** 'preferably,'
i. e. rather than to those who like me love their freedom.

XXXVIII.

I have not found any Greek fable corresponding to this in Halm; and it is not
in our Babrius.

1. torrente, abl. absolute, 'by the rushing of the river.' Verg. E. vii.
52 *torrentia flumina.* **coactus,** forced to quit the depths of the river,
where the water was sweet, for the salt water of the sea. By **stagnis** Av.
seems to mean the water at the bottom of the river, much as Vergil says
Aen. x. 765 *medii per maxima Nerei Stagna.* Ovid F. iii. 647, 8 *Corniger
hanc tumidis rapuisse Numicius undis Dicitur et stagnis occuluisse suis.* **2.
praeceps obibat,** 'darted to and fro.' **3. squamigerum agmen,**
'the scaly company.' So Lucretius uses *squamigeri* = *pisces,* i. 371, 378, cf.

squamigerum genus i. 162 (Munro).   **improbus,** ἀναιδής (Munro on Lucr.
iii. 1026). So XLII. 12.   **4. nobilitate,** 'gentility.'   **5. Non
tulit,** 'could not put up with the airs of the ejected fish.' Vergilian,
Aen. viii. 256, ix. 622, xii. 371.   **expulsum** represents the point of
view of the habitual occupants of the sea (**patrio sub gurgite**).   **phoecis** of *C* and the Carlsruhe fragm. accounts for *phocas,* the reading of most
MSS. It is another spelling of *phycis,* cf. *Poenicus Punicus, poeniceus puni-
ceus, moenia munia,* etc. (Roby L. G. i. p. 84). Pliny H. N. xxxii. 150
mentions the *phycis* as a *rock* fish (*saxatilium*), in ix. 81 as changing its hue
at different times, in spring parti-coloured, generally white: and as the
only fish which constructs a *nest* of sea-weed in which it brings forth its
young. Pliny's description is throughout of a *sea-fish,* which also suits the
etymology (φῦκος *alga*) Oppian Ἁλιευτ. i. 122 sqq. cited by Cannegieter
Πέτραι δ' ἀμφίαλοι πολυειδέες· αἱ μὲν ἔασι Φύκεσι μυθαλέαι, περὶ δὲ μνία πολλὰ
πέφυκε, Τὰς ἤτοι πέρκαι καὶ ἰουλίδες, ἀμφί τε χάννοι Φέρβονται, σάλπαι τε μετὰ
σφίσιν αἰολόνωτοι, Καὶ κίχλαι ῥαδιναὶ καὶ φυκίδες, οὖς θ' ἁλιῆες Ἄνδρος ἐπωνυ-
μίην θηλύφρονος ηὐδάξαντο (*cinaedi*).   **6. cum salibus** MSS against
metre. The Gale MS, as reported by Bährens, gives *cum sociis,* a manifest
interpolation, and without much point, for the force of the fable lies
greatly in the sharp contrast of the *two* fishes. *Pet*[2] has *cum reprehensionibus* written over *cum salibus;* possibly this gloss has remained after the
word it explained had become corrupted; and for *salibus* we should read
sannis, 'derisive scoffs.' Juvenal (vi. 306) and Persius (i. 62, v. 91) both
use the word: the Schol. on Pers. i. 62 explains *Sanna dicitur os distortum
cum uultu : quod facimus cum alios deridemus.* Like μυχθισμός *sanna* expresses
the act of forcing the breath through the nostrils and the scornful sound
thus produced, '*reuocato naribus spiritu insultare*' Schol. Juv. l.c.   **7.
laboratis,** 'studied' to give what he said a look of *plausibility* (Cannegieter). The idea is perhaps an extension of this, 'magniloquent.' Or
is it 'fabricated' and so 'unreal'?   **8. Quaeque,** i.e. *uana mendacia et
quae refutari queant.* See on XXXIII. 2.   **refutari,** 'disproved.'
Mamertin. Grat. Actio Iuliano v *Si enim comminisci aliqua flagitia temp-
tassent, facile ipso splendore laudis et gloriae refutarentur.*   **te quoque
teste,** 'by the evidence of your own eyes' (Canneg.).   **9. eat** is
Bährens' emendation for *erit* of MSS: which however can hardly be
considered certainly wrong in the Latin of Av. There is, too, something unusual, perhaps over-pompous, in eat; cf. however XVII. 6.   **10.
Si pariter,** i.e. should both be taken in some fisherman's net.   **umida lina trahant,** from Vergil G. i. 142 *pelagoque alius trahit umida
lina.*   **11. nobilior,** of rank or consideration. See on XXIII. 3,
4 *Nobilis hunc ... Mercari cupiens.*   **12. simul,** 'eodem tempore,'
Wopkens. The word points the contrast.   **aere breui,** 'for a brass
farthing.'   **debile,** XVI. 12. The sense seems to be 'insignificant,'
but I have not been able to find it elsewhere, unless this is the meaning of
Capitolinus Vit. Maximi et Balbini xiv *Cum Balbinus Maximum quasi ignobilem
contemneret, Maximus Balbinum quasi debilem calcaret.* In Stat. Theb. iii. 563
nos prauum ac debile uulgus Scrutari penitus superos, the best MSS seem to
give *flebile.* The *phycis* is often mentioned by the writers of the Middle
and New Comedy as a good fish for eating. Diphilus of Siphnos in his
work περὶ τῶν προσφερομένων τοῖς νοσοῦσι καὶ τοῖς ὑγιαίνουσι (directions for
food in health and disease) said τῶν πετραίων ὁ φυκὴν καὶ ἡ φυκὶς ἁπαλώτατα
ἰχθύδια ὄντα ἄβρωμα καὶ εὐφθαρτά ἐστιν Athen. 355 b. Cf. Alexis fr. 110
Kock, Antiphanes fr. 132 K., Ephippus fr. 12 K., Mnesimachus ap. Athen.
403 b. Anaxandrides in his Protesilaus introduced *boiled* phycides (Athen.
131 e). Their being so often alluded to by Athenaeus is a proof of the
high estimation in which they were held by epicures.

XXXIX.

Fab. Aesop. 386 Halm, 131 Kn.

This fable is not in our Babrius. Gitlbauer, following Lachmann, has attempted to reconstruct the prose version of the Bodl. Paraphrast (131 Kn.) in Babrian scazons (171 ed. Gitlbauer).

AESOP. 386 HALM.

Σαλπιγκτὴς στρατὸν ἐπισυνάγων καὶ κρατηθεὶς ὑπὸ τῶν πολεμίων ἐβόα ‘μὴ κτείνετέ με, ὦ ἄνδρες, εἰκῆ καὶ μάτην· οὐδένα γὰρ ὑμῶν ἀπέκτεινα· πλὴν γὰρ χαλκοῦ τούτου οὐδὲν ἄλλο κτῶμαι.’ οἱ δὲ πρὸς αὐτὸν ἔφασαν· ‘διὰ τοῦτο γὰρ μᾶλλον τεθνήξῃ, ὅτι σὺ μὴ δυνάμενος πολεμεῖν, τοὺς πάντας πρὸς μάχην ἐγείρεις.’

BODL. PARAPHR. (131 KN.).

Ὅτι πλεῖον πταίουσιν οἱ τοὺς κακοὺς καὶ βαρεῖς δυνάστας διεγείροντες πρὸς τὸ κακοποιῆσαι.

Σάλπιγγός τις ἦν ἐπιστήμων στρατὸν συνάγων εἰς συμβολὰς πολέμων. οὗτος αἰχμάλωτος ληφθεὶς ἱκέτευε μὴ κτείνειν αὐτόν, ὡς μήτε τινὰ φονεύοντα μήτε κουρσεύοντα, πλὴν τὸ χαλκοῦν τοῦτο βύκινον εἰδέναι. οἱ δὲ εἶπον ‘Διὰ τοῦτο μᾶλλον τεθνήξῃ ὅτι σὺ μηδὲν ἰσχύων τοὺς ἄλλους διεγείρεις.’

1. **Vouerat.** Florus (ii. 4. 4) cited by Canneg. of the Gauls *Mox Ariouisto duce uouere de nostrorum* (= Romanorum) *militum praeda Marti suo torquem. Intercepit Iuppiter uotum. Nam de torquibus eorum aureum tropaeum Ioui Flaminius erexit. Viridomaro rege Romana arma Vulcano promiserant : aliorsum uota ceciderunt.* **attritus per proelia,** 'battered in many a fight.' Pacatus Paneg. Theodos. v *attritam pedestribus proeliis Batauiam referam?* Amm. Marc. xvii. 13. 28 quoted by Heinsius on Claud. Nupt. Honor. et Mar. 179 *Quados Sarmatis adiumenta ferentes attriuimus.* **2. suppositis ignibus dare,** 'to light a pyre and consign to it.' *Supponere ignem* is Vergilian, Aen. xi. 119, and so Ovid M. ii. 810 *cum spinosis ignis supponitur herbis,* F. iv. 803, 4 *tectis agrestibus ignem Et cessaturae supposuisse casae.* **dare,** XXII. 11, 12. The construction *igni dare* is Macrobian, vii. 7. 5. **3. moriens,** falling in combat. **4. capi** followed by **ab** would more naturally mean to be taken *by* than *from*. Hence Canneg. conj. *rapi.* The MS reading however may be defended even from Cic. Verr. v. 48. 127 *In urbe nostra pulcherrima atque ornatissima quod signum, quae tabula picta est, quae non ab hostibus uictis capta atque deportata sit?* **5. uotis fors affuit,** 'chance favoured his hopes.' Symmachus has similar combinations Epp. iv. 18 *si fors uotum iuuet,* v. 69 *si fors uotis effectum secundet.* The opposite is *fortuna defuit* Val. M. iii. 2. 3. **memor,** 'recalling his vow.' **6. singula,** 'piece by piece.' **7. deflectens,** 'repelling,' and so 'deprecating.' This is the reading of the best MSS: but the use is rare. *defendens* is comparatively common-place. **murmure,** 'boom.' Lucr. iv. 543 *Cum tuba depresso grauiter sub murmure mugit, Et reboat raucum retro (regio* Munro) *cita barbara bombum.* **8. esse prius** MSS. **isse pyrae** is the joint conjecture of myself and Fröhner. 'Explains that it had come to the flames of the pyre for no fault of its own.' I prefer this to Fröhner's *Inmeritum in flammis s. d. esse pyrae,* as less tame and prosaic. But it is possible that Cataldo Iannelli was right in retaining *prius* (sc. *Inmeritum*), which with *isse* would give a fair sense, 'explains that it had come to the fire without having committed any fault up to that time.' **10. tamen** leaves a doubt whether Av. means 'cruel as is your action, you might *yet* allege as a plea for it that I had aimed a dart at you,' or 'though the dart did not strike or hurt you, you might *yet* say it was thrown by me,' with which cf. Plin. H. N. viii. 51 *eum uero qui telum quidem miserit, sed*

tamen non uolnerauerit. It marks something which is regarded as a set-off or compensation. See my note on Catull. ci. 7.   **11. uentis et can- tibus,** ' with blasts of wind and sounding tones,' a sufficiently apt phrase to express the function of a trumpet. None of the modern emenda- tions *uanis ego cantibus* Lachm., *suetis ex c.* Bährens, are as plausible as the interpolated reading of the Brit. Mus. Reg. 15 A. vii *uentis erranti- bus.*   **arma coegi,** στράτον συναγήοχα εἰς συμβολὰς πολέμων, as the Bodleian Paraphrast words it. It is a variation on Vergil's *totamque sub arma coactam Hesperiam* Aen. vii. 43.   Ovid's *arma coacta,* 'unavoidable war' (Trist. iv. 9. 8) is quite different.   **12.** 'And even this only with a subdued sound, be the stars themselves my witness.' The trumpet is hardly loud enough for the stars to hear.   **summisso,** like *summittere uocem, orationem* in Quintilian. *R* glosses the word by *humili.*   **13. resultantem addens,** 'jerking on the fire and making it rebound.' I see no reason for believing with Unrein p. 42 that *resultare* here = *recusare* or *aduersari* in which sense it is used by Cassiodorius Hist. Eccles. v. 11 *Iudaei teutabant resultare Romanis,* and Gregory of Tours Hist. Franc. x. 15 *Resultare coepimus dicentes, quod non accederemus ad hunc locum:* to which add Sidon. viii. 14 *difficultas resultat optatis,* vii. 2 *ueritati resultantia.*   **flammis crepitantibus.** Lucretian, vi. 155 *laurus Terribili sonitu flamma crepitante crematur.* Verg. G. i. 85 *crepitantibus urere flammis.*   **14. Nunc,** 'now,' after what you have confessed.   **maior,** ' an extra severity of punishment and pain.'   **dolor- que :** possibly *calorque,* as suggested by *B*'s *colorque,* is right, ' fiery punish- ment '?   **15. temptare,** ' try anything aggressive.'   **ausis,** as my excellent Brit. Mus. MS *B* gives, is clearly right. No greater proof of its value could be, for all the other, even the earliest MSS, have *au- sus.*   **16. Saeuior hoc,** ' you are a fiercer foe to deal with in so far as you make others quarrel.'   **hoc,** ' for this reason,' referring to quod **facis.** The omission of *es* after **Saeuior** is unusual : see on XXXIV. 1. In the somewhat later Commonitorium of Orientius it is tolerably frequent.

XL.

A fine fable on the frailness of beauty in comparison with mental gifts. The Babrian original is lost, but is almost recoverable in the prose version of the Bod- leian Paraphrast [1]. See Eberhard 137, Gitlbauer 172.

A very similar fable, but in which the interlocutors are a wolf and a fox, is still extant No. 101 in our Babrius. There a wolf that from his fine size and shape was called ' lion ' by his brother wolves, quits their society for the company of lions (τῶν δὲ συμφύλων Ἀποστατήσας τοῖς λέουσιν ὡμίλει). A fox meets him and remarks ' I pray to be saved from your delusions : among wolves you *may* be a lion, but among lions you are assuredly a wolf.'

Fab. Aesop. 42, 42[b] Halm = Bodl. Paraphr. 132 Kn.

CXXXII. KN.

Στικτή ποτε πάρδαλις ἐκαυχᾶτο φορεῖν ἁπάντων ζώων ποικιλωτέραν δέρριν. Πρὸς ἣν ἡ ἀλώπηξ εἶπεν ' Ἐγώ σοι τῆς δορᾶς κρείττονα καὶ ποικιλωτέραν γνώμην ἔχω.'

' Once a leopard spotted gaily and beauteous of breast went to parade himself among his fellow-beasts. But finding that the lions were surly and had no rich colour on their skins, that instant he concluded them to be a sorry breed. The other brutes he damned for a mean-looking lot, and found he was himself the one sole pattern of nobility. A wily fox seeing him so proud of his spring-like attire took him to task and showed that his fine

----

[1] I have attempted to restore this to Babrian scazons in Excursus II.

COMMENTARY. 125

markings were a delusion. "Go thy ways," said he, "put the prodigal's trust in thy blazon'd youth, if thou wilt : only let me have the fairer possession, understanding ; and let us own the fascination that comes of mental adornment rather than of glittering personal advantages." '

1. **maculis.** Plin. H. N. viii. 62 *Panthera et tigris macularum uarietate prope solae bestiarum spectantur. Pantheris in candido breues macularum oculi.* Il. x. 29 παρδαλέη ποικίλη. **pectore,** the reading of all early MSS, is to be preferred to *corpore* (1) from the pleasing alliteration **pulchro pectore pardus**; (2) from the fine contour of the leopard's neck and chest. **pardus.** Leopards and panthers, from their combined grace of form, colour, and movement, are natural types of beauty. Wordsworth Ruth 37 *He was a lovely youth! I guess The panther in the wilderness Was not so fair as he.* From the earliest period of the Roman Empire to the latest no gift was more acceptable to the Roman people than these graceful but fierce habitants of the jungle. Mamertinus in his Panegyric addressed to Maximianus says of the Persian King (c. x) *Offert interim uaria miracula, eximiae pulcritudinis feras mittit.* **2. consimiles** seems to express the Babrian σύμφυλοι (ci. 4). Lachm. went on to infer that the rest of Av.'s verse must correspond to the Babrian τῶν δὲ συμφύλων Ἀποστατήσας τοῖς λέουσιν ὡμίλει, and conj. for the corrupt **ibat inira** of the earliest MSS *abnuit ire;* which is accepted by Schenkl. With Bährens, I doubt the soundness of this emendation. For (1) **Sed** in 3 is then awkwardly explained by the negative *idea* in *abnuit,* instead of marking a distinct opposition, as it surely ought ; (2) **ibat** is the recurring ᾖει of Babrius (Rutherford's Index gives five examples) and the prose fables. What then is **inira** for which *P* gives *mira, RT inire; A m. sec.,* the two Peterhouse MSS, my *X,* and the valuable *B, ibat in arua?* It seems hardly probable that *in arua* should appear in the strange form of *in ira ;* and there is some force in Withof's objection that the pard would be more likely to go into the *jungle* than the fields. Withof's own conj. *honore,* 'his co-mates in distinction' would have a significance if we regard the fable as aimed at the *purpurati* and gaily-drest officials of the Imperial Court of the fourth and fifth centuries: *honore* indeed would suggest both ideas, official rank and splendid exterior (see on XV. 9). On this point of view we might illustrate from the Panegyrici. Mamertin. Grat. Act. Iuliano xxx *Paene intra ipsas palatinae domus ualuas lecticas consulares iussit inferri et cum honori eius uenerationique cedentes sedile illud dignitatis amplissimae recusaremus, suis prope nos manibus impositos mixtus agmini togatorum praeire pedes coepit . . . Credet hoc aliquis qui illa purpuratorum uidit paulo ante fastidia ? qui ideo tantum honorem in suos ne inhonoros contemnerent conferebant.* Yet there is something forced and unlike Av.'s ordinary style in **ibat** standing thus isolated : may the right reading be *in ora ?* The pard went *to parade himself* among the beasts his compeers. A similar corruption of letters is found in XXXVII. 8 where for *abire* was at first written in *C abore.* For the sense cf. Ovid Pont. iv. 6. 18 *Vestra procul positus carmen in ora dedi ;* similarly *in ore* Trist. iv. 1. 68 Güthling *Viuere quam miserum est inter Bessosque Getasque Illum qui populi semper in ore fuit.* Prop. iii. 13. 12 *Et spolia opprobrii nostra per ora trahit.* Symm. Epist. x. 32 *sit in ore plurimorum,* of Praetextatus to whom a statue was to be erected. **3. nulla.** See on XXXVI. 7. Calp. Ecl. iii. 5 *Iam dudum nullis dubitaui crura rubetis Scindere.* **graues** might seem here to mean ' strong-scented,' for Pliny describes the lion as having *grauem odorem, nec minus halitum* H. N. viii. 46. The v. would then carry a double reproach, ' the lions had a noisome smell and showed no fine colours in their skin.' This would agree with the fact stated also by Pliny (viii. 62) that the peculiar odour of the panther has a strange attraction (*mire solicitari*) for all other quadrupeds: and the

contrast of the two animals would be complete.   On the other hand,
lightness and agile grace of movement is as marked a characteristic of
the panther and the leopard as a grave and even heavy demeanour of
the lion : qualities which again part off into *sprightliness* on one side,
surliness on the other.   **uariarent terga,** 'spotted their backs' = *uari-
ata t. haberent.*   Pliny mentions as one kind of pard *uaria* viii. 63 and
64.   **4. Protinus,** 'he concluded without more ado' : as we might
say, leapt to his conclusion.   **miserum,** δείλαιον, 'sorry' or 'paltry.'   **5.**
sordenti uultu MSS, 'as mean-looking.'   Martial has *Dum nulla teneri
sordent lanugine uultus* i. 32. 5 : but this ill defends the MS reading, as there
sordent = ' is discoloured.'   Hence Lachm.'s emend. *cultu* is probable, cf.
amictu in 7 : the attire is of course the skin.   **damnans,** absolutely
' rejecting, vilipending,' our ' damning,' as several times in Pliny xx. 77 *in
totum damnauit serim,* xi. 4 *fastidio damnare.*   Sil. vi. 448 *patrios damnare
penates Absiste.*   This is more natural than to take **uultu** as abl. after **damnans,** ' condemning of,' ' holding guilty of ' an ignoble look : though this is
common enough.   **6.** ' Was himself the one sole pattern of aris-
tocratic breeding.'   in **exemplum** : frequent in Quintilian. ii. 1. 41
Vnam de schola controuersiam proponam in exemplum.   xii. 2. 27 *In exemplum
bene dicendi facundissimum quemque preponet sibi ad imitandum.*   v. 12. 21
*Cum corpora quam speciosissima fingendo pingendoue efficere cuperent, numquam
in hunc ceciderunt errorem ut Bagoam aut Megabyzum aliquem in exemplum
operis sumerent sibi.*   **7. arguta,** 'shrewd' : from which quality the fox
was called κερδώ, κιδάφη, κιδαφίων.   **nouo,** hardly ' rare,' ' strange,' like
noua figura oris Ter. Eun. ii. 3. 25, which expresses the opposite of a common or every-day beauty (Donatus *in loc.*), *arbor mira et noua* Fronton.
Epist. ii. 11 Naber, but 'fresh.'   The pard was in the first flush of his
youthful beauty.   **uulpis** is guaranteed by *C* and the Trèves MS : and cf.
XXXV. 14.   Otherwise the remarkable v.l. of *B, gädentem uulgus,* might
seem to point to a different reading, *fraudantem* or *ludentem uulgus,* like Ovid's
Indoctum uana dulcedine fallere uulgus M. v. 308.   We must then suppose
that **arguta,** 'the shrewd one ' = *uulpes,* like *paruula,* 'the ant,' XXXIV.
15, *auritulus,* 'the ass,' *laniger,* 'the sheep,' in Phaedrus i. 11. 6, i. i. 6,
domiporta, 'the snail,' = Hesiod's φερέοικος E. κ. 'H. 571, ἀνόστεος, 'the cuttle-
fish,' ib. 524.   **8. uanas,** 'neutiquam eius momenti de quibus merito
sic se iactare pardus possit.' Wopkens.   **approbat,** ' shows convincingly.'
Wopkens quotes Lamprid. Vit. Alex. Seueri 19 *Quasi falsi rei* (Casaubon
falsarii) *adprobati.*   Spartian. Vit. Getae 6 *Vt postea nece Pertinacis est
adprobatum.*   Add Veget. ii. 19 Lang *Tunc enim difficile commeatus dabatur
nisi causis iustissimis adprobatis.*   **9.** *Vade age,* but not **Vade** alone, is
Vergilian.   **pictae.**   Canneg. quotes Mart. i. 105. 1 *Picto quod iuga
delicata collo Pardus sustinet.*   The word aptly expresses the painted coat
of the panther.   **iuuentae,** as we might say ' the rich blazon of thy youth.'
Those who would substitute *figurae* would convert poetry into prose.
Merobaudes ii. 1 Nieb. *pulchram domini sortita iuuentam.*   **10. pul-
chrius** suggests the bodily beauty with which the mental adornment of
wise counsel is here contrasted.   **esse queat** has its full meaning ' so
long as I am *permitted to* surpass you in fine counsel.'   Wopkens wrongly
explained it as a pleonasm for *sit :* cf. XLII. 9.   I cannot think Fröhner's
rear, though admitted by Schenkl, necessary.   **11. Miremurque**
depends on **Dum.**   **12. corporeis bonis,** 'advantages of person.'
For the sentiment cf. Mamertin. Grat. Act. Iuliano xi *Facile fuit iuueni
dignitati corporis decorem animi praeponenti et candorem decolorare et oris nito-
rem alti inpressis cicatricibus deuenustare.*   Sidon. Epist. v. 10 *Erubescebat
. . . formae dote placuisse quippe cui merito ingenii suffecisset adamari, et uere
optimus quisque morum praestantius pulchritudine placet.*

XLI.

Fab. Aesop. 381 Halm, 124 Kn.

381 HALM.

Ποταμὸς δι' αὐτοῦ βύρσαν φερομένην ἰδὼν ἠρώτησε τίς καλεῖται· ἡ δὲ εἶπε ' ξηρά.' Ἐπικαχλάσας δὲ τῷ ῥεύματι εἶπεν· '"Αλλο τι ζήτει καλεῖσθαι. Ἀπα- λὴν γὰρ ἐγὼ ἤδη ταχὺ ποιήσω σε.'

The skin in this prose fable takes the place of the jar in Avianus. Whether Babrius was here Av.'s model is uncertain.

1. Inpulsus. It is the clouds, rather than the rain-shower, which strictly speaking are pushed by the force of the winds. Lucr. vi. 509 *Con-fertae nubes ui uenti certant Dupliciter ; nam uis uenti contendit et ipsa Copia nimborum turba maiore coacta* ('when a greater mass than usual has gathered,' Munro), *Virget de supero premit ac facit effluere imbres.* **pressa nube coactus,** ' driven into a mass by the pressure of the clouds upon each other.' Lucr. vi. 517 *Sed uemens imber fit, ubi uementer utraque Nubila ui cumulata premuntur et impete uenti,* a passage which describes the same two sources of heavy rain as Av.: (1) the accumulated pressure of the clouds, (2) the impetuous shock of the wind. **2. Ruperat se** with **hibernis aquis,** 'had burst in a fall of winter rain.' *Se ruperat* is Vergilian, Aen. xi. 548 *tantus se nubibus imber Ruperat.* Cf. G. i. 446. **3. effusas,** ' wide-spread,' to mark the far-reaching extent of the inundation. Tac. Germ. 30 *Non ita effusis ac palustribus locis ut ceterae ciuitates in quas Ger-mania patescit.* Luc. viii. 369 *effusaque plano Tigridis arua solo.* But it is not to be denied that the v. seems to be an imitation of Vergil's *effuso stag-nantem flumine Nilum* G. iv. 288, and it is possible Av. meant not so much ' wide-spread ' or ' open,' as *spreading into a flood* with the gradual increase of the rainy deluge. **stagnaret,** covered the land like a lake or pool, the consequence of the overflow. Conington on G. iv. 288. **4. Ex-positum,** 'set in the open air.' **fictile opus,** 'a jar of earthen-ware.' **pressit:** not ' sank ' as Canneg. thought, for a dialogue follows : but ' bore down upon ' nearly = ' struck or smote upon.' **5. Mobile,** 'plastic,' as in Vergil's *mobilis aetas* G. iii. 165, and so the younger Pliny, Epist. vii. 9. 11 *Vt laus est cerae, mollis cedensque sequatur Si doctos digitos ius-saque fiat opus . . . Sic hominum ingenium flecti ducique per artes Non rigidas docta mobilitate decet.* The other sense of ' moving in a wheel,' ' whirl-ing,' is commoner, especially in Prudentius, e. g. Apoth. 210 *Cuius ad arbitrium sphera mobilis atque rotunda Voluatur ;* but here the clay has already passed through the wheel and assumed its shape. *Nobile,* a v.l. mentioned by Iannelli would be quite classical. Pliny, when speaking of *uasa figlina,* says xxxv. 160 *Retinet hanc nobilitatem et Arretium in Italia . . . Habent et Trallis ibi opera sua et in Italia Mutina, quoniam et sic gentes nobilitantur.* It would be ' rare.' **instruit,** ' forms,' ' prepares.' **7. perquirit,** classical from Plautus onwards. **8. Immemor sui,** ' forgetting itself ' in its presumption, and assuming the style and title of a finished jar of the largest size. The hiatus after **sui** is probably as Av. wrote the v., since there is no other sign of disturbance as there seems to be in XXVIII. 12, XXVII. 10. Else it would be easy to read *Immemor olla sui est ' Amphora dicor ' ait ;* and Iannelli found *est* in his MS. **9. docta manus,** ' crafts-man's hand': Pliny's *docti digiti.* **Nunc,** 'as you see me now,' ' under pre-sent circumstances' deprecatingly. The jar appears to hint ' the state in which you see me is on the way to something more complete. I am already shaped to become when baked a perfectly tempered amphora.' This proves the jar was not yet broken, and still retained the fine shape and outline given it by the wheel. **rapiente uolumina gyro,** 'as the wheel speeds on in its revolution.' Ovid M. ii. 71 *celerique uolumine torquet.* **gyro,** ' the *rota* ' (Plin. xxxv. 159), or *orbis* (Plin. vii. 198), a wheel used in making pottery. **10. Molliter** with **obliquum,** ' has given my side a gentle inclination,' i.e. not a coarse or gross shape, but a finely convexed, gradually sloping, outline. **11. Hactenus,** ' up to this time and no longer.' Pacat. Paneg. Theodos. xlvii *Hactenus memet, Imperator Auguste, praeteritas res tuas attrectare fas fuerit.* Verg. Aen. vi. 62 *Hac Troiana tenus fuerit fortuna secuta.* **figura,** perhaps '*fine* shape,' as in Cat. lxiii. 62. **12. subiectam,** ' shall plunge you in its waters and wash you away.' Whatever the source of Cabeliauius' *pelluet,* it would not be the right word here: for according to Fronto p. 64 Naber *Os colluere dicam, pauimentum autem in balneis pelluere, non colluere: lacrimis uero genas labere dicam, non pelluere neque colluere.* accepto uiolentius amne **fatiscens.** Vergilian, Aen. i. 123 *Accipiunt inimicum imbrem rimisque fatiscunt.* **uiolentius** with **accepto,** ' drawing in the flood with a rush and cracking open.' **14.** ' It gave way and dashed head-long into the flowing waters.' **tenues,** as an epithet of **aquas,** occurs twice in the Georgics, iii. 335 *Tum tenuis dare rursus aquas,* iv. 410 *Aut in aquas tenuis dilapsus abibit.* Conington on this last passage compares the Homeric ὑγρόν, and this is obviously Av.'s meaning, ' flowing.' The edition of 1494 glosses the word by *liquidas.* **uicta.** Withof compares Val. Fl. iv. 48 *Victa fatiscit aquis donec domus, haustaque fluctu est.* **15. Infelix, quae.** Verg. Aen. ii. 345 *Infelix quae non sponsae praecepta furentis Audierit.* **magna,** the proud style of an Amphora. **16.** **pharetratis** MSS, and so in the verses on the winds printed in Reyfferscheid's Suetoni Reliquiae p. 305 *Mollior occiduos zephirus lambendo Britannos, (Dicitur Italiae sed et iste fauonius orae) Arma pharetratae labefactat uitrea brumae.* The clouds discharge from their full quivers the arrows of storm. Merobaudes Paneg. Actii 123 *Mox iaculum petiere manus, lusitque gelatis Imbribus et siccis imitatus missile lymfis Temptauit pugnas* shows that the resemblance of stiff icicles to pointed darts was sufficiently familiar to be introduced as a poetical conceit. The Trèves MS glosses *faretrate dicuntur nubes quod imbres atque fulmina de se emittant.* Yet there is some plausibility in the conj. *Ausa erat iratis* (Ellis, after Fröhner), cf. *O miserum, cui peccare licebat!* Cicero ap. August. de C. D. v. 27, or *Ausa foret tantis* (Bährens, after Wopkens). **17, 18** are considered spurious by Lachm. If *ut* in 18 were indubitable, metre would be a strong argument against their genuineness: and the fable ends sufficiently well with v. 16. But *B* gives **ne** for *ut,* as Withof subsequently conjectured, and **ne** is also in the ed. of 1494. Hence I have not ventured to mark them as suspicious. **17.** ' This may serve as a warning to the weak, not to place their destiny in the power of the great, and then deplore its unhappiness.' **miseros,** in a general sense ' mean men,' i.e. of no consideration ' debiles,' ed. 1494: or possibly like δειλοί, ' base born,' in opposition to high rank (*nobilibus*). This is the view of the commentator of ed. 1494: ' Reprehenduntur in hoc apologo omnes de infimo et uili genere exeuntes et de clara parentela se esse mentientes.'

XLII.

Fab. Aesop. 273 Halm.

Λύκος ἀρνίον ἐδίωκε· τὸ δὲ εἴς τι ἱερὸν κατέφυγε. Προσκαλουμένου δὲ αὐτὸ τοῦ λύκου καὶ λέγοντος ὅτι θυσιάσει αὐτὸ ὁ ἱερεύς, εἰ καταλάβῃ, τῷ θεῷ, ἐκεῖνο ἔφη· ''Ἀλλ' αἱρετώτερόν μοί ἐστι θεῷ θυσία γενέσθαι, ἢ ὑπὸ σοῦ διαφθαρῆναι.'
Ὁ λόγος δηλοῖ ὅτι οἷς ἐπίκειται τὸ ἀποθανεῖν, κρείττων ἐστὶν ὁ μετὰ δόξης θάνατος.

This is the same fable as Av.'s, but substitutes a lamb for the Latin poet's kid. It seems to have been written while sacrifices in heathen temples were still permitted, i.e. between 341 A.D. when a law of Constantius forbade *sacrificiorum insaniam* and the edicts of Theodosius by which the same law was reenacted under severer penalties at the close of the fourth century.

1. **melior cursu** like Vergil's *pedum melior motu* Aen. v. 430, *pedibus longe melior* Aen. ix. 556 (Koch-Georges Wörterbuch p. 53). The Bodl. MS *R* glosses the word by *uelocior*. **deluserat**, 'had baffled.' Hor. S. ii. 2. 56 *coruum deludet hiantem*. 2. **uicinis** seems to be dat. after **Proxima**, 'fields nearest to huts adjoining,' where the kid would be in reach of protectors, and the wolf would have to keep out of sight. **uicinis** is thus scarcely more than an amplification of **Proxima**. **dum petit**, sc. *haedus*. **casis**, straw-roofed huts used by herdsmen or rustics. Sidon. vii. 21, 22 *Angulus iste placet paupertinusque recessus Et casa cui culmo culmina pressa forent*. Isid. Origin. xv. 12. 1 *Casa est agreste habitaculum palis atque uirgultis harundinibusque contextum, quibus possint homines tueri a ui frigoris uel caloris iniuria*. 3. **fugam tendens**, Vergilian, Aen. ix. 781 *Quo deinde fugam, quo tenditis? inquit*. **in moenia** is explained by **urbem** in 5, a walled town where there was no fear of wolves or depredators. 4. **astitit**, all the best MSS. There seems to be hardly more force in the preposition than in Verg. Aen. ii. 328 *Arduus armatos mediis in moenibus adstans Fundit ecus* where Servius notes 'pro *stans*.' It is perhaps truer to say that Av. has followed the Vergilian use by which the word is combined with another preposition followed by a case *ante oculos adst*. Aen. iii. 150, *iuxta genitorem adst*. vii. 72. **astitit**, from this point of view, repeats the notion of **Inter**. (See Koch-Georges s.u.) 5. **Inpiger secutusque**, untiring, and therefore following the kid right into the city. See on XVII. 13. Fröhner's *mediam usque secutus* is clever but unnecessary. Mamertin. Paneg. Maximian. x *Regionem quam saepe uno die impiger uiator emensus est*, 'an active or brisk traveller.' Ovid M. i. 778 *Aethiopasque suos, positosque sub ignibus Indos Sidereus transit, patriosque adit impiger ortus*. **raptor**, Verg. Aen. ii. 355 *lupi ceu Raptores*. 6. **compositis**, 'studied,' 'artificial': a frequent use in Quintilian. Spalding cites viii. Pr. 23 *ficta atque composita*. 7. **cunctis**, VIII. 10, XIX. 10. The wolf tries to frighten the kid by appealing to his immediate surroundings. They are in a city, therefore with temples visible everywhere around them: in *every one* of these temples a victim bleeds. **uictima**, in combination with **cunctis templis**, points to a time before Paganism had succumbed to Christianity. See above on XXIII. 5. 8. **Inmitem**, 'relentless,' taking no notice of the blood that falls upon it. **regemens** *ORST*, *regimens P*, of which *redimens* in *C* is only a farther corruption. The word is used twice by Statius, from whom Sidonius has borrowed it. Theb. v. 388 *dat operta fragorem Pinus et abiunctis regemunt tabulata cauernis*, viii. 17 *Tunc regemunt pigrique lacus uastaeque paludes*. Sid. C. xi. 123 *per bifores regemunt caua buxa cauernas*. **cruentet**, as *tendantur*, *Luxuriet* in XXXVII. 3, 4. The indicative *cruentat* (*BPSX*) would be like Vergil's *Nonne uides croceos ut Tmolus odores India mittit ebur?* 9. **Quod nisi**, not before Cic. Verr. ii. 66 *Quod nisi Metellus hoc tam grauiter egisset*, Dräger Histor. Synt. ii. p. 490, who adds four other instances from Cicero. It is found in Vergil Ecl. ix. 14, G. i. 155. **securo**, as applied to a safe *place*, is not very common. Forc. quotes Liv. xxxix. 1 *Hostis leuis et uelox et repentinus qui nullum usquam tempus, nullum locum quietum aut securum esse sineret*. **ualeas** is not otiose as Wopkens thought; the sense is 'unless you succeed in escaping from the city with its temples and sacrifices to the undisturbed seclusion of the fields.' 10. I follow Lachm. in writing **Ei mihi** with *R* in preference to *Hcu mihi* which

has most of the earlier MSS to support it.　The instances of *heu* followed
by an accus. pronoun and an adj. in agreement with it *heu me miserum*, etc.,
are undoubted ; *heu misero mihi* Ritschl's MSS in Merc. iii. 4. 76, *heu miserae mihi* Merc. iv. 3. 2 : but in Prop. i. 3. 37, iv. 1. 58, iv. 8. 48, the Neapoli-
tanus reads *ei mihi :* and in Verg. Aen. xi. 57 none of Ribbeck's primary
MSS give *heu mihi*.　In 10 passages of Ovid's Tristia Mr. S. G. Owen's
three best MSS give *Ei hei i* or *et mihi*, never *heu*.　If *Heu mihi* was sometimes substitued for *Hei mihi*, the cases are exceptional, and not generally
supported by early MSS.　It is unfortunate that Prudentius who several
times uses *heu* alone, does not seem to combine either *heu* or *ei* with a personal pronoun ; had he done so the question might have been almost
settled by the invaluable Paris codex.　　　**uittata.**　Verg. G. iii. 486 *stans
hostia ad aram Lanea dum niuea circumdatur infula uitta.*　　　**11. Ille refert,** Vergilian.　　**Modo quam** MSS, changed unnecessarily by Lachm.
to *mihi quam*.　It is however not easy to decide whether **modo** is to be
constructed with **metuis,** 'you have just been apprehending,' 'you have
just explained your fears of,' cf. *aduenis modo* Ter. Hec. iii. 5. 8, *modo* thus
expressing 'tempus tam proximum ut pro praesenti haberi possit,' Hand
Tursellin. iii. p. 643 ; and for the position of **modo** before **quam** Cic. Phil.
xiv. 22 *Supplicationem modo qui decreuit ;* or, as Canneg. thought, with the
imper. **exue,** 'just,' dismissing the wolf's suggestion with some contempt, as
in *i modo tace modo age modo uide modo caue modo ;* cf. Vergil's *Necte Amarylli
modo* Ecl. viii. 79.　　　**exue.**　I again follow Lachm. in preferring this to
exime of all the early MSS.　It is true that *eximere* is often joined with
curam metum and corresponding words (Hor. C. iii. 14. 13, 14, Epp. i. 5. 18,
Cic. Tusc. Disp. ii. 12. 29), but in the sense of withdrawing cares from *others :*
on the other hand **exue** = ' drop ' from your own mind ; and this is obviously
Av.'s meaning.　So Mart. x. 30. 3, Ovid M. i. 622.　　　**12. uiles,**
' paltry.'　　　**minas,** 'forebodings,' 'praedictiones malorum,' Wopkens,
quoting Verg. Aen. iii. 540 *Bello armantur equi, bellum haec armenta minan-
tur.*　　　**13. sat erit,** ' I shall be content,' is not to be changed to the
weak *satius*, but stands in the same relation to **Quam** as *Proderit* in XXXVI.
15.　　　Vergil G. i. 68 and Columella R. R. vi. 3. 6 *sat erit pondo quadragena
singulis dari*, vi. 5. 3 *portione aequa per triduum cum uino dedisse sat erit* use
the words in a sense like the medical use of *sat, satis est* in prescriptions
(Celsus *passim*) ; and there may be this under-notion here : the kid's *perfect
cure* for the threatened but unreal danger of sacrifice is the thought of the
real danger from the wolf's jaws.　　　**sacrum,** 'sacrificial.'　Catull. lxviii.
75 *sanguine sacro*, Verg. Aen. v. 333 *sacro cruore*.　　　**14–16.** The Old
English translation of Avianus is worth quoting here.　' I had rather to shed
all my blood for the love of the gods, and to be sacrificed to them, than to
be eaten and devoured of thee.　And therefore he is full of wisdome and
prudence, who of two great evills, may escape the greatest of both.'　　　**14.**
Quam with no *magis potius* or similar word preceding has parallels in law
language, as well as in classical writers generally.　Roby, Introd. to Justinian,
ccxviii.　Dräger, Hist. Synt. ii. p. 618.

EXCURSUS I.

Praesumere.

Though the sense of 'anticipating' can alone claim to be classical, as early as Tacitus *praesumere* was already on its way to the later meaning of 'presuming,' 'arrogating,' which it still retains from the writers of the fourth, fifth, and subsequent centuries. Thus in Hist. i. 62 *Torpebat Vitellius et fortunam principatus inerti luxu ac prodigis epulis praesumebat* the meaning '*anticipated* his imperial fortune' is not far removed from 'presumed upon.' Tertullian seems to be the earliest writer who distinctly used it in this later sense. De Cultu Feminarum ii. 2 *Qui praesumit, minus ueretur, minus praecauet, plus periclitatur.* Possibly it was an Africanism. In the time of Constantine it was quite common, and except in elaborate poetry seems almost to have banished the more correct use. Inc. Paneg. Constantin. (ix Bährens) ii *Tene imperator tantum animo potuisse praesumere ut bellum tantis opibus, tanto consensu auaritiae, tanta scelerum contagione, tanta ueniae desperatione conflatum, quiescentibus cunctantibusque tunc imperii tui sociis primus inuaderes?* Inc. Paneg. Maximian. et Constantin. vii *Hoc iam tum diuina mente praesumpseras.* Porfirius Optatianus x. 10 ed. L. Müller *Ludere fas nobis, praesumere, dicere metra,* where the editor notes 'praesumere audere, ex more deterioris aetatis.' It does not seem to occur in Ausonius or Prudentius: but their contemporaries Symmachus and Pacatus both employ it, the former frequently. Symm. Epp. iv. 36 *Praesumptum de te officium operi meo uindicaui,* 'the courtesy which I had counted upon,' viz. of writing to me. vii. 47 *securitatis de tua mente praesumptae,* 'the secure feeling I assumed as to your disposition.' Pacat. Paneg. Theodos. xlii *Si nec praesumere ueniam reus, nec sperare fugam clausus, nec mortem potuit timere moriturus.* It is not avoided by the careful writer Vegetius in his treatise De Re Militari iv. 44 Lang *qui de uirtute praesumunt;* but no instance is found in Claudian, who introduces the word once, in its classical sense of anticipating, de iv Cons. Honorii 165 sqq. *Saepe tuas etiam iam tum gaudente marito Velauit regina comas, festinaque uoti Praesumptum diadema tulit,* a passage very like that above cited from the Histories of Tacitus. After 400 A.D. it is of very frequent occurrence, e. g. in Salvianus De Gubernatione Dei and Ennodius' Letters. Salv. de G. D. iii. 1 Pauly *recte etiam a nobis incolumitas aedificii praesumitur, cuius status subsidiis immortalibus continetur.* Ennod. Epp. v. 8 Hartel *quantum praesumo, nec fides in diligentia nec ad unguem ductus sermo uos deserit in loquela.* Libell. pro Synodo Praef. (p. 288 Hartel) *animus habendi cupidine subiugatus praesumptum aestimat iam habere conpendium,* 'the gain it counts upon getting.' Vit. Epiphani (p. 371 H.) *Audi Italorum supplicum uoces et de te praesumentium preces serenus admitte,* 'of those who count on your help.' Dictio iv. p. 436 *nec praesumimus aliquid nec timemus.* On the other hand, it is remarkable that Ennodius in one of his poems introduces *praesumere* in its strictly classical sense. De Castitate p. 404 *Ad me currentes puerum seponite factis* (put aside the boy = boyish habits), *Deque meo, iuuenes, canam praesumite uitam,* anticipate by early sobriety the life of old men. The general elevation of Avianus' style inclines me to believe that he uses *praesumptus* in V. 10 similarly in a sense if not classical (see Commentary) at least short of that claimed for the passage by Barth, Wopkens, and Unrein.

K 2

EXCURSUS II[1].

CONIECTURAE BABRIANAE.

XII. 16, 17, Rutherford:

$$τί σε δροσίζει νῶτον ἔννυχος στίβη,$$
$$καὶ καῦμα θάλπει, πάντα καὶ κατακναίει;$$

Perhaps καὶ καῦμα θάλπει (dative) πανταχῇ κατακναίει.

XVIII. 3:

The following passage from Amm. Marcellinus is not noticed by Rutherford. xvi. 5. 5 *Ex tapete et sisura quam uulgaris simplicitas susurnam appellat.*

XLV. 8: τὰς δ' ἰδίας ἀφῆκε μακρὰ λιμώττειν.

It seems possible that ἰδίας is a mistake for ἡμέρας, the tame goats. He has just before mentioned the other αἶγας κερούχους ἀγρίας πολὺ πλείους 'Ων αὐτὸς ἦγε.

LIX. 12: ὡς ἂν βλέποιτο τὸν πέλας τί βουλεύοι.

Rutherford reads after Gitlbauer:

ὡς ἂν βλέποι τὸ τοῦ πέλας τί βουλεύοι

against the Babrian rules of rhythm. It would be better to retain βλέποιτο as a passive, and reading τοῦ πέλας, make the genitive depend on the substantival notion contained in τί βουλεύοι, 'that so might be seen in one's neighbour, what he was purposing ' = ' one's neighbour's intention.'

LXXXIX. 5: ἐγὼ οὐ περυσινός· ἐπ' ἔτος ἐγεννήθην.

Rutherford seems right in supplying a negative to ἐγεννήθην; but I would then recast the verse as follows:

ἐγὼ περυσινός ; ἐπ' ἔτος οὐκ ἐγεννήθην.

I do not believe Babrius could have admitted so faulty a rhythm as οὐκ ἐπ' ἔτος ἐγεννήθην.

XCV. 75: καὶ νῦν ἐκεῖνος πλεῖον ἢ σὺ θυμοῦται.

θυμαίνει is an obvious correction.

XCIX. 2, 3: χὠ λέων τί κωλύει;
πρὸς αὐτὸν εἶπεν, ἀλλ' ἐνέχυρον δώσεις
τὠκυπτέρω σου μὴ μεθιέναι πίστιν.

Rutherford writes ἀλλ' ἐπ' ἐνεχύρῳ δώσεις and adds in his note that he considers this conjecture certain. I should much prefer, taking a feather from his own wing, to write

ἀλλ' ἐνέχυρον οὐ δώσεις
τὠκυπτέρω σου μὴ μεθιέναι πίστιν;

' But won't you give your two quill-feathers as a pledge of your fidelity ? '

CLXXII, Gitlbauer (137 Eberhard) :

I would write this fable as follows:

στικτή ποτ' ἐξηυχῆσε πάρδαλις ζώων
φορεῖν ἁπάντων ποικιλωτέραν δέρριν.
πρὸς ἣν ἀλώπηξ ' ἀλλὰ σῆς δορὰν κρείττω
γνώμης τ' ἔχω 'γὼ ποικιλωτέραν γνώμην.'

---

[1] Reprinted, with some slight alterations and additions, from the *American Journal of Philology*, vol. iv. p. 210.

INDEX.

L

THE END.

January. 1887.

Clarendon Press, Oxford

A SELECTION OF

BOOKS

PUBLISHED FOR THE UNIVERSITY BY

HENRY FROWDE,

AT THE OXFORD UNIVERSITY PRESS WAREHOUSE,

AMEN CORNER, LONDON.

ALSO TO BE HAD AT THE

CLARENDON PRESS DEPOSITORY, OXFORD.

[*Every book is bound in cloth, unless otherwise described.*]

LEXICONS, GRAMMARS, ORIENTAL WORKS, &c.

ANGLO-SAXON.—*An Anglo-Saxon Dictionary*, based on the MS. Collections of the late Joseph Bosworth, D.D., Professor of Anglo-Saxon, Oxford. Edited and enlarged by Prof. T. N. Toller, M.A. (To be completed in four parts.) Parts I and II. A—HWISTLIAN. 4to. 15*s.* each.

CHINESE.—*A Handbook of the Chinese Language.* By James Summers. 1863. 8vo. half bound, 1*l.* 8*s.*

—— *A Record of Buddhistic Kingdoms*, by the Chinese Monk FÄ-HIEN. Translated and annotated by James Legge, M.A., LL.D. Crown 4to. cloth back, 10*s.* 6*d.*

ENGLISH.—*A New English Dictionary, on Historical Principles:* founded mainly on the materials collected by the Philological Society. Edited by James A. H. Murray, LL.D., with the assistance of many Scholars and men of Science. Part I. A—ANT. Part II. ANT—BATTEN. Imperial 4to. 12*s.* 6*d.* each.

—— *An Etymological Dictionary of the English Language.* By W. W. Skeat, M.A. *Second Edition.* 1884. 4to. 2*l.* 4*s.*

——Supplement to the First Edition of the above. 4to. 2*s.* 6*d.*

—— *A Concise Etymological Dictionary of the English Language.* By W. W. Skeat, M.A. *Second Edition.* 1885. Crown 8vo. 5*s.* 6*d.*

[9]   B

GREEK.—*A Greek-English Lexicon*, by Henry George Liddell, D.D., and Robert Scott, D.D. Seventh Edition, Revised and Augmented throughout. 1883. 4to. 1*l.* 16*s.*

—— *A Greek-English Lexicon*, abridged from Liddell and Scott's 4to. edition, chiefly for the use of Schools. Twenty-first Edition. 1884. Square 12mo. 7*s.* 6*d.*

—— *A copious Greek-English Vocabulary,* compiled from the best authorities. 1850. 24mo. 3*s.*

—— *A Practical Introduction to Greek Accentuation*, by H. W. Chandler, M.A. Second Edition. 1881. 8vo. 10*s.* 6*d.*

HEBREW.—*The Book of Hebrew Roots*, by Abu 'l-Walîd Marwân ibn Janâh, otherwise called Rabbî Yônâh. Now first edited. with an Appendix, by Ad. Neubauer. 1875. 4to. 2*l.* 7*s.* 6*d.*

—— *A Treatise on the use of the Tenses in Hebrew.* By S. R. Driver, D.D. Second Edition. 1881. Extra fcap. 8vo. 7*s.* 6*d.*

—— *Hebrew Accentuation of Psalms, Proverbs, and Job.* By William Wickes, D.D. 1881. Demy 8vo. stiff covers, 5*s.*

ICELANDIC.—*An Icelandic-English Dictionary*, based on the MS. collections of the late Richard Cleasby. Enlarged and completed by G. Vigfússon, M.A. With an Introduction, and Life of Richard Cleasby, by G. Webbe Dasent, D.C.L. 1874. 4to. 3*l.* 7*s.*

A List of English Words the Etymology of which is illustrated by comparison with Icelandic. Prepared in the form of an APPENDIX to the above. By W. W. Skeat, M.A. 1876. stitched, 2*s.*

—— *An Icelandic Primer*, with Grammar, Notes, and Glossary. By Henry Sweet, M.A. Extra fcap. 8vo. 3*s.* 6*d.*

— - *An Icelandic Prose Reader*, with Notes, Grammar and Glossary. by Dr. Gudbrand Vigfússon and F. York Powell, M.A. 1879. Extra fcap. 8vo. 10*s.* 6*d.*

LATIN.—*A Latin Dictionary*, founded on Andrews' edition of Freund's Latin Dictionary, revised, enlarged, and in great part rewritten by Charlton T. Lewis, Ph.D., and Charles Short, LL.D. 1879. 4to. 1*l.* 5*s.*

MELANESIAN.—*The Melanesian Languages.* By R. H. Codrington, D.D., of the Melanesian Mission. 8vo. 18*s.*

SANSKRIT.—*A Practical Grammar of the Sanskrit Language*, arranged with reference to the Classical Languages of Europe, for the use of English Students, by Sir M. Monier-Williams, M.A. Fourth Edition. 8vo. 15*s.*

—— - *A Sanskrit-English Dictionary*, Etymologically and Philologically arranged, with special reference to Greek, Latin, German, Anglo-Saxon, English, and other cognate Indo-European Languages. By Sir M. Monier-Williams, M.A. 1872. 4to. 4*l.* 14*s.* 6*d.*

SANSKRIT.—*Nalopákhyánam.* Story of Nala, an Episode of the Mahá-Bhárata: the Sanskrit text, with a copious Vocabulary, and an improved version of Dean Milman's Translation, by Sir M. Monier-Williams, M.A. Second Edition, Revised and Improved. 1879. 8vo. 15*s.*

—— *Sakuntalá.* A Sanskrit Drama, in Seven Acts. Edited by Sir M. Monier-Williams, M.A. Second Edition, 1876. 8vo. 21*s.*

SYRIAC.—*Thesaurus Syriacus:* collegerunt Quatremère, Bernstein, Lorsbach, Arnoldi, Agrell, Field, Roediger: edidit R. Payne Smith, S.T.P. Fasc. I-VI. 1868-83. sm. fol. each, 1*l.* 1*s.* Fasc. VII. 1*l.* 11*s.* 6*d.*

Vol. I, containing Fasc. I-V, sm. fol. 5*l.* 5*s.*

- *The Book of Kalilah and Dimnah.* Translated from Arabic into Syriac. Edited by W. Wright, LL.D. 1884. 8vo. 21*s.*

GREEK CLASSICS, &c.

Aristophanes: A Complete Concordance to the Comedies and Fragments. By Henry Dunbar, M.D. 4to. 1*l.* 1*s.*

Aristotle: The Politics, with Introduction, Notes, etc., by W. L. Newman, M.A., Fellow of Balliol College, Oxford. Vols. I. and II. *Nearly ready.*

Aristotle: The Politics, translated into English, with Introduction, Marginal Analysis, Notes, and Indices, by B. Jowett, M.A. Medium 8vo. 2 vols. 21*s.*

Catalogus Codicum Graecorum Sinaiticorum. Scripsit V. Gardthausen Lipsiensis. With six pages of Facsimiles. 8vo. *linen,* 25*s.*

Heracliti Ephesii Reliquiae. Recensuit I. Bywater, M.A. Appendicis loco additae sunt Diogenis Laertii Vita Heracliti, Particulae Hippocratei De Diaeta Libri Primi, Epistolae Heracliteae. 1877. 8vo. 6*s.*

Herculanensium Voluminum Partes II. 1824. 8vo. 10*s.*

Fragmenta Herculanensia. A Descriptive Catalogue of the Oxford copies of the Herculanean Rolls, together with the texts of several papyri, accompanied by facsimiles. Edited by Walter Scott, M.A., Fellow of Merton College, Oxford. Royal 8vo. *cloth,* 21*s.*

Homer: A Complete Concordance to the Odyssey and Hymns of Homer; to which is added a Concordance to the Parallel Passages in the Iliad, Odyssey, and Hymns. By Henry Dunbar, M.D. 1880. 4to. 1*l.* 1*s.*

—— *Scholia Graeca in Iliadem.* Edited by Professor W. Dindorf, after a new collation of the Venetian MSS. by D. B. Monro, M.A., Provost of Oriel College. 4 vols. 8vo. 2*l.* 10*s.* Vols. V and VI. *In the Press.*

—— *Scholia Graeca in Odysseam.* Edidit Guil. Dindorfius. Tomi II. 1855. 8vo. 15*s.* 6*d.*

B 2

Plato : Apology, with a revised Text and English Notes, and
a Digest of Platonic Idioms, by James Riddell, M.A. 1878. 8vo. 8*s.* 6*d.*

—— *Philebus*, with a revised Text and English Notes, by
Edward Poste, M.A. 1860. 8vo. 7*s.* 6*d*

—— *Sophistes and Politicus*, with a revised Text and English
Notes, by L. Campbell, M.A. 1867.ʼ 8vo. 18*s.*

—— *Theaetetus*, with a revised Text and English Notes,
by L. Campbell, M.A. Second Edition. 8vo. 10*s.* 6*d.*

—— *The Dialogues*, translated into English, with Analyses
and Introductions, by B. Jowett, M.A. A new Edition in 5 volumes, medium
8vo. 1875. 3*l.* 10*s.*

—— *The Republic*, translated into English, with an Analysis
and Introduction, by B. Jowett, M.A. Medium 8vo. 12*s.* 6*d.*

Thucydides : Translated into English, with Introduction,
Marginal Analysis, Notes, and Indices. By B. Jowett, M.A. 2 vols. 1881.
Medium 8vo. 1*l.* 12*s.*

THE HOLY SCRIPTURES, &c.

STUDIA BIBLICA.—Essays in Biblical Archæology and Criti-
cism, and kindred subjects. By Members of the University of Oxford. 8vo.
10*s.* 6*d.*

ENGLISH.—*The Holy Bible in the earliest English Versions*,
made from the Latin Vulgate by John Wycliffe and his followers : edited by
the Rev. J. Forshall and Sir F. Madden. 4 vols. 1850. Royal 4to 3*l.* 3*s.*

[**Also reprinted from the above, with Introduction and Glossary
by W. W. Skeat, M.A.**

—— *The Books of Job, Psalms, Proverbs, Ecclesiastes, and the
Song of Solomon :* according to the Wycliffite Version made by Nicholas
de Hereford, about A.D. 1381, and Revised by John Purvey, about A.D. 1388
Extra fcap. 8vo. 3*s.* 6*d.*

—— *The New Testament in English*, according to the Version
by John Wycliffe, about A.D. 1380, and Revised by John Purvey, about A.D.
1388. Extra fcap. 8vo. 6*s.*]

ENGLISH.—*The Holy Bible:* an exact reprint, page for page, of the Authorised Version published in the year 1611. Demy 4to. half bound, 1*l*. 1*s*.

—— *The Psalter, or Psalms of David, and certain Canticles,* with a Translation and Exposition in English, by Richard Rolle of Hampole. Edited by H. R. Bramley, M.A., Fellow of S. M. Magdalen College, Oxford. With an Introduction and Glossary. Demy 8vo. 1*l*. 1*s*.

—— *Lectures on Ecclesiastes.* Delivered in Westminster Abbey by the Very Rev. George Granville Bradley, D.D., Dean of Westminster. Crown 8vo. 4*s*. 6*d*.

GOTHIC.—*The Gospel of St. Mark in Gothic,* according to the translation made by Wulfila in the Fourth Century. Edited with a Grammatical Introduction and Glossarial Index by W. W. Skeat, M.A. Extra fcap. 8vo. 4*s*.

GREEK.—*Vetus Testamentum* ex Versione Septuaginta Interpretum secundum exemplar Vaticanum Romae editum. Accedit potior varietas Codicis Alexandrini. Tomi III. Editio Altera. 18mo. 18*s*.

—— *Origenis Hexaplorum* quae supersunt; sive, Veterum Interpretum Graecorum in totum Vetus Testamentum Fragmenta. Edidit Fridericus Field, A.M. 2 vols. 1875. 4to. 5*l*. 5*s*.

—— *The Book of Wisdom:* the Greek Text, the Latin Vulgate, and the Authorised English Version; with an Introduction, Critical Apparatus, and a Commentary. By William J. Deane, M.A. Small 4to. 12*s*. 6*d*.

—— *Novum Testamentum Graece.* Antiquissimorum Codicum Textus in ordine parallelo dispositi. Accedit collatio Codicis Sinaitici. Edidit E. H. Hansell, S.T.B. Tomi III. 1864. 8vo. half morocco. Price reduced to 24*s*.

—— *Novum Testamentum Graece.* Accedunt parallela S. Scripturae loca, etc. Edidit Carolus Lloyd, S.T.P.R. 18mo. 3*s*.

On writing paper, with wide margin, 10*s*.

—— *Novum Testamentum Graece* juxta Exemplar Millianum. 18mo. 2*s*. 6*d*. On writing paper, with wide margin, 9*s*.

—— *Evangelia Sacra Graece.* Fcap. 8vo. limp, 1*s*. 6*d*.

—— *The Greek Testament,* with the Readings adopted by the Revisers of the Authorised Version:—

(1) Pica type, with Marginal References. Demy 8vo. 10*s*. 6*d*.
(2) Long Primer type. Fcap. 8vo. 4*s*. 6*d*.
(3) The same, on writing paper, with wide margin, 15*s*.

—— *The Parallel New Testament,* Greek and English; being the Authorised Version, 1611; the Revised Version, 1881; and the Greek Text followed in the Revised Version. 8vo. 12*s*. 6*d*.

The Revised Version is the joint property of the Universities of Oxford and Cambridge.

GREEK.—*Canon Muratorianus:* the earliest Catalogue of the
Books of the New Testament. Edited with Notes and a Facsimile of the
MS. in the Ambrosian Library at Milan, by S. P. Tregelles, LL.D. 1867.
4to. 10s. 6d.

—— *Outlines of Textual Criticism applied to the New Testament.* By C. E. Hammond, M.A. Fourth Edition. Extra fcap. 8vo. 3s. 6d.

HEBREW, etc.—*The Psalms in Hebrew without points.* 1879.
Crown 8vo. 3s. 6d.

—— *A Commentary on the Book of Proverbs.* Attributed
to Abraham Ibn Ezra. Edited from a MS. in the Bodleian Library by
S. R. Driver, M.A. Crown 8vo. paper covers, 3s. 6d.

—— *The Book of Tobit.* A Chaldee Text, from a unique
MS. in the Bodleian Library; with other Rabbinical Texts, English Translations, and the Itala. Edited by Ad. Neubauer, M.A. 1878. Crown 8vo. 6s.

—— *Horae Hebraicae et Talmudicae,* a J. Lightfoot. A new
Edition, by R. Gandell, M.A. 4 vols. 1859. 8vo. 1l. 1s.

LATIN.—*Libri Psalmorum* Versio antiqua Latina, cum Para-
phrasi Anglo-Saxonica. Edidit B. Thorpe, F.A.S. 1835. 8vo. 10s. 6d.

—— *Old-Latin Biblical Texts: No. I.* The Gospel according
to St. Matthew from the St. Germain MS. (g,). Edited with Introduction
and Appendices by John Wordsworth, D.D. Small 4to., stiff covers, 6s.

—— *Old-Latin Biblical Texts: No. II.* Portions of the Gospels
according to St. Mark and St. Matthew, from the Bobbio MS. (k), &c.
Edited by John Wordsworth, D.D., W. Sanday, M.A., D.D., and H. J. White,
M.A. Small 4to., stiff covers, 21s.

OLD-FRENCH.—*Libri Psalmorum* Versio antiqua Gallica e
Cod. MS. in Bibl. Bodleiana adservato, una cum Versione Metrica aliisque
Monumentis pervetustis. Nunc primum descripsit et edidit Franciscus Michel,
Phil. Doc. 1860. 8vo. 10s. 6d.

FATHERS OF THE CHURCH, &c.

St. Athanasius: Historical Writings, according to the Bene-
dictine Text. With an Introduction by William Bright, D.D. 1881. Crown
8vo. 10s. 6d.

—— *Orations against the Arians.* With an Account of his
Life by William Bright, D.D. 1873. Crown 8vo. 9s.

St. Augustine: Select Anti-Pelagian Treatises, and the Acts
of the Second Council of Orange. With an Introduction by William Bright,
D.D. Crown 8vo. 9s.

Canons of the First Four General Councils of Nicaea, Constantinople, Ephesus, and Chalcedon. 1877. Crown 8vo. 2s. 6d.

—— *Notes on the Canons of the First Four General Councils.* By William Bright, D.D. 1882. Crown 8vo. 5s. 6d.

Cyrilli Archiepiscopi Alexandrini in XII Prophetas. Edidit P. E. Pusey, A.M. Tomi II. 1868. 8vo. cloth, 2l. 2s.

— – *in D. Joannis Evangelium.* Accedunt Fragmenta varia necnon Tractatus ad Tiberium Diaconum duo. Edidit post Aubertum P. E. Pusey, A.M. Tomi III. 1872. 8vo. 2l. 5s.

—— *Commentarii in Lucae Evangelium* quae supersunt Syriace. E MSS. apud Mus. Britan. edidit R. Payne Smith, A.M. 1858. 4to. 1l. 2s.

—— Translated by R. Payne Smith, M.A. 2 vols. 1859. 8vo. 14s.

Ephraemi Syri, Rabulae Episcopi Edesseni, Balaei, aliorumque Opera Selecta. E Codd. Syriacis MSS. in Museo Britannico et Bibliotheca Bodleiana asservatis primus edidit J. J. Overbeck. 1865. 8vo. 1l. 1s.

Eusebius' Ecclesiastical History, according to the text of Burton, with an Introduction by William Bright, D.D. 1881. Crown 8vo. 8s. 6d.

Irenaeus: The Third Book of St. Irenaeus, Bishop of Lyons, against Heresies. With short Notes and a Glossary by H. Deane, B.D. 1874. Crown 8vo. 5s. 6d.

Patrum Apostolicorum, S. Clementis Romani, S. Ignatii, S. Polycarpi, quae supersunt. Edidit Guil. Jacobson, S.T.P.R. Tomi II. Fourth Edition, 1863. 8vo. 1l. 1s.

Socrates' Ecclesiastical History, according to the Text of Hussey, with an Introduction by William Bright, D.D. 1878. Crown 8vo. 7s. 6d.

ECCLESIASTICAL HISTORY, BIOGRAPHY, &c.

Ancient Liturgy of the Church of England, according to the uses of Sarum, York, Hereford, and Bangor, and the Roman Liturgy arranged in parallel columns, with preface and notes. By William Maskell, M.A. Third Edition. 1882. 8vo. 15s.

Baedae Historia Ecclesiastica. Edited, with English Notes, by G. H. Moberly, M.A. 1881. Crown 8vo. 10s. 6d.

Bright (W.). Chapters of Early English Church History.
1878. 8vo. 12s.

Burnet's History of the Reformation of the Church of England.
A new Edition. Carefully revised, and the Records collated with the originals,
by N. Pocock, M.A. 7 vols. 1865. 8vo. *Price reduced to* 1l. 10s.

Councils and Ecclesiastical Documents relating to Great Britain
and Ireland. Edited, after Spelman and Wilkins, by A. W. Haddan, B.D.,
and W. Stubbs, M.A. Vols. I. and III. 1869-71. Medium 8vo. each 1l. 1s.

> Vol. II. Part I. 1873. Medium 8vo. 10s. 6d.

> > Vol. II. Part II. 1878. Church of Ireland ; Memorials of St. Patrick.
> > Stiff covers, 3s. 6d.

Hamilton (John, Archbishop of St. Andrews), The Catechism
of. Edited, with Introduction and Glossary, by Thomas Graves Law. With
a Preface by the Right Hon. W. E. Gladstone. 8vo. 12s. 6d.

Hammond (C. E.). Liturgies, Eastern and Western. Edited,
with Introduction, Notes, and Liturgical Glossary. 1878. Crown 8vo. 10s. 6d.

> An Appendix to the above. 1879. Crown 8vo. paper covers, 1s. 6d.

John, Bishop of Ephesus. The Third Part of his Eccle-
siastical History. [In Syriac.] Now first edited by William Cureton, M.A.
1853. 4to. 1l. 12s.

—— Translated by R. Payne Smith, M.A. 1860. 8vo. 10s.

Leofric Missal, The, as used in the Cathedral of Exeter
during the Episcopate of its first Bishop, A.D. 1050-1072 ; together with some
Account of the Red Book of Derby, the Missal of Robert of Jumièges, and a
few other early MS. Service Books of the English Church. Edited, with Introduction and Notes, by F. E. Warren, B.D. 4to. half morocco, 35s.

Monumenta Ritualia Ecclesiae Anglicanae. The occasional
Offices of the Church of England according to the old use of Salisbury, the
Prymer in English, and other prayers and forms, with dissertations and notes.
By William Maskell, M.A. Second Edition. 1882. 3 vols. 8vo. 2l. 10s.

Records of the Reformation. The Divorce, 1527-1533. Mostly
now for the first time printed from MSS. in the British Museum and other libra-
ries. Collected and arranged by N. Pocock, M.A. 1870. 2 vols. 8vo. 1l. 16s.

Shirley (W. W.). Some Account of the Church in the Apostolic
Age. Second Edition, 1874. Fcap. 8vo. 3s. 6d.

Stubbs (W.). Registrum Sacrum Anglicanum. An attempt
to exhibit the course of Episcopal Succession in England. 1858. Small 4to.
8s. 6d.

Warren (F. E.). Liturgy and Ritual of the Celtic Church.
1881. 8vo. 14s.

ENGLISH THEOLOGY.

Bampton Lectures, 1886. *The Christian Platonists of Alex-*
andria. By Charles Bigg, D.D. 8vo. 10s. 6d.

Butler's Works, with an Index to the Analogy. 2 vols. 1874.
8vo. 11s.

Also separately,

   Sermons, 5s. 6d.   *Analogy of Religion*, 5s. 6d

Greswell's Harmonia Evangelica. Fifth Edition. 8vo. 1855.
9s. 6d.

Heurtley's Harmonia Symbolica: Creeds of the Western
Church. 1858. 8vo. 6s. 6d.

Homilies appointed to be read in Churches. Edited by
J. Griffiths, M.A. 1859. 8vo. 7s. 6d.

Hooker's Works, with his life by Walton, arranged by John
Keble, M.A. Sixth Edition, 1874. 3 vols. 8vo. 1l. 11s. 6d.

—— the text as arranged by John Keble. M.A. 2 vols.
1875. 8vo. 11s.

Jewel's Works. Edited by R. W. Jelf, D.D. 8 vols. 1848.
8vo. 1l. 10s.

Pearson's Exposition of the Creed. Revised and corrected by
E. Burton, D.D. Sixth Edition, 1877. 8vo. 10s. 6d.   •

Waterland's Review of the Doctrine of the Eucharist, with
a Preface by the late Bishop of London. Crown 8vo. 6s. 6d.

—— *Works*, with Life, by Bp. Van Mildert. A new Edition,
with copious Indexes. 6 vols. 1856. 8vo. 2l. 11s.

Wheatly's Illustration of the Book of Common Prayer. A new
Edition, 1846. 8vo. 5s.

Wyclif. *A Catalogue of the Original Works of John Wyclif*,
by W. W. Shirley, D.D. 1865. 8vo. 3s. 6d.

—— *Select English Works*. By T. Arnold, M.A. 3 vols.
1869-1871. 8vo. 1l. 1s.

—— *Trialogus*. With the Supplement now first edited.
By Gotthard Lechler. 1869. 8vo. 7s.

HISTORICAL AND DOCUMENTARY WORKS.

British Barrows, a Record of the Examination of Sepulchral
Mounds in various parts of England. By William Greenwell, M.A., F.S.A.
Together with Description of Figures of Skulls, General Remarks on Pre-
historic Crania, and an Appendix by George Rolleston, M.D., F.R.S. 1877.
Medium 8vo. 25*s*.

Britton. A Treatise upon the Common Law of England,
composed by order of King Edward I. The French Text carefully revised,
with an English Translation, Introduction, and Notes, by F. M. Nichols, M.A.
2 vols. 1865. Royal 8vo. 1*l.* 16*s*.

Clarendon's History of the Rebellion and Civil Wars in
England. 7 vols. 1839. 18mo. 1*l.* 1*s*.

Clarendon's History of the Rebellion and Civil Wars in
England. Also his Life, written by himself, in which is included a Con-
tinuation of his History of the Grand Rebellion. With copious Indexes.
In one volume, royal 8vo. 1842. 1*l.* 2*s*.

Clinton's Epitome of the Fasti Hellenici. 1851. 8vo. 6*s.* 6*d.*

  — *Epitome of the Fasti Romani.* 1854. 8vo. 7*s*.

Corpvs Poeticvm Borcale. The Poetry of the Old Northern
Tongue, from the Earliest Times to the Thirteenth Century. Edited, clas-
sified, and translated, with Introduction, Excursus, and Notes, by Gudbrand
Vigfússon, M.A., and F. York Powell, M.A. 2 vols. 1883. 8vo. 42*s*.

*Freeman (E. A.). History of the Norman Conquest of Eng-
land;* its Causes and Results. In Six Volumes. 8vo. 5*l.* 9*s.* 6*d.*

  —— *The Reign of William Rufus and the Accession of*
Henry the First. 2 vols. 8vo. 1*l.* 16*s*.

Gascoigne's Theological Dictionary ("Liber Veritatum"):
Selected Passages, illustrating the condition of Church and State, 1403–1458.
With an Introduction by James E. Thorold Rogers, M.A. Small 4to.
10*s.* 6*d.*

Magna Carta, a careful Reprint. Edited by W. Stubbs, D.D.
1879. 4to. stitched, 1*s*.

Passio et Miracula Beati Olaui. Edited from a Twelfth-
Century MS. in the Library of Corpus Christi College, Oxford, with an
Introduction and Notes, by Frederick Metcalfe, M.A. Small 4to. stiff
covers, 6*s*.

Protests of the Lords, including those which have been expunged, from 1624 to 1874; with Historical Introductions. Edited by James E. Thorold Rogers, M.A. 1875. 3 vols. 8vo. 2*l*. 2*s*.

Rogers (J. E. T.). History of Agriculture and Prices in England, A.D. 1259–1793.

Vols. I and II (1259–1400). 1866. 8vo. 2*l*. 2*s*.

Vols. III and IV (1401–1582). 1882. 8vo. 2*l*. 10*s*.

Saxon Chronicles (Two of the) parallel, with Supplementary Extracts from the Others. Edited, with Introduction, Notes, and a Glossarial Index, by J. Earle, M.A. 1865. 8vo. 16*s*.

Stubbs (W., D.D.). Seventeen Lectures on the Study of Medieval and Modern History, &c., delivered at Oxford 1867–1884. Demy 8vo. half-bound, 10*s*. 6*d*.

Sturlunga Saga, including the Islendinga Saga of Lawman Sturla Thordsson and other works. Edited by Dr. Gudbrand Vigfússon. In 2 vols. 1878. 8vo. 2*l*. 2*s*.

York Plays. The Plays performed by the Crafts or Mysteries of York on the day of Corpus Christi in the 14th, 15th, and 16th centuries. Now first printed from the unique MS. in the Library of Lord Ashburnham. Edited with Introduction and Glossary by Lucy Toulmin Smith. 8vo. 21*s*.

Statutes made for the University of Oxford, and for the Colleges and Halls therein, by the University of Oxford Commissioners. 1882. 8vo. 12*s*. 6*d*.

Statuta Universitatis Oxoniensis. 1886. 8vo. 5*s*.

The Examination Statutes for the Degrees of B.A., B. Mus., *B.C.L., and B.M.* Revised to Trinity Term, 1886. 8vo. sewed, 1*s*.

The Student's Handbook to the University and Colleges of *Oxford.* Extra fcap. 8vo. 2*s*. 6*d*.

The Oxford University Calendar for the year 1886. Crown 8vo. 4*s*. 6*d*.

The present Edition includes all Class Lists and other University distinctions for the five years ending with 1885.

Also, supplementary to the above, price 5s. (pp. 606),

The Honours Register of the University of Oxford. A complete Record of University Honours, Officers, Distinctions, and Class Lists; of the Heads of Colleges, &c., &c, from the Thirteenth Century to 1883.

MATHEMATICS, PHYSICAL SCIENCE, &c.

Acland (H. W., M.D.. F.R.S.).　Synopsis of the Pathological Series in the Oxford Museum. 1867. 8vo. 2s. 6d.

De Bary (Dr. A.).　Comparative Anatomy of the Vegetative Organs of the Phanerogams and Ferns. Translated and Annotated by F. O. Bower, M.A., F.L.S., and D. H. Scott, M.A., Ph.D., F.L.S. With 241 woodcuts and an Index. Royal 8vo., half morocco, 1l. 2s. 6d.

Goebel (Dr. K.).　Outlines of Classification and Special Morphology of Plants. A New Edition of Sachs' Text-Book of Botany, Book II. English Translation by H. E. F. Garnsey, M.A. Revised by I. Bayley Balfour, M.A., M.D., F.R.S. With 407 Woodcuts. Royal 8vo. half Morocco, 21s.

Müller (J.).　On certain Variations in the Vocal Organs of the Passeres that have hitherto escaped notice. Translated by F. J. Bell, B.A., and edited, with an Appendix, by A. H. Garrod, M.A., F.R.S. With Plates. 1878. 4to. paper covers, 7s. 6d.

Price (Bartholomew, M.A., F.R.S.).　Treatise on Infinitesimal Calculus.

    Vol. I. Differential Calculus. Second Edition. 8vo. 14s. 6d.

    Vol. II. Integral Calculus, Calculus of Variations, and Differential Equations. Second Edition, 1865. 8vo. 18s.

    Vol. III. Statics, including Attractions; Dynamics of a Material Particle. Second Edition, 1868. 8vo. 16s.

    Vol. IV. Dynamics of Material Systems; together with a chapter on Theoretical Dynamics, by W. F. Donkin, M.A., F.R.S. 1862. 8vo. 16s.

Pritchard (C., D.D., F.R.S.).　Uranometria Nova Oxoniensis. A Photometric determination of the magnitudes of all Stars visible to the naked eye, from the Pole to ten degrees south of the Equator. 1885. Royal 8vo. 8s.6d.

—— *Astronomical Observations* made at the University Observatory, Oxford, under the direction of C. Pritchard, D.D. No. 1. 1878. Royal 8vo. paper covers. 3s. 6d.

Rigaud's Correspondence of Scientific Men of the 17th Century, with Table of Contents by A. de Morgan. and Index by the Rev. J. Rigaud, M.A. 2 vols. 1841–1862. 8vo. 18s. 6d.

Rolleston (George, M.D., F.R.S.).　Scientific Papers and Addresses. Arranged and Edited by William Turner, M.B., F.R.S. With a Biographical Sketch by Edward Tylor, F.R.S. With Portrait, Plates, and Woodcuts. 2 vols. 8vo. 1l. 4s.

Westwood (J. O., M.A., F.R.S.).　Thesaurus Entomologicus Hopeianus, or a Description of the rarest Insects in the Collection given to the University by the Rev. William Hope. With 40 Plates. 1874. Small folio, half morocco, 7l. 10s.

The Sacred Books of the East.

TRANSLATED BY VARIOUS ORIENTAL SCHOLARS, AND EDITED BY
F. MAX MÜLLER.

[Demy 8vo. cloth.]

Vol. I. The Upanishads. Translated by F. Max Müller.
Part I. The *Kh*ândogya-upanishad, The Talavakâra-upanishad, The Aitareya-âra*n*yaka, The Kaushîtaki-brâhma*n*a-upanishad, and The Vâgasaneyi-sa*m*hitâ-upanishad. 10s. 6d.

Vol. II. The Sacred Laws of the Âryas, as taught in the
Schools of Âpastamba, Gautama, Vâsish*th*a, and Baudhâyana. Translated by Prof. Georg Bühler. Part I. Âpastamba and Gautama. 10s. 6d.

Vol. III. The Sacred Books of China. The Texts of Con-
fucianism. Translated by James Legge. Part I. The Shû King, The Religious portions of the Shih King, and The Hsiâo King. 12s. 6d.

Vol. IV. The Zend-Avesta. Translated by James Darme-
steter. Part I. The Vendîdâd. 10s. 6d.

Vol. V. The Pahlavi Texts. Translated by E. W. West.
Part I. The Bundahis, Bahman Yast, and Shâyast lâ-shâyast. 12s. 6d.

Vols. VI and IX. The Qur'ân. Parts I and II. Translated
by E. H. Palmer. 21s.

Vol. VII. The Institutes of Vish*n*u. Translated by Julius
Jolly. 10s. 6d.

Vol. VIII. The Bhagavadgîtâ, with The Sanatsugâtiya, and
The Anugîtâ. Translated by Kâshinâth Trimbak Telang. 10s. 6d.

Vol. X. The Dhammapada, translated from Pâli by F. Max
Müller; and The Sutta-Nipâta, translated from Pâli by V. Fausböll; being Canonical Books of the Buddhists. 10s. 6d.

Vol. XI. Buddhist Suttas. Translated from Pâli by T. W.
Rhys Davids. 1. The Mahâparinibbâna Suttanta; 2. The Dhamma-*k*akkappavattana Sutta; 3. The Tevigga Suttanta; 4. The Âkankheyya Sutta; 5. The *K*etokhila Sutta; 6. The Mahâ-sudassana Suttanta; 7. The Sabbâsava Sutta. 10s. 6d.

Vol. XII. The *Satapatha-Brâhmaṇa*, according to the Text of the Mâdhyandina School. Translated by Julius Eggeling. Part I. Books I and II. 12s. 6d.

Vol. XIII. Vinaya Texts. Translated from the Pâli by T. W. Rhys Davids and Hermann Oldenberg. Part I. The Pâtimokkha. The Mahâvagga, I IV. 10s. 6d.

Vol. XIV. The Sacred Laws of the Âryas, as taught in the Schools of Apastamba, Gautama, Vâsishṭha and Baudhâyana. Translated by Georg Bühler. Part II. Vâsishṭha and Baudhâyana. 10s. 6d.

Vol. XV. The Upanishads. Translated by F. Max Müller. Part II. The Kaṭha-upanishad. The Muṇḍaka-upanishad, The Taittirîyaka-upanishad, The Bṛhadâraṇyaka-upanishad, The Svetasvatara-upanishad, The Prasṇa-upanishad, and The Maitrâyaṇa-Brâhmaṇa-upanishad. 10s. 6d.

Vol. XVI. The Sacred Books of China. The Texts of Confucianism. Translated by James Legge. Part II. The Yî King. 10s. 6d.

Vol. XVII. Vinaya Texts. Translated from the Pâli by T. W. Rhys Davids and Hermann Oldenberg. Part II. The Mahâvagga, V-X. The Kullavagga, I-III. 10s. 6d.

Vol. XVIII. Pahlavi Texts. Translated by E. W. West. Part II. The Dâdistân-î Dînîk and The Epistles of Mânûskîhar. 12s. 6d.

Vol. XIX. The Fo-sho-hing-tsan-king. A Life of Buddha by Asvaghosha Bodhisattva, translated from Sanskrit into Chinese by Dharmaraksha, A.D. 420, and from Chinese into English by Samuel Beal. 10s. 6d

Vol. XX. Vinaya Texts. Translated from the Pâli by T. W. Rhys Davids and Hermann Oldenberg. Part III. The Kullavagga, IV XII. 10s. 6d.

Vol. XXI. The Saddharma-puṇḍarika; or, the Lotus of the True Law. Translated by H. Kern. 12s. 6d.

Vol. XXII. Gaina-Sûtras. Translated from Prâkrit by Hermann Jacobi. Part I. The Âkârâṅga-Sûtra. The Kalpa-Sûtra. 10s. 6d.

Vol. XXIII. The Zend-Avesta. Translated by James Darmesteter. Part II. The Sîrôzahs, Yasts, and Nyâyis. 10s. 6d.

Vol. XXIV. Pahlavi Texts. Translated by E. W. West. Part III. Dînâ-î Maînôg-î Khirad, Sikand-gûmânîk, and Sad-Dar. 10s. 6d.

Second Series.

Vol. XXV. Manu. Translated by Georg Bühler. 21s.

Vol. XXVI. The Satapatha-Brâhmana. Translated by Julius Eggeling. Part II. 12s. 6d.

Vols. XXVII and XXVIII. The Sacred Books of China. The Texts of Confucianism. Translated by James Legge. Parts III and IV. The Lî Kî, or Collection of Treatises on the Rules of Propriety, or Ceremonial Usages. 25s.

Vols. XXIX and XXX. The Grihya-Sûtras, Rules of Vedic Domestic Ceremonies. Translated by Hermann Oldenberg.

> Part I (Vol. XXIX), 12s. 6d. *Just Published.*
> Part II (Vol. XXX). *In the Press.*

The following Volumes are in the Press:—

Vol. XXXI. The Zend-Avesta. Part III. The Yasna, Visparad, Âfrînagân, and Gâhs. Translated by the Rev. L. H. Mills.

Vol. XXXII. Vedic Hymns. Translated by F. Max Müller. Part I.

Vol. XXXIII. Nârada, and some Minor Law-books. Translated by Julius Jolly. [*Preparing.*]

Vol. XXXIV. The Vedânta-Sûtras, with Sankara's Commentary. Translated by G. Thibaut. [*Preparing.*]

** The Second Series will consist of Twenty-Four Volumes.

Clarendon Press Series

I. ENGLISH, &c.

A First Reading Book. By Marie Eichens of Berlin; and
edited by Anne J. Clough. Extra fcap. 8vo. stiff covers, 4d.

Oxford Reading Book, Part I. For Little Children. Extra
fcap. 8vo. stiff covers, 6d.

Oxford Reading Book, Part II. For Junior Classes. Extra
fcap. 8vo. stiff covers, 6d.

An Elementary English Grammar and Exercise Book. By
O. W. Tancock, M.A. Second Edition. Extra fcap. 8vo. 1s. 6d.

An English Grammar and Reading Book, for Lower Forms
in Classical Schools. By O. W. Tancock, M.A. Fourth Edition. Extra
fcap. 8vo. 3s. 6d.

Typical Selections from the best English Writers, with Introductory Notices. Second Edition. In 2 vols. Extra fcap. 8vo. 3s. 6d. each.

Vol. I. Latimer to Berkeley.   Vol. II. Pope to Macaulay.

Shairp (J. C., LL.D.). Aspects of Poetry; being Lectures
delivered at Oxford. Crown 8vo. 10s. 6d.

—

A Book for the Beginner in Anglo-Saxon. By John Earle,
M.A. Third Edition. Extra fcap. 8vo. 2s. 6d.

An Anglo-Saxon Reader. In Prose and Verse. With Grammatical Introduction, Notes, and Glossary. By Henry Sweet, M.A. Fourth
Edition, Revised and Enlarged. Extra fcap. 8vo. 8s. 6d.

A Second Anglo-Saxon Reader. By the same Author. Extra
fcap. 8vo. *Nearly ready.*

An Anglo-Saxon Primer, with Grammar, Notes. and Glossary.
By the same Author. Second Edition. Extra fcap. 8vo. 2s. 6d.

Old English Reading Primers; edited by Henry Sweet. M.A.
I. Selected Homilies of Ælfric. Extra fcap. 8vo., stiff covers, 1s. 6d.
II. Extracts from Alfred's Orosius. Extra fcap. 8vo., stiff covers, 1s. 6d.

First Middle English Primer, with Grammar and Glossary.
By the same Author. Extra fcap. 8vo. 2s.

Second Middle English Primer. Extracts from Chaucer,
with Grammar and Glossary. By the same Author. Extra fcap. 8vo. 2s.
Just Published.

Principles of English Etymology. First Series. By W. W.
Skeat, Litt.D. Crown 8vo. *Nearly ready.*

The Philology of the English Tongue. By J. Earle, M.A.
Third Edition. Extra fcap. 8vo. 7s. 6d.

An Icelandic Primer, with Grammar, Notes, and Glossary.
By the same Author. Extra fcap. 8vo. 3s. 6d.

An Icelandic Prose Reader, with Notes, Grammar, and Glossary.
By G. Vigfússon, M.A., and F. York Powell, M.A. Ext. fcap. 8vo. 10s. 6d.

A Handbook of Phonetics, including a Popular Exposition of
the Principles of Spelling Reform. By H. Sweet, M.A. Extra fcap. 8vo. 4s. 6d.

Elementarbuch des Gesprochenen Englisch. Grammatik,
Texte und Glossar. Von Henry Sweet. Extra fcap. 8vo., stiff covers, 2s. 6d.

The Ormulum; with the Notes and Glossary of Dr. R. M.
White. Edited by R. Holt, M.A. 1878. 2 vols. Extra fcap. 8vo. 21s.

Specimens of Early English. A New and Revised Edition.
With Introduction, Notes, and Glossarial Index. By R. Morris, LL.D., and
W. W. Skeat, M.A.

> Part I. From Old English Homilies to King Horn (A.D. 1150 to A.D. 1300).
> Second Edition. Extra fcap. 8vo. 9s.

> Part II. From Robert of Gloucester to Gower (A.D. 1298 to A.D. 1393).
> Second Edition. Extra fcap. 8vo. 7s. 6d.

Specimens of English Literature, from the 'Ploughmans
Crede' to the 'Shepheardes Calender' (A.D. 1394 to A.D. 1579). With Introduction, Notes, and Glossarial Index. By W. W. Skeat, M.A. Extra fcap.
8vo. 7s. 6d.

The Vision of William concerning Piers the Plowman, in three
Parallel Texts; together with *Richard the Redeless*. By William Langland
(about 1362–1399 A.D.). Edited from numerous Manuscripts, with Preface,
Notes, and a Glossary, by W. W. Skeat, Litt.D. 2 vols. 8vo. 31s. 6d. *Just
Published.*

The Vision of William concerning Piers the Plowman, by
William Langland. Edited, with Notes, by W. W. Skeat, M.A. Third
Edition. Extra fcap. 8vo. 4s. 6d.

Chaucer. I. *The Prologue to the Canterbury Tales;* the
Knightes Tale; The Nonne Prestes Tale. Edited by R. Morris, Editor of
Specimens of Early English, &c., &c. Extra fcap. 8vo. 2s. 6d.

—— II. *The Prioresses Tale; Sir Thopas;* The Monkes
Tale; The Clerkes Tale; The Squieres Tale, &c. Edited by W. W. Skeat,
M.A. Second Edition. Extra fcap. 8vo. 4s. 6d.

—— III. *The Tale of the Man of Lawe;* The Pardoneres
Tale; The Second Nonnes Tale; The Chanouns Yemannes Tale. By the
same Editor. Second Edition. Extra fcap. 8vo. 4s. 6d.

Gamelyn, The Tale of. Edited with Notes, Glossary, &c., by
W. W. Skeat, M.A. Extra fcap. 8vo. Stiff covers, 1s. 6d.

Minot (Laurence). Poems. Edited, with Introduction and
Notes, by Joseph Hall, M.A. Extra fcap. 8vo. *Nearly ready.*

c

Spenser's Faery Queene. Books I and II. Designed chiefly
for the use of Schools. With Introduction, Notes, and Glossary. By G. W.
Kitchin. D.D. Extra fcap. 8vo. 2s. 6d. each.

Hooker. Ecclesiastical Polity, Book I. Edited by R. W.
Church, M.A. Second Edition. Extra fcap. 8vo. 2s.

OLD ENGLISH DRAMA.

The Pilgrimage to Parnassus with *The Two Parts of the
Return from Parnassus.* Three Comedies performed in St. John's College,
Cambridge, A.D. MDXCVII–MDCI. Edited from MSS. by the Rev. W. D.
Macray, M.A., F.S.A. Medium 8vo. Bevelled Boards, Gilt top, 8s. 6d.

*Marlowe and Greene. Marlowe's Tragical History of Dr.
Faustus,* and *Greene's Honourable History of Friar Bacon and Friar Bungay.*
Edited by A. W. Ward, M.A. 1878. Extra fcap. 8vo. 5s. 6d. In white
Parchment, 6s.

Marlowe. Edward II. With Introduction, Notes, &c. By
O. W. Tancock, M.A. Extra fcap. 8vo. 3s.

SHAKESPEARE.

Shakespeare. Select Plays. Edited by W. G. Clark, M.A.,
and W. Aldis Wright, M.A. Extra fcap. 8vo. stiff covers.

The Merchant of Venice. 1s.	Macbeth. 1s. 6d.
Richard the Second. 1s. 6d.	Hamlet. 2s.

Edited by W. Aldis Wright, M.A.

The Tempest. 1s. 6d.	Midsummer Night's Dream. 1s. 6d.
As You Like It. 1s. 6d.	Coriolanus. 2s. 6d.
Julius Cæsar. 2s.	Henry the Fifth. 2s.
Richard the Third. 2s. 6d.	Twelfth Night. 1s. 6d.
King Lear. 1s. 6d.	King John. 1s. 6d.

Shakespeare as a Dramatic Artist; a popular Illustration of
the Principles of Scientific Criticism. By R. G. Moulton, M.A. Crown 8vo. 5s.

Bacon. I. *Advancement of Learning.* Edited by W. Aldis
Wright, M.A. Second Edition. Extra fcap. 8vo. 4s. 6d.

—— II. *The Essays.* With Introduction and Notes. By
S. H. Reynolds, M.A., late Fellow of Brasenose College. *In Preparation.*

Milton. I. *Areopagitica.* With Introduction and Notes. By
John W. Hales, M.A. Third Edition. Extra fcap. 8vo. 3s.

—— II. *Poems.* Edited by R. C. Browne, M.A. 2 vols.
Fifth Edition. Extra fcap. 8vo. 6s. 6d. Sold separately, Vol. I. 4s.; Vol. II. 3s.

In paper covers :—

Lycidas, 3d.	L'Allegro, 3d.	Il Penseroso, 4d.	Comus, 6d.

Samson Agonistes, 6d.

—— III. *Samson Agonistes.* Edited with Introduction and
Notes by John Churton Collins. Extra fcap. 8vo. stiff covers, 1s.

Bunyan. I. *The Pilgrim's Progress, Grace Abounding, Rela-*
tion of the Imprisonment of Mr. John Bunyan. Edited, with Biographical
Introduction and Notes, by E. Venables, M.A. 1879. Extra fcap. 8vo. 5s.
In ornamental Parchment, 6s.

—— II. *Holy War*, *&c.* Edited by E. Venables, M.A.
In the Press.

Clarendon. *History of the Rebellion.* *Book VI.* Edited
by T. Arnold, M.A. Extra fcap. 8vo. 4s. 6d.

Dryden. *Select Poems.* Stanzas on the Death of Oliver
Cromwell; Astræa Redux; Annus Mirabilis; Absalom and Achitophel;
Religio Laici; The Hind and the Panther. Edited by W. D. Christie, M.A.
Second Edition. Extra fcap. 8vo. 3s. 6d.

Locke's *Conduct of the Understanding.* Edited, with Introduction, Notes, &c., by T. Fowler, M.A. Second Edition. Extra fcap. 8vo. 2s.

Addison. *Selections from Papers in the Spectator.* With Notes.
By T. Arnold, M.A. Extra fcap. 8vo. 4s. 6d. In ornamental Parchment, 6s.

Steele. *Selections from the Tatler, Spectator, and Guardian.*
Edited by Austin Dobson. Extra fcap. 8vo. 4s. 6d. In white Parchment, 7s. 6d.

Pope. With Introduction and Notes. By Mark Pattison, B.D.

—— I. *Essay on Man.* Extra fcap. 8vo. 1s. 6d.

—— II. *Satires and Epistles.* Extra fcap. 8vo. 2s.

Parnell. *The Hermit.* Paper covers, 2d.

Gray. *Selected Poems.* Edited by Edmund Gosse. Extra
fcap. 8vo. Stiff covers, 1s. 6d. In white Parchment, 3s.

—— *Elegy and Ode on Eton College.* Paper covers, 2d.

Goldsmith. *The Deserted Village.* Paper covers, 2d.

Johnson. I. *Rasselas; Lives of Dryden and Pope.* Edited
by Alfred Milnes, M.A. (London). Extra fcap. 8vo. 4s 6d., or *Lives of*
Dryden and Pope only, stiff covers, 2s. 6d.

—— II. *Vanity of Human Wishes.* With Notes, by E. J.
Payne, M.A. Paper covers, 4d.

Boswell's *Life of Johnson.* *With the Journal of a Tour to*
the Hebrides. Edited, with copious Notes, Appendices, and Index, by G.
Birkbeck Hill, D.C.L., Pembroke College. With Portraits and Facsimiles.
6 vols. Medium 8vo. *Nearly ready.*

Cowper. Edited, with Life, Introductions, and Notes, by
H. T. Griffith, B.A.

—— I. *The Didactic Poems of* 1782, with Selections from the
Minor Pieces, A.D. 1779–1783. Extra fcap. 8vo. 3s.

—— II. *The Task, with Tirocinium,* and Selections from the
Minor Poems, A.D. 1784–1799. Second Edition. Extra fcap. 8vo. 3s.

Burke. Select Works. Edited, with Introduction and Notes, by E. J. Payne. M.A.

—— I. *Thoughts on the Present Discontents; the two Speeches on America.* Second Edition. Extra fcap. 8vo. 4s. 6d.

—— II. *Reflections on the French Revolution.* Second Edition. Extra fcap. 8vo. 5s.

—— III. *Four Letters on the Proposals for Peace with the* Regicide Directory of France. Second Edition. Extra fcap. 8vo. 5s.

Keats. Hyperion, Book I. With Notes by W. T. Arnold, B.A. Paper covers. 4d.

Byron. Childe Harold. Edited, with Introduction and Notes. by H. F. Tozer, M.A. Extra fcap. 8vo. 3s. 6d. In white Parchment, 5s.

Scott. Lay of the Last Minstrel. Edited with Preface and Notes by W. Minto. M.A. With Map. Extra fcap. 8vo. Stiff covers, 2s. Ornamental Parchment, 3s. 6d.

—— *Lay of the Last Minstrel.* Introduction and Canto I., with Preface and Notes, by the same Editor. 6d.

II. LATIN.

Rudimenta Latina. Comprising Accidence, and Exercises of a very Elementary Character, for the use of Beginners. By John Barrow Allen, M.A. Extra fcap. 8vo. 2s.

An Elementary Latin Grammar. By the same Author. Forty-second Thousand. Extra fcap. 8vo. 2s. 6d.

A First Latin Exercise Book. By the same Author. Fourth Edition. Extra fcap. 8vo. 2s. 6d.

A Second Latin Exercise Book. By the same Author. Extra fcap. 8vo. 3s. 6d.

Reddenda Minora, or Easy Passages, Latin and Greek, for Unseen Translation. For the use of Lower Forms. Composed and selected by C. S. Jerram, M.A. Extra fcap. 8vo. 1s. 6d.

Anglice Reddenda, or Easy Extracts, Latin and Greek, for Unseen Translation. By C. S. Jerram, M.A. Third Edition. Revised and Enlarged. Extra fcap. 8vo. 2s. 6d.

Anglice Reddenda. Second Series. By the same Author. Extra fcap. 8vo. *Nearly ready.*

Passages for Translation into Latin. For the use of Passmen and others. Selected by J. Y. Sargent, M.A. Fifth Edition. Extra fcap. 8vo. 2s. 6d.

Exercises in Latin Prose Composition; with Introduction, Notes, and Passages of Graduated Difficulty for Translation into Latin. By G. G. Ramsay, M.A., LL.D. Second Edition. Extra fcap. 8vo. 4*s.* 6*d.*

Hints and Helps for Latin Elegiacs. By H. Lee-Warner, M.A. Extra fcap. 8vo. 3*s.* 6*d.*

First Latin Reader. By T. J. Nunns, M.A. Third Edition. Extra fcap. 8vo. 2*s.*

Caesar. The Commentaries (for Schools). With Notes and Maps. By Charles E. Moberly, M.A.

    Part I. *The Gallic War.* Second Edition. Extra fcap. 8vo. 4*s.* 6*d.*
    Part II. *The Civil War.* Extra fcap. 8vo. 3*s.* 6*d.*
    The Civil War. Book I. Second Edition. Extra fcap. 8vo. 2*s.*

Cicero. Catilinarian Orations. By E. A. Upcott, M.A., Assistant Master in Marlborough College. *In the Press.*

Cicero. Selection of interesting and descriptive passages. With Notes. By Henry Walford, M.A. In three Parts. Extra fcap. 8vo. 4*s.* 6*d.*

        Each Part separately, limp, 1*s.* 6*d.*

    Part I. Anecdotes from Grecian and Roman History. Third Edition.
    Part II. Omens and Dreams: Beauties of Nature. Third Edition.
    Part III. Rome's Rule of her Provinces. Third Edition.

Cicero. De Senectute. Edited, with Introduction and Notes, by L. Huxley, M.A. Extra fcap. 8vo. 2*s.*

        Or separately, Text and Introduction, 1*s.* Notes 1*s.*

Cicero. Selected Letters (for Schools). With Notes. By the late C. E. Prichard, M.A., and E. R. Bernard, M.A. Second Edition. Extra fcap. 8vo. 3*s.*

Cicero. Select Orations (for Schools). In Verrem I. De Imperio Gn. Pompeii. Pro Archia. Philippica IX. With Introduction and Notes by J. R. King, M.A. Second Edition. Extra fcap. 8vo. 2*s.* 6*d.*

Cornelius Nepos. With Notes. By Oscar Browning, M.A. Second Edition. Extra fcap. 8vo. 2*s.* 6*d.*

Horace. Selected Odes. With Notes for the use of a Fifth Form. By E. C. Wickham, M.A. In two Parts. Extra fcap. 8vo. *cloth,* 2*s.*

        Or separately, Part I. Text, 1*s.* Part II. Notes, 1*s.*

Livy. Selections (for Schools). With Notes and Maps. By H. Lee-Warner, M.A. Extra fcap. 8vo. In Parts, limp, each 1*s.* 6*d.*

    Part I. The Caudine Disaster. Part II. Hannibal's Campaign in Italy. Part III. The Macedonian War.

Livy. Books V–VII. With Introduction and Notes. By A. R. Cluer, B.A. Extra fcap. 8vo. 3*s.* 6*d.*

Livy. Books XXI, XXII, and XXIII. With Introduction and Notes. By M. T. Tatham, M.A. Extra fcap. 8vo. 4*s.* 6*d.*

Ovid. Selections for the use of Schools. With Introductions and Notes, and an Appendix on the Roman Calendar. By W. Ramsay, M.A. Edited by G. G. Ramsay, M.A. Third Edition. Extra fcap. 8vo. 5s. 6d.

Ovid. 'Tristia. Book I. The Text revised, with an Introduction and Notes. By S. G. Owen, B.A. Extra fcap. 8vo. 3s. 6d.

Plautus. Captivi. Edited by W. M. Lindsay, M.A. Extra fcap. 8vo. *In the Press.*

Plautus. The Trinummus. With Notes and Introductions. Intended for the Higher Forms of Public Schools. By C. E. Freeman, M.A., and A. Sloman, M.A. Extra fcap. 8vo. 3s.

Pliny. Selected Letters (for Schools). With Notes. By the late C. E. Prichard, M.A., and E. R. Bernard, M.A. Extra fcap. 8vo. 3s.

Sallust. With Introduction and Notes. By W. W. Capes, M.A. Extra fcap. 8vo. 4s. 6d.

Tacitus. The Annals. Books I–IV. Edited, with Introduction and Notes for the use of Schools and Junior Students, by H. Furneaux, M.A. Extra fcap. 8vo. 5s.

Terence. Andria. With Notes and Introductions. By C. E. Freeman, M.A., and A. Sloman, M.A. Extra fcap. 8vo. 3s.

—— Adelphi. With Notes and Introductions. Intended for the Higher Forms of Public Schools. By A. Sloman, M.A. Extra fcap. 8vo. 3s.

Tibullus and Propertius. Selections. Edited by G. G. Ramsay, M.A. In two Parts. Extra fcap. 8vo. In one or two vols.' 6s. *Just Published.*

Virgil. With Introduction and Notes. By T. L. Papillon, M.A. Two vols. Crown 8vo. 10s. 6d. The Text separately, 4s. 6d.

Virgil. The Eclogues. Edited by C. S. Jerram, M.A. In two Parts. Crown 8vo. *Nearly ready.*

Catulli Veronensis Liber. Iterum recognovit, apparatum criticum prolegomena appendices addidit, Robinson Ellis. A.M. 1878. Demy 8vo. 16s.

—— A Commentary on Catullus. By Robinson Ellis, M.A. 1876. Demy 8vo. 16s.

Catulli Veronensis Carmina Selecta, secundum recognitionem Robinson Ellis, A.M. Extra fcap. 8vo. 3s. 6d.

Cicero de Oratore. With Introduction and Notes. By A. S. Wilkins, M.A.
Book I. 1879. 8vo. 6s.   Book II. 1881. 8vo. 5s.

—— Philippic Orations. With Notes. By J. R. King, M.A. Second Edition. 1879. 8vo. 10s. 6d.

Cicero. Select Letters. With English Introductions, Notes, and Appendices. By Albert Watson, M.A. Third Edition. Demy 8vo. 18*s*.

—— *Select Letters.* Text. By the same Editor. Second Edition. Extra fcap. 8vo. 4*s*.

—— *pro Cluentio.* With Introduction and Notes. By W. Ramsay, M.A. Edited by G. G. Ramsay, M.A. 2nd Ed. Ext. fcap. 8vo. 3*s*. 6*d*.

Horace. With a Commentary. Volume I. The Odes, Carmen Seculare, and Epodes. By Edward C. Wickham, M.A. Second Edition. 1877. Demy 8vo. 12*s*.

—— A reprint of the above, in a size suitable for the use of Schools. Extra fcap. 8vo. 5*s*. 6*d*.

Livy, Book I. With Introduction, Historical Examination, and Notes. By J. R. Seeley, M.A. Second Edition. 1881. 8vo. 6*s*.

Ovid. P. Ovidii Nasonis Ibis. Ex Novis Codicibus edidit, Scholia Vetera Commentarium cum Prolegomenis Appendice Indice addidit, R. Ellis, A.M. 8vo. 10*s*. 6*d*.

Persius. The Satires. With a Translation and Commentary. By John Conington, M.A. Edited by Henry Nettleship, M.A. Second Edition. 1874. 8vo. 7*s*. 6*d*.

Juvenal. XIII Satires. Edited, with Introduction and Notes, by C. H. Pearson, M.A., and Herbert A. Strong, M.A., LL.D., Professor of Latin in Liverpool University College, Victoria University. In two Parts. Crown 8vo. Complete, 6*s*. *Just Published.*

Also separately, Part I. Introduction, Text, etc., 3*s*. Part II. Notes, 3*s*. 6*d*.

Tacitus. The Annals. Books I-VI. Edited, with Introduction and Notes, by H. Furneaux, M.A. 8vo. 18*s*.

Nettleship (H., M.A.). Lectures and Essays on Subjects connected with Latin Scholarship and Literature. Crown 8vo. 7*s*. 6*d*.

—— *The Roman Satura :* its original form in connection with its literary development. 8vo. sewed, 1*s*.

—— *Ancient Lives of Vergil.* With an Essay on the Poems of Vergil, in connection with his Life and Times. 8vo. sewed, 2*s*.

Papillon (T. L., M.A.). A Manual of Comparative Philology. Third Edition, Revised and Corrected. 1882. Crown 8vo. 6*s*.

Pinder (North, M.A.). Selections from the less known Latin Poets. 1869. 8vo. 15*s*.

Sellar (W. Y., M.A.). Roman Poets of the Augustan Age. VIRGIL. New Edition. 1883. Crown 8vo. 9*s*.

—— *Roman Poets of the Republic.* New Edition, Revised and Enlarged. 1881. 8vo. 14*s*.

Wordsworth (J., M.A.). Fragments and Specimens of Early Latin. With Introductions and Notes. 1874. 8vo. 18*s*.

III. GREEK.

A Greek Primer, for the use of beginners in that Language.
By the Right Rev. Charles Wordsworth, D.C.L. Seventh Edition. Extra fcap.
8vo. 1s. 6d.

Easy Greek Reader. By Evelyn Abbott, M.A. In two
Parts. Extra fcap. 8vo. 3s. *Just Published.*
The Text and Notes may be had separately, 1s. 6d. each.

Graecae Grammaticae Rudimenta in usum Scholarum. Auc-
tore Carolo Wordsworth, D.C.L. Nineteenth Edition, 1882. 12mo. 4s.

A Greek-English Lexicon, abridged from Liddell and Scott's
4to. edition, chiefly for the use of Schools. Twenty-first Edition. 1884.
Square 12mo. 7s. 6d.

Greek Verbs, Irregular and Defective; their forms, meaning,
and quantity; embracing all the Tenses used by Greek writers, with references
to the passages in which they are found. By W. Veitch. Fourth Edition.
Crown 8vo. 10s. 6d.

The Elements of Greek Accentuation (for Schools): abridged
from his larger work by H. W. Chandler, M.A. Extra fcap. 8vo. 2s. 6d.

A SERIES OF GRADUATED GREEK READERS:—

First Greek Reader. By W. G. Rushbrooke, M.L. Second
Edition. Extra fcap. 8vo. 2s. 6d.

Second Greek Reader. By A. M. Bell, M.A. Extra fcap.
8vo. 3s. 6d.

Fourth Greek Reader; being Specimens of Greek Dialects.
With Introductions, etc. By W. W. Merry, M.A. Extra fcap. 8vo. 4s. 6d.

Fifth Greek Reader. Selections from Greek Epic and
Dramatic Poetry, with Introductions and Notes. By Evelyn Abbott, M.A.
Extra fcap. 8vo. 4s. 6d.

The Golden Treasury of Ancient Greek Poetry: being a Collection of the finest passages in the Greek Classic Poets, with Introductory
Notices and Notes. By R. S. Wright. M.A. Extra fcap. 8vo. 8s. 6d.

A Golden Treasury of Greek Prose, being a Collection of the
finest passages in the principal Greek Prose Writers, with Introductory Notices
and Notes. By R. S. Wright, M.A., and J. E. L. Shadwell, M.A. Extra fcap.
8vo. 4s. 6d.

Aeschylus. Prometheus Bound (for Schools). With Introduction and Notes, by A. O. Prickard, M.A. Second Edition. Extra fcap. 8vo. 2s.

—— *Agamemnon.* With Introduction and Notes, by Arthur
Sidgwick, M.A. Second Edition. Extra fcap. 8vo. 3s.

—— *Choephoroi.* With Introduction and Notes by the same
Editor. Extra fcap. 8vo. 3s.

Aristophanes. In Single Plays. Edited, with English Notes, Introductions, &c., by W. W. Merry, M.A. Extra fcap. 8vo.

I. The Clouds, Second Edition, 2s.

II. The Acharnians, 2s.   III. The Frogs, 2s.

Cebes. Tabula. With Introduction and Notes. By C. S. Jerram, M.A. Extra fcap. 8vo. 2s. 6d.

Demosthenes. Olynthiacs and Philippics. Edited by Evelyn Abbott, M.A. Extra fcap. 8vo. In two Parts. *In the Press.*

Euripides. Alcestis (for Schools). By C. S. Jerram, M.A. Extra fcap. 8vo. 2s. 6d.

—— *Helena.* Edited, with Introduction, Notes, etc., for Upper and Middle Forms. By C. S. Jerram, M.A. Extra fcap. 8vo. 3s.

—— *Iphigenia in Tauris.* Edited, with Introduction, Notes, etc., for Upper and Middle Forms. By C. S. Jerram, M.A. Extra fcap. 8vo. cloth, 3s.

—— *Medea.* By C. B. Heberden, M.A. In two Parts. Extra fcap. 8vo. 2s.

    Or separately, Part I. Introduction and Text, 1s.
              Part II. Notes and Appendices, 1s.

Herodotus, Selections from. Edited, with Introduction, Notes, and a Map, by W. W. Merry, M.A. Extra fcap. 8vo. 2s. 6d.

Homer. Odyssey, Books I–XII (for Schools). By W. W. Merry, M.A. Twenty-seventh Thousand. Extra fcap. 8vo. 4s. 6d.

    Book II, separately, 1s. 6d.

—— *Odyssey,* Books XIII–XXIV (for Schools). By the same Editor. Second Edition. Extra fcap. 8vo. 5s.

—— *Iliad,* Book I (for Schools). By D. B. Monro, M.A. Second Edition. Extra fcap. 8vo. 2s.

—— *Iliad,* Books I–XII (for Schools). With an Introduction, a brief Homeric Grammar, and Notes. By D. B. Monro, M.A. Second Edition. Extra fcap. 8vo. 6s.

—— *Iliad,* Books VI and XXI. With Introduction and Notes. By Herbert Hailstone, M.A. Extra fcap. 8vo. 1s. 6d. each.

Lucian. Vera Historia (for Schools). By C. S. Jerram, M.A. Second Edition. Extra fcap. 8vo. 1s. 6d.

Plato. Selections from the Dialogues [including the whole of the *Apology* and *Crito*]. With Introduction and Notes by John Purves, M.A., and a Preface by the Rev. B. Jowett, M.A. Extra fcap. 8vo. 6s. 6d.

Sophocles. For the use of Schools. Edited with Introductions and English Notes. By Lewis Campbell, M.A., and Evelyn Abbott, M.A. *New and Revised Edition.* 2 Vols. Extra fcap. 8vo. 10*s.* 6*d.*
Sold separately, Vol. I, Text, 4*s.* 6*d.*; Vol. II, Explanatory Notes, 6*s.*

Sophocles. In Single Plays, with English Notes, &c. By Lewis Campbell, M.A., and Evelyn Abbott, M.A. Extra fcap. 8vo. limp.
Oedipus Tyrannus, Philoctetes. New and Revised Edition, 2*s.* each.
Oedipus Coloneus, Antigone, 1*s.* 9*d.* each.
Ajax, Electra, Trachiniae, 2*s.* each.

—— *Oedipus Rex:* Dindorf's Text, with Notes by the present Bishop of St. David's. Extra fcap. 8vo. limp, 1*s.* 6*d.*

Theocritus (for Schools). With Notes. By H. Kynaston, D.D. (late Snow). Third Edition. Extra fcap. 8vo. 4*s.* 6*d.*

Xenophon. Easy Selections (for Junior Classes). With a Vocabulary, Notes, and Map. By J. S. Phillpotts, B.C.L., and C. S. Jerram, M.A. Third Edition. Extra fcap. 8vo. 3*s.* 6*d.*

—— *Selections* (for Schools). With Notes and Maps. By J. S. Phillpotts, B.C.L. Fourth Edition. Extra fcap. 8vo. 3*s.* 6*d.*

—— *Anabasis,* Book I. Edited for the use of Junior Classes and Private Students. With Introduction, Notes, etc. By J. Marshall, M.A., Rector of the Royal High School, Edinburgh. Extra fcap. 8vo. 2*s.* 6*d.*

—— *Anabasis,* Book II. With Notes and Map. By C. S. Jerram, M.A. Extra fcap. 8vo. 2*s.*

—— *Cyropaedia,* Books IV and V. With Introduction and Notes by C. Bigg, D.D. Extra fcap. 8vo. 2*s.* 6*d.*

———————

Aristotle's Politics. By W. L. Newman, M.A. [*In the Press.*]

Aristotelian Studies. I. On the Structure of the Seventh Book of the Nicomachean Ethics. By J. C. Wilson, M.A. 8vo. stiff, 5*s.*

Aristotelis Ethica Nicomachea, ex recensione Immanuelis Bekkeri. Crown 8vo. 5*s.*

Demosthenes and Aeschines. The Orations of Demosthenes and Aeschines on the Crown. With Introductory Essays and Notes. By G. A. Simcox, M.A., and W. H. Simcox, M.A. 1872. 8vo. 12*s.*

Head (Barclay V.). Historia Numorum: A Manual of Greek Numismatics. Royal 8vo. half-bound. 2*l.* 2*s.* *Just Published.*

Hicks (E. L., M.A.). A Manual of Greek Historical Inscriptions. Demy 8vo. 10*s.* 6*d.*

Homer. Odyssey, Books I–XII. Edited with English Notes,
Appendices, etc. By W. W. Merry, M.A., and the late James Riddell, M.A.
1886. Second Edition. Demy 8vo. 16*s.*

Homer. A Grammar of the Homeric Dialect. By D. B. Monro,
M.A. Demy 8vo. 10*s.* 6*d.*

Sophocles. The Plays and Fragments. With English Notes
and Introductions, by Lewis Campbell, M.A. 2 vols.

> Vol. I. Oedipus Tyrannus. Oedipus Coloneus. Antigone. 8vo. 16*s.*
>
> Vol. II. Ajax. Electra. Trachiniae. Philoctetes. Fragments. 8vo. 16*s.*

IV. FRENCH AND ITALIAN.

Brachet's Etymological Dictionary of the French Language,
with a Preface on the Principles of French Etymology. Translated into
English by G. W. Kitchin, D.D. Third Edition. Crown 8vo. 7*s.* 6*d.*

—— *Historical Grammar of the French Language.* Translated into English by G. W. Kitchin, D.D. Fourth Edition. Extra fcap.
8vo. 3*s.* 6*d.*

Works by GEORGE SAINTSBURY, M.A.

Primer of French Literature. Extra fcap. 8vo. 2*s.*

Short History of French Literature. Crown 8vo. 10*s.* 6*d.*

Specimens of French Literature, from Villon to Hugo. Crown
8vo. 9*s.*

MASTERPIECES OF THE FRENCH DRAMA.

Corneille's Horace. Edited, with Introduction and Notes, by
George Saintsbury, M.A. Extra fcap. 8vo. 2*s.* 6*d.*

Molière's Les Précieuses Ridicules. Edited, with Introduction
and Notes, by Andrew Lang, M.A. Extra fcap. 8vo. 1*s.* 6*d.*

Racine's Esther. Edited, with Introduction and Notes, by
George Saintsbury, M.A. Extra fcap. 8vo. 2*s.* *Just Published.*

Beaumarchais' Le Barbier de Séville. Edited, with Introduction
and Notes, by Austin Dobson. Extra fcap. 8vo. 2*s.* 6*d.*

Voltaire's Mérope. Edited, with Introduction and Notes, by
George Saintsbury. Extra fcap. 8vo. cloth, 2*s.*

Musset's On ne badine pas avec l'Amour, and *Fantasio.* Edited,
with Prolegomena, Notes, etc., by Walter Herries Pollock. Extra fcap.
8vo. 2*s.*

> The above six Plays may be had in ornamental case, and bound
> in Imitation Parchment, price 12*s.* 6*d.*

Sainte-Beuve. Selections from the Causeries du Lundi. Edited by George Saintsbury. Extra fcap. 8vo. 2s.

Quinet's Lettres à sa Mère. Selected and edited by George Saintsbury. Extra fcap. 8vo. 2s.

Gautier, Théophile. Scenes of Travel. Selected and Edited by George Saintsbury. Extra fcap. 8vo. 2s.

L'Éloquence de la Chaire et de la Tribune Françaises. Edited by Paul Blouët, B.A. (Univ. Gallic.). Vol. I. French Sacred Oratory Extra fcap. 8vo. 2s. 6d.

Edited by GUSTAVE MASSON, B.A.

Corneille's Cinna. With Notes, Glossary, etc. Extra fcap. 8vo. *cloth,* 2s. Stiff covers, 1s. 6d.

Louis XIV and his Contemporaries; as described in Extracts from the best Memoirs of the Seventeenth Century. With English Notes, Genealogical Tables, &c. Extra fcap. 8vo. 2s. 6d.

Maistre, Xavier de. Voyage autour de ma Chambre. Ourika, by *Madame de Duras;* Le Vieux Tailleur, by *MM. Erckmann-Chatrian;* La Veillée de Vincennes, by *Alfred de Vigny;* Les Jumeaux de l'Hôtel Corneille, by *Edmond About;* Mésaventures d'un Écolier, by *Rodolphe Töpffer.* Third Edition, Revised and Corrected. Extra fcap. 8vo. 2s. 6d.

Molière's Les Fourberies de Scapin, and *Racine's Athalie.* With Voltaire's Life of Molière. Extra fcap. 8vo. 2s. 6d.

Molière's Les Fourberies de Scapin. With Voltaire's Life of Molière. Extra fcap. 8vo. stiff covers, 1s. 6d.

Molière's Les Femmes Savantes. With Notes, Glossary, etc. Extra fcap. 8vo. *cloth,* 2s. Stiff covers, 1s. 6d.

Racine's Andromaque, and *Corneille's Le Menteur.* With Louis Racine's Life of his Father. Extra fcap. 8vo. 2s. 6d.

Regnard's Le Joueur, and *Brueys and Palaprat's Le Grondeur.* Extra fcap. 8vo. 2s. 6d.

Sévigné, Madame de, and her chief Contemporaries, Selections from the Correspondence of. Intended more especially for Girls' Schools. Extra fcap. 8vo. 3s.

Dante. Selections from the Inferno. With Introduction and Notes. By H. B. Cotterill, B.A. Extra fcap. 8vo. 4s. 6d.

Tasso. La Gerusalemme Liberata. Cantos i, ii. With Introduction and Notes. By the same Editor. Extra fcap. 8vo. 2s. 6d.

V. GERMAN.

Scherer (W.). A History of German Literature. Translated
from the Third German Edition by Mrs. F. Conybeare. Edited by F. Max
Müller. 2 vols. 8vo. 21*s.*

Max Müller. The German Classics, from the Fourth to the
Nineteenth Century. With Biographical Notices, Translations into Modern
German, and Notes. By F. Max Müller, M.A. A New Edition, Revised,
Enlarged, and Adapted to Wilhelm Scherer's 'History of German Literature,'
by F. Lichtenstein. 2 vols. crown 8vo. 21*s.*

GERMAN COURSE. By HERMANN LANGE.

The Germans at Home; a Practical Introduction to German
Conversation, with an Appendix containing the Essentials of German Grammar.
Second Edition. 8vo. 2*s.* 6*d.*

The German Manual; a German Grammar, Reading Book,
and a Handbook of German Conversation. 8vo. 7*s.* 6*d*

Grammar of the German Language. 8vo. 3*s.* 6*d.*

German Composition; A Theoretical and Practical Guide to
the Art of Translating English Prose into German. 8vo. 4*s.* 6*d.*

Lessing's Laokoon. With Introduction, English Notes, etc.
By A. Hamann, Phil. Doc., M.A. Extra fcap. 8vo. 4*s.* 6*d.*

Schiller's Wilhelm Tell. Translated into English Verse by
E. Massie, M.A. Extra fcap. 8vo. 5*s.*

Also, Edited by C. A. BUCHHEIM, Phil. Doc.

Becker's Friedrich der Grosse. Extra fcap. 8vo. *In the Press.*

Goethe's Egmont. With a Life of Goethe, &c. Third Edition.
Extra fcap. 8vo. 3*s.*

—— *Iphigenie auf Tauris.* A Drama. With a Critical Introduction and Notes. Second Edition. Extra fcap. 8vo. 3*s.*

Heine's Prosa, being Selections from his Prose Works. With
English Notes, etc. Extra fcap. 8vo. 4*s.* 6*d.*

Heine's Harzreise. With Life of Heine, Descriptive Sketch
of the Harz, and Index. Extra fcap. 8vo. paper covers, 1*s.* 6*d.*; cloth, 2*s.* 6*d.*

Lessing's Minna von Barnhelm. A Comedy. With a Life
of Lessing, Critical Analysis, etc. Extra fcap. 8vo. 3*s.* 6*d.*

—— *Nathan der Weise.* With Introduction, Notes, etc.
Extra fcap. 8vo. 4*s.* 6*d.*

Schiller's Historische Skizzen; Egmont's Leben und Tod, and
Belagerung von Antwerpen. With a Map. Extra fcap. 8vo. 2s. 6d.

—— *Wilhelm Tell.* With a Life of Schiller; an his-
torical and critical Introduction, Arguments, and a complete Commentary,
and Map. Sixth Edition. Extra fcap. 8vo. 3s. 6d.

—— *Wilhelm Tell.* School Edition. With Map. 2s.

Modern German Reader. A Graduated Collection of Ex-
tracts in Prose and Poetry from Modern German writers :—
Part I. With English Notes, a Grammatical Appendix, and a complete
Vocabulary. Fourth Edition. Extra fcap. 8vo. 2s. 6d.
Part II. With English Notes and an Index. Extra fcap. 8vo. 2s. 6d.

Niebuhr's Griechische Heroen-Geschichten. Tales of Greek
Heroes. Edited with English Notes and a Vocabulary, by Emma S. Buchheim.
School Edition. Extra fcap. 8vo., *cloth*, 2s. *Stiff covers*, 1s. 6d.

VI. MATHEMATICS, PHYSICAL SCIENCE, &c.

By LEWIS HENSLEY, M.A.

Figures made Easy : a first Arithmetic Book. Crown 8vo. 6d.

Answers to the Examples in Figures made Easy, together
with two thousand additional Examples, with Answers. Crown 8vo. 1s.

The Scholar's Arithmetic : with Answers. Crown 8vo. 4s. 6d.

The Scholar's Algebra. Crown 8vo. 4s. 6d.

Aldis (W. S., M.A.). A Text-Book of Algebra. Crown 8vo.
Nearly ready.

Baynes (R. E., M.A.). Lessons on Thermodynamics. 1878.
Crown 8vo. 7s. 6d.

Chambers (G. F., F.R.A.S.). A Handbook of Descriptive
Astronomy. Third Edition. 1877. Demy 8vo. 28s.

Clarke (Col. A. R., C.B., R.E.). Geodesy. 1880. 8vo. 12s. 6d.

Cremona (Luigi). Elements of Projective Geometry. Translated by C. Leudesdorf, M.A. 8vo. 12s. 6d.

Donkin. Acoustics. Second Edition. Crown 8vo. 7s. 6d.

Euclid Revised. Containing the Essentials of the Elements
of Plane Geometry as given by Euclid in his first Six Books. Edited by
R. C. J. Nixon, M.A. Crown 8vo. 7s. 6d.
Sold separately as follows,
Books I-IV. 3s. 6d.   Books I, II. 1s. 6d.
Book I. 1s.

Galton (Douglas, C.B., F.R.S.). The Construction of Healthy Dwellings. Demy 8vo. 10s. 6d.

Hamilton (Sir R. G. C.), and J. Ball. Book-keeping. New and enlarged Edition. Extra fcap. 8vo. limp cloth, 2s.
  Ruled Exercise books adapted to the above may be had, price 2s.

Harcourt (A. G. Vernon, M.A.), and H. G. Madan, M.A. Exercises in Practical Chemistry. Vol. I. Elementary Exercises. Third Edition. Crown 8vo. 9s.

Maclaren (Archibald). A System of Physical Education : Theoretical and Practical. Extra fcap. 8vo. 7s. 6d.

Madan (H. G., M.A.). Tables of Qualitative Analysis. Large 4to. paper, 4s. 6d.

Maxwell (J. Clerk, M.A., F.R.S.). A Treatise on Electricity and Magnetism. Second Edition. 2 vols. Demy 8vo. 1l. 11s. 6d.

—— *An Elementary Treatise on Electricity.* Edited by William Garnett, M.A. Demy 8vo. 7s. 6d.

Minchin (G. M., M.A.). A Treatise on Statics with Applications to Physics. Third Edition, Corrected and Enlarged. Vol. I. *Equilibrium of Coplanar Forces.* 8vo. 9s. Vol. II. *Statics.* 8vo. 16s.

—— *Uniplanar Kinematics of Solids and Fluids.* Crown 8vo. 7s. 6d.

Phillips (John, M.A., F.R.S.). Geology of Oxford and the Valley of the Thames. 1871. 8vo. 21s.

—— *Vesuvius.* 1869. Crown 8vo. 10s. 6d.

Prestwich (Joseph, M.A., F.R.S.). Geology, Chemical, Physical, and Stratigraphical. Vol. I. Chemical and Physical. Royal 8vo. 25s.

Roach (T., M.A.). Elementary Trigonometry. Crown 8vo. *Nearly ready.*

Rolleston's Forms of Animal Life. Illustrated by Descriptions and Drawings of Dissections. New Edition. (*Nearly ready.*)

Smyth. A Cycle of Celestial Objects. Observed, Reduced, and Discussed by Admiral W. H. Smyth, R.N. Revised, condensed, and greatly enlarged by G. F. Chambers, F.R.A.S. 1881. 8vo. *Price reduced to* 12s.

Stewart (Balfour, LL.D., F.R.S.). A Treatise on Heat, with numerous Woodcuts and Diagrams. Fourth Edition. Extra fcap. 8vo. 7s. 6d.

Vernon-Harcourt (L. F., M.A.). A Treatise on Rivers and
Canals, relating to the Control and Improvement of Rivers, and the Design,
Construction, and Development of Canals. 2 vols. (Vol. I, Text. Vol. II,
Plates.) 8vo. 21s.

—— *Harbours and Docks;* their Physical Features, History,
Construction, Equipment, and Maintenance; with Statistics as to their Com-
mercial Development. 2 vols. 8vo. 25s.

Watson (H. W., M.A.). A Treatise on the Kinetic Theory
of Gases. 1876. 8vo. 3s. 6d.

Watson (H. W., D. Sc., F.R.S.), and S. H. Burbury, M.A.
I. *A Treatise on the Application of Generalised Coordinates to the Kinetics of
a Material System.* 1879. 8vo. 6s.

II. *The Mathematical Theory of Electricity and Magnetism.* Vol. I. Electro-
statics. 8vo. 10s. 6d.

Williamson (A. W., Phil. Doc., F.R.S.). Chemistry for
Students. A new Edition, with Solutions. 1873. Extra fcap. 8vo. 8s. 6d.

VII. HISTORY.

Bluntschli (J. K.). The Theory of the State. By J. K.
Bluntschli, late Professor of Political Sciences in the University of Heidel-
berg. Authorised English Translation from the Sixth German Edition.
Demy 8vo. half bound, 12s. 6d.

Finlay (George, LL.D.). A History of Greece from its Con-
quest by the Romans to the present time, B.C. 146 to A.D. 1864. A new
Edition, revised throughout, and in part re-written, with considerable additions, by the Author, and edited by H. F. Tozer, M.A. 7 vols. 8vo. 3l. 10s.

Fortescue (Sir John, Kt.). The Governance of England:
otherwise called The Difference between an Absolute and a Limited Mon
archy. A Revised Text. Edited, with Introduction, Notes, and Appendices,
by Charles Plummer, M.A. 8vo. half bound, 12s. 6d.

Freeman (E.A., D.C.L.). A Short History of the Norman
Conquest of England. Second Edition. Extra fcap. 8vo. 2s. 6d.

George (H. B., M.A.). Genealogical Tables illustrative of Modern
History. Third Edition, Revised and Enlarged. Small 4to. 12s.

Hodgkin (T.). Italy and her Invaders. Illustrated with
Plates and Maps. Vols. I—IV., A.D. 376-553. 8vo. 3l. 8s.

Kitchin (G. W., D.D.). A History of France. With numerous
Maps, Plans, and Tables. In Three Volumes. *Second Edition.* Crown 8vo.
each 10s. 6d.

Vol. 1. Down to the Year 1453.
Vol. 2. From 1453-1624.   Vol. 3. From 1624-1793.

Payne (E. J., M.A.). A History of the United States of America. In the Press.

Ranke (L. von). A History of England. principally in the Seventeenth Century. Translated by Resident Members of the University of Oxford, under the superintendence of G. W. Kitchin, D.D., and C. W. Boase. M.A. 1875. 6 vols. 8vo. 3*l*. 3*s*.

Rawlinson (George, M.A.). A Manual of Ancient History. Second Edition. Demy 8vo. 14*s*.

Select Charters and other Illustrations of English Constitutional History, from the Earliest Times to the Reign of Edward I. Arranged and edited by W. Stubbs, D.D. Fifth Edition. 1883. Crown 8vo. 8*s*. 6*d*.

Stubbs (W., D.D.). The Constitutional History of England, in its Origin and Development. Library Edition. 3 vols. demy 8vo. 2*l*. 8*s*.

Also in 3 vols. crown 8vo. price 12*s*. each.

—— *Seventeen Lectures on the Study of Medieval and Modern History*, &c., delivered at Oxford 1867-1884. Demy 8vo. half-bound, 10*s*. 6*d*.

Wellesley. A Selection from the Despatches, Treaties, and other Papers of the Marquess Wellesley, K.G., during his Government of India. Edited by S. J. Owen, M.A. 1877. 8vo. 1*l*. 4*s*.

Wellington. A Selection from the Despatches, Treaties, and other Papers relating to India of Field-Marshal the Duke of Wellington, K.G. Edited by S. J. Owen, M.A. 1880. 8vo. 24*s*.

A History of British India. By S. J. Owen, M.A., Reader in Indian History in the University of Oxford. In preparation.

VIII. LAW.

Alberici Gentilis, I.C.D., I.C., De Iure Belli Libri Tres. Edidit T. E. Holland, I.C.D. 1877. Small 4to. half morocco, 21*s*.

Anson (Sir William R., Bart., D.C.L.). Principles of the English Law of Contract, and of Agency in its Relation to Contract. Fourth Edition. Demy 8vo. 10*s*. 6*d*.

—— *Law and Custom of the Constitution.* Part I. Parliament. Demy 8vo. 10*s*. 6*d*.

Bentham (Jeremy). An Introduction to the Principles of Morals and Legislation. Crown 8vo. 6*s*. 6*d*.

Digby (Kenelm E., M.A.). An Introduction to the History of the Law of Real Property. Third Edition. Demy 8vo. 10*s*. 6*d*.

Gaii Institutionum Juris Civilis Commentarii Quattuor; or, Elements of Roman Law by Gaius. With a Translation and Commentary by Edward Poste, M.A. Second Edition. 1875. 8vo. 18*s*.

Hall (W. E., M.A.). International Law. Second Ed. 8vo. 21s.

Holland (T. E., D.C.L.). The Elements of Jurisprudence.
Third Edition. Demy 8vo. 10s. 6d.

—— *The European Concert in the Eastern Question,* a Collection of Treaties and other Public Acts. Edited, with Introductions and Notes, by Thomas Erskine Holland, D.C.L. 8vo. 12s. 6d.

Imperatoris Iustiniani Institutionum Libri Quattuor; with Introductions, Commentary, Excursus and Translation. By J. B. Moyle, B.C.L., M.A. 2 vols. Demy 8vo. 21s.

Justinian, The Institutes of, edited as a recension of the Institutes of Gaius, by Thomas Erskine Holland, D.C.L. Second Edition. 1881. Extra fcap 8vo 5s.

Justinian, Select Titles from the Digest of. By T. E. Holland, D.C.L., and C. L. Shadwell, B.C.L. 8vo. 14s.

Also sold in Parts, in paper covers, as follows

Part I. Introductory Titles. 2s. 6d.　　Part II. Family Law. 1s
Part III. Property Law. 2s. 6d.　Part IV. Law of Obligations (No. 1). 3s. 6d.
Part IV. Law of Obligations (No. 2). 4s. 6d.

Lex Aquilia. The Roman Law of Damage to Property: being a Commentary on the Title of the Digest 'Ad Legem Aquiliam' (ix 2). With an Introduction to the Study of the Corpus Iuris Civilis. By Erwin Grueber, Dr Jur., M.A. Demy 8vo. 10s. 6d.

Markby (W., D.C.L.). Elements of Law considered with reference to Principles of General Jurisprudence. Third Edition. Demy 8vo 12s.6d.

Twiss (Sir Travers, D.C.L.). The Law of Nations considered as Independent Political Communities.
Part I. On the Rights and Duties of Nations in time of Peace. A new Edition, Revised and Enlarged. 1884. Demy 8vo. 15s.
Part II. On the Rights and Duties of Nations in Time of War. Second Edition Revised. 1875. Demy 8vo 21s.

IX. MENTAL AND MORAL PHILOSOPHY, &c.

Bacon's Novum Organum. Edited, with English Notes, by G. W. Kitchin D.D. 1855. 8vo. 9s. 6d.

—— Translated by G. W. Kitchin, D.D. 1855. 8vo. 9s. 6d.

Berkeley. The Works of George Berkeley, D.D., formerly Bishop of Cloyne: including many of his writings hitherto unpublished. With Prefaces, Annotations, and an Account of his Life and Philosophy, by Alexander Campbell Fraser, M.A. 4 vols. 1871. 8vo. 2l. 18s.
The Life, Letters, &c. 1 vol. 16s.

—— *Selections from.* With an Introduction and Notes. For the use of Students in the Universities. By Alexander Campbell Fraser, LL.D. Second Edition. Crown 8vo 7s. 6d.

Fowler (T., D.D.). The Elements of Deductive Logic, designed mainly for the use of Junior Students in the Universities. Eighth Edition, with a Collection of Examples. Extra fcap. 8vo. 3*s.* 6*d.*

—— *The Elements of Inductive Logic,* designed mainly for the use of Students in the Universities. Fourth Edition. Extra fcap. 8vo. 6*s.*

Edited by T. FOWLER, D.D.

Bacon. Novum Organum. With Introduction, Notes, &c. 1878. 8vo. 14*s.*

Locke's Conduct of the Understanding. Second Edition. Extra fcap. 8vo. 2*s.*

Danson (J. T.). The Wealth of Households. Crown 8vo. 5*s.*

Green (T. H., M.A.). Prolegomena to Ethics. Edited by A. C. Bradley, M.A. Demy 8vo. 12*s.* 6*d.*

Hegel. The Logic of Hegel; translated from the Encyclopaedia of the Philosophical Sciences. With Prolegomena by William Wallace, M.A. 1874. 8vo. 14*s.*

Lotze's Logic, in Three Books; of Thought, of Investigation, and of Knowledge. English Translation; Edited by B. Bosanquet, M A., Fellow of University College, Oxford. 8vo. *cloth,* 12*s.* 6*d.*

—— *Metaphysic,* in Three Books; Ontology, Cosmology, and Psychology. English Translation; Edited by B. Bosanquet, M.A. 8vo. *cloth,* 12*s.* 6*d.*

Martineau (James. D.D.). Types of Ethical Theory. Second Edition. 2 vols. Crown 8vo. 15*s.*

Rogers (J. E. Thorold, M.A.). A Manual of Political Economy, for the use of Schools. Third Edition. Extra fcap. 8vo. 4*s.* 6*d.*

Smith's Wealth of Nations. A new Edition, with Notes, by J. E. Thorold Rogers. M.A. 2 vols. 8vo. 1880. 21*s.*

Wilson (J. M., B.D.), and T. Fowler, D.D. The Principles of Morals (Introductory Chapters). 8vo. *boards,* 3*s.* 6*d.*

X. ART, &c.

Hullah (John). The Cultivation of the Speaking Voice. Second Edition. Extra fcap. 8vo. 2*s.* 6*d.*

Ouseley (Sir F. A. Gore, Bart.). A Treatise on Harmony. Third Edition. 4to. 10*s.*

—— *A Treatise on Counterpoint, Canon, and Fugue,* based upon that of Cherubini. Second Edition. 4to. 16*s.*

—— *A Treatise on Musical Form and General Composition.* Second Edition. 4to. 10*s.*

Robinson (J. C., F.S.A.). A Critical Account of the Drawings by *Michel Angelo* and *Raffaello in the University Galleries, Oxford.* 1870. Crown 8vo. 4s.

Ruskin (John, M.A.). A Course of Lectures on Art, delivered before the University of Oxford in Hilary Term. 1870. 8vo. 6s.

Troutbeck (J., M.A.) and R. F. Dale, M.A. A Music Primer (for Schools). Second Edition. Crown 8vo. 1s. 6d.

Tyrwhitt (R. St. J., M.A.). A Handbook of Pictorial Art. With coloured Illustrations, Photographs, and a chapter on Perspective by A. Macdonald. Second Edition. 1875. 8vo. half morocco, 18s.

Upcott (L. E., M.A.). An Introduction to Greek Sculpture. Crown 8vo. 4s. 6d.

Vaux (W. S. W., M.A.). Catalogue of the Castellani Collection of Antiquities in the University Galleries, Oxford. Crown 8vo. 1s.

The Oxford Bible for Teachers, containing supplementary HELPS TO THE STUDY OF THE BIBLE, including Summaries of the several Books, with copious Explanatory Notes and Tables illustrative of Scripture History and the characteristics of Bible Lands; with a complete Index of Subjects, a Concordance, a Dictionary of Proper Names, and a series of Maps. Prices in various sizes and bindings from 3s. to 2l. 5s.

Helps to the Study of the Bible, taken from the OXFORD BIBLE FOR TEACHERS, comprising Summaries of the several Books, with copious Explanatory Notes and Tables illustrative of Scripture History and the Characteristics of Bible Lands; with a complete Index of Subjects, a Concordance, a Dictionary of Proper Names, and a series of Maps. Crown 8vo. *cloth,* 3s. 6d.; 16mo. *cloth,* 1s.

——+——

LONDON: HENRY FROWDE,
OXFORD UNIVERSITY PRESS WAREHOUSE, AMEN CORNER,

OXFORD: CLARENDON PRESS DEPOSITORY,
116 HIGH STREET.

The DELEGATES OF THE PRESS *invite suggestions and advice from all persons interested in education; and will be thankful for hints, &c. addressed to the* SECRETARY TO THE DELEGATES, *Clarendon Press, Oxford.*